MRS. DEMMING AND
THE MYTHICAL BEAST

FAITH SULLIVAN

Mrs. Demming and the Mythical Beast

MACMILLAN PUBLISHING COMPANY   *New York*

*All persons, incidents, and institutions
in this book are fictitious.*

*Macmillan Publishing Company
866 Third Avenue, New York, N.Y. 10022
Collier Macmillan Canada, Inc.*

*Library of Congress Cataloging in Publication Data
Sullivan, Faith.
Mrs. Demming and the mythical beast.
I. Title.
PS3569.U3469M7 1985   813'.54   85-10589
ISBN 0-02-615450-1*

10 9 8 7 6 5 4 3 2 1

Printed in the United States of America

For Daniel

MRS. DEMMING AND
THE MYTHICAL BEAST

I

The first time I saw him, I didn't really see him. That is, I thought I saw someone, a glimpse of someone, a pair of eyes, but basically I just had a *feeling* of seeing someone.

If nothing more had happened, I would have blamed the feeling on a bad bottle of mead. Harry Arneson, owner and publisher of *The River Courant,* had given me a bottle of his homemade mead. Every summer when we came out to Belle Riviere, Harry gave me a bottle of mead. Mead gave my husband, Bart, a terrible headache, so Harry didn't even bother to put Bart's name on the card. For years Harry and I had carried on a mild and innocent flirtation, so the card always read something like, "To Larissa, whose eyes are like bits of unconsumed anthracite." I didn't know what the hell Harry had in mind, but it was nice that he took the trouble.

The day I saw the eyes, I'd packed lunch and a bottle of mead into the canoe and paddled across the river to enjoy a solitary picnic. The river is Belle Riviere. It was named by a French explorer and, in the best tradition of English-speaking people, the local population has always called it Belle Riviere River. Beautiful River River. Long ago I gave up trying to correct them. I was just trying to act educated, Arch Bergquist told me. Arch runs the local movie house, the Little Palace, where last summer a three-week Gene Autry festival ran for two weeks. Since I was only a summer person, it seemed pointless to make a moral issue of Belle Riviere River.

It was June, mid-June, and after months of numbing winter, the landscape was still tender and emerging. In Minnesota there's a tentativeness about early summer, as though a harsh word or sudden movement might cause it to change its mind and disappear.

Despite the clear, strong sunlight, a frill of coolness edged the day. When I beached on the opposite shore, I unloaded my basket on the sand where the sun shone unobstructed, rather than back under the trees on the mossy bank. I came to this side of the river to picnic because the trees didn't grow as close to the water as they did in front of our cabin. There was a strip of sandy beach to lie on. Also, this side, the eastern bank, was protected by law from development, so there were no cabins and one could hope to picnic or read without interruption.

I spread the big beach towel I used for a picnic cloth and lay down on my stomach to read *Murder at Montmorency,* an English-country-weekend mystery. When I feel unsettled, a mystery in which sophisticated, chatty Londoners motor down to someone's place in the country for a fatal house party usually settles me. At least it gives me a false sense of order and that's nearly as beneficial. Lately I had been awash in unsettlement.

For half an hour I read *Murder at Montmorency,* then set the book aside. I needed something left of it to see me through bedtime. Sitting up, I pulled a thin slice of French bread from the basket and spread it with runny Brie. Pouring a paper cup full of mead, I took a deep drink and sighed.

Across the river our six-room cottage sat on the bluff, nearly hidden by birch and pine trees. On that side of the river Bart labored alone with his writing, as he had done for twenty summers. Increasingly, the cottage held only Bart and me. Bart's study was filled full of him. The other rooms were nearly empty of life. Myself divided among them was scant life to occupy them, and I lived mostly here on the opposite shore, reading, writing letters, and sketching or painting.

Since our children, Clark and Miranda, had graduated from high school, they'd spent less and less time on Belle Riviere. College summers had been taken up by classes and travel with friends. And now it was only an occasional weekend when they could drive up. This was the course of things. The family was no longer the focus of their lives. I didn't rue their evolution, but I missed the warmth and noise they'd shared with me.

I wanted to repay Miranda for the pleasure of her childhood. The debt I felt toward her, let alone the love, wouldn't allow me to sit idly by while she blithely threw away the world, presuming it well lost. But how did one tell a twenty-four-year-old woman with a master's degree in business, and her feet planted firmly on the thick carpeting of an investment banking firm, that she shouldn't marry a twenty-eight-year-old attorney who had his head screwed on tightly and a nice way with children and animals?

If one were to do it at all, one ought to be at a safe distance, thereby avoiding flying objects—words, pocket calculators, or whatever. I could call Miranda tonight. Or I could write a letter. That was the safest, most cowardly, and appealing way to handle it.

Desperate feelings about Miranda's marriage were making me meddlesome and conniving. A year ago I'd tried to reason with Clark. He'd married Sarah anyway. I would try to reason with Miranda, but if reason failed I would try something unreasonable. She was too young. Clark had been too young. I could do nothing about Clark, but Miranda was still free.

"Unnnh," I grunted and reached for another slice of bread. I'd just spread it with cheese and had it to my mouth when I heard a soft rustling up in the woods behind me. I turned, thinking I might spot a deer coming to the water to drink. Nothing of that sort was visible. Without moving, I searched the greenery, up- and downstream. Perhaps my scent had frightened it. I opened my mouth to take a bite—and heard it again. My heart thumped loudly. I don't know why. It wasn't at all unusual to encounter animals—deer, raccoon, beaver, even an occasional bear—in these woods.

With eyes "like bits of unconsumed anthracite," I bored through the trees—and, for the briefest part of a second, saw eyes like burning bituminous boring back.

Drying my hands, I removed my apron, hung it on a peg, and turned to Bart. After dinner he'd remained at the kitchen table with a second cup of Sanka and a sheaf of notes on ancient India.

"Have you decided whether you want to go to the movies?" I interrupted. If one didn't interrupt Bart's reading or writing, one might go without conversation for intolerable stretches.

He put an index finger on the page to mark his spot and looked up at me abstractedly. "Did you say something?"

"I asked if you wanted to see the movie."

"What was the movie again? Did you say?"

"I said. We discussed it briefly this morning. It's a French film from several years ago. Filmed in Greece. Do you want to go?"

His gaze fogged with bemusement as he refocused his mind. "Oh, yes. I remember now. Something about the Greek civil war, didn't you say?"

"That's what *The River Courant* said."

"What time does it start?"

"Seven-thirty."

"And what time is it now?"

I glanced at the kitchen clock. "Six-thirty."

"Six-thirty." He seemed to be subtracting six-thirty from seven-thirty. "Yes, all right. Why not? What time will we leave?"

"Seven?"

"Seven."

"That should be time enough."

"I'll just check a couple more pages here," he said, remembering the carefully placed index finger.

For nearly twenty-seven years Bart had taught ancient history courses at the university. To the young—anyone five years younger than I was—Bart would probably seem ancient history himself. A year ago last March he had attempted to ignore his fiftieth birthday. Ignoring it somehow drew more attention than simply blowing out the candles and getting drunk. Stoicism frets one's family.

"I'll call you when it's time," I told him. "Do you want to change clothes or anything?"

"I don't think so. It's never a very dressy crowd at the Little Palace. I wonder how they came by a French film."

"Arch Bergquist's wife speaks a little French, about fourteen words. Those fourteen words get us an occasional French film." Arch had always suspected that any movie without horseflesh and long shots of the Badlands was arty and possibly subversive.

I glanced at Bart as I prepared to leave the kitchen. Once again his head was bent over the notes. A handsome man, in a British way, he had dark reddish-brown hair, beginning to gray, and a lovely mustache that was doing the same. When he removed his tortoiseshell-rimmed glasses, he revealed mellow blue eyes, startlingly set off by long, dark lashes. Women found Bart attractive. And they imagined that he was shy. People often suppose shyness masks a deeply sensual nature. Women regarded Bart with sidelong glances, speculating about the volcanic passions he held in strained check.

Bart was not, in truth, shy. He was preoccupied. He had been preoccupied for as long as I had known him and even before that, I'm told. His mother said he first showed signs of preoccupation at about age three. Aside from oatmeal with raisins, which still preoccupied him on occasion, I didn't presume to know what ideas and pleasures held him locked in their embrace at age three. I did know that for the past three years, when he hadn't been lecturing, he'd been occupied and preoccupied with writing a novel about ancient India.

Throughout our marriage we'd tried to support each other's enthusiasms, however trivial or tedious. The writing of a novel I did not consider trivial, and only Bart could have said whether it was tedious. I guess the word I would have used for this latest preoccupation of Bart's was "unlikely." It seemed an unlikely enthusiasm for him. Several years ago he'd written a well-received text called *Art and Artisans of Ancient Cultures*, proving that he could put a sentence together with certainty and grace. But a novel? Set in ancient India? He didn't want any of us to read it until it was finished. Secretly, I didn't look forward to reading it at all. What if it were chaste and scholarly?

People who are preoccupied invite protection. One is always afraid that, in their preoccupation, they'll do themselves harm. I felt that way about this damned novel. I didn't want anyone to laugh at Bart. I didn't want to read supercilious reviews by moonlighting thirty-year-old instructors of freshman composition whose lack of tenure made them enthusiastically nasty.

Shaking my head, I went along to the bedroom Bart and I shared. The light was dimly soft in this southeast corner room. The woods on three sides of the cottage pulled twilight in at an early hour.

I snatched a cardigan from the bureau. It might be cool by the time we drove home, especially if I could persuade Bart to stop in Belleville. He'd never been awfully fond of the town, hadn't the time. We'd come to the river each year at the end of spring quarter so that he could escape friends, fellow faculty members, and the constant small intrusions of city life, and devote his time to writing. In the early years, he'd written papers for journals, then it was the text, and now it was the novel. It wouldn't have done to allow the locals to tax his time or fragment his preoccupation.

I was fond of Belleville. It was a pretty little place, clean and green, clinging to the western bank of Belle Riviere. Its east-west streets, running to and from the river, were so steeply pitched that, walking up or down, one was nearly in peril of falling off. Though we'd never come here in winter, I imagined one could sled from the top of the slope, down through the village, onto the frozen river and across to the next county.

However pretty Belleville might be, it was the river that dominated the countryside. For a mile or more south of Belleville, naked palisades rose on either side of its pools; then giant rocks, tumbled haphazardly at the water's edge, held out against the lush green of oak and pine, maple and birch. These gave way, as the river twisted, to softly rounded hillocks, sensuous as sleeping bodies sprawled easily along the shore. Suddenly dense growth reclaimed the verge, as well as the receding hills that were piled upon one other. Along its length Belle Riviere was by turns fierce and quiet, but everywhere it demanded a passionate eye.

I picked up a brush from the bureau and ran it quickly through my hair. Catching my own gaze in the mirror, I paused, recalling for the dozenth time what I'd seen from the beach that afternoon. Recalling it, I noted briefly and without surprise that I'd failed to mention it to Bart. Slowly returning the brush to the dresser, I continued staring, not seeing the eyes in the mirror, but those watching from behind thick, swaying foliage. I trembled, not quite from fear. And giggled, not quite from mirth.

"Larissa! Bart!" From the back of the Blue Ox the resonant bellow of Harry Arneson good-naturedly commanded us as we stood just inside the door surveying the Wednesday-night crowd.

Slowly we picked our way among a cluster of summer-vacationing college boys roistering self-consciously, eager to remind us of the privileges of their youth; then among several old men, regulars waiting with quiet resentment to secure one of the pool tables; and half a dozen tourists lounging against booths and earnestly lying to one another about the day's catch of bass.

Signaling to us above the heads of other customers, Harry, who'd been sitting alone at the long bar, picked up his schooner of beer and headed toward the empty back booth.

"Bring a pitcher of tap beer and a couple of glasses, Benjy," he called back to bartender Benjy Bledsoe.

When Bart and I were seated across from him, Harry filled one of the glasses and slid it toward me. "How're the kids?" he asked, filling the second glass for Bart.

Inquiring about the "kids"—twenty-four and twenty-five, respectively—was a ritual gambit for Harry. In his subconscious, Harry had determined that his innocence could be established and maintained if he began a conversation with me by discussing my children. Any flirting that might ensue was pre-absolved by close attention to the details of Clark and Miranda's progress. For twenty years this artless scheme had served him well. Our affair was still standing on a siding in a place called Marking Time. Up to now it had been sufficiently satisfying to both of us.

"Fine," I said.

The River Courant, the weekly newspaper Harry published, went to press on Wednesday. Wednesday was a long day for Harry and when the paper was finally to bed, he unwound—as much as Harry ever unwound—at the Blue Ox. Not that he was a noticeably tense person. On the contrary, he appeared a big, affable buoy, seldom overturned or submerged by events, a man of voluble conviction who knew how to ride out a squall.

But Harry was never at *rest.* His was the heartiness of an essentially lonely person. He looked like a football player in anxious search of a game from which he'd become inexplicably separated. When he hailed you across a room, there was puzzlement and inquiry in his eyes. Where were the others? Gone to the showers? Somewhere the game went on without Harry. If life were lived by rules half as fair as those of football, Harry would be in the thick of whatever he'd lost. All this about him appealed to me. Without his ever understanding why, Harry owned my sympathy and devotion. I longed to see him peaceful, not merely resigned. In the meantime, I appreciated his formless sense of dispossession and the restless bonhomie it produced.

"Been to the movie?" Harry asked.

"Yes."

"How's the book going, Bart?"

"All right."

Bart hated to be asked how the book was going. It made him peevish. And that made him feel guilty, which made him more peevish. What Bart liked was for everyone to pretend they didn't know he was writing. Then one day he could produce a whole and perfect project as though from a hat, and we could all tip back on our heels, roll our eyes up in our heads, and cry, "My God, how do you do it?" It was a perfectly human frailty.

I knew Bart didn't want to talk about his writing, but of course Harry couldn't be expected to know. I jumped in to fill the void. "The movie was filmed in Greece, Harry. It was beautiful. I had no idea Greece was that beautiful. I've never been there."

Harry interrupted his own thoughts to smile benignly at me. "When you leave Bart, that's where we'll head," he assured me. Something else was on his mind, however. His fingers nervously tapped the edge of the table. Finally, he took a slow breath and looked very directly at us, first me, then Bart. "Have you heard about Belle Rive Estates?" he asked as though it were something of which people were dying like flies.

Bart and I shook our heads.

"You will," Harry continued. "You will. There's a front-page piece in tomorrow's *Courant*. Also an editorial."

"Well, what *is* it?"

"A huge condominium project to be built upriver."

"How huge and how far up?" I asked.

"About two hundred units. About four miles up."

"My God!" Bart exclaimed. "That's a small *town*."

Harry nodded unhappily.

"Who's building it?"

"A Dallas outfit. Would you believe—Valhalla Projects?" The very name set his teeth on edge.

"Can you begin at the beginning, Harry?"

He filled his glass and drank off half of it. "I don't know where the beginning is. Or the middle or the end. It's the damnedest maze you ever saw. The outfit behind this condo thing has gone to enormous lengths to keep people from finding out about it. I know that Ernie Duffy sold his farm along the river. He didn't have a choice. Like plenty of others, he was going under. When the sale went through, it was thought around here that the buyer was Harold Falworth of Dallas, Texas. But Harold Falworth, Inc., is the name of a real estate development outfit."

"How did you find out?"

"Ever since he sold out, Ernie Duffy's been half-soused. When I came in here after work last Wednesday, he was shooting off to the old boys about a hand-delivered check for half a million bucks from the Harold Falworth *Company*. The more I questioned him, the more suspicious the whole business sounded. Next morning I called a woman in Dallas who graduated from Columbia with me. She's on the Dallas *Times-Herald*."

Delores Apple, cashier at the Little Palace Theater, winked at Harry and cracked her gum as she flounced past on her way to the Ladies'.

"My friend in Dallas," Harry went on, nodding absently to Delores, "checked on Harold Falworth. Harold Falworth, Inc., locates, buys, and develops real estate properties, but it's under the control of a holding company, Valhalla Projects. And Valhalla Projects is owned by a small group of wealthy Arabs. Very wealthy Arabs."

"Arabs?"

"Arabs."

"You mean Ernie Duffy's farm was bought by Arabs?" I asked, incredulous.

"You might say."

"But the two-hundred-unit condo, how do you know that's what they're planning?" I pursued.

"Barbara, my friend on the *Times-Herald,* called her ex. He's with a big architectural firm, Davis, Price, and O'Flaherty. If any kind of architectural job had been given out in Dallas that related to this property, she thought he might have heard about it. She hit the jackpot. Davis, Price, and O'Flaherty are designing a two-hundred-unit condo, Belle Rive Estates, for Harold Falworth and Valhalla Projects."

"Why all the secrecy?" Bart wanted to know.

"In a part of the world where families budget for heating fuel before their kids' education, oil-rich Arabs will be about as popular as a rabid skunk at a Sunday school picnic."

I could hear the clicking of snooker balls at the other end of the room. Delores Apple came out of the Ladies', ignored me, and smiled at Bart as she passed. What would Delores Apple think when she read in *The River Courant* that Arabs were building a 200-unit condo on Belle Riviere, four miles above Belleville?

I didn't blame Ernie Duffy for selling his farm. His back was against the wall. And there was always a pack of jackals waiting. When a farmer went down, the others grew older and quieter, listening for the cries of carrion-eaters, who crouched along the boundary of every farmer's vulnerability.

Not many words passed between us as Bart and I drove back to the cottage. We were absorbing what we'd learned about Belle Rive Estates. Although Bart didn't ordinarily concern himself with local problems, this one was difficult to ignore. It seemed fairly certain Belle Rive Estates would affect a lot of lives, including our own.

In a sleepy rural area, the addition of four to six hundred new inhabitants would mean change, congestion, and, doubtless, new business. But what about Belle Riviere? Not the least important consideration was the environmental impact the project would have. Wouldn't the river become noisy and polluted? Although our cottage was south of town and Belle Rive Estates was to be located north of Belleville, what began up there would soon flow down here.

There was something else. Over the years, we'd discussed selling the house in Minneapolis when Bart retired. The cottage was only an hour from the city. We would winterize it and live on the river year-round. Would Belle Rive Estates affect that? Wading through damp grass from car to cottage, I grunted angrily.

"Step in something unpleasant?"

"Belle Rive Estates."

"Yes." He sounded none too pleased himself. "Well, put it away for tonight. In the morning, when you're fresh, you'll worry more effectively."

I laughed and reached for the kitchen door. I envied my husband his calmness and objectivity, like a safe battlement from which to watch the distant war.

Bart was asleep. I turned out the lamp. Then, remembering, I turned it on again. From under *Murder at Montmorency* on the bedside table, I pulled a postcard. The color photo on the front was of a rodeo cowboy on a bucking horse. "Welcome to the Calgary Stampede," it said. The postmark on the back was Edmonton. He might have had the card in his satchel for months. Who knew?

> Larissa,
> May come south this winter and check in with you over the holidays. I wonder how that would strike you.
> It's a grand big world, but the places are starting to look the same.
>
> Love,
> Jamie

"Hmmmph," Bart had said, "I should think they *would* look the same. He's been at it long enough. Thirty years. My God, you'd think the man would be tired of playing hooky."

It was ten years since Jamie's last visit. My chest still tightened up like the shell of a mollusk when I thought of him. It was worse when one of these cards came, prising between the delicate pink lips of the shell, forcing entry to a dark chamber which ought to be mine alone. I turned out the light and withdrew into sleep.

2

A big black country mailbox with DEMMING stenciled on the side stood on a weathered post where our drive joined the narrow, rutted river road stretching out from Belleville along Belle Riviere.

Rising early, Bart had fetched the mail, and it was waiting on the breakfast table when I got up. From the study came the erratic clicking of his typewriter. An empty juice glass and a plate with buttery crumbs were in the sink. Bart was not sentimental about breakfast.

I poured myself a cup of coffee, put an English muffin in the toaster, and sat down to see if there were letters in the mail. The first thing to hit my eye was *The River Courant* headline, "Belle Riviere Condo Project Revealed." Hastily I covered it with a bill from the electric company and pretended I hadn't seen it. Noon was my best hour for adversity.

From Miranda:

Mom and Dad,
    A brief note, scribbled during yet another unnecessary and time-consuming conference.
    Wedding is set for October 2 at St. Mark's. Have arranged for photographer, engaged string quartet and caterer for reception. Mrs. Bird is making my gown as well as the bridesmaids' dresses.
    Invitations, announcements, thank-you notes, and calling cards are on order. Patterns have been registered at Dayton's, Hudson's, and elsewhere.
    I mention all of this, Mother, only to indicate the confidence and determination with which Dennis and I are moving ahead.

We may drive up for July 4th weekend. If you're in town before that, call and we'll have lunch.

Kisses,
Miranda

Oh, Miranda. Impatiently I tossed the note on the table. I had only Bart and myself to blame for the way Miranda and her brother, Clark, had turned out: capable, ambitious, self-confident, and decent. Also, reactionary. For the latter I blamed myself entirely.

If I hadn't encouraged nonconformity, preached liberalism, and condoned experimentation, we wouldn't be in the mess we were in today—Clark a CPA, married and expecting a child in September; Miranda an investment banker engaged (a marquise-cut diamond!) to a bright young attorney who would have a judge-ship by forty-five.

It was I who had urged the child Miranda to try out for Little League. Miranda had steadfastly continued ballet lessons. It was I who had argued for the glamorous dark green satin prom gown, Miranda who'd insisted on pale yellow organdy. I had hoped she and Bobby Arneson would spend the summer in Europe together at the end of their junior year at the university. Miranda determined to enroll for yet another course in corporate tax law.

Well, and wasn't I to blame for her interest in money? When the children were small, I'd painted daily. It was escape and a small income. Daisy Fitzroy had a gift shop in Belleville, and she sold my watercolors of the river to tourists and locals. For several years I enjoyed a modest vogue in the area. Then came Daisy's car accident and the business was closed.

We hadn't needed the extra income, so I'd put my earnings in the bank. When Miranda was thirteen or fourteen, she became interested in the stock market. If she studied the market for six months, she asked, would I let her invest part of the painting money? I said yes and that we would split the profits, should any accrue.

Her first purchase was ten shares in a tiny computer company based in California. Within ten years the stock went from ten dollars a share to one hundred. It split and, inside of three years, again climbed over a hundred. In the meantime, based on what she'd read about the founder, Miranda bought shares in a new pharmaceutical firm that was to develop revolutionary techniques in administering drugs. By the time she graduated from high school, Miranda had earned each of us twenty thousand dollars.

That, I suppose, had been the beginning of her career. Instead of saving her from the awful drowning death of conventionality, I'd practically driven her into it. Without a backward glance, she and Clark had given up freedom to throw themselves into an abyss of respectability.

How could I save her? Jumping from the table, I snatched a charred muffin from the toaster and opened the window over the sink to dissipate the acrid smoke that caused my eyes to brim and my nose to run as if I were crying.

Dressed in jeans and an old sweater, I sat beneath a pale noonday sun and dug my toes into the cold sand. The can of light beer, held in my two hands, was cold too. I shivered and set the beer aside. I'd be glad when it was high summer.

Gazing miserably into the middle distance, I mulled. And at length I dug a pad and pencil from the picnic basket. After a number of wrong starts, I wrote:

Darling Miranda,

You are beautiful, loving, and intelligent. You are also sensible. You're proud of being sensible, and why not? It's a talent, I think, and one I envy. You're a marvel at organizing time and activity, at handling friendships and budgeting money. My own undertakings and emotions are undisciplined and tend to overpower me. As I've watched you march, neatly and in perfect time, through life, I've shaken my head in wonder and gratitude that you could learn so much that I was unable to teach you.

You've been terribly sweet about my inadequacies in these areas, much more understanding than many girls would have been. For that and all your dear qualities, I love you madly.

I have just taken a deep drink of Belle Riviere air and stuck my pencil in my ear, because I don't know how to proceed. Now I have taken a deep drink of beer. Let's see if that helps.

Miranda, I think there's a beast in everyone that needs to be let out to run. It isn't necessarily a dangerous beast but it might grow so, if we didn't acknowledge it.

Some people never open the cage to look in until the beast has grown old and mean. You may recall your father's Aunt Cass and the guru from Omaha, for instance. If Aunt Cass had taken that beast for a walk when she was eighteen or twenty-

---

13

five, he'd have been a dear woolly thing to keep her warm in her old age. But by the time he was let out, he was ready to eat her alive.

Am I accusing you of having been too good? If I am, forgive me. I'm proud of you, Miranda. But I would feel easier if you were going into marriage having met your beast and having learned, perhaps, to love him a little.

Could you be persuaded to postpone the wedding just for six or eight months? Spring weddings are nice, too.

If you and Dennis come for the Fourth of July weekend, I promise not to mention the wedding once, unless, of course, you should bring it up first.

Your selfless and adoring,
Mother

I returned the pad and pencil to the picnic basket. Wrapped in a checkered napkin in the basket were three Ritz cracker sandwiches with peanut butter inside. I took them out and ate them, wiped the corner of my mouth with the napkin, and finished the open can of beer, which had grown warm while I wrote.

I felt a little better, having written to her. A mother must do the awful things a mother must do. I must prevent Miranda's marriage.

Brushing away cracker crumbs with a self-satisfied gesture, I snapped open *The River Courant* with a flourish to read the Belle Rive Estates story while my emotional pendulum was on the upswing.

The front-page story was essentially what we'd already learned from Harry. In his editorial he spoke of environmental considerations and suggested that the residents of the area have an opportunity to vote on the project. After all, an undertaking of these proportions would affect the entire county, and while Belle Rive Estates would mean more taxes for the county and more business for the community, it would also mean greater expenditures and congestion and disruption of a cherished rural life-style. The newspaper would be in close contact with local and state authorities to ascertain whether laws or regulations were being broken by the proposed construction.

I put the paper aside. This was just the beginning. There was going to be a war. I wondered how the sides would line up, who would stand by whom.

Suddenly, behind me, wings flapped and birds remonstrated. Close by, an owl flew out of the trees, hooting mournfully as he glided over the river. On the opposite shore, he veered and swung back into the woods on this side, seventy or a hundred yards downstream.

A startled doe bounded from between two pines, spotted me, and turned south along the bank, leaving dainty hoofprints in the damp sand. This small drama of fear and flight would be repeated thousands of times during the construction of Belle Rive Estates. If that came to pass.

What had caused this particular disturbance? I wondered, folding *The River Courant* and packing it into the basket. A bear? A hiker? A chill breeze scudded across the water, piercing my sweater. The eyes. I'd forgotten. Miranda and Belle Rive Estates—and Jamie's postcard—had eclipsed them. Now, remembering, I slowly turned to face the woods.

Biking into town to mail Miranda's letter, I sheepishly recalled having paddled home as though the Devil slavered behind me, straining to clutch me to him. I'd go back tomorrow and poke around. There would be tracks of whatever was hanging about.

After I dropped the letter at the post office, I left my locked bike in the stand outside, and drifted down Main Street, half expecting to hear heated exchanges as impassioned citizens contended over Belle Rive Estates. But, except for a handful of tourists, Main Street was nearly deserted.

I was disappointed. I wanted to know people's reactions. Reaching the corner of Main and River Avenue, I turned left, heading toward *The River Courant* office. River Avenue was Belleville's primary east-west artery, one of its most steeply pitched streets, and I was glad I hadn't brought the bike.

When River Avenue reaches the water, it bids farewell to Belleville in Beau Bois County, becomes River Avenue Bridge, stretches across Belle Riviere, and on the opposite bank finds itself in the village of Blind Moose in Three Toes County. It is still called River Avenue there. In fact, all the east-west streets in Blind Moose have the same names as the east-west streets in Belleville, as if, like a sled, they'd pushed off at the top of the slope in one village, hurtled downhill across a frozen river and up the other side, before coming to rest.

Pushing open the door to the *Courant,* I passed the front counter, where a couple of women were placing ads in next week's classified section, and made my way back to Harry's glassed-in office at the rear. The presses were in the building next door, as was a thriving printing business run by Harry's wife, Roberta, and his son, Bobby.

Harry saw me coming, rose, still cradling the phone against his shoulder, and motioned me in. I entered, closed the door behind me, and stood with my back to him, studying the room beyond, where three women and a man worked at desks. I wasn't the least interested in them, but I wanted to give Harry a pretense of privacy in his phone conversation. I hoped it wasn't his wife on the line. Roberta made me purse my lips in a manner so unattractive that it was hard to forgive her.

It wasn't Roberta. "Yes, Sam," Harry was saying, "yes, I agree. I'd appreciate your doing that. And, if I were you, I'd call Hoot Bergen and see what he thinks."

Out on River Avenue it was late spring, the air light, thin-feeling on the skin and in the nostrils, yet in this room it was high summer, hot, the air moist and heavy-feeling as suede. The still, humid heat of midsummer was my favorite weather, the antithesis of the too-long, too-cold, singing whip of winter. Most civilized people preferred spring's wan innocence or the autumnal flash in the pan, but I hungered for the sharpest contrast, the hottest hot. I longed for clothes to cling damply, hair to gather in ribbons of curl around the face, breathless afternoons of cicadas and thick nights of crickets. That kind of summer was already in this room. Why should that be? I wondered.

Harry's conversation was winding down. I turned from the glass wall and sat beside his desk in a faded brown leather chair. The wall to the right of the desk was entirely covered by shelves. They were crammed with reference books; battered and dogeared personal reading; and, here and there, mementos: a stained baseball, seams coming unsewn; a framed snapshot, brittle and blurry, of Harry Truman as he stood on the band shell in Humphrey Park, smiling and waving; and another candid picture, this one enlarged and mounted in a heavy walnut frame: a young, smiling Harry Arneson, squinting against the sun, big, muscular torso bare except for a droopy-looking pair of swim trunks, his hand on the shoulder of a boy, maybe eight years old, who held up a string of bass for the camera to record. The boy was Bobby. To his left a slim, attractive woman mugged for the camera, holding her nose and pointing to the fish. Roberta.

"Okay, Sam. Thanks again. Keep me posted." Harry replaced the receiver on its cradle, clasped his big hands behind his head, and leaned back in the oak swivel chair, grinning. "You've come to enlist."

"Enlist?"

"Save the River. Sam Fergus is setting up an ad hoc committee to fight Belle Rive Estates. He'll be in touch with you. May ask you to do some artwork for him—posters, circulars. He might ask Bart to write something for the literature they're putting together. At the very least he'll hit you for a nominal financial contribution."

"Harry..."

"The *Courant* only came out this morning and already..."

"Harry?"

"Yes?"

"Slow down and back up. I didn't come to enlist. I don't know which side I'm on."

Unclasping his hands, he sat forward, leaning toward me in disbelief. "You don't know which side you're on?"

"That's right. After we left the Blue Ox last night, I thought a lot about Belle Rive Estates. I read the paper today and thought about it some more, and I still don't know which side I'm on."

"I don't understand." On a dusty, disorderly filing cabinet, beside an open window facing on an alley, were a couple of bottles, one gin and one bourbon, and a stack of Dixie cups. Rising slowly, Harry moved to the filing cabinet. He poured himself a shot of bourbon and looked out on the alley, leaning an elbow on the filing cabinet. Finally, he turned. "Sorry, would you like a drink?"

"A shot of gin would be nice."

He poured one and handed it across the big desk to me, inquiring, "Why don't you know whose side you're on?"

I was baffled by the tone of voice. It said my indecision was a *personal* rejection. That wasn't like Harry. We'd differed on issues before, enjoyed the arguments, never assumed that because we were friends, we should always be allies. "Harry, it's not *whose* side, it's *which* side. We're talking about an issue, not a person. If I had to choose between a bunch of wealthy Arabs in Savile Row burnooses and Harry Arneson in his L. L. Bean corduroys, I'd choose Harry Arneson every time."

Grunting softly, he pushed the chair back and sat down.

"In any case, Harry, I'm only a summer person and I'm not convinced that summer people have a right to get involved in this battle," I told him.

"You own property here. That gives you a tangible right, in addition to the moral responsibility."

"You think the issues are clear-cut," I pointed out crisply. "I don't. Until someone does an environmental study, we don't know how severely this condo project will affect the river. It may not be all that bad. It's bound to help local business.

"And another thing," I went on, gesturing extravagantly. "Keeping people out, well, I'm not sure that's too moral—or democratic. We—you and I—love the river and the life we have here. So may others. Why don't they have a right to it?" I took a dainty swig of gin.

"It's true we need an environmental-impact study," Harry agreed. "But I can tell you now the news won't be good. The argument that everyone opposed to Belle Rive Estates wants to prevent others from enjoying the river is a pile of horse apples. In Beau Bois County alone, there are two sizable campgrounds on Belle Riviere. Anyone can use them, not just the crowd with money for condos. But if this project goes through, there'll be other projects, and pretty soon we'll have our own Coney Island. The water won't be fit for anything—including fish. The woods'll be destroyed and the wildlife killed or driven off. I damned well am going to do whatever *I* can to see that that doesn't happen." Harry's voice had risen and I wondered if the three women and one man beyond the glass were straining to hear us. *I* would be.

He drank from his Dixie cup. Setting the cup down, his hand remained clasped around it, his gaze fastened on it. "I need you on my side."

He said this humorlessly, no trace of a mocking smile lurking in the eyes or around the mouth. "I need you on my side." It was right out of an old Frank Capra movie. Crusading small-town newspaperman turns to the woman he loves and says...

Oh, my God. Some realizations do not dawn all at once, but come creeping over the horizon a bit at a time. The realization that Harry was in love with me arrived in this way. The Harry I had known would never have entreated, "I need you on my side," in just that way. He'd have laughed and predicted, "If you don't play ball on our team, you'll be sorry as hell when we take the pennant."

When had things changed? Why hadn't I known? My head hummed with guilt, not only because I'd somehow caused Harry to fall in love with me, but also because I was not disappointed to discover it. Love was a soaring delight in its pure, abstract form, a form in which it might remain for about fifteen minutes.

Alarm resounded through my nervous system. *Run,* it warned. *Run for your life, for sanity, for innocence. Run.* I looked at Harry. His wary, wanting face swept away the underpinnings of my resolve. I smiled the most comforting smile I could manage. "I need to think, Harry."

"Yes, well, hell, I understand," he said with false bluffness. He grinned ruefully and steered the conversation down a side street. "Hollis Gibney is heading up the opposition to Save the River."

"I'm sure you knew you'd be opposed."

"Yes."

"You should be glad it's Hollis. He's a bit dim."

"Hollis will just be a titular head, as they say. Who do you think's really running it?"

"Who?"

"Roberta."

So this was why he "needed" me. His wife had pulled the rug from under him and he was casting about for comfort. I felt slightly sick with disappointment. It was insane. I'd been thrown into a state of panic at the prospect of Harry's loving me. And now that it appeared he was only using me for solace, I was miserable instead of relieved.

His head slightly lowered, Harry regarded me as though he were looking over the top of eyeglasses, bringing me into closer scrutiny, sharper focus. "It's as well, really, about Roberta," he explained without apparent emotion. "I'd rather she fought me outright than sabotaged me."

Though he'd often been provoked, never before had I heard Harry indict his wife. He drank the last of his bourbon and said no more about her. Crushing the empty paper cup and tossing it into the wastebasket, he observed, "Most of the merchants in town are going to support Belle Rive Estates. Simple economics."

"I suppose so."

"But I'd foolishly assumed," he began quietly, swiveling his chair sideways to face me more directly, "that you would be in the trenches with *me.*"

His disappointment thrilled me. My face grew hot. I held the

Dixie cup tightly against my knee to keep it from shaking. His gaze was unwavering. I wanted to touch him. I wanted to run my hands over his face and say loving things to him. I was not sure if that was because he was in pain or because it would be very pleasant. I guessed I'd better get the hell out of there.

Rising stiffly, I backed away, still clutching the cup in my hand. When I reached the door, I managed to whisper, "Thanks for the gin, Harry." I turned. The three women and one man were staring at me. I drank the rest of the liquor, which was most of it, and walked out, snorting and coughing as it went down the wrong pipe.

3

Across the tiny table from me sat my closest friend, Daisy Fitzroy. Daisy and her husband, George, are year-round residents of Belleville. George is an accountant, a very good one, who draws clients from several counties. Daisy is a full-time do-gooder in the best sense of that abused expression. Daisy does good.

She is small, slender, and blond, with the exquisite features of a nineteenth-century doll. Although I have little opportunity to show it, I feel protective toward her, as though Fate had assigned me the sacred task of keeping Daisy from harm. The feeling dates back, I'm sure, to the time years ago when she was nearly killed in a car accident and afterward lay for months, bedridden, full of irony and gaiety, reassuring me as much as herself. Whatever the origin of my protectiveness, it hasn't worked out in practice. Daisy often as not has looked after me.

I'd ordered beer. Daisy was drinking white wine with a maraschino cherry. We were on the patio of Sadie's Salad Emporium, a spot from which, due to the sharp angle at which the town rises from the river's edge, one can glimpse Belle Riviere over the roof of the Soo Line depot.

"There's no reason a woman shouldn't disagree with her husband, God knows. But this public repudiation of Harry is just another in a long line of humiliations Roberta has handed him." Daisy opened the menu, glanced briefly at it, and set it aside.

I'd been explaining to Daisy that Harry's wife, along with Hollis Gibney and I didn't know who else, was publicly opposing Harry and Sam Fergus and their Save the River Committee.

"I have known Roberta since I was a girl, Larry, and not one day of those many years have I liked her." Daisy paused. "I take that back. The day of the Senior Prom she came down with chicken pox. *That* day I liked her, I think." She picked up her wineglass. "What're you having?"

"Asparagus salad. Why does he put up with it, Daisy?"

"Sure as hell beats me. I think it used to be for Bobby's sake. Now—well, maybe he can't find the time for a divorce. You know, lots of people stay married because they just don't have time to sort it all out and argue over it. It wasn't Georganna who kept George and me together. It was our collection of matchbooks and theater programs."

"How is Georganna?" Daisy's daughter, the same age as my son Clark, was studying painting in Paris.

"Skinny." Holding the maraschino cherry by the stem, she pointed it at me. "Since she started living over there, she looks as though she'd been drawn by Daumier on an off day. An entire 747 lifts off weekly, loaded with chocolate chip cookies and rice crispy bars, and bound for Georganna Fitzroy. Still she's gaunt."

"Is she happy?"

"Unaccountably. But I worry. It's so far away. And she doesn't take care of herself. And her friends are all escapees from someplace. Everyone she knows is a mental defective or a political refugee. That's where the rice crispy bars go, I know." She sighed the blithe sigh of a woman who in her heart is not the least disappointed in her child's choices.

"She's right in the messy thick of what she wants. Don't you envy her?"

"Well, of course." She grinned broadly, looked away toward the river, then at me. "You know, Larry, a woman struggling up the executive ladder in banking is in the thick of it, too."

"Yes. It's not Miranda's career I object to. It's the marriage."

"You like Dennis. You've told me so."

"Dennis is a brick. But Miranda is too young to set aside the options of girlhood. She needs adventures. She needs pratfalls, a worthless man or two, and at least one daring risk."

Daisy hesitated. "Did you have those?"

"Probably not. Or maybe I thought Bart was a daring risk." I tried not to sound sardonic. "You have to remember, he was a brilliant young professor and I an impressionable coed."

"I'd forgotten."

"He was practically a prodigy—had his Ph.D. before he was twenty-four. I was only three years younger than he was." I sounded defensive, too eager to explain and justify.

"Was he terribly dashing?"

"He was very handsome. I suppose I thought that was the same thing. And maybe I wanted to..." I played absently with my knife, turning it over and over. "Well, I don't know what," I concluded abruptly.

She glanced at me obliquely, an eyebrow raised slightly. The waitress appeared with our food. Daisy ordered more wine and I asked for another beer. I was glad she'd called this morning. It had been a rough night.

At 3 A.M. the sound of my own moaning had awakened me from a dream more erotic than most of my erotic dreams. Not surprisingly, it had been about Harry. When the dream began, we were running through the darkened streets and alleys of Belleville, escaping and hiding from whom I never discovered. I only knew that I was impelled by fear so powerful it made my chest ache.

Harry and I ran hand in hand until we reached Humphrey Park and I could run no farther. I stumbled and swayed and begged Harry to go on without me. He picked me up and ran through the shadowy park carrying me in his arms. On the stage of the band shell he put me down and we both lay on the gray enameled floor waiting for Harry Truman.

Beyond the band shell the night was full of eyes. We slid across the floor into the deeper darkness at the back of the shelter. By a trick of the shadows I thought someone was standing over me. I opened my mouth to scream and Harry covered it with his. Immediately I was aroused and began to writhe beneath him.

Harry pulled back so that I could remove my clothes. I stood and began unbuttoning my blouse, moving my body in a teasing way. I had my blouse off and was unfastening my brassiere when I heard a whisper in the park. I didn't know if it was Harry Truman or Bart or my father. I continued to undress, aware of the audience and excited by it.

When I'd removed all my clothes, I did a slow, obscene dance and concluded it by pulling Harry down on top of me. The moment he penetrated me I came, and woke instantly, moaning.

Recovering slowly, I glanced across at Bart. He slept like a loaf of lead. I wanted to get up and make tea, but I was afraid to wake him. I couldn't face him just then, so I turned over and went back to sleep.

I should have made tea. Before dawn I woke from a second dream, this one a thoroughgoing nightmare. I dreamed we had a storm cellar in the yard, like the one on a cousin's farm when I was little. Miranda was visiting and I said to her, "I've stored a basket of beautiful apples in the storm cellar. Let's get some."

She followed me across the damp grass to the hatch door in the earth. I grasped the iron ring and pulled. It was heavy and unwilling. If I hadn't been absolutely bent on having the apples I wouldn't have bothered. But I'd told Miranda about them, so I tugged until I'd raised the door.

From the cavity below a thick mist billowed and roiled. It was too dense for us to see shapes beyond it, but a pale light shone through. The light stirred in me a deep unease, black and viscous as tar. At the time I understood why. Miranda was beside me, however, and I mustn't let her see how terrified I was becoming. My skin was as cold as the ring in my hand. I let the door slam and stepped back away from it.

"Is that where you keep the beast, Mother?"

I woke in a stiff and clammy sweat and jumped out of bed as though it were on fire. Seated at the kitchen table with a cup of tea, a sweet early-morning breeze cooling my fever, I began to see how comical it was. The dream had grown out of the letter I'd written Miranda. I thought I'd tell her about it. She'd laugh and say it served me right.

Then recalling the earlier dream, the one with Harry in the band shell, I laughed aloud. Setting my cup on the table, I threw my head back and laughed and couldn't stop.

With the nether creatures of dreams on my mind, I finished the tea and put the cup in the sink. When the sun was higher, I would row across the river to look for animal tracks. But at nine-thirty Daisy had called and suggested lunch.

"Could we make it tomorrow?" I'd asked.

"Tomorrow is out for me. I'm hauling a load of kids down to Minneapolis."

So I had quickly agreed and we'd settled on Sadie's Salad Emporium. As Sadie's waitress moved away from the table, I asked, "What kids are you hauling and why?"

"The four oldest Purvis children, to see the city. It's an hour away and they've never been there. Can you believe it? We're going to stay overnight at the Holiday Inn and come home Sunday."

"Is George going?"

"Three of George's old college buddies are flying up from Chicago to go fishing in some godforsaken place near the Rainy River. They'll spend four days drinking beer, and losing half their fishing tackle in the lake. And they'll begin to imagine that they were in the war together." She smiled indulgently. "Well, bless them, it *does* beat being in the war. But I'd rather be with the Purvis children in the Holiday Inn."

"Daisy, are you going to get involved with Save the River?" I asked suddenly.

"Yes." She pushed her empty plate away and rested her elbows on the table. "In fact I thought I'd call Harry tonight. You and I can work together. What would you like to do? The two of us could throw a cocktail party or kaffeeklatsch."

Daisy Fitzroy could make a gala occasion out of gravedigging. No one had ever told her that work wasn't fun. "If we had a party in our backyard, we could string Japanese lanterns..."

"Daisy, I'm not going to work for Save the River."

She looked up from the napkin she'd been folding and cocked her head. "Really?"

"Bart and I are outsiders. I'm not even sure I'm opposed to the condos except on environmental grounds, and we don't know the scope of that yet."

"You told Harry this?"

"Yes."

"What did he say?"

"That we had a right because of our river property, that the project would upset the environment, pollute the river, and drive off wildlife. And that it would destroy the nature of the community."

"And you don't agree?"

"I don't know. I only know I feel guilty trying to keep people out."

She looked skeptical. "There isn't any other reason?"

"I don't think so."

"Is there a chance you'll change your mind?"

"Of course. But I have to give it more thought."

We faced the river, two blocks east, below us. Scanning the

vista north and south, we saw yellow cliffs and deep woods and pale, graceful pastures.

"There aren't many rivers as wild and unspoiled as this. Not in this country. If civilization comes to every place, where can anyone go to get away from it?" She turned and studied me. "Was Harry hurt?" she asked.

"Yes."

"For years you two have played with matches," she said, not unkindly. Shaking her head, she added with disbelief, "You've always imagined they would never light."

If Harry and I had been playing with matches all these years, I thought, guiding the car around the worst of the potholes in River Road, why hadn't I known?

A flock of blackbirds slid down through the sky in an arc and lighted along the telephone wires. I'd left Daisy outside Sadie's with her questions unasked. She wanted to know how aware I was of the involvement between Harry and me. Did I realize how serious it had grown or would I wake up one morning and find my life pulled up by the roots?

But I'd only fallen in love yesterday. It was too soon for discussing. And when I had it all in hand it would be too late, except when we were old and it could be talked of as though it had been humorous. *Remember, Daisy, when Harry and I thought we were in love?*

What I should have told Daisy to ease her mind was that nothing was going to come of Harry and me. We were both married people with the days of great risk taking behind us.

A cloudless sky covered everything, the same as yesterday. Gravelly dust blew around the Volvo as I swung off the road and into our backyard. I grabbed my bag from the front seat and legged it toward the kitchen door. When one thought about it, really nothing had happened between Harry and me. Nothing would happen. One had a will.

"Bart, how would you like to take a trip this summer?"

He was seated in his favorite old armchair, wearing his favorite old house slippers, and sucking on his favorite old pipe. The study was dark except for the corner where he sat. The floor lamp behind the chair circumscribed him possessively with its glow. I felt like an intruder, which I was, actually, since he'd been poring over a very large book of ancient Indian art when I came to the door.

"A trip?"

"Yes. We haven't been anywhere for years. I'd like to get away. What do you think?"

"But you *love* the river. You'd miss it, you know."

"I would miss it, but we'll be here again next summer. It isn't as though we weren't coming back."

"Why not wait till winter? We'll go at the winter break. I've been thinking I'd like to see India before I send the book off to the publisher. Just to check out certain settings, you know." There was such genuine enthusiasm in his voice, I hated to be negative.

"That would be nice, yes, but I'd like to get away this summer. It's kind of hit me all of a sudden."

"Where did you want to go?"

"Far away. Uh, Greece, maybe. It looked lovely in the film the other night. You were there years ago, but it must be worth a second trip."

"I'm sure it is. Unfortunately, I can't go. I've got to stick here and work on the book, or I won't have it finished by the first of the year, when it's due. Wait till winter break and we'll stop in Greece on our way back from India."

"Maybe I'll go alone," I mused aloud, not having thought of such a possibility before, but intrigued now that I'd said the words. "Would you mind?"

"Of course not. You deserve a trip." He seemed relieved that I'd thought of it and eager to return to his interrupted research. "You can still go to India in the winter," he said absently, adjusting his glasses and slipping away again into the tome of ancient art.

4

The small parking lot beside Samuelson's Market was nearly full on Saturday mornings. In the second row, I found an empty space and turned the Volvo into it.

To the right of the market's IN door, a card table had been set up. Lying on it was a pile of leaflets and sitting beside it was Roberta Arneson, the many gold bracelets on her slender wrist announcing her persona with a thin jingle.

Roberta's smooth black hair was pulled back from a ruler-sharp center part and secured by a green grosgrain bow at the nape of a graceful neck. Her eyes were green and fringed by black lashes beneath exquisitely arched brows. Her nose was long, but not too long, and her lips well shaped and full. She wore pale lipstick and cheek color so subtle only a keen and jaundiced eye like my own could recognize that it wasn't natural. A fine-looking woman was Roberta Arneson.

She was dressed in a green-and-white-striped Lacoste polo shirt and white wraparound skirt, and on her feet she wore Bernardo thongs. Her aging preppie voice, thin and jingling like her bracelets, hailed me.

"Larry, shame on you. Why haven't you called? How long have you been at the cottage?"

"Only a week."

"Let's have lunch at the club next week." The "club," located a mile or so east of Blind Moose, was a quasi–country club with a nine-hole golf course. Membership came from both Blind Moose and Belleville. The food was notorious. Roberta probably had a new golf skirt.

"Let me check the schedule, Roberta."

"Robby," she corrected. "You always forget to call me Robby."

I didn't forget. It was just that she and her son Bobby were frequently in tandem, and "Robby and Bobby" sounded improbably infantile. Once or twice I'd tried, but it was no use.

I had never liked Roberta and she had never liked me. I'd always thought her a brittle, snobbish conniver. And that was when I felt generous. She'd pulled her son Bobby nearly in two trying to gain his undivided loyalty. She'd used him to hurt Harry when it served her purposes. She criticized Harry for the way he ran the *Courant* and most especially for the paper's editorial policies.

Her opinion of me was as ruthless as mine of her. I was a flirt (which was perfectly true). I was bohemian. Only in a village like Belleville, upright as a white picket fence, would anyone conceive of me as bohemian. On what did she base this epithet? That I was an artist. I didn't call myself that, Roberta did. And in her mouth the word became a subtle derogation: one understood of course that a certain moral ambivalence and emotional instability attached to the word "artist," and one must make allowances.

But calling me an artist was a sly insult to Harry as well: you didn't have to be anything special for an artist to find you attractive.

Artists were a notoriously goatish breed. And: only a man as obtuse as Harry would fail to see what everyone else certainly did—that I was unconventional and possessed of the artist's natural disdain for society. Nestled cozily into Roberta's assessment of me was the hint that someone like myself was a lighted fuse.

I was amused and pleased that Roberta saw me as bohemian. One would have to be a consummate Babbitt to be any more conventional in one's public behavior than I was. But it was convenient for her to think of me this way since it explained why I found her crowd dull.

She had assembled a coterie of those whose friendships tended along business lines. From an inconsiderable distance it resembled a commercial trade association. There was nothing wrong with that, but because Roberta was an exemplar, the others were slightly failed imitations of her. And a herd of Robertas was nothing one would care to be stampeded by.

Roberta's dislike of me had little effect on my summers in Belleville. Because her husband and I were friends, occasionally her life and mine overlapped, but when they did, we threw on disguises and played at being friends. This may seem hypocritical, but it's the sort of flimflam that keeps the homicide rate in villages low.

Roberta was sunshine itself this morning, eager to enlist me in the fight against Harry. What a triumph that would be. While I had no intention of signing up with her, my righteousness toward Harry's wife was currently flaccid. I would hear her out politely.

"I suppose you've heard about Belle Rive Estates, Larry. It's going to turn this town around, I'm convinced. Absolutely turn it around. You know—jobs and a bigger tax base and that sort of thing. Bobby and I are terribly excited." She handed me one of the leaflets from the table. "Hollis Gibney has organized a group to spread the good news. Bobby and I have volunteered our humble services. We printed these," she said, indicating the leaflets. "I think they're awfully good-looking, don't you?"

The work turned out by Robby and Bobby was always impeccable. The graphics on these were clean, bold, attention-demanding. Robby, Bobby, and Hollis must have started this work immediately after Harry Arneson learned about Belle Rive Estates and Valhalla Projects. Had Roberta been in touch with Valhalla Projects?

Tossing her head in a strangely unabashed gesture, Roberta said, "It's been painful having to oppose Harry on this. I searched my conscience, Larry, and sought the advice of friends. In the end it was Hollis who showed me my moral duty." She inspected her perfectly manicured nails and found them not wanting. "As Hollis pointed out, it's money that frees men to do good, and if Belle Rive Estates brings a lot of money into our little community, we're all bound to be better people for it. When I saw that, I threw myself and Arneson Printing on the side of the angels." She looked up from her nails. "Naturally, Bobby joined me." Having given Roberta and his son Arneson Printing when Bobby graduated from college, Harry was being hoisted on his own generosity.

Roberta pointed to the leaflet in my hand. "If you read that, Larry, I know you'll throw yourself on the side of the angels, too."

I realized with a stab of chagrin that my mouth was pursing in the unattractive manner that Roberta inspired.

As I slouched along in the checkout line, the woman ahead of me explained to Vera Samuelson at the cash register that she'd once known a Gladys Falworth who moved to Sioux City, Iowa. She guessed that her Gladys Falworth probably was no relative of Harold Falworth, Inc., of Dallas, Texas. On the other hand, she might have been a second or third cousin. But Gladys had stopped exchanging Christmas cards some years ago, probably because postage had gone sky-high, so it would no doubt remain a mystery whether she'd been related to Harold Falworth, Inc., of Dallas, Texas, who had bought Ernie Duffy's farm to put up condominiums.

"Mrs. Demming, how are you? Enjoying the river?" Vera Samuelson chatted as she rang my groceries on the register. "What do you think about the condominiums? Exciting, isn't it?"

"I'm not sure what to think. I worry about the river, what will happen to it."

"Well, yes, I know what you mean," she said, packing the groceries in a bag. "I'm sure we all feel that way. But when it comes down to it, I think we have to ask ourselves which is more important—people or rivers, don't you?" She smiled as though I were an eight-year-old who'd missed a particularly obvious point in the Bible lesson. In all the years of summering here, I'd never grown used to the way local tradespeople treated summer residents like exotic children of modest intelligence.

I picked up my bag of groceries, bid her a pleasant day, and

---

strode through the automatic OUT door, hoping Vera would drop a roll of half-dollars on her foot.

So far Samuelson's Market, Arneson Printing, and Gibney Chevrolet were, as Roberta had expressed it, "on the side of the angels." A heavenly choir of some proportions was beginning to assemble. And since Clete and Vera Samuelson and Hollis and Ginger Gibney were part of Roberta's clique, it looked as though she were forming the nucleus of Harry's opposition in the palm of her hand.

Hollis Gibney had taken over for Roberta, passing out leaflets to Saturday shoppers and assaulting the gentle morning air with a fusillade of empty laughter. Hollis was a paranoid, resentful, unlovable boy, grown portly, pink, and middle-aged. Pale hair that gave the appearance of being freckled, like his skin, grew sparse over a pink dome. And his body oozed sweat and oil as though it were trying to melt itself down.

At one time Hollis had eyed the political arena with hope and longing. He yearned to have power over more than his wife, Ginger, and the half-dozen men he employed at the Chevrolet garage and dealership. He hungered for power over events and power over people, a power which those people could not evade by locking themselves in the spare bedroom or quitting his employ. In short, Hollis dreamed of dictatorship. It crossed my mind that he might see Belle Rive Estates as an issue from which to springboard into public office. Spying me as I tried to slip past like someone he didn't know, he crowed, "Larry. Good to see you." A man of overweening jocularity, half of Hollis's words were chortled, as though every banality were a rich bon mot.

"Hollis," I acknowledged, nodding my head.

"Don't rush off," he convulsed. "Take one of our leaflets home with you." He stood and thrust his body across the table, leaflet in hand.

"I have one, thank you."

"This," he said, placing a strong, beefy finger on one of the leaflets lying on the table, "is the side of the angels, and we're going to make things just a leee-e-tle hot for the fellas who don't want to pluck harp strings with us." He slapped the table and guffawed. "We'll use economic sanctions, if need be, to see that the common good prevails." He held his head on one side in a boyish way and grinned broadly, coldly.

"What sort of sanctions?" I asked, fighting the impulse to retreat a step, as from a snake in my path.

"That would depend on the business. But to give you a forinstance, if a fellow was running a newspaper, he'd be pretty dependent on his advertisers, wouldn't you say? And if a few of them were to take their ads out of the paper, they'd probably have the fellow by the short hairs. Now that's just a, you know, random example, but there's legal ways of making folks see the common good." He smirked self-righteously.

I shifted the bag of groceries, which was growing heavy, and leaned over the table until our faces were close. Imagining that I was going to share some cozy, gossipy item, possibly concerning Save the River, Hollis's smirk stretched wider, and he turned a large, red, freckled ear toward me, to catch every juicy drop.

Into his ear I cooed, "Hollis, take your harp and shove it where angels fear to tread."

"Economic sanctions!" With the tip of the paddle, I pushed the canoe sharply away from the dock. "Economic sanctions!" Paddling across Belle Riviere, I was throbbing with fury.

I wanted to crush Hollis like a huge pink beetle whose armor would collapse with a brittle, satisfying snap beneath my heel. It was Harry and *The River Courant* that Hollis had in mind for economic sanctions. Hollis and the others would withdraw their advertising and carry it across the river to the *Blind Moose Mirror,* which was little more than a shopper's guide and ran no risk of upsetting them with editorial policy. If enough business people went along, Harry would be ruined.

Grinding my teeth, I let the canoe come hard aground. Pulling it up on the beach, I grabbed the beach towel, threw it on the bank, and stomped along the water's edge, kicking up sand and cursing.

I wished Daisy Fitzroy weren't in Minneapolis with the Purvis children. How rotten of her to be gone.

Seizing a gray and twisted stick from the beach, I whacked it against the water, punishing Harry's enemies, as I rammed along the river's margin.

Was Roberta deliberately trying to ruin Harry? If Harry's son followed his mother, the paper was all Harry had left. What would become of him if the paper went under?

Gaining the farthest reach of negotiable beach, where trees

grew down to the water, I turned back toward the canoe. I hurled the stick into the river and kicked recklessly at the smooth, water-licked pebbles in my path. The second kick met an immovable rock, submerged in sand and water. A hammer stroke of pain shot up my leg. I cried out and fell to the sand, clutching the foot like a baby. Tears of pain and self-pity trickled down my cheeks. I sat huddled, facing the woods, rocking and keening, like a widow in an Irish tragedy.

A sound, as of someone clearing his throat, intruded upon my hysterics. The undergrowth ahead of me trembled and whispered. My heart beat as wildly as a piece of cheap machinery out of control. Slowly I stood, ignoring the painful foot.

"Goddamn you!" I hobbled up the slope like a madwoman. Beating aside the foliage, I broke into the forest. "How dare you!" My glance darted from tree to tree, bush to bush. "Where...?"

Forty feet away, watching with ancient, impenitent composure, naked body insolent in repose as he leaned against a gnarled oak, he waited.

5

The bathroom was stifling, clogged with steam. A tight, harsh spray of uncomfortably hot water stung my body. Turning slowly beneath it, I was flailed, back and front, but I couldn't get warmed through. I let the shower run until the hot water was exhausted and the stream grew tepid. But when I stepped out and wrapped myself in a huge bath sheet and then a warm gown and robe, I was cold.

The scene in the woods had stopped my blood or turned it to icewater. My mind was a foreign country. If this...thing I'd found roamed in it, what else lurked in its wildwood? The cold space between the sheets was a cave to shelter me.

I pulled the covers tightly around my neck so that only my head stuck out above them, and I clung to myself, trying to find some body heat to warm my limbs. The sides of my face ached with constant effort to prevent my teeth chattering. Just as they did in winter if I was insufficiently wrapped up, the muscles in my abdomen twisted into a painful knot from the cold. The temperature in the room must have been eighty-five.

At five Bart wandered in with a martini in his hand. "Under the weather?"

I nodded.

"What's wrong?"

"Cold . . . cold." I heard this as though from another room.

"Coming down with the flu?"

I nodded.

"I'll fix myself dinner. Can I get you anything?"

I shook my head.

"Call me if you need me." He tiptoed out, closing the door softly behind him.

I slept. When I didn't sleep, it was very much like sleep. And then it was morning. Time passed, but it was time without shape. Bart brought tea and things to eat, toast or canned chicken soup. I ate without remembering that I did.

When the sun shone and it was Monday, I was still cold. By Tuesday afternoon my mind was like a fist that could no longer be held clenched. Unwelcome pictures insinuated themselves. To prevent them, I filled my head with the immediate environment. Part of the immediate environment was Bart.

I watched him execute his simple, unhurried routines. He functioned quite neatly, quite satisfactorily without me. He lived his life compactly, successfully, accomplishing his goals, enjoying the accomplishment. His life proceeded on schedule, as undeviating as the German railway system.

It was not unpleasant to observe him succeeding. It was rather noninvolving in any practical or deeply emotional sense. I saw that my function in life was to observe Bart succeeding. There was no irony in the discovery.

Aside from light housekeeping and observing, I served little purpose in his household. On the contrary, I perceived that I interrupted the quiet, the concentration, the smoothly advancing order in his days. While he *was* preoccupied, he was not the classic absentminded professor. Not by any means. He was a person of intense focus. I jiggled the lens and threw the focus out of whack. Wasn't he actually quite patient and tolerant not to have pointed this out?

From the uncustomary and detached sickbed perspective, I thought our marriage looked like a dead horse. One I'd been daily currying and propping up.

Wednesday morning, when Bart brought in the tray, I caught his hand. "Is everything going well? I know you don't like to discuss the book, but are you . . . pleased?"

"Oh, yes." He smiled with childlike satisfaction. "Since you've been sick, I've played catch-up with my schedule. It's clicking along beautifully."

Wednesday night I determined to face what had happened in the woods. First time around, I paced off the morning and my encounter with Roberta and Hollis. Second time, I marched into the afternoon and through the injury to my foot out on the beach.

Then I halted. My cold hands worked nervously at the hem of the sheet. My hands looked very old. I turned my gaze away from them.

Outside the windows, birch and pine stood silhouetted against the gray-lavender of late evening. Slowly I slid my legs out of bed. Standing at the window, I could just make out the river below. The opposite shore threatened, or maybe beckoned. I shivered and climbed back into bed.

Hours later, after Bart was long asleep, I woke and lay staring and restless. Getting up, I padded into the bathroom. Leaning over the basin, I examined the face in the mirror with apprehension. Did it look tetched? Vacant and staring?

I turned slightly to the side, to catch the face unawares. But observed objectively in this most cruel of all lights, the late-night bathroom light, the face was reassuring. It was no longer young, it was presently haggard, but it was not daft-looking. I was grateful.

I tiptoed to the kitchen. The bulb in the refrigerator was yellow and cordial, revealing half a bottle of rosé on the top shelf. I carried it to the table and sat down close to the window. Dotted-swiss curtains were pulled back and warm night air gathered around, lenient and abetting.

I looked at the moon, white as untanned buttocks. It seemed to shed an inordinate amount of light on the scene: crooked fence posts bordering the field opposite, telephone wire strung low across the sky, a pale backyard blanket of grass.

No place or time would be more supportive than this for remembering. I drank quickly from the bottle of rosé, then set it away from me.

In plain, hard-edged words, I had seen a Mythical Beast in the woods. Part human, part—goat? In memory I saw the satyr again, a tall, swarthy-skinned animal leaning against an oak, arms folded insouciantly across a great, broad chest; thick, pointy black brows lifted as though in mild surprise to see me. But he wasn't surprised, of course. Up and down his face tiny ripples of amusement played, and I can't say how I knew it from that distance but I did.

I dropped to my knees in a swoon of terror, the paralyzing terror of nightmare, when one begs to wake or die. From that moment on, memory became half conjecture. I imagined that he'd thrown back his immense head, covered with sooty curls, and laughed a laugh ringing with accumulated grief and mystery. And I imagined, too, that close to me I saw hoofs like milky-veined marble, pale against the brown earth, with fur above them white and soft as swansdown, feathering out in graceful frills where it met each hoof. And as I fell, I was caught in a cradling hammock of potent darkness.

6

Why would Larissa Maureen McClanahan Demming create a Mythical Beast? I asked a coolly detached half-bottle of rosé. I had been, to outward appearances, a sane and ordinary woman, trying since my marriage to fashion myself into something smooth and blameless as an egg, trying not to be a mistake my husband would rue. To perform as trouble-free as his Olivetti, comfort as unstintingly as his fleece-lined house slippers, and reflect his good taste as eloquently as his silk ties—this had been my resolve.

I was a faculty wife, collector for fund drives, Democratic Party canvasser, rummage sale volunteer, chronicler of family history. All this did not bespeak a woman who falls down mad one day at the feet—hoofs—of a Mythical Beast.

I pulled the bottle to me and drank. There was an unopened bottle of Burgundy in the cupboard.

How did a run-of-the-mill forty-seven-year-old woman come

by a creature like that? My mother? Had I inherited him from Marie Anderson McClanahan, dead over thirty years?

Marie Anderson, only child of a Lutheran minister, had at the age of eighteen married James (Jamie) John McClanahan in a Roman Catholic nuptial mass, thus distancing herself from a family which hitherto in modern history claimed not a single Catholic.

It was a pity the Andersons took it so heavily, since it was only rarely that Jamie or Marie went to mass. My own interest in the faith was desultory. I never experienced the free-flight sensation one was said to earn with confession and absolution, and after my mother's death I had reason to give it up altogether.

Marie Anderson had been distilled by the passing years to a slender volume of facts and close-mouthed illustrations. This because she'd lived life not on the surface, where it could be noted and recalled by others, but beneath a seamless countenance. She had been a beautiful woman, with fine hair, only slightly darker than cream, pulled tightly back from features of cameo perfection. Mounted as they were in so pale a setting, her eyes, nearly black, were startling and demanding. They were occasional discoursers. But like a child who has read an adult book and recognized the words without comprehending the story, I hadn't grasped the narrative in them. If she suffered monsters, they remained her secret. And if I inherited one of them, that and her black eyes and a legacy of five thousand dollars were all I inherited.

Draining the nearly empty bottle of wine, I sat in the dark trying to conjure up Marie Anderson. Reason told me that she had been lonely, cut off from her family, and never forming a cohesive bond with her husband. She'd been the pale, cool, silent moon set distant from the blustering, lyrical west wind that was Jamie. Against her reserve had been his blarney and impudence.

Little though I'd understood his relationship to my mother, I'd been enchanted by him, so much that after my mother's death I wondered if I hadn't wished her dead so that I could have him to myself. With his black curls and ice-blue eyes, he'd been larger and more tempting than life. He had sung to me, danced with me, recited poetry, encouraged my sketching and, very important, named me. He had seen the name Larissa on a map of Greece. "It's the fairest name a lass ever had," he'd crooned in the sly brogue he affected as a kind of joke on himself.

After my mother's death Jamie had seen me through high

school, sold the house and three thriving hardware stores in Minneapolis, and begun to buck and wing his way around the world. At the university I lived year-round in the dorm. Sometimes he called, rarely he stopped over, and occasionally he posted sketchy, unsatisfactory accounts of his odyssey.

Now I didn't know where he was. The last postcard said Edmonton, which seemed to indicate a progress of sorts toward home (though there was no "home"), but that assumption could prove premature. Jamie could as lief turn around and head for Vladivostok, or he might stay in Alberta a year or more. There were any number of places in the world where he had holed up a year or two. I didn't think it likely we would see him soon.

Rising abruptly, noisily from the table, I grabbed the Burgundy down from the cupboard. Rummaging clumsily through a drawer, I found a corkscrew and carried it to the table. The Burgundy had a harsh edge to it and made my mouth feel coated.

Enough of Jamie. The less, the better.

With the bottle of wine in one hand and a waterglass in the other, I padded through the cottage out to the screened porch overlooking the river. Staring down into the black of trees, I grimaced and sniggered to find I was weeping. *Oh, Christ.* It was embarrassing. To feel such self-pity, even in the dark and alone, was sordid.

Wiping my eyes on the sleeve of my gown, I lowered myself onto the porch swing. With my foot I set it in motion. *Ah, well,* I pointed out frankly, in the manner of a Dutch uncle, *it may not be the worst thing, being crazy.* I thought about that for a while. *Starvation, maybe? Cancer? Losing a child? At any rate I have the comfort of knowing I'm rather narrowly crazy. It's nearly Thursday (the sky would soon pale over there behind the woods) and no further delusion has come forward. Only the Beast.* I poured Burgundy into the glass. *Harpy and griffin have I none.*

At seven I woke with a hung-over head and a crick in my neck from sleeping in the swing. Recorking the wine, I put it in the refrigerator, throwing what remained in the tumbler down the sink. Bart was up and working in his study. I put coffee on and at seven-thirty he came out to pour himself a cup.

"Feeling better?" he inquired, stirring half-and-half into his cup.

"Yes. I'm going to get up today."

"Good. I was beginning to worry," he said and picked up cup and saucer. "I'll toddle off then." And he went back to his work.

I sat at the table staring after him. Had Bart really wanted to marry me? I suddenly wondered. I found that I couldn't recall clearly how he'd behaved before we were married. Had he pursued me? Had I pursued him? At that moment it seemed the strangest thing in the world that we were married, that we had been married for twenty-six years! More bizarre and far more unreal than the Beast.

Now, *really*, I thought, *stop this!* I went to the cupboard to find aspirin. From beyond the window came the crunch of the mail truck stopping in the graveled road, the thunk of the day's allotment being tossed into the black metal box and then a little snick as the door was flipped shut. I waited until the truck had growled away in low gear before letting myself out the back door and wading through the wet morning grass.

Crazy or not, what was there to do but to pick up your two feet and put them down, read the paper, cook the dinner, and try to find a spare room in life for a Mythical Beast?

The part of me that was essentially female and pragmatic, and therefore optimistic of solutions and accommodations, began preparing a room: I observed again that only *one* apparition had visited me; I didn't own a whole zoo full of delusions. If I was very clever and circumspect, and assuming things didn't get a whole lot worse, I could probably keep people from finding out. Certainly it shouldn't be hard to keep from Bart. And finally, there might be some positive use for the...Beast.

Oh, I knew it wasn't *that* easy. Beneath this soldierly management of my insanity, I knew that I was more frightened than I had ever been. At any moment the cold shakes could grab me again. But in the meantime I picked up my two feet and put them down. And in the mailbox found an electric bill from Northern States Power Company and *The River Courant*.

The sunlight beating slantwise against the porch floor was hot and brilliant. From a table in the living room I fetched sunglasses. I'd been too many days in the half-light of the bedroom.

The paper contained more news of Belle Rive Estates. A private marina was part of the plan, the *Courant* said. Depressing, but not surprising.

"A meeting of the Save the River Committee is scheduled for this evening, June 24, 7:30 P.M., at the home of Daisy and George Fitzroy, 127 Fleur Street, Belleville. Anyone interested in preserving the quality of our community life and the unspoiled nature of the river environment is invited to attend. For further information call 391-1020."

I rose from the wicker chair and faced Belle Riviere. The water glittered around the dock below me. From the dock one could see mossy pebbles in the shallows and small fish swimming among them. A marina upstream, pouring gasoline, oil, and other manner of pollution into the water would alter this. I frowned. That day in Harry's office he'd said, "The water won't be fit for anything— including fish. The woods'll be destroyed and the wildlife killed or driven off."

The wildlife. My gaze moved across the water and came to rest on the trees along the other bank. What effect would this new intrusion by civilization have on a Mythical Beast? A dangerous and misconceived monster it might be, but it was mine.

7

Daisy's home was an imposing three-story Victorian, heavily adorned with gingerbread, stained glass, and treillage, and towering over the village like a dowager empress over a tea table. High on the slope it sat, looking out over streets and river. From the cupola, Daisy said you could see 1893 and the retreating figure of Grover Cleveland. Softening its dignity were masses of red geraniums, petunias, or zinnias in ample white wooden boxes on the wrap-around porch and in smaller boxes on the broad steps leading down to the front walk.

Though the sky was wisteria-colored when I climbed the steps with a basket of cookies in hand, the gas lamp at the end of the walk was lit, as were the carriage lamps on either side of the front door.

Daisy, in a blue handkerchief-linen shirtdress, held the screen door for me.

"Am I the first?"

"Except for Harry and Sam Fergus."

She took the cookies and headed for the kitchen. "Cup of coffee?"

"Yes." I followed.

In the big blue-and-white kitchen Daisy handed me a silver tray and set the basket on the table. "Arrange the cookies on this while I get the coffee."

"Do you have any idea how many people will show up?"

"Not a clue," she said. "Several have called and said they'd come, but how many will show up, I don't know."

"Did you get any idea, from the calls, what *sort* of people are interested?"

"Well, one was a teacher at the high school. I forget what she said her name was. I wrote it down. Last year was her first here." Daisy sat on a stool and ticked people off on her fingers. "One was a retired farmer. One was the young minister at the Methodist Church, Mark Braun. No, I guess there's not much of a pattern."

We heard the old-fashioned brass doorbell and Daisy jumped up and ran to answer it. Until the meeting came to order at seven-forty-five, I remained in the kitchen rearranging cookies I'd already arranged. Although I was determined to be at the meeting, in the wake of my five-day dropout I felt shaky, insubstantial, and not quite of this world. Also, I was afraid to see Harry.

About fifty people were crowded into the Fitzroy living room and adjoining formal dining room when Sam Fergus strode briskly to the front of the living room and rapped a gavel on the library table, getting business under way.

Sam, a retired district judge and widower, was seventy-two. Well-read, witty, and aggressively dapper, he was a shamelessly fought-over extra man at dinner parties, in both Belleville and the metropolitan area of Minneapolis and St. Paul, "the Twin Cities," or as they're known in the provinces, "the Cities."

I glanced around to see what sort of people shared a desire to save Belle Riviere. No one age, sex, or economic group predominated. There were a number of farmers who'd left the fields early in order to make the meeting, their wives, a dozen or so college kids home for the summer, senior citizens who'd pulled up in a van marked BELLEVILLE SENIOR COMMUNITY (the "Community" was a high-rise apartment building at the north end of Main Street), several teachers, a retired doctor, and so it went. No discernible pattern except for a poor representation of merchants, and no bankers that I could see.

Across the dining room, near the window—in fact trying to blend into the voluminous chintz draperies—was Roberta Arneson's best friend, Brenda Bergquist. She was without husband Arch, owner of the Little Palace movie house, and she appeared to have arrived alone. She scanned the gathering furtively, looking for some specific person or taking notes. Gliding her hand into her bag, she glanced around to see if she was observed, then looking as though she might pull a weapon, she pulled instead a small spiral pad and a pen and began to scratch notes on the paper.

She was spying. She of the fourteen-word French vocabulary and imitation Louis XV furniture upholstered in pink vinyl would gladly fix her star more securely in Roberta's firmament by volunteering an evening of cloak and dagger.

Brenda's presence sent a thrill of foreboding through me. Was the battle for Belle Riviere to be a dreadful little war of espionage, character assassination, and neighborly nastiness from which we might none of us come quite clean? I turned toward the living room.

"Welcome. I'm Sam Fergus. I'm pleased and grateful to meet you." He gave us a shard of shy smile. A genuinely kind and warm man, he was nonetheless as wily as a Jimmy Stewart naif. "I like fancy duds, as you can see. If I were to tell you I'm just a simple country boy, you'd snicker and put me down for a damned liar. But if a country boy is someone who loves the country, who'd like to preserve its integrity for himself and others to enjoy, then I *am* a country boy. If not a simple one, then a sophisticated one. And so must we all be if we hope to hang on to Nature and not see her snatched out of our grasp and destroyed. We must be sophisticated in our knowledge of what is valuable and vulnerable, sophisticated in our methods of preserving and protecting it.

"The value of Belle Riviere is twofold: the protective habitat it provides animal life, and the joy it gives humans. The sloughs formed by the river's overflow are an unsurpassed breeding area for waterfowl, many species of which we've all but eliminated from a world that was as much theirs as ours. The shores of the river are home to deer, raccoon, beaver, and bear. Once these animals kept men alive. Now men must return the favor.

"We're afraid that two hundred condominiums and a marina will destroy the beauty, the serenity, the sanctuary of the area. We are asking that an independent study be commissioned to determine what the impact would be, and that after the results of the study are published, residents of the community be allowed to determine the future of Belle Rive Estates.

"We hope that the cohesion of our community will not be a victim of Valhalla Projects. We are not here tonight to divide a community or to set one neighbor against another. We are here to save the river. It is part of our inheritance, one of the primary reasons our parents, grandparents, and great-grandparents settled here, invested their lives here. It provided food, transportation, and recreation. And...heart's ease. You all have felt that at some time." He concluded, "There is a spiritual value to the river which we must not blush to recognize or hesitate to give estimation to." With a deferential nod to his audience, Sam moved to one side to allow Harry the floor.

Harry looked drawn. He'd come directly from the paper to the meeting. The pale-blue button-down shirt he wore was limp, and the sleeves were rolled above his elbows. The tan chinos looked slept-in and there was a memory of spilled coffee above one knee.

Harry began explaining the nuts and bolts of the committee's work; the subcommittees that must be named and headed up, the funds that must be raised, and so forth.

"Daisy Fitzroy is overall chairperson and any suggestions you come up with can be filtered through her. I'll be handling publicity until some kind person relieves me of the job. Sam is our one-man legal staff at the moment and will need clerical help immediately. He is currently checking laws—local, state, and federal—to determine what our options are. He'll also be examining the course Valhalla Projects has taken, and intends to pursue, with regard to zoning and environmental laws."

I stood at the side of the dining room, near the door to the kitchen, watching Harry, listening to him conclude his remarks and begin answering questions from the audience. I had not shrugged the dim, floating world of the past five days. My mind persisted in drifting and muddling the scene as if vacillating between wakefulness and sleep. I couldn't get a locking hold on the here and now. Another image kept melting over the one before me. Another male figure, large and strong like Harry, but ancient and artful and frightening, even from a distance of five days.

It was for him that I was here. He, as much as the deer and bear, would be protected if we were successful. Wasn't it singular, I thought, how I'd set myself to guard him rather than exorcise him?

Harry's figure came into focus once more, picking up a pile of leaflets from the table and handing them to the first person in the front row. "Take one or several of these and pass them along, please."

Harry stepped back again to the table and slumped his weight against it. His eyes burned with exhaustion and he looked like a zealot, strung out on fervor. Was this battle for the river the game for which I'd imagined him searching? His voice when he continued was calm, however. "There is an event already in the planning that will kick off our fund raising. Friday night, July second, Daisy and George Fitzroy will host a party in their backyard. Admission will be ten dollars per person. There will be a no-host bar and live music donated by Sam Fergus's grandson, Dave Fergus, and his group, Backwater. Anyone who'd like to help with this project can speak to Daisy tonight or call her in the next few days."

"One last question, Mr. Arneson." An elderly woman, one of those from the Belleville Senior Community, rose with the help of a cane. Leaning slightly toward the speaker's table, she looked fragile as tissue paper, but she was intent. "This outfit—Valhalla Projects—they're Arabs?" She inclined her head to catch the answer with her good ear.

For twenty minutes *Robert's Rules of Order* went out the window. It's difficult for anyone not living in a hard climate to understand life-and-death dependence on gas and oil, or the victimization felt by those who must pay half or more of a small income to keep from freezing.

"Please. Please." The judge rapped his gavel. Slowly the group resumed their seats. "I know your frustration. But we mustn't lose sight of why we're here. It's the river. *Whoever* threatened it, it would be just as imperative to save it."

Daisy's husband, George, slipped into the dining room through the door beside me. He gave me a nod. "Sam'll adjourn it now. Want to give me a hand?"

I followed him through the swinging door. The kitchen was heady with the aroma of strong coffee. We loaded a large urn, paper cups and napkins, cookies and cream and sugar onto a mahogany tea cart.

"Things were hot out there for a minute," I said. "It's going to be messy, isn't it?"

"Yes. That's what it'll be." He added plastic spoons to the load. "You signing on? Daisy wasn't sure you were interested."

"I've gotten a new perspective since I talked to Daisy last week."

We wheeled the cart into the dining room. People were milling around. Some were asking questions. Others were signing committee sheets. Still others were gathered in fervent little knots of concern. Nodding and listening intently to the arguments of several villagers, Harry rested his weight against the speaker's table, arms crossed in front of him.

Pouring myself a cup of coffee, I noted Brenda Bergquist making her way with theatrical stealth to the foyer and presumably out the front door. Within her crowd she would dine out on this until even her closest chums would go rigid and vacant-eyed with boredom every time it was resurrected.

I returned to the kitchen and checked the sink to see if there were dirty dishes I could wash. Unfortunately, there were none. How long would Harry stay? Maybe I should go out the back way and call Daisy in the morning.

"Larissa!"

I looked up from the now-cold cup of coffee as Harry bounded into the kitchen.

"You've changed your mind, Daisy just told me. How come you're hiding in the kitchen?"

"I'm not hiding," I lied.

"Well, come out and have a drink. Everyone's left except the hard drinkers—Sam and me and of course Daisy and George."

He put a big hand on my back and led me down the hall and into the living room. My skin beneath Harry's hand was hot and seemed to leap to meet his skin. A reckless surge of excitement lifted me free of the earth and pulled me along, helpless but consenting.

8

Lifting the second damp sheet from the laundry basket, carefully so it wouldn't trail in the grass, I removed a clothespin from between my teeth and fastened the sheet to the clothesline. It was a small wash: a few towels and the bed linens. Our sheets had looked unsoiled, but I washed them to freshen them in the summer sun. Having huddled five days between those same sheets, I might have expected them to be in a good deal worse condition.

Five days. Only yesterday I'd gotten up, but already the five days seemed months ago. The Beast was fresh and sharp in my memory, however. His image was so real it felt like a thing of weight and mass that I carried around inside me.

I fastened the last clothespin and picked up the laundry basket. I felt heavy and ungainly as a pregnant ox. Last night's reckless, lightsome mood was gone. Slowly I lowered the basket to the grass and then my great, heavy self as well. Bart's study window was only ten or twelve feet away. It didn't matter. He wouldn't notice. I sat in the grass beneath the clothesline and thought how my mood swung violently up and down and how I tried to catch and hold it as it soared or plummeted, but could only observe helplessly as it slipped through my hands.

Get up, I told myself. *Put the basket away. Have a cup of coffee.* I heard the mail van coming along the road. It stopped beside our box and the postman hesitated, unsure whether I would walk over and take the mail from him. I stayed where I was. I didn't want him to see my face. Finally, he leaned out of the van, opened the box, and tossed the mail into it.

"'Lo. Nice morning." He pulled on the peak of his cap in a kind of salute.

"Yes. Nice." My arms locked tightly around the laundry basket held on my lap.

"Well, have a good day." He put in the clutch, shifted into low, and was gone.

I sat until all the dust had settled again to earth, then urged myself up. Carrying the basket, I plodded over to the box. Maybe there would be an invitation. To what? *I don't know. I can't think of everything.*

One letter. The return address was Miranda's, but the letter in the box was addressed solely to me. That was noteworthy. I threw it into the basket and walked around the cottage to the front porch. My feet dragged in the long grass. I sat on the porch swing and picked the letter open slowly, meticulously, as though I might want to seal it up again.

> Selfless and Adoring Mother!
>
> In the past I've dismissed your eccentricity as fey, even charming. But it's become disturbing. Reading your recent letter, I was angry that you were trying to run my life and insulted that you'd think I could be moved by such nonsense as your "Beast." But I was also concerned by the distance you're putting between yourself and reality.
>
> I don't mean to be cruel, Mother, but I live and work in the *real* world. You've lived your life in a shadow world, first in Granddad's shadow, then Dad's. You've never fought, as I do, for a place in the sun. What gives you the right to question my judgment?
>
> Dennis and I will not alter our plans by a day. If you continue interfering and disapproving, you'll find yourself very much outside of things. I don't want to exclude you. It's your choice.
>
> I didn't show Dennis your letter. I have no reason, therefore, to cancel our July 4 plans. We'll drive up after work Friday, the 2nd, and return very early Tuesday. If you mention anything about postponing the wedding or letting my Mythical Beast run free, I'll pack my bag and leave.
>
> I don't like to think that there are monsters in your life, Mother. Have you had a physical recently? This may all be some sort of midlife hormone imbalance. Make an appointment with Dr. Minnelli.
>
> And why don't you get a pet or something to occupy you?
>
> Love,
> Miranda

For a long time I sat, empty and inanimate, staring across the sunny room at nothing. At last I lifted the letter and shifted my staring gaze to it.

"Eccentricity?" *What* eccentricity? Even as one layer of brain reacted angrily, however, another was simpering with self-conscious delight, *Me? Really?* A brain that had for years felt obliged to smooth out its wrinkles couldn't avoid relishing the label "Eccentric."

But the letter was pontifical and stuffy and cruel. "Shadow world!" That I resented through and through. It was true, of course, but because it was true, and dreadful, and past undoing, it shouldn't have been said. And what Miranda didn't see was that life was as real in the shadows as it was in that mythical "place in the sun." What a hackneyed phrase. My daughter had attended one too many Republican fund-raisers.

I would find myself "outside of things," she threatened. "Outside of things" was a weapon honed sharp as a razor. And if she thought that beasts weren't real...

My brain leapt frenziedly thus from one word or phrase to another, stabbing itself with them again and again, sometimes dropping the bloody things only to return seconds later, pick them up and plunge them in again.

"Oh, God," I cried aloud. Lunging up and running to the bedroom, I dropped the letter in a bureau drawer among my sweaters. A minute later I was in the canoe, thrusting its bow toward the opposite shore. Through a scrim of tears, the shore had an unreal, faintly alienating look, like a piece of grainy film.

Pulling the craft out of the water. I threw myself down on the hot, dry sand and wept as I hadn't wept since I was a girl, profoundly, convulsed, half-drowned, unable to stop. She would put me "very much outside of things" if I didn't acquiesce. It was my own fault. But I didn't think I was wrong. I might be crazy but I understood some things. Fifteen years from now Miranda would climb out of bed one day to find herself awake but no longer alive.

Depression finally blunted the peaks of pain. A torpor, a nullity overcame me and I lay insensible. When I tried to sit up, my limbs were reluctant, my head clumsy. I persevered because the alternative was to sink into the sand and unresistingly take root.

I stood gazing sightlessly into the woods, willing myself to the top of an incline of purpose so that I might roll down it with an impetus that would carry me back across the river.

Suddenly, there was a crackling, thudding, shooshing series of sounds. Someone retreated hurriedly through the woods.

"Wait!" I screamed, and hurled myself up the embankment

and through the outer fringe of greenery. How heartless to spy and scorn and run away. I stalked through the trees and brush, gaining the narrow slough. Launching into it, I was slowed by mud above my sneakers, then water above my knees. Emerging into the ooze at the opposite side, my sneakers made sucking sounds as I plodded. I climbed a shallow rise and paused to catch my breath. Gnats and mosquitoes buzzed, imprisoned in my hair.

"Damn you," I cried, "wait for me." I pursued, running raggedly. For a city block, vaulting fallen logs, thrusting aside brambles, praying not to fall, I followed him, straining to hang on to the sounds of his retreat. I mustn't lose the bastard. I could hear him and I was gaining on him.

Ahead, through the trees, I saw a greater intensity of light. A clearing. Nearly there, I gasped for air, my throat strangling, chest pounding like a great, pulverizing piston.

"Stop!" I hadn't enough breath to scream. The word emerged in a thin rasp. As I staggered into the open, fifteen yards away a figure collapsed in the tall, shimmering, indifferent grass.

I'd run him to ground. Him and his frightening, naked body. "Stand up!" I demanded hoarsely. I stood, swaying, hands on hips, barely able to keep my head upright on its yielding stem. I wiped away tears with my forearm, and the salt from my sweaty arm seared my eyes.

He didn't move. I wanted to beat him senseless. My legs trembled. Sinking to my knees, I crawled toward the darkness in the grass that I knew was him.

"Missus," he wheezed, "missus, please. I'm sorry."

A shoe, large, coarse, the leather dry and split, was the first I saw of him. After that, a filthy gray twill trouser leg. A smell of urine.

"Missus, I didn't mean to bother," the man pleaded, sweat glistening on his grizzled face. He held a torn duffel bag before him like a shield.

"Are you all right, old man?"

He nodded frantically, trying to move himself away from me.

"Are you sure?"

"Fer Christ's sake, yes, you crazy bitch."

He wasn't the Mythical Beast.

* * *

The hash-brown potatoes in the iron skillet were perfectly golden. The outer crust resembled starched lace, delicate and crisp, while the fluffy interior was steaming and salty. I had tended the potatoes in a trance of concentration. Single-minded absorption in simple-minded routine provided something firm under my feet while the rest of the universe tilted and reeled beyond my control. I fried the potatoes faultlessly and burned the chops.

"Sorry about the chops."

"They're fine."

"They're burned."

"The Chablis is good."

"Thank you."

Bart ate European-style, never shifting his fork from left hand to right. Most of the time I didn't notice, but if I was off my feed, the sight of him pushing perfectly golden hash-brown potatoes with a knife held in his right hand, onto a fork held in his left, then lifting the fork to his mouth with the genteel, somewhat precious refinement one associates with certain academics, was nearly sufficient cause for me to tip the table over on him. I would have done it if I hadn't had to clean up the mess.

"Miranda and Dennis are coming for the Fourth of July weekend," I said, finding it difficult to unfasten my gaze from Bart's unhurrying, scrupulous hands. "They're driving up after work on Friday."

"How long are they staying?"

"Until early Tuesday," I replied, studying his precisely masticating jaws. Bart chewed his food twenty-four or thirty-six or however many times medical science recommended. I fought the urge to reach across the table and say, "That's enough. You'll chew away your fillings." I continued, "If we clean out the barbecue pit, we can have a cookout Saturday."

He was inhaling his Chablis and lost in its fumes.

"Bart?"

"Well, we'll have to have a cookout while they're here," he said. "I suppose the barbecue pit needs attention. Do we have charcoal?"

"I'll get some at Samuelson's. We can take Miranda and Dennis to the Save the River party if they aren't too tired after the drive. They'd enjoy it, don't you think?"

"Save the River party?"

"At Daisy's. To raise money for the committee."

"Oh, yes, certainly."

The food on my plate looked unreal, like those dead-looking things, made of plaster of Paris or plastic, in restaurant windows. I carried it to the sink, dumped the potatoes and salad into the garbage, and set the chop aside on a saucer. "Will you need the car tomorrow?"

"No."

"I'm driving to Minneapolis."

"Could you bring back the other typewriter? This one's developed a couple of sticky keys." He finished his wine, poured another half-glass, and got up from the table. Passing me on his way out of the kitchen, he bussed my cheek. "That'll be fine, old girl. That'll be just fine."

9

Shades drawn, drapes closed, the house in the city was cool and dark and unfamiliar. Estranged by our absence, it held itself aloof. I would have to pay it some attention before it would cozy up to me again. Finding that I was tiptoeing, I picked out a Duke Ellington cassette and put it in the player. Would that break the ice?

I went to Bart's study, found the typewriter already in its case, and set it beside the front door. Returning to the study, I paused in the doorway, perusing the room, scrutinizing it as I imagined a detective might—Hercule Poirot?—entering it for the first time. What did it reveal of the man who labored in it? Were there telling clues which I might have passed, unseeing, a thousand times, that to a trained eye disclosed Bart's deepest nature, secret terrors, or untold hopes?

To the left was a chair, nearly identical to the one at Belle Riviere, old and colorless and comfortable. On three sides of the room bookshelves reached to the ceiling. Unlike Harry's shelves at the *Courant*, these held almost no memorabilia, although there were framed pictures of Miranda and Clark and me, pictures I framed and placed there, now that I recalled. Did husbands ever do that for themselves? During the Fourth of July weekend, we must have someone take a picture of us all, a family picture.

With my fingertips I caressed the top of an enormous oak rolltop desk, "as big as County Clare," that dominated the fourth wall. A present from Jamie McClanahan to Bart during his first visit following my marriage, it had been salvaged from an old Milwaukee Railroad depot that was being torn down. It was scarred and darkened by years of service. "And so you don't die of thirst before you finish your correspondence," Jamie had said, opening the lower right-hand drawer to reveal a bottle of Bushmill's. He'd arrived with the desk, his only real effort to please Bart. Bart wasn't all that willing to be pleased in any case.

"You find him 'dashing,'" he'd observed in a private moment during Jamie's visit.

"Yes. Don't you?"

"He's your father, of course. I find him rather...bravura, a one-man parade—all that singing and jigging and his constant talk-talk-talk about the places he's been. Aren't you exhausted by it?"

"No. What else does he have to talk about?"

"He's pretty damned critical, too, don't you think? Didn't like your haircut. Your dress was the wrong color. What else? Oh, yes, the fish should have been poached instead of fried."

"He isn't usually critical. Something's stuck in his craw." I didn't say, *It's really you he can't stand, so he's punishing me.* I couldn't let Bart see how upset I was by Jamie's little attacks. He shouldn't know the power Jamie wielded. It would give him further reason to dislike my father, and maybe say something that would keep him away.

Little more was said about Jamie during those few days he was with us. But Bart became suddenly demanding, wanting to be waited on and pampered. In bed he was insistent and heedless, taking more and enjoying it less, as though it weren't the enjoying that mattered, but the taking.

I reached down now to open the lower right-hand drawer. There was a pint of Jack Daniel's and a shot glass. Pouring out a shot, I returned the bottle to the drawer and began slowly, glass in hand, to circle the room, reaching out occasionally to touch something, as though it might speak to my hand.

There were no books strewn or left open to gather dust on their white pages; no old, unanswered correspondence littering the desk; no postcards from someone abroad, tacked up on the wall.

I parted the drapes at the French window beside the desk and gazed out at the tiny flagstone terrace and the deep, narrow, tree-shaded yard. After three weeks untended, it was shaggy as a country dell. Its disorder was reviving after the sterile composition of the room.

Memory of the old man, all filth and consternation, lying in the tall grass of another dell, raised a hot flush to my cheeks and I laughed hard and drank the Jack Daniel's. Closing the drapes and returning the glass to the drawer, I drew the door behind me, no more intimate with Bart's stored yearnings than when I'd arrived. *C'est tout, Hercule?*

Before leaving the house, I went up to our bedroom and found the flowing red dress I meant to wear to Daisy's party. I tossed it on the bed and picked up the telephone to invite Sarah and Clark for next weekend.

"Sarah? Larry. I'm in town. Thanks, dear, but I have to get back to the river. I just wanted to see if you and Clark would come up next weekend. Miranda and Dennis are coming after work Friday. That's lovely. I've saved you a call, then. No, don't bring anything but yourselves. We're going to a party Friday night at Daisy Fitzroy's. You remember Daisy. It's a fund-raiser. I'll explain it all when I see you. If you feel up to the party, bring a sundress or something like that. How are you feeling? Are your ankles swelling? Wonderful. We're just fine. Everything's very usual. Give Clark a hug. See you Friday."

Locking the house, I got in the Volvo and drove across town to the university. After spending a couple of hours in the library, I came away hardly more satisfied than before. In an off-campus bookstore, I picked up W. H. D. Rouse's *Gods, Heroes, and Men of Ancient Greece*, a paperback Bulfinch, and a couple of other promising-looking volumes.

In the pleasant airiness of the New French Café, I sat before a green salad and opened one, then another of the books I'd purchased. How little information there was on the subject of my research. While waiting for my coffee to cool, I used the phone to dial a colleague of Bart's, a classics professor. As I waited, the number ringing, I pondered briefly why I was calling Dr. Fiedler. Why not ask Bart?

Fiedler came on the line, fatherly and a little patronizing. He was curious about my sudden interest in Greek mythology, curious as well to know why I hadn't gone to Bart with my questions. I put him off and said good-bye. The patronage of men like Fiedler had begun to irritate me. Why it should after so many years of tolerating it, I couldn't see.

On the back of a shopping list, I had scribbled a couple of titles that Fiedler had suggested. From the cottage I would drop a note to an old friend at the university bookstore and request help obtaining them. Climbing back into the Volvo after lunch, I headed toward Marquette Avenue. Miranda's bank was on Marquette. I had a sudden hunger to look at her, the sweet contours of her Renaissance face. I longed, whenever I saw her, to touch her high, rounded brow, cool and luminescent as a pearl. Maybe I would only walk through the bank. I didn't want to bother her, and I wasn't sure I had any small talk. From a distance she wouldn't notice me. She sat in her own office, behind a glass wall, always busy.

I left the car in a ramp around the corner. Strolling up Marquette, I decided that if there was no one with Miranda in her office, I would say hello and apologize briefly for the letter that had upset her. Maybe she would have time for a cup of coffee. I could tell her about the party at the Fitzroys' and that she should bring a dress if she planned to attend. Until I devised a way of convincing her to postpone her wedding, I would keep things light. I had by no means given up hope of convincing her.

The enormous brass handle of the bank door didn't yield when I grasped it. It was locked. Today was Saturday, of course, and Miranda's bank wasn't open.

I turned away slowly, re-orienting, considering what to do next. Call her? I didn't think so. Unpleasantness came to one in such a pure form on the telephone. There was only a mouth, an ear, and the wire connecting them. The slim essentials of injury.

Well, let's see, there was still a good deal of shopping I'd promised to do for the committee party. I would walk over to Nicollet Avenue, and do that now. Glancing up and down Marquette, my eye was held by the gold lettering on a window across the street— FARAWAY PLACES. I jaywalked directly toward that beckoning window.

* * *

Later, sitting in Loring Park, I looked at one of the books I'd bought and the largest of the Greek travel pamphlets. "He and his retinue roamed the fields and forests. He was especially fond of Arcadia on the Peloponnese, though it is said he wandered through the mainland also.

"He was attended by nymphs as well as by those who resembled himself in aspect, and all of them loved to sport and dance, often to the irresistible music he provided on the pipes (syrinx).

"During the midday hour they would find a shaded spot and there lie down to rest and renew their spirits for later revels. Mortals coming upon them unawares were often frightened witless for, in addition to the enchanting music of the pipes, the god could render a cry so fearsome it caused the earth to tremble and stout men's courage to fly." When I met the Beast again, I would have the small advantage of my research.

I ducked as a Frisbee sailed close overhead. A leggy, attractive girl ran to fetch it and apologize in a sweet breathless way for the near collision. She reminded me of Miranda.

I loved all the lakes and parks in the city, but this one had been an especial favorite from years before when the adjacent blocks were deep in apartment buildings for the middle class and, later, as the buildings aged, for the lower middle class and poor. Although our house was nearer the park surrounding Lake Calhoun, I'd often brought Clark and Miranda to this one when they were little. Nestled into a raw, has-been setting, it was as unexpected as a bejeweled and crenellated castle. Maintaining this exquisitely designed green gem in what became a neighborhood of welfare and social security incomes, disenfranchised, and stubborn holdouts, had seemed one of those acts of drop-dead magnanimity that only an unselfconsciously and profligately noble city performs. In a world that rarely took note or compensated them, the park had been a small but significant requital to the failed, the aged, and the powerless.

The land on which the old apartment buildings stood had grown increasingly valuable because of the park and the proximity of the business core of the city and the burgeoning metropolitan population. Eventually most of the careworn buildings came down, to be replaced by chic, expensive condominiums and apartments. In one of them Miranda lived.

I wondered where the evicted had fled. The old man I'd frightened in the woods might, a few years ago, have lived in this neighborhood and dozed on this bench. Now he'd joined the bears and the Mythical Beast.

I took up the book beside me and opened it to the place where I'd inserted the pamphlet as a bookmark. "God of woods and pasture meadows, he looked after those who tended flocks and caused the flocks themselves to increase. His pursuit of pleasure and nymphs notwithstanding, there was a general benevolence in his nature toward the creatures of his realm, men and beasts."

IO

I rose early Sunday morning and dashed off a note to Miranda. I knew that she liked things spelled out, in writing if possible. I assured her that nothing more would be said about postponing her wedding. Certainly, nothing would be said over the long weekend. She could relax and enjoy herself. I also advised her to bring a dress.

When I'd sealed the note, I knocked lightly on the study door. "Bart, may I come in?"

He was sitting in the easy chair writing longhand.

"It's a glorious morning. Wouldn't you like to pull your chair over to the window?" I raised the sash and a warm breeze played with the cotton voile curtain.

"No, I prefer this spot. Fewer distractions."

"Could you take a break or is this a bad time? I'd like to drive into town and have brunch at the Kaffee Kafe. I want to pick up the Sunday paper and drop a load of party supplies at Daisy's. Any of that appeal to you?"

"All of it, but I'm on a roll here," he said, indicating the writing pad, "and I think I'd better stay with it."

"Can I bring you something?"

"Two of the very large glazed doughnuts. The ones that cause heart disease and bad skin."

I blew him a kiss.

Driving to town, I was perched atop the same calm plateau of mood as yesterday, gazing sagely and imperturbably for miles in all directions of my life. It seemed incredible, even unlikely (had I dreamed it?) that for days I'd been heaved about like a rag doll. Well, today I was the old Larissa. Calm, calm, calm. But eccentric? Fey? My faith in who I had been all these married, motherhood years had been shaken by Miranda. *Now, Larissa, don't go slidin-n-n-g dow-w-n-n-n again-n-n. Think crisp, airy Belgian waffles, real butter, thick, hot maple syrup. Whipped cream.*

The Kaffee Kafe, at the edge of town on the main highway to the Cities, was the Sunday-morning gathering place for Belleville and Blind Moose. Helen Wilhelm's Belgian waffles and cinnamon coffee drew customers despite the glare of Formica and the stainless-steel aspect of Helen herself. She was a chill, gray, thoroughly utilitarian woman who operated with a whine rather than a whir and, when pricked, bled brine.

The waitress who brought me a mug of cinnamon coffee, along with a menu, was a college girl who'd been working summers in the Kafe since she was a sophomore in high school.

"How are you, Mrs. Demming?"

"Fine, thank you. How's school?"

"Great. I love it."

"What year are you?"

"I'll be a junior this fall."

The news made me feel like a hoary monument. "What's your major?"

"Electrical engineering."

"That's wonderful!" I exclaimed. When I was young, had girls studied electrical engineering? "What kind of work will you do?"

"Some area of energy conservation. A lot depends on the economy."

Envy fluttered through me. Smiling abstractedly, I looked down at the menu and ordered French toast. "Coming to the Save the River party? Special rates for students, I understand."

"I can't."

"I'm sorry." While I waited for the French toast, I strolled to the cash register and bought a Sunday paper from the stack beside the register. Helen Wilhelm made change for me.

"Nothin' in there but bad news," she remarked of the newspaper. "People out of work. No money around. Damned Japs drivin' us out of business."

I turned quickly away.

"Good morning, Larry." Sam Fergus and a young man were sitting several booths beyond mine. "You know my grandson, Dave, don't you?" Sam asked as I approached.

"I don't think so. I'm happy to meet you."

"Do you have a minute?" the judge asked.

I sat down.

"There was a meeting last night at Roberta Arneson's. The Belleville Welcoming Committee."

"What's that?"

"You didn't see the notice in Thursday's paper? They're 'the friendly citizens dedicated to opening community doors and hearts to newcomers.'"

"The friends of Belle Rive Estates."

"Right."

"I guess it was going to happen," I observed. "It's hard to believe they met at Roberta's, though."

"What's hard to believe about that?" The judge, who had finished eating, slid his plate away and drew the coffee mug toward him. In a lowered voice he proclaimed, "Roberta Arneson is a consummate bitch." He explained, "After our gathering at the Fitzroys' last Thursday, I went home and compared the ads in Thursday's *Courant* with those in the previous week's. Roberta and Hollis have been busy. Harry's revenues are hurting worse than he'll admit." He added, "And the fighting's just begun."

"What can we do?"

"I don't know. I think there's a natural ebb and flow to these things and eventually what Harry's doing will attract new advertisers and some old ones will come back. In the meantime he could go under."

"What's Roberta getting out of this?"

"Only Roberta could say. But we can count on her vindictiveness. We should be prepared." There was warning in the look he gave me.

He suspects that Harry and I are having an affair, I thought. *He's warning me that if we are, Roberta will use it to drive Harry out of business and taint the Save the River campaign.* In midwestern villages, politics was still a vestal pastime.

"Mrs. Demming, your French toast is ready." My waitress stood beside me.

"What? Oh, yes, of course. I'd forgotten. I'll be right there. Sam, I'll talk to you later," I said and hurried away.

The waitress hesitated beside the booth. "Mrs. Demming," she began, lowering her voice so that she couldn't be overheard. "I'd really like to go to the party Friday night. I mean, I'm on your side about the river. But if I went and the Wilhelms found out, I'd lose my job." She darted a glance over her shoulder to be certain Helen Wilhelm was at the cash register.

"You're not serious."

"I am. The Wilhelms are freaky on the subject. You should have heard them yesterday, talking to some people from Blind Moose. They've stopped running their ad in the *Courant*, they said, and they're buying more space in the *Blind Moose Mirror* and some other little papers. Just because Mr. Arneson's trying to stop the condominiums. They said anyone who's against the condos is an Antichrist." Again, she glanced at Helen Wilhelm. "I'd better get to work." She moved away, fetching a carafe to refill mugs.

Antichrist?

Behind me the front door opened. Like a flourish of trumpets, Roberta Arneson's voice parted the clatter of heavy restaurant china. "...Besides," she was reminding son Bobby and Hollis and Ginger Gibney, "Arnold and Helen are on the side of the angels." It was proprietors Arnold and Helen Wilhelm, of course, to whom she referred.

"Hi, Helen," she trilled. "Coffee, please. *Je suis fatigué.*"

A high giggling voice, like an answering echo, sang across the room, "*Très, très fatigué.*" Brenda Bergquist, using two of her fourteen French words.

I hadn't noticed Brenda and Arch Bergquist sitting in a booth beyond the horseshoe-shaped counter which filled the center of the room. Having learned from Sam Fergus of last night's meeting of the Belleville Welcoming Committee, I surmised that the company now assembled on the opposite side of the Kaffee Kafe was the central committee of that organization. Since Arnold and Helen Wilhelm were "on the side of the angels," doubtless they too were members.

Waving acknowledgement to Brenda, Roberta and her party made their way around the room to occupy a booth adjacent to the

Bergquists. Either Roberta didn't notice me and Sam Fergus, or we were receiving our first snub since signing on with Save the River.

My French toast, when at length I turned to it, had grown cold. It hardly mattered. The appetite I'd brought from home was gone, and my stomach was filled with worry. If Sam Fergus suspected an affair between Harry and me, so must others.

The waitress brought fresh, hot coffee and carried away my plate. Sam and Dave Fergus said good-bye. Before my coffee was cool, Vera and Clete Samuelson walked past and around the counter toward Roberta. Was I the only one in the restaurant who represented the river?

"Vera! Clete!" Roberta hallooed. "Here, take the booth next to us, with Brenda and Arch. Isn't this fun?"

Folding the *Tribune* and leaving a tip on the table, I gathered my things together and proceeded to the cash register. I dropped my check and ten dollars on the rubber mat beside the register and waited for Helen Wilhelm.

Chatting and chumming uncharacteristically, she leaned against the booth where the Bergquists and now the Samuelsons were convened. Helen Wilhelm, meagerly educated, gaunt and stern, was suddenly comrade to Roberta Arneson, prosperous, educated, and superior.

Roberta rose, laughing and flushed.

"Well, gang," she bubbled to those in her booth and the adjacent one, "there are five accounts here who no longer advertise in the *Courant*."

I strained to hear what she said.

"More than anyone," she continued, "*I* am sorry to see what's happening to Harry, but being on the side of the angels means having to harden one's heart. As Hollis said, our little committee is going to put food on the dinner plate and shekels in the collection plate and that," she concluded righteously, "is no sin."

Helen Wilhelm added an amen, but Roberta wasn't finished. "Economic pressure will force Harry to back off. The majority will have its way."

I'm not sure what finally propelled me—Roberta's smug assumption that she was part of a majority; the implication that even the shabbiest angel in heaven was on the side of a sexist bastard like Arch Bergquist (known to pinch, goose, and otherwise victimize the high school girls who worked for less than minimum wage at the Little Palace); or the systematic ruin of Harry under the guise of Christian principles. But suddenly I was planted before the Belleville Welcoming Committee.

"Roberta," I began, more peremptorily than I had intended, "if there's any more talk about economic sanctions against the *Courant,* I'm going to take an ad in the paper and explain to the whole town what you and your friends are up to. I might even urge a boycott of the businesses involved in these shenanigans. I don't believe any self-respecting angel wants to be on the side of people who'd ruin a man's career to silence him."

Arch Bergquist jumped to his feet, interrupting, "Who gave *you* the right to tell us what to do? You don't have to make a living in this town. You only live here three months of the year, for God's sake. Go peddle your papers somewhere else." Realizing that he'd come close to being clever, he repeated, "Yeah, that's right, go peddle the *Courant* someplace else, lady."

Ginger Gibney hid behind a menu, and Bobby Arneson, Harry's son, studied me openly, expressionlessly. But the others glared— not impotently, but with faces like weapons.

"I'll buy the ad," I told them again, "if the campaign against Harry goes on."

It was Hollis Gibney this time. "Is Harry sending another fella's wife out to fight his battles these days?"

"Larry's in love with my husband," Roberta explained. "She's thrown herself at him for years. Now she'll try to *buy* him. I don't intend to be intimidated. I won't put my ad back in the *Courant.*"

Embarrassment for myself and Roberta made my stomach turn over, but I stood rooted. Roberta might not be intimidated but I thought the others would.

"I'll read next Thursday's *Courant* with interest," I said, looking into each face in turn. As my gaze came to rest on Harry's wife, I admonished, "You can suit yourself, Roberta."

Turning, I walked away as though I were being played by Bette Davis.

"Give me a glass of your strongest water," I told Daisy, dumping shopping bags of party supplies on her kitchen table, then collapsing on a stool.

"What's happened?" She left to get water, but returned with a

Bloody Mary. Sitting down opposite me, she demanded, "What's happened?"

By the time I'd finished replaying my sordid little tale, Daisy was bent over with laughter.

"A hundred years from now, we'll look back and laugh at this," I told her. Ignoring me, she continued to giggle. "That's a hundred years from now," I repeated.

"Sorry, Larry. I know it's not as funny to you as it is to me."

"Not nearly."

"You mustn't let what happened upset you."

"I really wouldn't give a damn what people thought," I told her, "but I don't want to hurt Harry or Bart. And I don't want this to affect Save the River."

"Tell Bart what happened. You'd better tell Harry, too. As for Save the River, we'll just have to wait and see." She put a hand on my arm. "What you did was right."

As she let me out the front door, I asked, "Am I fey and eccentric?"

But she just laughed and shooed me on my way.

It was one o'clock when I left Daisy. I'd called Bart to tell him not to worry. He hadn't. "How much trouble could you get into at the Kaffee Kafe?"

I told him I would see him later. Leaving the Fitzroys' I drove toward River Avenue, turned right, and headed down the long slope, across the River Avenue Bridge and into Blind Moose. At the first intersection I took a left and drove along a narrow blacktop road that followed the river north out of Blind Moose.

When I'd spoken to Bart, Daisy had said, "Now call Harry. I think you should talk to him before someone else does."

"I suppose you're right."

"He's probably at the office. He can come here. No one will think anything of that."

"But you and George won't be here." They were driving to St. Paul for an afternoon jazz concert.

"What difference?"

"The neighbors will see you leave and then see Harry's car and mine in front of your house..."

"Don't you think you're being overly circumspect?"

I laughed ruefully.

"Well, call him and meet him someplace."

I was meeting him someplace. Al's Place. Al's Place was eight miles north of Blind Moose. The parking lot was nearly empty: the only vehicles were a dusty old pickup with a faded Goldwater sticker on the bumper, Harry's VW, and a red Ford sedan that must belong to Al. I parked as far from Harry's car as possible, around on the side, beyond Al's Ford.

Sitting there with the ignition turned off, the afternoon so quiet I could hear the tiny metallic sounds of the engine cooling down, I assured myself, *This is not "sneaking around." This is an innocent thing that you're doing.* I cleared my throat, wiped my palms on my skirt, checked my lipstick in the rearview mirror and took several deep breaths. *An innocent thing.*

It was dark in Al's Place. I looked into the first booth. There were two old fellows drinking Schlitz. "Aw, hell," one said to the other, "Jake don't know a damned thing about catching bullheads. Last time we was out, he barely got his limit. Mornin', missus," he said to me, doffing an old red hunting cap.

"Good morning."

"Can I help you?" someone asked, tapping my shoulder.

I jumped. "I was...I was looking for someone."

"Your husband?" He eyed me askance.

"No. No, I'm not looking for my husband. I'm meeting someone. A friend."

"The next booth, I think."

"Thank you."

Harry stood. "Hi," he said.

"You want to order something?" Al asked.

I sat. Harry was drinking Bud. I didn't want beer.

"Do you have coffee?"

"Not until the girl comes at four."

"Well, then, I guess I'll have a Bloody Mary."

He left, glancing from Harry to me and back again, before turning away.

"Does he know you?" I asked.

"Slightly."

"Will he think this is...hanky-panky?"

Harry laughed. "Tell me what's happened that's so terrible?" he asked, ignoring my question.

Again I recited my tale of the Kaffee Kafe, stopping in the

middle when Al brought the Bloody Mary, and concluding with, "Harry, please don't laugh."

He took my hand. "I'm sorry, Larissa. You're worried about Bart. I shouldn't laugh, but I'd give a helluva lot to have seen their faces—Hollis and Arch and the bunch of them—when you said you were going to take an ad and expose them. I'd bet better than even money they're on the phone before ten tomorrow morning, putting their damned ads back in the paper."

"I hope so, Harry."

"Would you like me to talk to Bart?"

"No."

"He's such a hermit these days, he might never find out about this."

"I don't want to take a chance."

"No. I suppose not." He still held my hand. "Thanks for everything."

"Don't thank me, Harry. Everyone in town is going to look sideways at you tomorrow. According to Roberta, I've been throwing myself at you for years."

"If you had, wouldn't I have caught you?" he teased.

"I didn't deny it, Harry." I swung my bag over my shoulder. "I have to get home. I'll . . . I'll be in touch."

The front booth was empty. The two old men had left. At the door I glanced out to see Bobby Arneson's yellow Jeep turn into the parking lot. For a moment I froze, unsure what to do. As I stood staring, the Jeep swung around in a U-turn and drove back to the blacktop. Bobby must have spotted his father's car. But why did he leave? He couldn't have seen my car since it was behind Al's. I pushed the door open and left.

Sliding into the Volvo, I suddenly realized that Al's car was gone. The Volvo was exposed. How could that be? Al was at the bar when I headed for the door. The red car must have belonged to the two old men. In any case, Bobby knew that Harry and I were together.

The day was increasingly farcical but not funny.

Bart wasn't laughing. But of course I hadn't expected him to.

"I feel like a fool and a cuckold."

"But I haven't been throwing myself at Harry for years. You know that."

"The embarrassment for me is the same either way." His frown deepened. "Besides the embarrassment, this business is going to bring disorder to our lives."

He paused. We were sitting on the front porch with only the spilled glow from the living room doorway to light us. Bart was drinking a glass of white wine; at least he had been until I dropped my bomb. I was drinking straight shots of gin over ice. I would rue it in the morning.

Partly because I had to gather my courage and partly because I didn't want to disturb Bart's work, I'd waited until he put his writing aside before I told him about events at the Kaffee Kafe.

He continued, "Disorder. Yes. In some way it will bring disorder. My mother used to call sudden confusion, 'fruit basket upset.' Apples and oranges and grapes and the whole damned mess...all tumbling about. That's what I mind the most—the botheration— even more than the embarrassment. I want to order the events of my life, not have them thrust upon me. Things like this intrude, they interrupt one's concentration and rhythm. A life lived in this fashion doesn't scan. Do you know what I mean?"

"I've created a mess and you don't want to have to deal with it."

"Something like that."

"Cuckold." There was an old-fashioned word to make one's toes curl up with shame. I'd made Bart feel like a cuckold. Roberta and I squaring off in a crowd raised a blush to my own cheek.

After Bart went to bed, I sat on the porch listening to the river. The night was warm and still. Except for the crickets, all the sounds were whispers.

Before irreparable damage was done, I had to stop things dead with Harry. I had to fill my head with work and plans unrelated to him. When Clark and Miranda were children I'd told them that boredom was inexcusable. Everybody's head was filled with toys and stories, I'd counseled. If you were bored, you weren't using your head.

When Bart was asleep, I fetched a towel from the bathroom, let myself out the front door, and padded down to the water. Undressing on the dock, I left my clothes, towel, and sandals there, and waded into the water until it reached my thighs. Then I began to swim upstream. The water soon felt warm as I pulled against the current.

At this moment—what was it, twelve-thirty?—I was probably the only one swimming in the river. An entire river to myself. As my limbs grew heavy and weak, I turned on my back to float downstream to the dock. The sky was intensely dark and spangled, and closer than the trees.

Pulling myself out onto the dock, I wrapped the thick towel around me, sat down and drew my legs up close, imagining the others who were still awake—people, animals, and others of whatever sort there were.

The awake of the world were like a secret society. Hearing the muffled rumble of a distant jet on its way to the Minneapolis airport, I pictured the pilot and the attendants and the drowsy passengers.

The summer after my mother died, Jamie and I drove across the country to California. Stopping in all-night cafés, we played the songs on the Selectomatic and kidded with the waitresses and truck drivers, and said hello and how are you to families with sleepy children who were on their way to a job somewhere. Jamie liked to drive at night and sleep in the hot, glaring days, behind tightly drawn shades.

There was something easier about night, easier about the people in the truck stops and motels. They weren't always looking for your soft spot. There was a kind of low-key camaraderie, as though we were a convention of outcasts.

That summer, when I was fifteen, the weather was hot, very hot everywhere we drove. We both wore shorts and when he was driving, Jamie didn't bother with a shirt. He had a big, hard chest, tanned and with a soft mat of black curly hair beneath which his heart lay beating. I wore light cotton blouses with loose, gathered necklines, peasant blouses they were called. We must have looked like brother and sister. Jamie was only thirty-seven and he looked about twenty-five.

When he was very close, so that I could see the vein on the side of his neck throbbing, I would lay my fingers against it. "Pulse is scary, isn't it? Something in there drives us, doesn't it? I mean, it just pushes and pushes and our blood runs ahead of it like horses being whipped. And the only way we can stop it is to die."

Those days and nights with Jamie loomed like a mountain in the distance, lone and pure and perfect. I tried not to think of them, even after all these years; they were too painful in their inaccessibility. Sometimes they would glide into my mind as they did then on the dock, but I never grasped hold of them. I let them glide past, because the pain interfered with life. And if sometimes I was incautious, the pain became physical. It was in my throat and chest, as if I were a sword swallower who had forgotten and swallowed his sword.

I got to my feet suddenly. Slipping into my sandals and picking up my clothes, I hurried up to the cottage and quietly let myself in. I was hooking the screen door when he began to laugh. From across the water the sound came, filling the darkness. It had a rolling, echoing quality, like someone laughing down a vast well.

II

Sleep refused to come wholly to me. It flirted and teased, touching me lightly, then withdrawing. But into those fragments of sleep came pieces of dreams, and when the night was ended they made a whole.

A woman who was surely me running frightened down a mountain, running, running. Jagged mountains and blue sea vistas. Above, endless cerulean spaces where now a woman astride a white horse floated like a figure in a Chagall painting. How calm she was.

What it meant I didn't know, but waking, I was purposeful without caring why. I prepared a simple but perfect breakfast for Bart: berries and cream, a poached egg on toast, and strong coffee. Setting the tray on the bedside table, I raised the shade at the window to let in the early sun and the pleasant, slightly brackish air from Belle Riviere.

The alarm clock, which he never needed to set, said 6 A.M., the usual hour of his awakening. I sat on the margin of the bed and kissed him. I would begin making amends for yesterday's embarrassment.

He opened his eyes and was immediately clear-eyed and clear-headed. How admirable, always to know who and where you were first thing in the morning.

"Good morning. I've brought you a tray," I said, placing it in front of him as he sat up.

"So you have." He spread the napkin across his front. "It looks delicious." He glanced at me. "I'm sorry if I said anything to upset you last night."

"It's all right. After all, it was my fault."

He ate a spoonful of berries, wiped his mouth, and said, "Our lives have been so smooth. Upheaval was never my style and I'm not good at it."

"There isn't any reason you should be."

"I *will* be embarrassed facing people and knowing that they're wondering about you and Harry. I think any man in these circumstances would be, don't you?"

"Yes."

"But I'll get over it."

"You're being very good about it."

"However, I don't see why you got into a silly set-to at the Kaffee Kafe in the first place."

"You don't?"

"No."

"*You* wouldn't have been angry?"

"The whole thing could have been handled more appropriately."

"How?"

With a knife and fork he sliced off a corner of toast and popped it into his mouth, following this with the napkin again. "At the next meeting of your committee you could have brought up the advertising boycott and let the *committee* take an ad in the *Courant* explaining what was going on. Instead, you made a fool of yourself, of me, and of Harry in one schoolgirl gesture."

I didn't respond, because what he had said was true.

"If you want to be involved with Save the River, it's all right with me. I think it's probably worthwhile. I don't have the time for it myself, but I'm not opposed to it. And it gives you something to do with your time. But it musn't interrupt my work. I don't want to have to think about it."

"You'll go to the party at Daisy's, won't you?"

"Oh, yes. I meant I don't want any more unpleasantness or

any more involvement than attending a party. Until the book's finished, I'm incommunicado." He smiled and gave me a berry-flavored kiss. "You understand, don't you?"

"I understand, yes, perfectly."

By the time I'd finished cleaning out the barbecue pit and defrosting the ancient refrigerator, it was ten. I took a quick shower, toweled my hair, and drew on a pair of shorts and a shirt. The mailbox revealed a blank interior. Snapping the door shut, I paced slowly around to the front of the cottage, and continued, more quickly now, across the lawn to the head of the wooden stairs leading down the embankment to the dock. Eyes narrowed against the sun, I studied the length of the opposite shore as far as I could see in either direction, then turned about and headed back to the cottage.

From the top of the refrigerator I grabbed the picnic basket and set it on the counter beside the sink. Standing on the kitchen stool, I reached a small jar of caviar from the cupboard. That went into the basket along with a chilled bottle of champagne, thin slices of French bread, Brie, two apples, a knife, two glasses, and two cloth napkins. Three of the books I'd bought Saturday and my reading glasses were wrapped in a beach towel.

Lugging all of this down to the dock and lowering it into the canoe, I reassured and encouraged myself as if I embarked on an expedition both imperative and perilous.

What, after all, did I know about the Beast? I had only mythology as a reference and that, by its nature, was fiction or some combination of fiction, history, and conjecture. The Beast might be rapacious or murderous or both. Contrary to pictures and descriptions in books, in the flesh he was large and muscular, a formidable creature, whose forbearance and nobility, if he possessed any, would have to be invoked.

Giving a final glance back up at the cottage and girding my loins, I set out. On the opposite shore I peered about, waded into the shallows with the champagne bottle, and wedged it between a couple of rocks.

I sat down and tried to read. It gave me the appearance of being occupied, of being indifferent. After fifteen minutes I set the book aside and got to my feet on the pretext of checking the champagne to be certain it was still securely cradled among the rocks. It was. As I straightened, my eyes took in the trees and undergrowth in the near area. Nothing.

I returned to the towel and book. As time passed, my apprehension increased. At moments I was transfixed with terror. He was watching with bestial malevolence, preparing to drag me by my slender wrist into the bushes, to throttle me or tear me limb from limb or hurl me off the palisades.

And if his intent were lascivious rather than murderous, what would he do? And what would he expect *me* to do? I surveyed in my mind a gamut of sexual perversions, ranging from delightful to unthinkable. Whatever his predilection, I didn't want to be surprised.

Why, you wonder, did I remain on the beach waiting for him, heart hammering like a frightened rabbit's? Because I was more frightened of returning to the cottage. Whatever waited here with the Beast, it would be different from that other course.

Another fifteen minutes elapsed and agitation drove me to my feet again. Slipping off my sandals, I strolled barefoot down the narrow strand, throwing sidelong glances up the grassy incline to the left. I went, as I did on these strolls, as far south as where the embankment rose steeply and turned sharply toward the river. Here I must wade out into the water to pass, or turn back. I turned back.

I'd begun to have doubts. What did I know about conjuring delusions? My experience was slim and I had so far never consciously called him into being. He had simply appeared or laughed unbidden in the night.

Approaching the gaudy towel and Durant's *The Life of Greece,* which lay on it, I was struck by the pitiful asininity of what I was doing. My body folded downward, collapsed by the force of it. Unable to crawl as far as the towel, I lay on the hot sand, sand flies stinging my arms, sand burning my thighs.

The voice at first had no effect; it seemed removed, like a radio playing in another room where someone else listened.

"I have no taste for caviar," it said. "I am particularly fond of Brie and bread and champagne, however."

I had only a mild interest in this fragment of radio drama.

"My palate is as sophisticated as the next," it continued, "but whatever one spreads it on, caviar tastes like a corrective." It added peremptorily, "It makes no difference whether it's Russian, Greek, or Icelandic."

The voice was compelling. I made a slight effort.

"Beluga is a great fraud. There are, you know, conspiracies of taste." He paused as though expecting a comment, then continued, "It's rather a case of the emperor's clothes. Some fool with more power than wit declares that white sturgeon roe are a gift of the gods. Then all those owing fealty to this ignoramus hold their noses, close their eyes, and swallow quickly. They continue the exercise until they've learned to do it with a smile." He laughed contemptuously. "I can tell you for a fact, no god of my acquaintance messes about in fish eggs—sturgeon, salmon, carp, herring, whitefish, cod, or any other kind."

The voice was closer. I was moving toward it and it toward me.

"You're not likely to win any prizes as a hostess," it reproved in the offhand manner of those unimpeachably superior. "Mind what I'm doing here. I'm moving your towel and your book, do you see? I'm moving them up here beneath the trees."

The tone was neither coaxing nor patronizing but, rather, clinical and slightly exasperated. It was one Jamie had used when my temper or unhappiness exceeded what he considered safe limits, a tone implying, "You're too bright and resourceful to bore yourself and others with this self-indulgence."

I had no idea then how carefully the Beast had chosen his tone. I turned my head inches and opened my eyes to a narrow slit, which I shaded with my hand as if looking upon my delusion might be as dangerous as looking into the sun.

"You may have the caviar," he repeated and began to lay out the contents of the picnic basket.

"What kind of Greek...?" I muttered, breaking off, my head buzzing and crackling with static as I struggled to tune in to the Beast. "What kind of Greek doesn't like caviar?" It was an inane question, a substitute for "Testing, testing, one, two, three."

"My kind of Greek. Would you like me to help you up?" he asked, not moving, appreciating that, like his ancient love, Echo, I might dash into the water if he drew nearer.

"No."

"Do you want Brie on your bread and butter or do you prefer it spread on apple slices?" he inquired.

"I can't think."

"I'll do some of each." In a moment, he added, "I'm going to fetch the champagne now and uncork it. If you would come here and keep the flies from the food?"

I got slowly to my feet. Stumbling to the river, I waded in up to my calves and scooped up water to wet my face. When I turned I saw that he stood on the sand, poised anxiously lest I throw myself into the current.

Touched and vaguely amused by this concern, I smiled. "I won't drown myself."

A poignant shadow eclipsed his features and was gone. "Of course you won't."

With the sluggish, flaccid gait of someone dragged from bed and not fully awake, I trudged across the sand and up the shallow embankment to the meal laid out under the trees. He made his way down the beach to the rocks where I'd stored the wine. It was a loping, leisurely stride with which he moved. Not so delicate as a deer, nor lumbering as an ox. Something in it recalled the gainly, lunging grace of immense linemen in their unhurried canter onto the football field.

Though still dazed by my circumstances, I did wonder at his boldness, and my eyes slid up and down the far embankment, then up the river itself. No hikers or boaters were apparent.

I rearranged myself so that I sat leaning comfortably against the rough bark of a cedar. From the earlier plunge into depression, some lingering enervation remained. That, combined with the strangeness of the scene, filled me with a narcotic calm. I was no longer afraid, certainly not of the Beast. I was defenseless and without need of defenses, a state little known to women.

Returning from the river, he popped the champagne cork just as his hoofs reached the hem of the picnic towel. I handed him glasses and he caught the first spume from the bottle, laughing at his cleverness as he did.

"To generous women," he pledged, touching the rim of his glass to mine. There was no hint of irony in the words, nor hidden sexual slur. Lifting my glass in salute, I caught the trail of bubbles, rising with them on an ascendant mood.

12 ❧

"Hard-boiled eggs would have been good," he observed, reclining on his side, head propped against his arm. "Might you bring eggs and Greek olives next time? It's been some time since I've enjoyed Greek olives."

I had continually to adjust my perspective and remind myself that *I* was not nearly so exotic to him as he was to me, that this meal was nowhere near so fantastical for him as for me, and that his utterly prosaic references to food were perfectly congruous if one were looking at the world from his perspective.

I hadn't supposed that mythological figures lounged about discoursing in dactylic hexameter all day. Nevertheless, numerous reconcilements were required between what I had imagined a deity, even a minor one, to be and what this flesh-and-blood deity in fact was. But even with willing and alert adjustments, there were moments of incredulous silence on my side.

Glancing across at me, he broke the present incredulous silence. "You don't like hard-boiled eggs?"

"What? Oh...oh, yes. I like them well enough."

"And Greek olives?"

"Yes, I like those, too. I'm not sure I can get Greek olives in Belleville. I can call my daughter in Minneapolis and have her bring them on Friday when she comes to visit." Was I really talking about eggs and olives and daughters?

"How long will she be here?"

"Until the following Tuesday. Also her fiancé and my son and his wife. They're all driving up Friday evening and staying until early Tuesday morning."

"For the Fourth of July weekend."

"Yes." I glanced quickly at him. What had Beasts to do with Fourth of July weekends? Though my private invention, he was turning out to be his own Beast. Would a creature who dealt in national holidays ever speak heroic verse?

"How old are your children?"

"Miranda is twenty-four and Clark is twenty-five."

"And you?"

I hesitated. Why did I mind his knowing? And why did he ask since he must already know?

He looked at me from beneath half-lowered lids, the creases at the corners of his eyes showing amusement.

"Forty-seven."

"That's a good age."

"It's not one I'd choose."

"You'd rather be young?"

I thought for a moment. "I suppose. I'd like a chance to try harder. A chance not to acquiesce, but to hold on and struggle." His gaze was deep and kind. He understands it all, I thought. I refilled his glass. "How old are you?"

He laughed. Not the immense, rumbling laugh in the night, but a bounteous laugh nonetheless. "I don't know. Would it make a difference?"

"Probably not, but that's because you're immortal. If you were mortal and you were my friend or . . . lover, an actuarial table in my head would begin to calculate your remaining years of strength, lucid intelligence, sexual vigor, and good health. Not because I'd care less for you if those were of modest duration but because, I think, we begin to mourn the loss of a lover when we begin to love him. There's an expectation of loss built into love, don't you think?"

"The statistics are on your side," he said, a pensive, sardonic note creeping into his voice.

Surveying him with the eye of a part-time artist, I told myself, *You've created a masterpiece.* His torso had a tensile beauty, a continually flexed look. Flat planes of muscle, like slabs of marble, met curved surfaces no less hard. Light and shadow played on these as he moved, giving him a beauty in motion that was quite apart from his overall grace.

He was well over six feet tall, perhaps six feet four or five, and weighed, I believe, about two hundred and forty pounds, possibly a little less. His skin was caramel color and the depressions and junctures were dusky. "Done" in pastels, the hollows would have been a deep, tropical blue. If a line were drawn from hipbone to hipbone, curving downward in the center, it would trace the perimeter below which his glossy white fur grew luxuriantly. It curled, not in tight coils, but loosely in waves and was, at its longest, about three inches. Below the knee joint it was shorter but frilled out in long, silky wisps just above his hoofs. The hoofs were not so much like marble as alabaster, with a kind of white upon white lustrous depth to them and cloven in a way I never tired of studying.

His genitals, lying in the midst of this splendor, like fabulous eggs in a nest of velvety white feathers, were large but not unusually so for a creature of his stature. Having lived with them time out of mind, he wore them with as much ease and unsuspecting pride as a beautiful woman wears flawless skin.

All of the Beast's magnificence, however, culminated in the grand head that crowned his person. It bore a cap of raven curls, which he did not allow to grow long but kept trimmed to about two or three inches. Beneath, a broad forehead met brows, wide-set and arched, and these sat poised above large, slightly hooded eyes, carved from jet and catching secret light as though they possessed a thousand facets.

His nose was classically Greek, narrow and thrusting downward from the brow without indentation where it passed between his eyes. High, sharply sculpted cheekbones lent the face an appearance of greater length than it actually possessed. But a beard, black and springy to the touch as the hair on his chest, saved the contours from any hint of severity. Protected by the beard, his lips were sensual and expressive as a young boy's.

His appearance, however, was more than the sum of its parts. Like the faces of martyrs and archfiends, his face held knowledge that was not secret but, worse, was unknowable. And intermittently, humor and pain and impatience flashed across the features, like heat lightning briefly illuminating a moonless landscape.

For whatever private reasons, he had determined to share with me a portion of his worldly self. And for these same reasons, he was courting my acquaintance. A thoroughly complex creature had sprung from the Stygian swamp at the back of my mind.

"You were frightened half to death the first time you saw me," he said. "I apologize. Today you are braver."

"Bravery has nothing to do with it. Just the opposite. It was less frightening to be crazy than to be sane. In the end I think it will be less lonely also."

"Crazy?"

"Mad, insane, delusional."

"I understand the word. You think you're crazy?"

"If you met a satyr in the woods, wouldn't you?"

"Not just *any* satyr," he injected.

"Be that as it may—when I saw you, I was sane enough to know I was crazy. I'm not so far gone that I create satyrs and think they're real. I know you're not real. At first that scared the hell out of me. I felt helpless and embattled. But as time passed, I saw that you might be a stroke of good luck."

I hesitated. He bathed me in the warm encouragement of his smile and I was led, unresisting, to explain, "You see, I'm desperate for . . . distraction . . . escape. So desperate I was willing to risk whatever kind of Beast you might be." I got to my feet and moved off a short distance, closer to the water. He sat up abruptly, and I felt at my back the strength of his will, like the strength of the sun beating through one's shirt, able to heal or burn.

"Paddling across the river, I imagined that you might tear me to pieces," I admitted.

"You came anyway. I was right then, you *are* brave."

"No, even that wasn't brave, because it wasn't the most frightening prospect I could imagine. The most frightening prospect was staying on the other side."

"You see now that I'm not dangerous." His voice was soothing, coaxing, as though he lured me back from a precipice.

"I think you probably are dangerous—in many ways, some I haven't even begun to envision." I turned toward him. "But you are my Beast; I'm not going to abandon you," I said, an oddly maternal note coloring the words. "And you surely are an escape, however dangerous. Besides," I continued, shaping ideas from an amorphous jumble of feelings, "I don't think a person must abide by traditional scruples in using a fantasy. I think a person may do pretty much as she pleases with a fantasy. After all, who'll suffer? A fantasy is a tool. A person wouldn't scruple over the sensibilities of a car, for instance. I would drive my car where I pleased and never ask whether the car approved. So," I concluded, "I will use you as I please." I returned to the picnic cloth and lowered myself beside him, laying a hand on his thigh.

"And how will it please you to use me?" he teased dryly, sounding as though he were humoring me.

My God, I thought, *the brain is subtle. I'm being patronized by my own delusion.* "Surely you can imagine uses?" I poured the last of the champagne. "I've created a masterpiece," I said and raised my glass to him. "A useful masterpiece."

He chuckled, indulgently amused, as at the arguments of a child vehemently supporting the existence of Santa Claus. "I sprang full-blown a week ago last Saturday?"

"Yes."

"You have no doubts?"

"None."

He rose and paced a few steps away, then back. Stroking his beard, he seemed to search for the appropriate response. "A few moments ago you laid your hand on my thigh."

"Yes."

"What did you feel?"

"Aroused."

"No, no, I mean, what lay beneath your fingers?"

"Fur, very soft, like the throat of a pampered dog. Beneath that, muscle."

"That's right. And yet you don't believe the evidence of your own fingers?"

"Evidence of what?"

"That I'm not a delusion, that I exist outside your mind, just like this tree," he said, impatiently slapping the trunk of a young birch.

"But you see, I wondered about that, too," I told him reasonably. "I was sure I'd felt your fingers on my skin the day I fainted, so I went to the university library and did some research on delusions. All the senses, it turns out, can be incorporated into a delusion, including smell and taste. I could have *tasted* you and found you to taste like cinnamon, but you'd still be a hallucination." I tilted my head back and looked seductively up at him. "If I'd tasted your figs, you'd still be a figment." I giggled. I was beginning thoroughly to enjoy this. There was no need to beat about the bush with a delusion. One could get immediately down to pleasure. He was immeasurably more fun than a pet.

"Stop being so damned cute," he reproved. "This is serious."

"Don't you think I know that?"

"I don't mean your insanity. You're as sane as I am. I mean, your mistaken notion that I don't exist."

"Please don't." I was on my feet, panic crawling over my skin.

"What? Please don't what?" he asked quickly.

"Don't try to convince me that you're real." I moved away, trying to gain control of the situation.

"I don't understand you," he said. "I'd think you'd be relieved to know you're sane. Most people would be."

Ignoring this, I told him, "You're trying to take it all away."

"All what?" He moved a little toward me, but I stepped away, desperate to regain faith in my insanity, a faith he'd begun to undermine. "All what?" he repeated. "What am I trying to take away from you?"

"Yourself. And this," I said, spreading my hand to indicate the picnic we'd shared. "If you're real... Whatever is real, one has no control over."

"You'd rob me of my reality just to keep me for... for a toy?" he asked, his voice so quiet I strained to hear.

Put that way, it sounded dreadful, selfish. I felt immediate shame and great confusion. Did phantasms argue their reality, or was I sane, as he insisted? For forty-seven years I'd taken sanity for granted, and for a few days I'd taken insanity for granted. Now I could take neither for granted.

I felt betrayed, but by whom I couldn't say. Perhaps myself. Dazed, I returned to the picnic cloth, knelt, and began insensibly, mechanically to gather the gleanings into the basket. I poured the wine from my glass onto the ground, a libation to gods who despised me but must be appeased. Had I asked for too much? A single, happy delusion? Impotent rage palsied my hand, and the last drops flew wide and stained the cloth.

"Let me carry it," the Beast said and extended a hand to take the basket.

I sidestepped and hurried past him. Dropping the basket into the canoe, I prepared to shove the craft into the water. His hand fell on my forearm, holding it lightly, detaining me.

"Is it so disappointing if I'm real?"

"Yes."

"Why?"

"Because you'll have volition and it will take you away, and while you're here I'll have to have scruples, and—even worse— because I'm a married woman I'll have to have morals. I'll have to feel reticent toward you and embarrassed. If you try to make love to me, I'll have to be uncomfortable and make you uncomfortable.

Inevitably, I'll be anxious and sad about your leaving. It will be more of what life already is."

I studied the transcendently beautiful face bent close to mine. The authorship of that face would have been an achievement and reward giving meaning to any deprivation or any expenditure. A *chef d'oeuvre*.

"I'm fossilizing," I explained, "becoming a dry shell that looks much the same as when it was alive. I'm caught here because of compunctions or cowardice. In the end, it won't matter which. You were a possibly dangerous, but wholly *innocent* diversion. Isn't that the middle-age dream?"

"Don't you see," he said mildly, "that you would 'fossilize' *me* if you insisted on my being a fantasy? I'd be as inorganic as a cast bronze. However passionately a fantasy is shaped, it's only a piece of handiwork. Don't limit my uses to mere diversion."

With his free hand he took up the beach towel from the canoe where I'd tossed it. With the hand that lay on my arm he guided me back to the spot where we'd picnicked. Unfurling the cloth, he held chivalrously to my hand as I seated myself. When I was settled, legs folded beneath me, hands folded in my lap, resigned and inert, he stood staring down at me for several minutes.

Although I didn't look up, I knew he was taking some final measure of me and the results would determine his next words. I felt too removed to grow restive under his long appraisal. Concluding, he lifted a hoof to plant it more firmly and with this movement seemed to set himself on a course.

"My dear..."

"Larissa."

"My dear Larissa," he began, then clasping his hands together behind his back, he surveyed the river as though it were a flood of sorrows whose current had swept him helplessly beyond his landing. "Would you like to know how I came here?"

13 🌿

I didn't answer. I regret having repeatedly to mention my per-plexity, but it was a haze surrounding me, and his words reached me late and as though traveling through cotton batting.

Unfolding my legs, I stretched myself out and lay on my side, head propped against my hand. From the tone of the Beast's voice and his posture, one understood that he was embarking on a nar-rative. I was reminded of a childhood in which Jamie McClanahan sat at the side of my bed, spinning tales of gods and heroes and villains and victims.

"In the spring of eighteen ninety-five," he launched, "Alice Hazeltine toured Greece. Alice was the daughter of Alexander Hazeltine, lumber and railroad baron and all-around bad apple. But he's another matter. Alice was accompanied to Europe by her unmarried maternal aunt, Jessica, and a finishing-school chum, Selma Funston. They were all three extremely good-looking women. Alice and Selma were eighteen-year-old rosebuds, fresh and dew-covered, and Aunt Jessica, at forty-three, was a flower in full bloom." Lyrical warmth modulated his description and I glimpsed briefly his ancient nature, the delightable eye with which he'd pursued and studied women.

"They'd been to London and Paris and Vienna and the usual," he continued. "After a month in Italy, they sailed for Greece, which was to be the last splurge of sightseeing and classic indulgence before their return to the United States. They'd been abroad since the previous September and it was time now for the girls to journey home, and there be captured by captains of industry.

"Of the three, Alice was the most serious student of classical history, although Selma and Aunt Jessica were not far behind, and they all took an immense delight in the galaxy of immortals, traips-ing here and there and back again to visit the scenes of legendary crimes, heroics, and amours committed by gods and goddesses, major and minor.

79

"On the advice of an American friend, they had engaged as their guide a retired professor from Athens, himself old enough to remember firsthand half the events of Greek history since Pericles. For that time and their station in society, the three women were very modern, almost scandalous, in their rough-and-ready approach to travel and, frankly, the professor lent their travels a respectability and an appearance of scholarly intent they would not otherwise have had. The women had enormous American curiosity and wanted to go everywhere, preferably without hindrance, escort, or fussing over.

"I met up with them at the sanctuary of Zeus at Olympia. They were unfashionably tanned and lean as boys. Lovely. They packed food for their outing to the shrine, and after lunch Alice separated from her aunt and her friend to wander alone in the pines that grew among the ruins and up the side of Mount Kronos.

"The day was hot and she wore a simple pale-peach-colored dress. When she removed the sash, the garment fell smocklike from her shoulders, giving her the appearance of an over-tall child. The fabric, she said, was called lawn. It was a fine, thin cotton and I told her I would like a shirt of that stuff. She laughed at that, but later she had one made for me of the very same cloth."

Turning so that his face was in profile to me, he gazed downstream, as though his Victorian Alice might materialize there, strolling barefoot with delectable negligence through the warm sand. In that limpid moment, the wistful, yearning tilt of his perfect countenance wrenched the breath from me, and sent life careering off on an irreversible tangent.

He went on, "The pale peach against her tanned skin and sunbleached hair is one of my best and most detailed memories. She wore her hair down with a ribbon to hold it back and she carried a straw hat she'd purchased in Italy.

"Her face, with wide-set golden-colored eyes, was fragile above a slender neck and broad, delicate shoulders. A stripling girl, bending and swaying gracefully as she strolled through the pine trees.

"I was smitten. You'll laugh," he said, and swung partway around, "but I think she expected to find me there. To find *someone*. She was startled but not alarmed when I spoke to her. And although I wore only an animal skin caught up at the shoulders, somewhat like a chlamys, she didn't seem offended or frightened by my body. She was only a girl, remember, and was currently immersed in the lore of gods and heroes. The women had already visited numerous ruins and had allowed themselves susceptibility to the spirits and mysteries that linger in fallen temples and tread the remnants of ancient stoas. Alice was prepared to encounter me."

He was silent for a few minutes. Finally, he moved from his exposed position at the edge of the woods and lowered himself to the long grass ten or so feet from me. "Alice and I talked . . . of I don't know what, and didn't know even that day. The words, whatever they were, were merely a prosaic translation of the enchantment we both felt. A spell, like a golden net, had been cast over us. After two hours we forced ourselves to part. She had to return to the others, who lay napping and reading near the remains of the Temple of Zeus. She suggested returning to Olympia the following day on the pretext of having lost a ring which her mother, before her death, had given her. Alice and her party were staying at the home of a distant relative of the professor's, on the sea coast. It was a long ride. I told her that, instead, I would meet her near their village in two days' time.

"During the three weeks that followed, I trailed them as though pulled by a powerful lodestone, staying close enough that Alice could steal away, usually at night, to spend an hour with me. Drawing Selma into our affair, Alice told her friend that she'd fallen in love with a Greek youth she'd met at Olympia, someone of a well-regarded but impoverished family. I was amused by what seemed an ironic truth in that.

"When a young girl is in love, her happiness conspires to give her away. From the warm, high color in her cheek, to the very flutter of the bright ribbons on her straw hat, she is a walking advertisement for the sweet fabric in which she winds her soul. As the days passed, the aunt was increasingly aware of the changes in Alice, but she could discover nothing.

"Alice and her friend Selma together were able to purchase clothing for me. It wasn't a wardrobe that fit equally well in all its parts, but only what two girls inexperienced in these matters could gather. When we reached Athens, Alice located a wheelchair!

"She was determined that I should spend the summer in the United States. She was confident she could work out the details, and since she was an intelligent and determined person, with funds as well, I didn't doubt her. Also, there was in the land around her, in the crystal sunlight of the strand and the whispering shadows of antiquity, an air of possibility, as though a lover's scheme, however mad, might find favor with the gods. Well, Alice was in love and not ready to be tragically parted, like a star-crossed girl in a story, so she set her scheme sailing on the high tide of her hopes.

"She would take me to America with her and send me home to Greece in September or early October at the latest, she said." Lying on his side and resting his weight against his elbow, he looked at me, through me, and past me a good long way. "She never meant to send me home, I think." He was smiling, so I knew he didn't speak with bitterness.

"The only way we could manage the unwieldy plan was to pass me off as a wheelchair-confined cripple traveling to the United States by the same route and with similar accommodations to her own." Parenthetically he added, "This was because my feet and legs had to be kept under wraps, as you can understand. It was none of it easy despite Alice's money and ingenuity. The chair was painful for me, but Alice was in love and I couldn't bring myself to deny her."

His lips curved in reverie. "Lest I appear a dupe in all of this, I tell you that I was every bit as love-maddened as Alice. I, with eons of dalliance and several serious alliances behind me, was tossed beam-ends by her! She was beautiful. But I'd known many beautiful women. She was cheerful as a spring fair and she laughed a good deal, but she was not clever. No, clever would not apply to her as it does to one who instinctively sees the personal advantage in every situation. There was a purity of intent about her. She undertook nothing in life that she thought might injure another. In this regard, she was almost agonizingly circumspect. She was not, however, conventional, for she did undertake heresies when she was convinced they would harm no one else. Her love affair with me was certainly such a heresy.

"Alice's foremost feature, though, was her intelligence. It was deep and grave as a Druid. She should have been sent to a university, but conversational French and enough piano training to play a Liszt tune were the limits of Alexander Hazeltine's expectations regarding her education. To satisfy her craving for learning, Alice read. From our conversations and what I witnessed, I'm sure she'd read as many books as most professors and considerably more than the average university graduate. What she longed for was the seminar or tutorial situation, the opportunity to translate reading into creative thought. She dreaded the prospect of marriage, calling it 'death by comfort.'"

He lay back and folded his arms across his eyes. I respected his silence and waited for him to recover. After several minutes, he clasped his hands behind his head and once again picked up the narrative.

"We ended up spending an extra week in Athens while she used her wiles and influence to secure papers giving me an identity acceptable to the world. Jessica, who was a truly wise and good woman, made allowances, thinking that Alice had fallen in love and required time for a sweetheart's protracted farewell.

"At last we departed for America. Once we were at sea, our days were considerably less complicated. Alice managed to 'meet a dear, shy, unfortunate gentleman' toward whom she felt protective, almost maternal, as she explained to Jessica. And her aunt was relieved. The friendship would fill the hours Alice might otherwise spend tearfully recalling the youth in Greece, the one she was certain Alice had been infatuated with.

"The weather was ideal, the crossing an idyl. Alice wheeled me on the promenade deck, while Jessica observed us fondly and with that protective, maternal eye which Alice could only simulate.

"Selma was a silent heroine in this little drama. She must certainly have recognized on me the clothing she'd helped Alice purchase, clothing she'd been told was for an irresistible and noble youth of impoverished circumstances. She said nothing, nor did she comment on those occasions when, late at night, she woke to find Alice missing from her bed for an hour or more.

"My life has been too long to be remembered fully, but I'm sure there were no days in it happier than those on the ship and the ones following, here on Belle Riviere, before...before I lost Alice."

Again, he fell momentarily silent. After more than eighty years he was still trying to understand the course their lives had taken. "When we'd disembarked in New York, we traveled by train to St. Paul, site of the Hazeltine residence.

"Alice explained to her father that she and Jessica had invited me to spend a few days at the cottage on Belle Riviere before I continued to my destination, San Francisco. Of course I had no intention of going to San Francisco, but only Alice and I knew that.

"Selma's parents were expecting her to spend the remainder

of the summer at their summer place on Lake Minnetonka, west of Minneapolis, so she departed with them. Alice saw clearly in how many ways she'd become reliant upon Selma. Selma's presence had lent Alice confidence. Alice's father was a formidable man, harsh by nature, inscrutable by choice. She had always found it difficult to deal with him. Adding deceit to her dealings increased her discomfort immeasurably. She was anxious to get away from the St. Paul house, so we didn't linger in town.

"Taking with us one of the household staff, Irma Platt, a colorless, obsequious woman of middle years, to look after what housekeeping we would require, we headed for Belle Riviere— Alice, Jessica, myself, and Miss Platt. The train ride was short and pleasant, with glimpses of the river as we neared Good Hope, the village nearest the Hazeltine cottage.

"We would hire a horse and buggy at the livery, Alice pointed out. That would be used for the remainder of the summer unless more were required.

"The cottage, as everyone referred to it, was a mile and a half from Good Hope, so we were there and settled in quickly. The house was more in the style of a hunting lodge than any rude cottage or cabin. There were six bedrooms and as many baths on the second floor. On the ground floor there was the usual kitchen-scullery-pantry arrangement, four small rooms for servants, a library, large dining room, even larger parlor, and a screened porch that girdled all but the back of the house, which faced the stables.

"The place was built of stone and rough timbers and, while it could hardly be described as cozy, it was pleasant and comfortable. There was no elevator and the house hadn't been constructed with a wheelchair in mind, so I was put up in one of the servants' rooms on the ground floor and, lest Miss Platt's sensibilities be offended, she was settled into the smallest of the upstairs bedrooms, what had formerly been Alice's nursery.

"When we had unpacked, Miss Platt and Jessica drove the buggy to the village to order provisions and bring back what groceries would be needed until the order could be delivered. While they were away, Alice showed me the house, the grounds, and the outbuildings, including the stable and boathouse. There was a tennis court, somewhat overgrown, and a charming gazebo, which stood begging to be used as a rendezvous. Wandering back to the house, we hung about on the porch exchanging discreet caresses and light kisses, careful not to disturb the delicate counterbalance of elements that composed this perfect afternoon. When Jessica and the housekeeper returned, Alice and I were sitting on the porch, an atmosphere rich and golden as butter enveloping us in an amplitude of content.

"The older women made tea and with it served fresh-smelling baked goods brought from the village. The iceman, they said, would bring ice for the kitchen, so they'd carried home cream for tea. It was as thick and delicious as custard. Never had I had cream or attention so sweet, nor ever hoped to have again." His face was gilded by the sunlight of that other afternoon. At length he said, "That is enough for now. I will tempt you back with the remainder of the story." The truth was that his memories taxed him.

14

Sliding the meat loaf out of the oven, I set it on the counter to firm up, then stood, wineglass in hand, leaning my buttocks against the edge of the sink. I was still fairly sure that the Beast and his story were inventions, although I was in the dark as to how I'd invented the story. Oh, the part about Greece was easy enough since I'd recently been studying all of that. But Alice Hazeltine, her entourage, the summer place—where had I come by that?

I crossed to the phone and dialed Miranda's number in Minneapolis. If I didn't do it quickly and without pondering, I might not find the courage to do it at all. I didn't want to hear yet again that I should mind my own business. Maybe she wouldn't be home.

"Hello, dear. Sorry to bother you at dinner but I need a favor. Will you bring a case of Greek olives with you Friday?... Yes, that's right...I suppose in jars, yes. A case of them.... What?... Well, the largest jars they have, I think. It's all very complicated. I'll explain later.

"We're looking forward to seeing you and Dennis. Doesn't the party at Daisy's sound like fun? Most of our friends will be there,

I'm sure.... Bobby Arneson? I doubt it. That's a long story, too. We'll have a good gossip, you and I.

"Well, darling, I'll let you go. We're nearly ready to sit down. Dad sends his love.... Don't forget the Greek olives. Bye-bye." I sank weakly onto a kitchen chair and held a glass of Burgundy to my lips.

"Who was that?" Bart inquired, strolling into the kitchen.

"Miranda."

"How is she?"

"Fine." I roused myself. "She's working hard and looking forward to the long weekend."

"We'll have to clean out the barbecue pit, I think. And we'll need charcoal, of course."

"Yes, dear."

"I'm not much help these days." He sat down at the table and spread his napkin on his lap. "It's a good thing you're not busy."

I put a baked potato on his plate. "Sour cream?" Engrossed in his wine, he didn't answer. I sliced the meat loaf and placed the platter on the table. "Would you like ketchup or steak sauce?"

"What?"

"Ketchup or steak sauce?"

"Uh, no, I think not."

Sitting across from him, I asked, "Do you mind Miranda's getting married?"

"Why would I mind?"

"Well, she's young."

"A hundred years ago women ten years younger than Miranda were marrying and raising families and thinking nothing of it."

"They didn't have other careers."

"Why should Miranda's career prevent her from marrying? She's very capable."

"What if she finds out it was a mistake? What if Dennis turns out not to be the right man? If she were older, she'd have known more men. She could be more certain."

"People are always certain at the time, whatever age. Look at you. You were younger than Miranda."

"Yes." I poured myself more wine. "Will you be writing tonight?"

"Not writing, no. I'll be reading, though. I sent away for a book from the university library and it's come."

"About India?"

"Yes. That's all I have time to read these days. Nothing just for pleasure anymore. Although I must say, most of the research has been very pleasant."

"I may go into Belleville tonight, if you don't mind."

"Of course not."

I held the Burgundy to the fiery light of the setting sun. It was an extraordinary color. Brighter than blood, darker than fire. It reminded me of the Beast.

"Miranda asked about Bobby Arneson," I told him.

"Really? That surprises me."

"It surprised me, too."

I watched Bart disappear through the kitchen doorway, headed for the study with a cup of coffee in his hand. He was like a canny animal who locks himself in his cage to escape the threat of humans, dangerous, unpredictable, and essentially illiterate beasts that they are.

Paddling upstream toward the village was slow, exhausting labor, but it was reassuring to feel muscles strain and the canoe move steadily through the water, to know some things were hard and true and happened according to rules.

The village streetlights, in the nearly imperceptible haze of a warm river evening, looked white and fuzzy, like dandelion heads gone to seed. I walked through the park, angling toward the north-westernmost point, where the public library stood at the corner of Main Street and River Avenue.

Nellie Bergen was tidying up the day's accrual of public library mess, which threatened to engulf the checkout desk. There were still fifteen minutes until closing time, however, so I riffled through the card file, then poked among shelves at the back of the large room. Emerging with several heavy volumes full of improbably clear and brilliant photos of Greece and the Mediterranean, I plunked them down on the desk and asked, "How far back do your newspapers go?"

"The local paper?"

"Yes."

"Only to 1936. The library burned down that year and every-thing was lost. You could check the Blind Moose library or Good Hope. Was there something in particular?"

"Did you ever hear of a man named Alexander Hazeltine?"

"Oh, heavens, yes. He was one of the so-called robber barons of this part of the world. Lumber and railroads and milling, you name it. There was a big summer place on the river, down near Good Hope, that belonged to him. I remember people pointing it out to me when I was little. Of course he was long dead by that time, but it had been his. That burned down, too. Must have been, let's see, when I was in my teens. Maybe '29 or '30."

"Did you ever hear any stories about Hazeltine or his family?"

"Nothing personal. Not that I recall. If I run across anything, I'll set it aside for you."

She began checking out the books I'd selected. "Planning a trip?"

"Possibly. I want to go to Greece. Maybe after the condo dispute is settled."

"Are you involved, too?"

"I joined Save the River."

"I'm one of your comrades in arms." She looked up at the clock and announced to an old man and several teenagers that it was closing time. "Can you stop at the Blue Ox for a beer?"

We settled into the same back booth where Bart and I had sat listening to Harry describe the Belle Rive Estates project. When Benjy Bledsoe had deposited a pitcher of tap and two glasses on the table in front of us, Nellie said, "Hoot is working with Sam Fergus on the legal aspects of the condo mess."

Hoot Bergen, Nellie's husband, had spent over forty years studying and writing about midwestern rivers, from the Mississippi, Missouri, and Ohio rivers to tiny but significant creeks. He was in demand now as an environmental expert whose expertise was inland waterways. He would be an invaluable ally to Harry and Sam Fergus.

"If you don't mind my curiosity, Larry, what on earth put Alexander Hazeltine into your head?"

"I met someone recently who mentioned the name, and I realized how little I knew about local history."

"If you're interested in local history, you ought to go out and visit Grandma Mercy."

"Who?"

"Grandma Mercy. John Mercy's grandmother. She lives with John and Delia. They're about six miles west of town on County

Road 19. Grandma's way over ninety, but her mind's clear and she loves company. If you call and let her know you're coming, she'll bake biscuits and serve her strawberry and rhubarb preserves. Fit for the gods."

"Are you coming to the party at Daisy's?"

"Oh, my, yes. I was on the phone with Daisy this afternoon. I'm bringing my infamous paté puffs." She wiped a wet ring on the table with a cocktail napkin. "What do you think about Roberta Arneson?"

I was caught off-balance. It was inevitable that I'd be drawn into discussions of Roberta and Harry, and I'd better formulate a few glib, unimpassioned observations. At the moment I tried to look thoughtful, as though my silence were due to consideration of the question rather than impalement on it. "Well, Nellie, a woman has a right to disagree with her husband. Maybe their disagreement over the river proves how solid their marriage is."

"This goes beyond disagreement. She's bad-mouthing him all over the county and now I understand she's trying to ruin his business."

"I don't think that's going to come to anything, Nellie."

She held a silver-capped head defiantly. "I sure as hell hope not. Belleville owes Harry. The *Courant*'s the best small paper in Minnesota. That's not easy. Anybody can print legal notices and obituaries. But print the truth and you'll step on everybody's corns.

"Living cheek by jowl with a handful of other people the way you do in a village makes people wary of flat-out truth. There isn't the buffer from it that city-life anonymity provides. In a village everyone is directly implicated in the truth. If you read that bank president Joe Doe has played fast and loose with depositors' funds— it's *your* money. It's your kid he teaches Bible lessons to every Sunday morning in the basement of the Baptist church. It's your bridge club his wife has to 'tough it out' in. And it's your eyes Joe has to meet or look away from when you pass on the post office steps. It's all pretty intimate and people would rather pretend not to know. That's what gossip is about—knowing and pretending not to. A newspaper that won't hide pertinent truths of village life is a mirror of our corruptibility and silliness. Readers don't want to know they're corruptible or silly. They want miracle cures and two-headed cows and 'Couple Captured by Alien Midgets.' Instead, Harry says, 'This is Belleville and *you're* responsible for the quality of life here.'"

Nellie sighed. "Harry works like a dog and the average citizen thinks he's a nuisance. I guess that's what rankles Roberta. She hates being married to a nuisance. There's no social coinage in it." Smiling suddenly, she asked, "Why am I telling you all this? You know how things are with Harry."

At the bar Benjy Bledsoe laughed. "God, he was a mess, that old man. And scared? He was lookin' over his shoulder all the time he was here. He sat right there," Benjy said, indicating one of the stools in front of him, "drinking straight shots. Said he'd seen the Devil. Don't know where he got the money for the shots. No business of mine." He scooped up change from the bar and tossed it in the cash register. "Said he'd seen the Devil and the Devil's woman, too. Can you figure it? Said the Devil's woman chased him through the woods and knocked him on the ground. She was carryin' a club, and he kneeled and made a sign of the cross in front of her and figured she was gonna brain him then and there. He starts reciting the Our Father fast as he can, and she backs off into the woods."

A couple of old regulars who usually played snooker were sitting at the bar, snorting into their beer and slapping their knees at Benjy's story.

"I don't know what the old geezer saw," Benjy said, carrying their glasses away to put a head on them. "Probably fell asleep and had a nightmare. Maybe got hold of some bad liquor or spoilt food or something. That's all I can figure."

Nellie and I strained to hear. Fortunately, no one was playing the jukebox and the handful of customers, most of them townspeople, didn't consider it impolite to eavesdrop, so we all listened to the bartender's monologue.

"On the other hand," Benjy continued, "the old coot may just be crazy. You never know. There's plenty of loonies that ain't locked up. Unless you're homicidal or your family has you put away, there's nothing says you hafta be on the funny farm. This guy may have a habit of seeing the Devil and the Devil's woman. But, by God, he was one scared old tramp, I'll tell you."

"Well, now," one of the men at the bar began. He removed his cap, hit it against his thigh, placed it back on his head, adjusting it meticulously the way baseball players do, and cleared his throat. "Well, now, I do recall there was a story years ago, when I was a kid, about the Devil living in the dalles, but I thought that was an

Injun story. Maybe this old duffer heard of that and thought he'd pull your leg, Benjy."

"Naw. You shoulda seen him. He was still white as this here shirt when he came in here. He wasn't pullin' nobody's leg."

"Sounds like somebody pulled *his*, though," another of the old men added.

"Well, like I say," the man with the cap explained, "I heard the tale about the Devil in the dalles, but I never heard of no Devil's woman. That's a new one to me. I wish to hell they'd git themselves up to Ernie Duffy's place and scare the pants off the Ay-rabs when they show up."

Nellie and I finished the pitcher, used the rest room, and parted outside the Blue Ox about ten-thirty. "We'll see you Friday night, Nellie."

"Say hello to Bart." She turned north and I headed south to River Avenue.

You might think that, having overheard the story of "the Devil and the Devil's woman," and having discovered that there was, in fact, an Alexander Hazeltine, I would be convinced of my sanity. Didn't this information prove I was sane? No such thing. I began to wonder if everything on *both* sides of the river was mythology. Reaching River Avenue, I turned left and allowed my feet to carry me slowly toward Belle Riviere.

"Larissa."

I nearly jumped out of my sneakers.

"Sorry. I didn't mean to frighten you." It was Harry, coming out of *The River Courant* office. "Where are you headed at this hour? Can I give you a lift?"

"No thanks, Harry. I'm going down to the dock. The canoe's tied up down there."

"I don't like your being on the river after dark." He took the books from my arms and steered me across River Avenue and into the dim recesses of Humphrey Park. Stopping now, he suggested, "Look, why don't we get my car and I'll drive you home?"

"No. I want to take the canoe. It doesn't take any time to get home. It's a beautiful night." I might have added that Bart would take it amiss if, after yesterday's scene at the Kaffee Kafe, Harry were to bring me home. It would look as though I'd gone to town to meet him.

"Where have you been?"

"I came in to check some books out of the library," I told him, "and Nellie Bergen asked me to have a beer at the Blue Ox."

When we reached the dock, he placed the books on the seat of the canoe, removed the Mae West, and helped me into it.

"By the way," I asked, "do you know anything about a Hazeltine family who had a big place on the river near Good Hope? Particularly, about Alice Hazeltine? The house burned to the ground years ago, but I'd like to know more about the family."

"Why?"

"I've been thinking of trying a few watercolors of Belle Riviere at the turn of the century. The Hazeltine house has come up as a possible subject. I'll need photos. Alice Hazeltine would make a nice human element to inject into a painting of the property." What began as a white lie became, as I spoke, a commitment. "What do you think?"

"I think it's a first-rate idea. The paintings might even be used in some way—I'm not sure yet just how—to help Save the River. Would you mind that?"

"I'm rusty. I have no idea how long the project would take. Don't count on them until I see."

"Call Lydia Comstock. She's head of the County Historical Society. Good Hope's in Beau Bois County. I know they have a lot of old photographs and probably information on the Hazeltines."

We stood close and spoke in hushed voices. Our words were everyday words, but we'd lost the knack of being beer-drinking pals. What was the difference between friendship's love and lover's love, that one was effortlessly accepting, the other full of doubt and awkwardness? Something of value was gone now, and trouble had taken its place.

"Harry." I hesitated. "Bobby saw our cars in the parking lot at Al's Place."

"How do you know?"

"As I was leaving, he drove into the lot, turned right around, and drove out again. After just hearing his mother accuse me of being in love with you, finding us together won't convince him otherwise. I'm sorry. I'm making awful problems for you."

"Baloney. Maybe I'll talk to him about it. Don't worry."

"I'd better shove off."

"For Christ's sake, Larissa, be careful." He put a hand to my face and I put mine over it.

"I will."

"I'm going back to the office to wait. When you get home, call and let me know you're all right." He handed me into the canoe, and held my fingers for a moment. "Don't forget."

He untied the mooring rope and tossed it into the canoe. The craft moved with the current, slipping through the water like a hand through a satin sleeve. I skimmed past Humphrey Park and square shapes that were Burton's Feed and Seed, Harvey's Body Shop, Handelman's Ford, and the fire station. Then lights shone from rooms where people watched reruns of *M*A*S*H* or argued or washed their hair. I wondered if Bart had finished reading and would like a glass of wine. I hadn't meant to stay so late in town.

The village was soon behind me. Now I moved in the darkness that lay between the dalles, hundred-foot stone walls, hulking and primal, rising sheer and monolithic from the water. Before, I would have shivered, passing them late. But knowing the Beast had found a home there, I was grateful for their fierce and concealing face. (You had to live as though *everything* were real—otherwise you'd go crazy.)

Beyond the dalles, there was a farm on the right and then cabins, set rather far apart and—like ours—back up among the trees. From a considerable distance I could see our dock shining white in the moonlight. I'd just caught sight of it when I heard the music. It was a single instrument, a little like a flute or recorder, but sweeter than either. It flowed like skeins of silk ribbon, graceful loops of it reaching out to encircle me. I was caught by it and pulled toward the opposite shore. I recalled my promise to Harry. I couldn't keep him waiting and worrying. Struggling against the music, I reluctantly brought the canoe about and slid it smoothly up to the dock.

Bart undressed as I sat in bed reading *Five Clues in Surrey*. It was seldom, with his schedule, that I saw Bart undress. His body was neither muscular nor flabby. With the years it had acquired an unformed look, like an eight-year-old boy's.

When we'd married, he was, like Richard Cory, "imperially slim," slim and loose-jointed as a basketball player. Now he was a little thickened in the middle, which made his shoulders seem narrower. His body was not repulsive, nor in any way distinctive. It was the body of a middle-aged man. I was frankly unsure that in a roomful of naked men, all of them with flour sacks over their heads, I could pick him out. That was more my fault than his.

Returning from the bathroom after a quick shower, he climbed into bed, pajamaless, and reached for me. I flinched with a deep spasm of resentment, then was tranfused by guilt, rising from a limitless source, guilt strong enough to make me nauseated.

I embraced him, caressed and kissed him, feeling no desire, nor even desire *for* desire, but only a violent mating in my viscera of resentment and guilt.

I played out the event as best I could, knowing that it wasn't really good enough, that it hadn't been for a long time, and feeling guilt for that, but grateful that Bart didn't criticize. When it was over and I could lie by myself again, I felt a slight abating of the war inside me, as if in the sex act I'd paid a penance, not one large enough to carry off the guilt, only just enough so that I could sleep.

15

It was just past ten-thirty when I turned the Volvo into Humphrey Park and left it in the lot beside the County Historical Society building. The structure was a log cabin, which, a placard beside the door explained, had been moved from its original location on the Lars Borg farm northwest of Belleville to its present site in 1958. In 1855 it had been constructed by Per Borg and his wife, Inga, immigrants from Sweden.

Inside was a museum of pioneer life. A larger adjacent building had been added in recent years to house an overflow of farm implements, buggies and wagons, kitchenware, clothing, and every sort of county memorabilia. In this section, also, was a reading room for society members, visiting scholars, and others like myself who required research materials on local history.

Lydia Comstock met me at the door. I'd phoned her at ten, when the musuem opened, to explain my project and needs. She'd been receptive, suggesting particular collections that might yield the required information. Now she led me into the reading room.

"Mrs. Demming, I can't tell you how thrilled we'd be to have one of the paintings. You don't really have to do that, but it's terribly kind and we accept the offer."

Lydia was a plump, dark-haired woman with flawless skin and intelligent eyes. Settling me at a big oak table, she presented me with bound and unbound volumes of printed and photographic materials. In addition, there were personal letters and handbills and account books and even grammar school report cards.

"I'll leave you alone," she said. "If you have questions, holler."

I set to work on the old photo collections first, interrupting the search occasionally to sketch a scene or just a detail or two from a candid shot: the collar of a woman's dress, an oarlock on an old boat, or a gentleman's straw hat at a country picnic. By two o'clock my stomach was sending up pestering sounds. I stacked the books neatly, closed my sketch pad, and left the reading room.

"Thanks for your help," I told Mrs. Comstock. "I'll be back tomorrow morning."

"Would you like me to leave the things out on the table for you?"

"Yes. I'd appreciate that."

"Did you find what you need?" she asked, walking with me to the door.

"Between what you've got here and the river settings that are pretty much unaltered, I'll have plenty of material."

I dashed quickly in and out of the liquor store before heading home. Groceries would have to wait until tomorrow. It was getting late.

Arriving at the cottage, I threw fruit and hard rolls and wine in the basket. These, the books of Greece, and my Belle Riviere sketches I loaded into the canoe, then quickly rowed across the river. On the other side, I was unsure how to proceed. I hesitated to tramp through the woods, wine bottle in hand, calling, "Here, Beast!"

Spreading myself out on the big towel, I ate an apple and a roll and waited. I wished that I'd remembered to bring my pad and pencils. Finally, opening one of the books, I began to read the information accompanying the pictures of Greece. I checked the index for Arcadia. A small section of the book was devoted to it. It was breathtaking. There were several photos—two from Olympia, where Alice had found the Beast.

I looked through all the books, then through my sketches. It must have been past four. At length I lay down to wait. I dozed and when I woke, I was certain it was five. I had to start dinner.

The Beast had missed a fine picnic. Well, that would show him, I muttered, gathering everything back into the basket. I tried to be offhand, but I was frightened. Had he vanished into the Labyrinth of my brain?

If the Beast never returned, would that mean I was well? I spent the evening on the screened porch, fussing over sketches, and hoping by my light to attract his attention. I attracted a sizable group of moths who were nearly as jittery as I.

At ten I threw down my pencil, dumped some gin in a glass of ice, and strolled down to the dock. Nothing was there but moonlight and mosquitoes. No thundering laughter, no tender melody. So far, sane was a washout. At eleven I resigned myself to bed. Several times during a night of empty sleep, I woke to hear nothing.

Returning from town Wednesday morning, I showered and pulled on a fresh sleeveless blouse, a bright peasant skirt, and sandals. In the linen cupboard, I dug around, coming up with an old damask bedspread, pale ivory, a bit frayed with the years, but immeasurably more elegant than the gaudy beach towel, a relic of Miranda's teen years, which I'd been using for my solitary picnics.

Before dashing down to the canoe, I called my son Clark's wife, Sarah. "That's right. Ouzo—O-U-Z-O. And retsina. Two bottles of ouzo and half a dozen of retsina. They're for a friend. If you'll just bring them up Friday, I'll be grateful. Thank you very much, dear. Give our love to Clark. See you Friday. I hope you're remembering to put your feet up, at least half an hour a day. Good girl. Good-bye again."

The day being hot, I smoothed the bedspread out under the trees, in the shade. I felt dithery and kept straightening and re-arranging everything. I'd packed a fine picnic, much finer than the previous day's, and now waited, with a child's pathetic expectancy, as if the sheer merit of my effort entitled me to the Beast's presence. By my little ceremonies of preparation and games of will I was magicking his appearance.

The minutes stretched themselves to their utmost. Retrieving my pad and pencils from the canoe, I began idly to draw—a line, two. Soon I was engrossed, sketching quickly, smudging and crosshatching, closing my eyes for a moment to concentrate, then hurrying on. I set the sketch against a tree and stood back to judge. I grunted aloud with dissatisfaction and shook my head.

"Your husband?"

Whirling, I found the Beast directly behind me.

"Is that a portrait of your husband?"

"No."

"It looks a little like me, except the nose."

"Well, it's not." I grabbed up the pad, closed it, and laid it beside the basket. "I'm so glad you came," I announced without reserve. "Are you hungry?"

"Famished."

"Good. Sit down." The plates, napkins, and glasses were already laid out. From the basket I pulled bread, cheese, coarse sausage, an onion, a large, fragrant tomato, boiled eggs, strawberries, and melon. Handing him a knife, I slipped out of my sandals and ran to the river—lightly, like a child—to fetch a cold bottle of champagne.

"You've thought of everything," he said, taking the bottle to open it. "I wouldn't have ordered one thing differently."

"Thank you. I think you'll like the sausage. It's made locally by a butcher in Blind Moose."

He poured champagne and gave me a glass. Raising his, he pronounced, "Collaboration," and looked knowingly at me, as if I were his conspirator. I was mystified but raised my glass and drank.

When we finished eating, I packed everything but the champagne and glasses into the hamper. Reclining, he rested his shoulders against a log and I sat nearby, my back to a tree. For long, peaceful moments we sat, silent together, and it was impossible to recall the chill of fearing him lost in the folds of my mind.

Finally I said, "You were telling me about the Hazeltines Monday afternoon."

"I've never spoken to anyone else about those days. For many years I couldn't bring myself to discuss it, even when there was opportunity. More recently, there's been no one I trusted."

I was greatly flattered. I refilled his glass. When I'd filled my own and arranged myself comfortably, he took up the narrative. Once again we were at the Hazeltine summer house on Belle Riviere, outside of Good Hope. Alice, her aunt Jessica, and a domestic, Irma Platt, made up the household, along with the invalid guest from Greece.

It was the height of a warm, country summer at a time and in a place where days were delicious exercises in well-bred self-indulgence. Hours were tasted, ingredients adjusted, to attain a perfect blend of afternoon or evening. The excitement of the affair between Alice and the Beast was contrapuntal to the pervading atmosphere, and all the more thrilling. It was the dark bloom in a garden bouquet of pastels and baby's breath. Like all anomalies, however, it begged excising. Being uncommon is dangerous.

This afternoon, warm, lazy, and softly sibilant, must have mocked him with its likeness to those he spent with Alice. He stroked his beard idly and pulled together the threads of the past.

"Those days and nights, when I was a guest at the cottage, were surrounded by an aureola of grace. The air was winy with honeysuckle and pine. The sunlight was nearly as thick as the country cream. The night was aromatic with rich secrets, not the least of them mine and Alice's.

"The fresh and simple foods we ate couldn't have been more succulent had they been harvested on Olympus: tomatoes, plump, with the perfume of the vine still clinging; ears of corn, golden and bursting with sweet white milk; crisp peas, uncooked, stolen from the colander, tasting like dessert.

"Alice and I spent nearly every waking hour together, many of them in the gazebo, where she began teaching me to read English. My spoken English was broken and she tutored me in that as well. When lessons were done, she read—the Romantic poets, Shakespeare, Dickens, Jane Austen, and Whitman's *Leaves of Grass,* which, she explained simply, was supposed to be shocking.

"At the end of a week, I bid good-bye to Jessica and Miss Platt, and Alice drove me to town. She purchased a ticket to St. Paul, lest there be any question later. If the station master ever had occasion to deny putting me on the train, Alice would confess to having driven me to the next village rather than part while we were midway in a discussion of Byron's involvement in the Greek war of independence.

"Presenting me the ticket, as a souvenir of our charade, she climbed back into the buggy and drove into the country, half a mile or so beyond the Hazeltine cottage. The chance of our being seen was slim. The road was usually deserted and the area was sparsely populated in those days. Reining the horse, she helped me down and together we carried my things, including the wheelchair, into the woods. When she had left, I would find a way to hide them properly.

"Because the buggy stood in the road, she couldn't stay but promised to meet me after lunch where the grounds surrounding the cottage met the dense woods, perhaps a hundred yards beyond the gazebo.

"It was now the third week in July. If, as she had promised, she was to send me to Greece no later than early October, we had only two months remaining. Perhaps Alice feared I would refuse to stay in the United States. I don't know. Because of her father's harsh and critical nature, she was accustomed to keeping her own counsel. Whether she wished me to stay or go, she didn't say. That she loved me, she left no doubts.

"A frenzy of love and study began. She was determined to teach me reading as quickly as man was ever taught. And when we were not at our phonics, we were at our pleasure.

"As the days ran away with us, I grew melancholy. Me! It was centuries since I could remember being melancholy and what I remembered of it was not so sharp or black as this. I didn't want to leave. I had come to the United States for a lark. I was a bored adventurer, a minor deity recalling former glory like a fading matinee idol. I had never intended in the beginning to love Alice. Never intended to be melancholy.

"The lessons progressed well. At first we'd used primers from the public school, stories of good and bad little boys and girls who soiled their clothes and lost their dolls, or said their prayers and rolled hoops. We laughed as we read, trying to hold the future at bay.

"I had found a cave in the palisades upriver from here. I spent little time there but it was an ideal place to hide my belongings and myself, should that be necessary. During those summer days, however, I camped in the woods and Alice brought me all that I needed and more.

"Early in September Alice grew somber in looks and manner. I thought at first it was my impending departure that saddened her. I tried to cheer her up, urging that she and Jessica come again to Europe the following spring. There were many excuses she could make: friends who had invited her back, studies she wished to take up. When she returned, we would find a means of keeping her there.

"She smiled gravely, ran her hand along my cheek, and said nothing. Each day I saw a worsening in her state. Pale lavender-gray circles appeared around her eyes, and her body, always slender, grew thin, her face ill. I was beside myself. Life was escaping from her and I couldn't discover the reason.

"What was her illness? She swore she had none. Was she worried, then, about my leaving? I would do whatever she asked, including remain in the United States. Was she tired of me? I would leave immediately. She mustn't concern herself. At that she threw her arms around me and, laughing miserably, pulled me violently to her.

"Frequently she tried to dissemble, putting on a false show of gaiety and reciting lighthearted patter. The playacting made me weep inside, for I could see what it cost her. One day I turned aside and walked away in the middle of this invented chatter, desolate that she should feel a need for pretense.

"She wept then and I held her. She sobbed and couldn't stop. I worried that she would make herself weaker. She was feverish. Eventually, I went to the river and wet a cloth to bathe her face. I wanted to abduct her, carry her away from her anguish.

"At last she ceased even the dry sobs. She was calm and ethereal as she rested against me and spoke low.

"She was carrying a child, she confessed. It was only the slightest bit of thread, Clotho's work barely begun, but it was undeniable. Mine was a masculine reaction and one not taking into account Alice's anxieties. I was jubilant. For a moment I felt newborn.

"I forbade her to worry. She was to rest and eat and be happy. I would find a way to care for her and the infant. She lay quietly in my arms until it was nearly dinner hour. Then she kissed me lingeringly on the lips, on my eyelids and ears, my neck and hands. I longed to make love to her one last time before she left, but she said no, that Jessica would come searching for her. Reluctantly, I let her go and watched her slender back, light-brown hair falling loose to her waist, as she glided spectrally between the trees and out of the woods.

"That night she didn't come to me. About midnight by my reckoning I went to the edge of the woods. The house was ablaze with lights, upstairs and down. There was another buggy near the stable door and a second horse within. For several hours I remained on the grounds, trying to discover what was taking place inside the brightly lit rooms. No clue escaped from them and, shortly before dawn, I withdrew a scant fifty yards into the trees, where I drowsed lightly and uneasily.

"About seven o'clock I heard cries. Women's voices raised jaggedly and dying in moans. Then a man's shout. I ran toward the sounds, halting only when I reached the last line of trees concealing me from those standing on the dock: Jessica, Miss Platt, and Alexander Hazeltine. Hazeltine, dressed in pajamas and robe, plunged into the water and waded toward the end of the boathouse, where Alice's body floated, her gown caught on a piling. With painful, unhurried delicacy, her father freed the cloth and, gathering her up, roared like a maddened bear. He had loved her, too.

"For many hours and miles, blinded and crazed, I shattered the woods, screaming and tearing my flesh, detesting immortality. Death was mine to inspire but not to share. For the first time in all time, I felt that life was a deep pit from which I could not climb out.

"By evening I crawled back to the spot where we had lain, and tried to conjure her warmth. Far into the night I lay, trying to understand. Why had she died? Had she not trusted me? I had failed her.

"When I could endure the pain no longer, I got up and wandered aimlessly in the dark. An hour before dawn I found myself emerging from the trees near the gazebo.

"I climbed the steps and stood gazing around as though I half-expected to find her. There was a dark shape on the bench where we had sat working my lessons. I ran to see and found not one but several gifts. On top of the others, a piece of cloth. Holding it up, I saw that it was a shirt. My hands told me it was made of lawn and morning would reveal its pale-peach color. Beneath the shirt were the books, my primers and the volumes from which she'd read to me. Between the pages of the topmost book, there was a note, the paper protruding enough to catch the eye.

"I carried everything away into the woods and at the first light I read the note:

Dear Love—

Papa arrived from the city before dinner. I suspect that Aunt Jessica sent for him. She has been worried about my health, half-convinced I'd contracted consumption while we were abroad.

I hope you will understand that I had to tell Papa about the baby. I have limited resources until I am twenty-one and inherit from my mother. Jessica's income is small. Papa had supplemented it because of her care of me.

I prayed to Papa to send me to Europe to live, someplace out of the way where I wouldn't be a humiliation to him. I thought, dear love, that we could be together in the countryside, possibly near Mt. Chelmos, where you took me to see the falls of the Styx.

I could not anticipate with what disdain Papa would view this plan. He said that I would live in a convent until the baby came, and when it was born, it would be given for adoption. It is Papa's belief that once the baby was disposed of, I could marry and live the life intended.

What have I done to you, my love? I have brought you to a strange place, far from your home, and placed an impossible burden of responsibility on you.

In an envelope within the pages of this book you will find the cash I brought with me from St. Paul as well as money I took from Papa's wallet. I'm sorry it is so little, but I think, if you were quite careful you might find it sufficient to get you to France and from there perhaps you could make your way home.

I love you to desperation. For that I ask no forgiveness, but for all else I pray you forgive.

Alice

16

Finishing the story, he lay back and flung a forearm over closed eyelids. After long years he was still made wretched by his memories. He lay like that for twenty minutes or more, then sat up.

"Forgive me."

Ignoring the apology, I asked, "Why didn't you leave?"

"I couldn't leave without punishment. I needed around me constant reminders, like thorns, to prick my consciousness and prevent me growing comfortable and forgetful. When I finally might have left, it was too late."

"Too late?"

"How old do I look to you?"

I considered. I wasn't sure how old he looked. His face seemed older than his body. "Forty?"

"The papers with which I came to this country stated my age as thirty. I think perhaps I would still look thirty but for Alice's death. In any case, the authorities would certainly not accept that I had aged only ten years in the past eighty-six, even if they believed that I could still be alive. My age, according to the papers, would now be one hundred sixteen."

"Would you like to go back?"

"Yes. I would like to see Greece again." He paused, savoring his thoughts. "I long to roam Arcadia, to see how the shepherds have fared without me. Perhaps there are no longer shepherds there."

"I think there are," I assured him. "If you're a minor deity, an immortal, why is it that you can't work magic to return yourself to Greece?"

He smiled indulgently. "The only magic of a minor deity is a kind of sleight of hand. I have mental powers similar to those of a good hypnotist or stage magician. My magic is intelligence and tricks."

"What about Zeus or Dionysus? Couldn't you call upon them?" I spoke of Zeus and Dionysus as if they were king and plenipotentiary of a Third World nation. "Haven't you been missed? Don't they wonder what's become of you?"

"I doubt that any of the gods has noted my absence, even Dionysus. He has a sizable retinue and doesn't depend upon me. If I am missed at all, it will be by the shepherds and hunters. But if any god or goddess thought to look for me, they would conclude, I'm sure, that I had got my just deserts and must find my way back by my wits. No," he said, shrugging philosophically, "it is up to me."

I changed the subject, curious about another matter. "What happened to Alice's family? Do you know?"

"No. They didn't return to the cottage. It was put on the market and three different families owned it before it burned to the ground in 1929."

"Year after year alone here, haven't you gone a little crazy? I mean, don't you crave companionship?"

"Before the cottage was sold, I removed dozens of books from the library, many of them works that Alice had mentioned. They've been my chief companionship. I read aloud to myself. It provides practice in speaking."

"You haven't spoken to anyone since Alice died?" I asked incredulously. "Anyone other than me?"

"There was one," he said with a note of chagrin. "In 1925 people named Bartlet bought the cottage. He was a doctor in Minneapolis. Doctor Cyrus Bartlet. His young wife, Nancy, and two small children spent several summers at the cottage. Doctor Bartlet brought them in early summer, along with a housekeeper and nurse, and left them. He joined them every second weekend. It was lonely for Mrs. Bartlet.

"I'm not sure how necessary it was for Doctor Bartlet to spend nearly all his time in the city. From what I observed of him with the children's nurse on a number of occasions, I don't believe he was a man to be trusted at either end of the twice-monthly railroad trip.

"Observing the circumstances for a couple of summers, I decided that Mrs. Bartlet would benefit from company. After Alice, I was reluctant to give more than friendship to a mortal. You yourself said love has a built-in expectation of loss."

"Even for minor deities," I said, depressed by the thought.

"One does become cautious—the first sign of age. In any event, I needn't have worried, because Nancy was not a woman I was tempted to love.

"At eighteen Alice had character and grace. She possessed depth and subtlety and sensibility. Nancy Bartlet at twenty-six was shallow and spoiled and endlessly silly. Hers was a penny-dreadful intelligence.

"Although she'd been sent to expensive schools, she'd assiduously avoided education, and the extent of her liberation in that exciting postwar time was the smoking of cigarettes and drinking of bootleg liquor. She longed to be genuinely wayward but was too lazy or lacking in imagination to succeed even at misconduct. She hoped for someone to drop a load of decadence in her lap.

"When she encountered me, I seemed the answer to a prayer. Titillated by my form, she considered me the quintessential perversion." His glance turned toward me and he explained, "For countless centuries I've enjoyed my reputation. I've worn it like a sapphire in my navel, with confidence and good humor. How can I explain...?" He hesitated. "Will you understand when I say that Nancy made me feel dirty?"

I laughed aloud.

"I was afraid of that." He snatched up a pinecone and hurled it toward the river. "Decadence without intelligence is dangerous. It requires imagination to anticipate the consequences of one's corruption, and character to accept them." He added soberly, "Even gods make mortal mistakes.

"But to return to Nancy. I tried not to frighten her, but in the end it was she who frightened me. She first saw me, as you did, in the woods. Unlike you, she didn't imagine that I was a delusion. She thought I'd escaped from a traveling freak show.

"'Oh, you poor man,' she said. 'Can I help you?'" His voice assumed a breathy, insinuative tone.

"'No. I'm quite all right. Thank you,' I told her, looking up at her but not moving from where I sat reading beneath a tree. Impolite, perhaps, but she was impervious.

"She sidled forward. 'Was your mother frightened by a...'

"'Goat?'

"'...by a goat?' she inquired, perfectly seriously.

"'No, madam. My father assumed the form of a goat when he lay with my mother. I cannot say why. He's a playful sort. It doubtless seemed a clever ruse at the time. In any event, my mother was not in the least frightened by him.'"

"What did Mrs. Bartlet say to that?" I asked.

"That I was a lying fool or a depraved schizophrenic. In either case, she was aquiver with delight. I was just what the doctor's wife had ordered.

"I felt sorry for her. She was bored and neglected and lonely. It was obvious to me that Cyrus Bartlet had married her for money. Although she couldn't admit it, it was as obvious to her.

"When she was asleep, she was a beautiful woman, voluptuous, but not heavy, with masses of blue-black ringlets worn short in a boyish style. Her large gray eyes were thickly fringed by black lashes. There was a natural high color to her cheeks, though the rest of her skin was milky. A beauty when she slept. Awake she was petulant, self-serving, and exhausting." He sighed. "But I hoped to convince her to help me return to Greece. For that I needed her goodwill, so I tried to please her. It was fraudulent and whorish, I know, selling myself for return passage. But I was perfectly willing to give her full value." He caught my expression. "What is it?"

"With your reputation, you want me to believe that you were conscience-stricken over using Nancy Bartlet?"

"I've been a seducer and a deceiver and many other kinds of animal, but what I've done, I've done with affection," he told me with injured gravity. "I've tried not to victimize."

I said nothing.

"For a few weeks Nancy was pleased with me. I had no difficulty satisfying her sexual desires, but she was basically unimaginative, so that much of my talent was wasted. What impelled her, you see, was not sex but a formless hunger for excitement. She was not a person who could satisfy this through the subtleties of human relationships or other creative outlets, for she was empty of creativity. Whatever talents she'd been born with had long since atrophied for want of use."

Parenthetically, he pointed out, "A human and perhaps a god, no less, requires expression of self. It comes of being born with an ego. One needs to stand atop the mountain, or mere hillock, of one's work and cry, 'Look at me! Look at me! This is who I am.'

"But Nancy's lack of constructive expression drove her to instinctive, ill-considered foolishness. She liked, for instance, to hike upriver a mile or more from the house, to a point not far below where we sit now. There was a narrow spit of land projecting into the river then—it has since disappeared—where she demanded that we picnic. We were exposed on three sides to the eyes of anyone boating on the river or hiking along the opposite bank. Arriving there, she would make a great ceremony of undressing in full view. Once naked, she insisted upon public fornication before lunch." He hastened to add, "Mind you, I'm not a prude." He looked in my direction. "You find that amusing."

I was laughing hard. He was funny and tragic, childlike and wise. For someone so ancient and admittedly jaded, he was remarkably artless.

"I'm sorry," I apologized. "I will accept that you're not a prude."

"No, it wasn't simple prudery that put my back up. Her carryings-on placed me in jeopardy." He got to his feet and paced for a minute. Then, veering about, he eyed me shrewdly. "If you consider what might happen were the population convinced that a creature like myself existed in these woods, you'll see why I feared Nancy Bartlet's antics. I have a secure hiding place in the dalles, a place I'm certain no one knows of, but it isn't inconceivable that I could be hunted and hounded like the Loch Ness Monster or the Abominable Snowman if I were spied by enough people. I could be tracked and trailed and dogged into a corner. I might even be snared."

"No."

"It's possible. And then what? I would be the freak in an eternal traveling show, whatever happened."

"You'd certainly be an overnight celebrity."

"I already *am* a celebrity," he replied defensively. "I don't require every damned fool's recognition to validate my legend." Against his will a look of forlorn embattlement shadowed his features and his voice grew husky with a bleak emotion. "I don't want to be a public grotesque, Larissa."

Amazed by this unexpected susceptibility, I immediately rose and went to him. "No, of course not." Laying a hand on his arm, I swore fervently, "It won't happen."

Mischief followed pain across his features. Inclining his head so close that I felt the light caress of his beard on my cheek and then my ear, he chaffed, "I prefer to be a private novelty."

17

"That Nancy Bartlet had so little regard for me she would risk my freedom for a few moments of rebellion on the beach, grieved me. That I must endure it if I hoped to glimpse Arcadia, was galling. I was ashamed and afraid."

Returning to the ivory bedspread, the Beast sank down on it, took up his glass, and drank off the remaining champagne. The bottle was nearly empty, too, and I padded, still barefoot, to the water to fetch the second one, wedged between the rocks.

When he had filled our glasses and motioned me to join him on the damask cloth, he continued, "Nancy was not a woman with many close friends. She was too self-concerned. Occasionally, however, someone was drawn to her for a brief period. A timid or repressed soul, seeking vicarious danger, would attach herself to Nancy in hope of witnessing the hell-bent self-destruction toward which Nancy's impiety was headed.

"Two such young women came frequently to the cottage the summer Nancy and I consorted. Their names were Maude and Meredith Sontag, and they'd been three years to a religious college someplace in Iowa. They were the twin daughters of a local minister whose denomination I never learned. They were not unattractive girls, but their behavior was circumscribed by the rather narrow religion of their father.

"Before taking up the missionary vocation, they'd come home for a summer vacation. How and where Nancy met them, I don't know, but the Sontag girls, pale and pervious and wearing their skirts rather longer than the fashion, began showing up in the afternoon at the cottage.

"Usually they sat on the screened porch or in the gazebo, and Nancy served them lemonade. For an hour or two she chattered and laughed while Maude and Meredith murmured quiescently and glanced sideways at each other from under lashes lowered like discreet portieres. Frequently, Nancy played the phonograph and the Sontag girls were shocked and pleased by the unabashed sounds of speakeasy music.

"At first I feared Nancy might, for her own amusement, commit some bizarre and ungodly act simply to shock the girls. But as the afternoons slid past, one after the other, I concluded that she'd grown genuinely fond of them and enjoyed having someone to call friend. Perhaps the combined influence of the Sontag girls and myself (the alpha and omega of religious representation) was having a positive effect on Nancy. At any rate she continued pleasant to them and seemed almost sympathetic toward me. I began to entertain hope of seeing Greece before winter.

"When I spoke of my goal and financial needs, she listened. She still imagined that I was a fortuitous freak and nothing more, but freaks, too, had homelands toward which they tended.

"In August the Bartlets' two children, accompanied by the nurse-governess, journeyed to Chicago on the train to visit their paternal grandparents. At the end of the month, Nancy and Dr. Bartlet, traveling by the same railroad, were to follow, remaining with the senior Bartlets until after Labor Day and returning with the children and nurse, not to the river cottage, but to their home in Minneapolis. Before joining her husband in the city for their trip, Nancy would close the cottage for the season.

"The prospect of this seemed to cheer her. There was a suppressed excitement in her behavior as the time drew closer, and she was ever more sanguine toward me and my affairs, intimating that a solution to my difficulties was being worked out. By this I took her to mean that she was securing a passport and passage for me. She'd had a photographer out from town after the children had left and while the housekeeper was enjoying her day off, to take a simple, straightforward photo of me in clothes of the doctor's and with my lower extremities covered, of course. August was the pleasantest time I had known with her, and I was proud of the progress she appeared to be making in applying herself to the concerns of others.

"Several days before her departure, she told me she would like to prepare an intimate farewell dinner for me at the cottage the night before she left. 'You've been kind to me,' she explained, 'and I would like to show my appreciation.'

"I doubted seriously that she was capable of cooking the simplest meal, but I sensed that she wished to create a ceremony around the presentation of my passage to Greece. I accepted gratefully and without a hint that I guessed her motive.

"That last day Maude and Meredith Sontag drove out for a final social call. They stayed most of the afternoon and I strongly suspected that Nancy had put them to work preparing our dinner, for they remained indoors despite the day, which was of that lush, ripe, golden August sort whose perfection inspires rue.

"A church bell in Good Hope told me when it was six o'clock. Carrying flowers I'd purloined the previous night from the graveyard at the edge of the village, I made my way to the cottage, glancing carefully about as I crossed the broad lawn, lest someone appear unexpected and spy me.

"Nancy met me at the door and took the flowers, thanking me prettily. She told me to make myself comfortable while she went to the kitchen for wine and glasses. We sat on the porch, relaxing in the warm serenity of the red-and-mauve twilight. The next day someone would come from town, she told me, to carry the porch furniture to the stable for the winter. The Bartlets did not keep horses, but they still referred to the building as a stable, though it housed only automobiles. Chatting of such domestic matters, we passed the time until dinner.

"Nancy or the Sontags had prepared a cold dinner, simple but delicious. She poured a light French wine and when we were seated, raised her glass. 'To surprises,' she said, smiling, eyes bright, cheeks flushed. I cocked my head as if baffled by the toast, though naturally I was quite certain I knew the surprise. 'I have a surprise for you,' she laughed, '—later.'

"Following dinner we returned again to the porch and in the dark listened to music on the radio. I remember only 'What'll I Do?' which I later learned was by a man named Irving Berlin. It was a sweet, sad song and made me think of Alice. I closed my eyes and tried to imagine that she sat in the chair nearby.

"Eventually, Nancy got up and came to sit beside me on an oak settee. She spoke softly to me, saying that she would miss me and would always remember this summer. There was a finality in her phrases and I knew it was because I would be going away and not returning. I felt tender and loving toward her for what she was giving me.

"We kissed and caressed and she led me to her bedroom on the second floor. It was a large room with deep Aubusson carpets in pale colors. Lace and satin dressed the big open windows overlooking the moonlit lawn and river; more of the same draped the huge bed. The room was soft and easy as the inside of a loving woman. I wondered who had furnished it.

"Can you imagine," he sighed, "how it felt to lie on that immense, perfumed bed, with a down pillow beneath my head and consoling sheets blessing my ancient body? Such luxury and comfort after years of deprivation! I blush to tell you there were tears in my eyes as I lay down. I needed nothing more to complete the evening. But, to convey my gratitude, I made love to her, using every sexual skill I possessed.

"Later I reclined in euphoric exhaustion while Nancy found champagne and glasses. From below came the sound of the popping cork. I wondered that she hadn't asked me to open the bottle, then smiled, realizing that she was treating me as guest of honor. Up she came with full glasses and the bottle on a tray. It was not a very smooth vintage, but I drank politely and lay back against the lace-trimmed pillows, amused to find my scarred and hairy body cushioned in such splendor.

"I hoped she would soon bestow the 'surprise' upon me, as I was growing irresistibly sleepy. Again she excused herself and I slumbered as I waited her return.

"I'm uncertain how much time had elapsed when the snorting

vibrations of an automobile wove themselves into the fabric of my inconsequential dreams. I struggled unsuccessfully to reconcile the sound to the images passing through my mind. I nagged my consciousness, but I was having difficulty rousing it.

"Voices reached me, several voices, mostly female. They were—where? In the drive? Outside the bedroom door? Perhaps below, on the porch. One of them, Nancy's, penetrated my fog. 'He's upstairs.' Even in my stupor, the elation in her voice alarmed and prodded me.

"Lifting my head required unendurable effort and time. As the voices continued—'Reverend Sontag, you'll see it's him. It's *him*'—my mind ran panicking through fields of peril, begging my lethargic body to be up and away.

"Rolling onto my side, I struggled with my legs, pulling them to the edge of the bed, then dropping them, like bags of sand, over the side as I inched my torso up on my elbow.

"'Calm yourself, Mrs. Bartlet,' a masculine voice urged. 'You lead the way. The girls must remain here. You and I will go up and I will go into the room alone.'

"I was sitting on the edge of the bed, straining to push myself to my feet.

"'You'll see, Reverend Sontag,' Nancy promised. 'He has hoofs and horns. It's him!' She was drunk with jubilation. 'Oh, I can't wait! Hurry, please!'

"I swayed on my feet and reached for the window frame. Steadying myself, I gulped the night air and tried to plan. If Maude and Meredith were waiting on the porch, I didn't dare climb out this window and lower myself to the ground from the porch roof. Below stairs, voices moved into the house. Nancy and Sontag.

"Staggering, I made my way to the bedroom door and hoped I could negotiate the hallway before they began climbing the stairs. The last room on the right faced the stable rather than the river. It had a small balcony formed by the roof of the scullery.

"I lurched forward like a man on deck in a squall, clutching the balustrade surrounding the stairwell, using it for support as I shambled toward the far-off door. Nancy and Sontag were at the foot of the stairs, he counseling composure and prayer, she exhorting swift exposure of the demon.

"Their argument covered my clumsiness as I turned the knob of the bedroom door and let myself in. Closing it behind me, I heard Nancy, followed by the reverend, mount the open stairway. She was urging him to be quick before the drug she'd given me wore off.

"I steadied myself against a bed, then an armchair, finally a chest. I was at the French doors, groping first with the draperies, then the handle. There was a key in the lock! Could my fumbling hands hold and turn it? The effects of the draught were wearing thin, but there was numbness yet in my fingers.

"Slowly, and with prodigious concentration, I grasped the delicate key between my thumb and forefinger and gingerly began to turn it. I heard a click as the bolt slid back, but my trembling fingers knocked the key from the lock. Kneeling, I ran my hands hastily along the floor until I felt the small metallic object. Taking it between my teeth, I stood, opened the door and slipped out. An angry shriek from the opposite corner of the second floor told me Nancy had discovered my disappearance.

"I locked the French doors from the outside, climbed over the rail, and began to let myself down. In this, at least, I was fortunate. There were trellises against the wall on which purple clematis grew, and these supported my awkward descent.

"On the ground, I bolted for the woods and once within their protecting blackness, waited, out of sight, to discover what was taking place at the house. Several minutes passed while Nancy searched for me. I could imagine her frantic haste, her moans and cries—a frenzied termagant whirling cyclonelike from room to room.

"She burst out the front door, the minister behind her and, behind him, his puzzled and pious daughters, waiting an opportunity to be of help to someone. 'He's here somewhere, laughing. Find him! Help me!' She ran around the corner of the house, clothed now in a modest robe. 'I know he's here. He *was* here. I swear to you!'

"I heard her open the stable doors. Sontag, waving his arm like someone hailing a cab, ran after her, calling, 'I want to help you, Mrs. Bartlet. But I don't think we'll find him.'

"In his wake, the two girls, prompt to lend aid and decorum to whatever rite this might be, stepped ceremoniously along like pale priestesses in the moonlight. After an interval of possibly five minutes, the procession came around the far side of the house, Nancy sobbing and spewing out pleas and threats and demands, all incoherent. I'm not sure if she stumbled on the hem of her long robe or if she threw herself on the ground in a paroxysm of frustration, but she lay sprawled across the soft, damp grass. The others hurried to her side, the minister dropping down on one knee, Maude and Meredith standing opposite, waiting attendance.

"'Mrs. Bartlet, please. Let us help you. You're hysterical. Won't you sit up and look at me? You asked the girls to bring me here tonight. I came, to help you in your struggle against Satan. You spoke of his presence in your life. I sympathize. I want to help you turn your back on him and make Jesus the object of your love.'

"Nancy dragged herself to her knees, disheveled and distraught. 'He was here. The Devil was here and you missed him.' She looked into Sontag's eyes but gestured toward the cottage behind her. 'He brought me flowers and drank champagne. I put sleeping powder in his champagne. Don't you understand? Don't you believe me?' They were kneeling, facing each other. She clutched his sleeve and thrust her swollen face close to his. 'You damned fool, don't you believe me?' she screamed.

"Nancy knew that I wasn't Satan," he gravely pointed out. "I was a freak. And, I believe, a freak for whom she had fondness. But the dark viscosity of discontent boiled up in her, driving her to injure me.

"The anguish of being thwarted in this and, additionally, of being thought mad, touched off the breakdown I witnessed. The scene was like a narcotic dream, but the bark beneath my hand was rough and real; the slim shard of cloud crossing the moon wasn't of my imagining.

"I was saddened and turned away, wondering whether one of the great gods had rescued me. If it were so, I wished it might have been accomplished less destructively."

We sat for a long while not speaking, giving it time to settle, like old ashes stirred by the wind. I sipped champagne, reflecting on the irony of the drink itself. Finally I said, "But you *don't* have horns."

Gently he grasped my free hand and slowly raised it to his brow and upward beyond the hairline. There, beneath the black curls, my fingers touched first one and then another small mound, roughly the size of the end of one's thumb.

His breath was warm and smelled of champagne. He smiled and lowered my hand, holding it against his face as he did, so that it caressed his ruddy cheek.

18

With Bart's fog-bound consent, we ate an early dinner so that I could sketch on our dock while there was still good light. First paddling to the opposite bank, I dragged the canoe up on the sand and, for purposes of composition, shoved it this way, then that, until I'd achieved the juxtaposition of elements that I wanted. In the watercolor the apparently abandoned canoe would represent mystery and sharp loneliness.

Swimming back across the river, I quickly toweled off and began to draw. I only needed the basic lines and relationships today. Tomorrow, if I was satisfied with these, I would set colors to the scene.

When the light grew too dim, I hauled everything back to the cottage, dumped it in the living room, and swam across Belle Riviere to bring the canoe back. I half-expected to see the Beast, but he didn't appear.

Before taking a shower, I riffled through the evening's work and was on the whole satisfied with the studies of the beached canoe. My eye was caught by a sketch I'd done earlier of the Beast, only a few lines, little more than a caricature. I wanted to do a more detailed charcoal study. I would begin it tonight, working from this hasty portrait. In all likelihood I'd end up doing a series of drawings and paintings of him.

Studying the rough portrait in my hands, I knew I'd invented him. First of all, he looked like Jamie. He was too much what I would have ordered: not a squat, pug-nosed, crabapple-cheeked monster, but a creature well-proportioned and classic as the Hermes of Andros. There was nothing repugnant either in the various parts of him or the way they were assembled, unless one were repulsed by the improbable. In that case, one was bound to be offended by angels as well.

By ten-thirty my eyes burned. I stopped work and went to Bart's study. "Are you ready to call it a day? How about a glass of

Riesling?" We'd shared so little time in recent weeks, I felt like a polite stranger.

"I've set myself one more chapter to read tonight. I'll have to fall behind schedule while Miranda and Clark are here, so I'd like to finish this, if you don't mind."

I closed the door softly.

Slipping into a nightgown, I turned out most of the lights in the cabin and, restless, went to the kitchen to brew a pot of tea. Mine was the restlessness of insufficiency. When the tea was steeping, I carried it on a tray to the porch and sat in the dark, enjoying the smoky fumes of Lapsang soochong and the seductiveness of the warm night. Warm summer nights made me feel I might wake up young.

A fragment of melody, pianissimo but close by, rose from near the river. I stood and studied the dark landscape. There was no one on the pale beach across Belle Riviere. In any case, the music had been nearer. Another delicate motif from below. Then I made out a foreign shape at the end of the dock.

I turned toward the kitchen to fetch another cup and saucer and a box of Nabisco gingersnaps. Loading them on a tray, I pushed open the screen door and let it to behind me, catching it with my foot so that it didn't slam.

In the morning I spent two hours at the museum again, poring over old books, photo albums, scrapbooks, and newspapers. There were pictures of incredible mountainous logjams on the river, of excursion boats which plied Belle Riviere when it wasn't jammed. Some of these originated hundreds of miles away, as far as Lower Alton, Illinois, making their way up the Mississippi to that river's juncture with Belle Riviere and there steering into the waters of the smaller but no less spectacular stream.

I didn't find mention of the Devil of the dalles, though there were numerous photos and drawings of the cliffs and their inevitable climbers. Nor did I find any pictures of the Hazeltine house near Good Hope or the unhappy Hazeltines themselves.

As I prepared to leave, I told Lydia Comstock, "One more morning and I should have everything I need in the way of historical details, except for the Hazeltine house. I'll try to get in a couple of hours tomorrow." I hoped to conclude this part of the project before the long weekend.

Again, Lydia walked me to the door. Before I could open it, she laid a hand lightly on my shoulder. "Have you seen this morning's *Courant*?" she asked.

"No. Not yet."

"There's more about Belle Rive Estates." She made a small moue. "When you have time, read it."

"I will," I assured her.

After breakfast Nellie Bergen had called. "If you're in town today, drop by the library. I have a book for you."

Rushing from the museum with my sketchbook and notepads, I jumped into the Volvo and drove through the park to the library, half a block away. Nellie hadn't taken a lunch break, so she agreed to join me at Sadie's Salad Emporium. When we were seated on the patio she handed the book across to me—*A Pictorial History of the Belle Riviere Valley*.

"I remembered this after we talked the other night. Hoot and several others put it together. The state historical society commissioned it a number of years ago." She got up and came around the table. Flipping the pages of the big glossy book lying before me, she stopped on page 127. "You'll find this interesting."

There were three photographs that age had robbed of black and white. The scenes were gentled, misted grays, like dim memories. The first was of a large house, dark but not forbidding, with a big screened porch dominating its front and a broad lawn sloping down to the river. The Hazeltine cottage.

In the second picture three people holding croquet mallets were disposed informally before a gazebo. The man, substantial, intimidating, and robust in appearance, stood to the right and slightly apart from the two females. On the left a pale woman smiled as though it cost her great pain. Beside her, sitting on the bottom step of the gazebo, was a girl of possibly fourteen. Long hair, held off her face by a ribbon, fell around her shoulders. Her face was turned three-quarters to the camera and tilted down a bit, so that she seemed to be gazing out from a secret place, full of humor and intelligence. The Hazeltines before the death of Alice's mother.

The last of the pictures was taken in the drive at the rear of the cottage. Alice sat in the buggy, holding the reins, while an attractive, dark-haired woman, her arm across Alice's shoulders, laughed and waved a hat with cabbage roses on the brim. Behind them were the stables and to the left was the scullery with its little balcony and, even then, a vine-covered trellis.

That woman—Jessica, I felt sure—wasn't it a pity the Beast hadn't fallen in love with her? She looked warm and strong, not one to throw herself into a river. Poor Alice, gentle and loving. There was an agreeable piquancy in her upturned mouth and delicate features. I thought she would have grown into a strong woman like Aunt Jessica, had she lived.

"Nellie, these are wonderful. Thank you."

"You're welcome. Is this research leading someplace?"

"I've started a series of drawings and watercolors of Belle Riviere as it must have looked at the turn of the century. I keep finding later scenes I want to add, so it's turning into a larger retrospective than planned. I needed a picture of the Hazeltine cottage but there wasn't one at the museum. This is perfect."

"You must talk to Hoot about all this. He'll give you any information he can. And don't forget Grandma Mercy."

"I'm going to call her after the children leave."

Our table was at the far end of the patio, with its sweeping river view. We could see part of the dalles and the dark, encroaching woods that marched down the hillsides to the water. In the greater distance, like silk handkerchiefs thrown on the ground, were fields of sunflowers and corn.

"I've always thought Belle Riviere was... mysterious," Nellie observed. "I don't really know what I mean by that," she added. She stirred her coffee.

She went on, "The world disparages mystery. Spotlights are thrown on all our dark little havens. The very word 'secrecy' has taken on a purely negative meaning."

"You can probably blame Freud and television for that," I told her.

She smiled. "I suppose. The rage to reveal has filled the world with boring, empty people and dull information, hasn't it? I, for one, refuse to divulge my many secrets," she declared with light self-mockery.

"'Our souls refresh at pools of mystery,'" I proclaimed with a florid gesture.

"Who said that?"

"I did."

She laughed. "I've written it on my cuff."

"I'd have lent you my pad."

Nellie sighed and gazed at the panorama. "I hate the whole idea of Belle Rive Estates. It's one more beater moving through the tall grass, flushing what wants to be hidden."

I left Nellie at the library and headed up the hill to Daisy's.

"I'm at your disposal all day tomorrow," I told her, following her to the screened eating porch at the back of the house. "The kids don't get in till dinner and I'm going to let Bart fix that."

"Fine." She directed my attention beyond the porch. "The band will be there," she said, pointing to the back right-hand corner of the yard. "Since we have that big cemented area," she went on, indicating a patio and barbecue pit at the back left, "we might as well use it for dancing."

"Where are you getting tables and benches?"

"Renting them from the county. It's stuff they use for the County Fair. Hoot Bergen got us a truck to haul everything."

"What's the food situation?"

"About thirty women have volunteered to bring food. I specified things that could be eaten from small paper plates."

"Is there anything I can do today?"

"Do you have a watercolor you could part with, one of the river?"

"I have one I'm working on. But I don't know how good it's going to be. Why?"

"Go home and finish it. I want to sell chances on it. What about matting?"

"I've got some stock pieces."

"Fine. We'll put the painting on an easel by the entrance. There'll be someone there to sell chances and we'll have a drawing later in the evening. Clever? It'll be a reminder of what all this is about."

I began work on three different versions of the beached canoe. When they were completed, I would select the best for the fundraiser. I didn't like working with a tight time limit, but that couldn't be helped.

At four I put it all away. My concentration was going and, with it, critical judgment. The painting was proceeding well enough, and it was pointless to press. Grabbing the *Courant* from the kitchen table and packing it into the hamper, I made what was becoming a ritual trip across the river.

Spreading my portable world under the trees, I opened the newspaper. On page one Roberta Arneson's face beamed at me. A beaming Roberta never boded well and the heading was "Local Woman Accepts Position with Dallas Firm." My hands shook and I had to put the paper down on the bedspread to read it. "Valhalla Projects, Inc. of Dallas, Texas, has announced the hiring of Roberta Arneson of Belleville as public relations coordinator for the projected Belle Rive Estates Condominium Village, to be built approximately four miles north of Belleville on Belle Riviere." There was considerably more about the condominiums, Roberta's duties, and her impending trip to Dallas to confer with her new employers, but I chucked the paper violently aside.

A hand squeezed my shoulder. "Anything wrong?" the Beast wanted to know. He sat down beside me. At length he pointed out, "I've told you so much, isn't it selfish to share so little with me?"

Resisting the impulse to confess, I spoke only about Belle Rive Estates and events of the past two weeks, including the difficulties Harry was undergoing because of the *Courant*'s editorial position.

"You've been friends with this man Harry for many years," the Beast observed when I was done.

"Twenty."

"Twenty years is a long time—for people. You must know him well."

I shrugged.

"Maybe I can help you."

"What does that mean?" I asked charily.

He smiled. "I meant maybe I can help in the matter of the condominiums."

"How?"

"Remember, I am the protector of woods and pastures. If there are woods and pastures requiring my protection, I ought to protect them." He got up and rummaged through the hamper, opening a can of beer for each of us. "Let me think about it. Of course, it would be easier if Cladeus were here."

"Cladeus?"

"A neighbor back home. A river god."

"I'd rather you didn't involve yourself in this problem," I told him.

"Why not?"

"What if you were discovered?" I told him about the old tramp in the Blue Ox, who swore he'd seen the Devil and the Devil's woman. "I shudder to think what would happen if Roberta found you. By dinner, she'd have you on network news."

"The Devil's woman," he said, ignoring my consternation. "How did you feel about that?"

I accepted a bunch of grapes he handed me from the hamper. "Terrific."

"Hmmmph," he grunted, not displeased.

"Promise you won't do anything rash. Remember what you said. You don't want to be a public grotesque."

"I won't do anything rash." He lay on his side, leaning against his elbow. "This whole condominium story escaped me, I'm afraid."

"How could you have known about it?"

"I read the paper," he said, offended. "I've read *yours* many times. I simply help myself to it from the box and return it afterward."

I was bemused.

"Good Lord, I'm not an illiterate, you know. I try to keep up. I've even seen television several times. When people are away for the weekend, I house-sit, as you might say. So far I've been unlucky with television or perhaps I don't understand how to operate it properly. I never find anything of interest." He picked up the *Courant* I had tossed down. "May I keep this? I'll return it tomorrow."

"Keep it." Suddenly I asked, "What should I call you?" It was impossible to go on thinking of him as "the Beast."

"Call me? You should know, if you created me."

"What did Alice Hazeltine and Nancy Bartlet call you?"

"Why, they called me by my name. Pan. What else should they call me?"

I shrugged. "Have you ... have you watched me for some time, as you did Nancy Bartlet?"

"Many years."

"But you didn't show yourself until now."

"You were busy with children. The past couple of summers I've studied you more intently."

"And what did you conclude?"

"That you were alone a good deal. That you might be susceptible to a monster if he, too, were alone." He sat up and leaned toward me across the damask expanse. "Speaking aloud is not enough after a while. There must be someone to *hear*. I will hear you if you will hear me." He paused, then added, "It's a more serious commitment than sex, you know."

"I know." I didn't need to consider. "All right."

Changing the subject, he inquired, "When do your children arrive?"

"In time for dinner tomorrow."

"Then you'll be busy tomorrow."

"Yes. All day."

"What about Saturday?"

"I'll get away if I can."

"You're looking forward to seeing your children."

"Yes. Yes, I guess I am." He cocked his head. "I'm having my problems with Miranda. She's planning to be married in October."

"You don't approve?"

"She's too young, too certain. She thinks everything works out as she orders it, simply because it always has. She thinks..." I broke off. "Oh, God, what difference does it make *what* she thinks? She's going to be miserable. She's going to be buried alive." I drank off the last of my beer. "When she's forty-seven she's going to create a mythical beast."

He looked aslant at me. "Am I so dreadful, then?"

I laughed and rose to fetch us another beer. "You're the answer to a prayer." In the hamper I came across *A Pictorial History of the Belle Riviere Valley* and withdrew it. Opening it to page 127, I said, "There are some photos in this book that I think you'll want to see." Carrying the book with my finger holding the place, I knelt down and went on to explain, "There are three of the Hazeltine cottage, and Alice is in two of them." I handed him the open book, then got to my feet and moved away, to afford him privacy.

I looked out across Belle Riviere. The lowering sun made dark lace patterns through the birches in our yard. By a trick of the late afternoon light, that other shore seemed especially distant.

After several minutes, I turned back. The book was still open, but he stared away from it, tears on his cheeks. I ran to him. "Don't cry. Please, don't cry. I'm sorry. I shouldn't have shown you the pictures."

I took up the corner of the bedspread and wiped his eyes and cheeks. His brow was vulnerable and weary and as familiar as my own. I moaned with its familiarity, and kissed it. Holding his face gently but securely, as if it might melt once again from my grasp, I kissed his eyes and cheeks, his ears and neck and finally his mouth, which tasted like honeydew.

"Don't be sad," I pleaded. Grasping the hem of my shirt, I pulled it off over my head. "Let's not be sad."

19

Clark and Sarah unfolded themselves from the front seat of their Ford station wagon, Clark, handsome and, like his father, faintly British-looking in his rumpled tan seersucker suit with vest; Sarah, cool and pristine, even in her maternity garb and sensible espadrilles.

I ran out the back door, letting it slam. "Welcome."

Many years ago, when I was a senior at the university, I'd known a girl named Camille, who was a home economics major. Her collar was always immaculate, her skirt unwrinkled. I knew her egg whites were never watery, her correspondence never unanswered. When she married, there would be nothing of unknown origin in the back of her closet, or the back of her mind. Despite all this, I found it impossible to dislike Camille, and so it was with Sarah, who leaned slightly forward to plant a kiss on my cheek. Noting the simple perfection of everything about her, one knew instinctively that Sarah's herbs and spices were stored alphabetically, likewise her fantasies. One knew also that she would unearth ouzo and retsina in her neighborhood for you or know the reason why.

"The ouzo and retsina are in the back of the wagon," she told me. "Clark will bring them in."

I led her into the cottage, where a reviving breeze was finding its way from the river. "Now you must take off your shoes, dear girl, and put your feet up. Would you like to do that here on the couch and have something cool to drink or would you rather lie down in the bedroom? Clark, you can put those bags in your bedroom."

"I think I'll have something cool to drink and then nap for half an hour."

"Splendid. I have lemonade, iced tea, and all things alcoholic."

"Iced tea sounds good."

Sarah was not actually pretty, but she was a woman of such serenity and presence that she gave mere prettiness a bad name. I plumped a pillow to put at her back and went to get iced tea.

Later, while Sarah napped in the bedroom, Miranda and Dennis pulled into the yard, parking Dennis's gray BMW beside Clark's navy-blue Ford. I shook my head. The two cars looked like a pair of DAR matrons discussing the Fourth of July cake booth.

Dennis bounded around the car like a spaniel and gave me a hug that lifted my bare feet off the grass. I wondered if this was to compensate for the restrained, noncommittal greeting I'd had from Miranda. "Well, how *are* you, Mother Demming?" he inquired heartily while unloading their bags and the case of Greek olives.

"Dennis, darling, please don't call me Mother Demming to my face. It makes me feel like bread pudding. Call me Larry or Baby Snooks or any damned thing but that." I didn't dare point out that he was not yet my son-in-law. He was so four-square and guileless, there was no point in hurting his feelings.

"Okay, Baby Snooks."

Bart, who'd been lighting the charcoal in the barbecue pit, came over to carry one of the bags into the cottage. "Where would you like this?" he asked Miranda. "In your room?"

She glanced at the bag. It was Dennis's. "Dennis insists on sleeping in the living room on the sofa bed," she explained in an offhand voice, but with a tic of annoyance on her face. "I guess you might as well put it there."

"I'll get the folding luggage stand from the closet and we can set it on that," I told Bart, patting Dennis's arm and hurrying ahead into the cottage. It wasn't, after all, Dennis's fault that I wanted him out of Miranda's life.

A few minutes later I thrust icy beers into Dennis and Clark's hands and set Bart's scotch and soda on a table where steaks wrapped in plastic waited to be laid on the grill. "There you are."

Back in the kitchen I opened a beer for myself, put a kettle of water on the stove for sweet corn, and went along to Miranda's room. She was changing from office clothes to a swimsuit.

"I think I'll take a dip before we eat," she told me.

"Of course. Can I get you a cold beer or something?"

"I'll fix myself something when I come up from the river."

"All right." I sipped from the sweaty beer can. "Dennis understands that he's welcome to sleep in here with you?"

"Oh, yes. He doesn't think it would be...right," she said, not finding quite the word she sought.

"I don't want him to think it would, uh, prejudice me against him," I said, trying with absurd delicacy to refer to the wedding situation without actually referring to it.

"He knows you for an archliberal, Mother," she said with a trace of impatience. Whether impatience with me or with Dennis, I couldn't be at all sure. "Where does all that liberality come from? How is it you're always on the side of the misfits and heretics? What's the matter with us WASPs?"

Shrugging an ivory bracelet from her wrist, she set it on the bureau beside a matching pair of earrings. "Anyway, Dennis has what he calls 'The Code of the Brewsters,'" she explained, again with an edge of impatience that might have been directed at me or perhaps at Dennis for necessitating explanations. Miranda was generally of the "Never explain, never apologize" school. "He says his code is peculiarly his own and doesn't relate either to current mores or traditional morality," she went on. "In any case, it obliges him to sleep on the living room sofa bed."

I wasn't sure if I was meant to find this quaint and exasperating or noble and praiseworthy, so I said, "'The Code of the Brewsters.' That's rather clever—like P. G. Wodehouse's *The Code of the Woosters*—don't you see?" She looked at me as though I'd spoken pig Latin. "Well, I think in the end one's code must be peculiarly one's own," I said lamely. Then to change the subject, which was in need of changing, "Thank you for buying the olives. I know you're very busy."

"It wasn't any trouble." She grabbed a swimming towel from the back of the door where I'd hung it. "Want to come down to the dock?" she asked.

I was delighted but tried not to overreact. "Sure," I said, following her. "You go ahead. I'll turn down the fire under the kettle and be right with you." Hugging myself with pleasure, I called out the back door to Bart, "Hold off on the steaks for ten minutes. Miranda's going to take a quick swim."

Pulling herself out of the water and onto the dock, Miranda

looked seventeen. Her body was long, slender, and firm. She stood at the end of the dock, toweling off slowly, then turned and came to sit beside me, hanging her legs over the edge of the dock to let her feet play in the water. Her wide-set eyes, spiced with gold, were creased at the corners in a sweet, forgiving expression. "I'm sorry I was hard on you in my letter," she said.

I was touched. "I probably deserved it."

"We'll have to agree to disagree about Dennis."

"It's not about Dennis that we disagree," I started to explain. "It's only ... well, we won't get into that. I promised."

"You said you'd tell me about Bobby's not being at Daisy's tonight." She got suddenly to her feet, moving to the end of the dock to stand with her long straight back to me.

This reference to Bobby seemed a strange follow-up to Dennis, but I told her as briefly as I could about the rift between Harry and his wife over Belle Rive Estates and the ticklish position in which it placed Bobby.

When I'd concluded she said almost inaudibly, "Poor Bobby."

I thought she might amplify this simple response. Instead she murmured, "When I was little, I was afraid of the other side of the river—the woods."

"Really?"

"We used to go for picnics on the beach, you and Clark and I, and you took us on 'nature adventures,' but the woods were so dark and ... foreign. And the slough—that was the worst. It looked as if *anything* might grow in it."

"Well, that's the beauty of the slough, of course. Anything *does* grow in it, including great blue herons and bryozoans the size of cantaloupes."

She hugged her waist. "I was afraid of coming on something ... under the surface, something that would rise up from the ooze." Suddenly, mercurially, she flicked her shoulders and laughed unsuccessfully. "A banker's mentality. I don't like surprises. I want things to add up and come out even." Putting the river behind her, she strolled over and gave me a hand to my feet. "I'm hungry."

At the door to the cottage, I turned and my eyes touched the opposite shore. "A genuine monster is quite innocent, you know, and needs your love."

Abruptly, her goodwill fell away. "Not more monsters and beasts," she said sourly. I held the door for her to pass. "Can you wait dinner?" she asked. "I'm going to shower before we eat. It's chilly."

Of course it wasn't anything of the sort. It was hot. I watched her hurry from me. Poor little girl, afraid of things rising from the ooze.

20

We drove our Volvo and Clark's Ford to the party, so that Clark and Sarah could leave when she grew tired. Fleur Street was nearly full as we drew near, and we parked around the corner on Chestnut. Emerging slowly from the two cars, women checking to make sure their slips hadn't ridden up beneath thin summer dresses, men locking car doors and jingling change in their pockets as they waited, we began ambling toward the Fitzroy house, soft rock music luring and quickening us, making us shiver or giggle even as we appeared indifferent and in no hurry.

In George and Daisy's drive, at a small table beside my easel, Lydia Comstock chatted and smiled with effortless kindness at the trivial banter of a knot of people standing in line to buy chances. Bart and the children joined them while I called hello, squeezed past, and continued on, anxious to check the lights I'd strung around the yard that afternoon.

I'd begun painting shortly after dawn and, finishing before noon, I'd driven to town to help Daisy. I spent a good part of the afternoon stringing lights around the backyard and worrying about Harry. Roberta's job with Belle Rive Estates was known to nearly everyone in Beau Bois and Three Toes counties, thanks to Harry's piece in the *Courant*. It was going to be a long night for him, surrounded by neighbors, mere acquaintances, and total strangers, many of whom would have no interest in sparing his feelings. Some of them would have a lively interest in getting even for past embarrassments or tragedies of their own which had been published in the *Courant* and for which in some strange way they blamed Harry.

At the back gate, librarian Nellie Bergen came toward me. "We've reserved that long table over there," she said, indicating one that would easily accommodate fifteen. Hoot Bergen and Sam Fergus were already gathered at it, drinks in front of them.

While the sky was light we argued casually, joked seriously, and gossiped a little, first with one another at our own table, and then with others scattered around the yard. It was a noisy, self-congratulatory crowd, totaling upwards of four hundred as people came and went. From Blind Moose and Good Hope and as far away as Minneapolis and St. Paul, they came to lend support to the river's cause. Harry was there, of course. He'd shored up his defenses and he mingled resolutely, but beneath the joviality was wariness and fatigue.

With the sky deepening, couples began to crowd the dance floor. Bart took my hand. "The painting is really quite good," he told me. "Do you paint a great deal these days?"

"Yes."

"I'm glad you're finding things to do. What are you reading? There's a stack of books on your bureau."

"Mythology, local history, geography of Greece."

"That's nice—that you have interests you're pursuing while I'm working. I'm proud of you."

Everything he said annoyed me. I tried not to show it, but I wanted to grind my teeth until I wore them down to sharp edges. Instead, I smiled and squeezed his hand.

"You have a sudden interest in Greece," he remarked.

"I told you I wanted to see Greece, soon if possible."

"So you did."

"I've sent for a passport application."

"That sounds serious."

"Yes."

"Good girl. You've got initiative."

I told myself that we were merely out of practice in conversation. "Sarah looks wonderful, don't you think?"

"Yes. Yes, she does," he agreed.

"I wish they'd waited another year or so, don't you?"

"For what?"

"To have a baby."

"Why?"

"Well, to have more time alone."

"I don't know," Bart reasoned. "The baby will give them something to do together."

"Ah, yes. I hadn't thought of that," I said, whirling around the dance floor in a fume of gin and irony. The cold, smug way I despised my husband at times made me loathe myself.

I danced with Hoot Bergen and Dennis, then strolled up the path to the house to give the Purvises, Jeannine and Debby, a hand refilling platters and potato-chip bowls. With darkness the colored lights metamorphosed from pale bravery against a lavender sky to defiant panache against the black.

At nine-thirty the band fell silent. To a flourish of drums, Daisy, in a white linen dress, made her way to the microphone and welcomed the crowd. She spoke a few words about the hopes and purpose of Save the River. She explained briefly what steps the committee had taken and she thanked everyone present for their support. With drollery she noted that Mayor Smiley and all but two members of the village council had sent their regrets, pleading pressing commitments elsewhere.

From a revolving wire drum Sam Fergus drew the winning chance, and the painting was claimed by a St. Paul attorney who confessed to having purchased fifty chances to win it. Bart patted my back and the guests at our table congratulated me, while I tried vainly to appear modest.

Another drumroll and crash of cymbals concluded the business portion of the evening as the band broke for food and drinks.

Miranda had found several childhood friends, among them Cate Comstock, Lydia and Phil's daughter, up from Chicago for the long weekend. Miranda needed relaxation and friendship. She lived life without a margin for error.

Sitting on the steps of Daisy's back porch with Lydia Comstock, I glanced away toward the gate. Pausing there, his eyes searching the crowd, was Bobby Arneson. What could *he* want? I wondered. It must be fairly important to bring him into the enemy camp.

"Excuse me, Lydia." I got up and made my way past crowded tables. "Bobby, can I help you?"

He hesitated. "I ... I was looking for Miranda. Dad said she'd probably be here."

"She's over there, by the bar. Talking to Cate Comstock. Do you see her?"

"I'd like to say hello." He made no move.

"Do you want me to get her?"

"I'd appreciate it."

When I'd given Miranda the message, I continued along to our own table. Clark, who was preparing to take Sarah home, asked me to dance.

"Was that Bobby Arneson?"

"Yes. He wanted to say hello to Miranda."

He scowled.

"Anything wrong with that?"

"Doesn't he know she's engaged?"

"Clark, even engaged girls are allowed to speak to men."

"A gentleman would come in and meet her fiancé."

"Bobby and Roberta are opposed to Save the River. That's why he didn't come in." I peered over Clark's shoulder at Harry and Roberta's son. Was that why he didn't come in?

Bobby Arneson had his mother's black hair and thick, dark lashes, but where her eyes were green, his were an unexpected and unsettling gray, and they had a slightly smudged look about them as though he'd been several days without proper sleep. I had never learned what came between him and Miranda while they were at the university.

When Clark returned me to the table, Bobby had left and Miranda was walking slowly across the yard, playing abstractedly with a string of beads at her neck, her gaze fastened on some inward landscape.

I escorted my son and his wife to their car and kissed them each goodnight. When I strolled back into the party, Harry asked me to dance. I had hoped he wouldn't, but I couldn't refuse when I had accepted others at our table.

"Did you see Bobby?" I asked.

"Yes."

"What was that about?"

"What it was always about."

"Did you want Bobby to settle in Belleville?"

"No."

"What did you hope he'd do?"

"You mean, what did I *secretly* hope he'd do?"

"Yes."

"I hoped he'd end up a journalist, maybe in a foreign bureau, traveling, seeing the world. When he was sick of being rootless, I hoped he'd write books or find a spot on a big paper in this country."

"You didn't want him to run a small paper like the *Courant*?"

"I wouldn't want anyone I cared for to do that and especially not Bobby."

"And yet *you* stayed here." He didn't answer. "Bobby majored in journalism."

Harry nodded. "Journalism and design."

"I always hoped Clark would fall hopelessly in love with Georganna Fitzroy and follow her around the world until she loosened him up a bit."

"And Miranda? What did you hope for her?"

"Oh, God, I don't know...that she could love herself like a friend?" I laughed and added, "...that she could love me like a stranger."

Discovering our drinks gone when we returned to the table, we went along to the bar. One of the bartenders complained that he'd lost his bottle-opener, probably dropped it in the grass. Harry said he'd find him another.

Jeannine Purvis, hurrying past with a plate of Chinese chicken wings, paused. "Mrs. Demming, I can't find the other cans of mixed nuts and a lot of the dishes on the tables are empty. I don't want to bother Mrs. Fitzroy. She and Mr. Fitzroy are talking to the county attorney."

"I'll look," I told her as Harry handed me a gin and tonic.

The table adjacent to the bar was filled with a large contingent from Good Hope, or so Lydia Comstock had informed me. They were an agreeably voluble, free-spending group, given to hollering the length of the table or across the yard. In the general noise and confusion of the moment, I don't know how many others heard what was said at their table. Harry and I couldn't avoid hearing it and, because the bartenders stood between us and those who argued, the Good Hope men had no way of knowing that we heard.

"What kind of guy puts up with a bitch like that? Would *you?*"

"Hell, no, but he *had* to print the story. Everybody was going to find out anyway. He'd just look like a damned fool if he didn't print it and then everyone saw it in the other papers."

"Well, hell," the other man laughed, "she's made him look like a damned fool anyway." Then he added, "If she's so crazy about Arabs, someone oughta ship her over there."

I moved quickly away. "I'm going to look for the mixed nuts, Harry."

He picked up his glass, tossed money on the bar, and followed, mumbling something about the bottle-opener. At the top of the porch steps, I turned to hold the screen door for him. Coming up the steps, he raised his head and smiled a sardonic smile, anger compressing him into a tight package.

"Where would I find a bottle-opener?" he hissed.

"In one of the pantry drawers maybe." I led the way, my high heels clicking angrily on the kitchen tile. Pushing the swinging pantry door, I held it for him. He let it swing behind him. Opening and slamming cupboard doors at random, I told him, "I'm terribly sorry, Harry." Slamming the last door so hard it swung back at me, I pounded my fist on the cupboard and cried, "And...and...I don't know where the hell the damned mixed nuts are!"

He pulled me to him and kissed me. It was instinctive and I yielded involuntarily. I clung to him and kissed him as if each kiss were the last one left on earth. The sound of our irregular and gasping breaths and the murmuring as we tasted each other's faces and mouths was a sound so uniquely our own and new to us, it spurred desire.

His hair was clean and crisp in my fingers. His hands on my buttocks held me firmly, and I pressed against his hardness. I wanted him right then and there. On the floor, standing up, it didn't matter.

I didn't hear or see the door swing open. I did hear Miranda breathe, "Oh, my God."

And my voice, like an echo of my daughter's, breathing against Harry's ear, "Oh, my God."

21

There are moments so cataclysmic one cannot imagine that life will have the audacity to extend itself beyond them. But, boorishly, it goes on. One does not die of embarrassment or shame. At any rate, not often enough.

Waking Saturday morning at a quarter to five, my heart was so heavy I couldn't turn over in bed. What had I done to Miranda? I had run after her last night, trying to explain. She wouldn't let me near her. Bart didn't notice, thank heaven, and I knew she wouldn't tell him, wouldn't, in all likelihood, tell anyone. I wished she would talk to Dennis or Sarah. I couldn't bear that she was sad all by herself.

At length I turned over and stared at the ceiling. It's to my disgrace, I suppose, that I only regretted the minutes in the pantry because they had hurt Miranda. But for that, I would go right back and do it all over. Until she walked in, it had been unmixed bliss, an inevitable and culminating affair. It must necessarily be succinct as well. It had begun and ended there in the pantry.

But even if I promised that to Miranda, I was not sure she would forgive me. She'd seen me betray her father, and for all she knew, this was not a single incident but part of a full-blown liaison. It was possible things would never be right between us. I wondered if she would go to Bobby with this. She and Bobby went back a long way. When they were in high school he'd spent most of his summer days with us. I'd once been very fond of him. We were strangers now. We might be enemies before long.

Rolling slowly back on my side, I faced the window where the dawn's early light heralded Saturday, July 4. I groaned. At six Bart rose, made a pot of coffee, and a piece of toast. I pretended to be asleep. The smell of toast, betokening a guilt-free appetite, annoyed me.

Dragging myself from bed at seven, I pulled on slippers and scuffed quietly to the bathroom to brush my teeth and toss down a couple of aspirin. Tiptoeing, I passed a softly snoring Dennis, sprawling innocent and righteous on the living room sofa bed. What a pity that large, strong body and sweet nature hadn't been where they were needed last night, in Miranda's room.

When I'd reheated the coffee, I carried a mug to the porch and sat down in the rocker. The birches switched and swayed as though vexed. A blue jay studied me, reproved, and flew away.

Where was Jamie McClanahan this Fourth of July? The question was there before I saw it coming. Where was he? Far away, fleeing a beast, leaving me to make these dreadful mistakes.

After a breakfast during which Miranda assiduously avoided even eye contact with me, the children headed down to the river. Sarah sat in a deck chair in the sun and wrote letters, while Miranda and Clark swam and Dennis took the canoe out. The day was clear and warm. It promised to be hot and possibly sultry by afternoon. We would have a cold lunch on the porch. It was difficult to think of food, but something would have to appear on the table. Salade Niçoise, perhaps. The prosaic details of life led one by the hand through the morass.

Leaving the cottage, Sarah had turned back. "You're coming down, too, aren't you?"

"Maybe later. I'll work on my sketches for a while." But it was merely an excuse. I showered, pulled on a cool terry sundress, and moped through the cottage, too tormented to sit, too distraught to apply myself to anything. I had to talk to Miranda. I had never had the patience to leave a bad situation alone.

At eleven I peered through the screen door to see if Miranda was swimming. Lying on the dock sunbathing, she looked small and fragile. Oh, God.

"Miranda! Can you come here a minute? Just a minute and then you can go back."

Reluctantly she rose, a limb at a time, stepped into thongs, and headed up the stairs and through the ankle-deep grass to the door. Not until she reached the steps to the porch did she raise her head. "Yes?" she inquired dully.

I opened the door. "Come in, please."

She passed me, walked to an old wooden garden chair, and sat on the edge, ready for flight. "What is it?"

I closed the door to the living room and sat on the rocker opposite her. "Please don't say anything until I can get out a sentence or two," I told her and wished I'd gone over what I wanted to say one more time before calling her. "What happened last night between Harry and me—it's never happened before. It won't happen again. I could try to explain all that, set the stage for it, but it wouldn't change anything. Harry is going through an awful time. We've been friends for many years and I hate seeing him suffer. Last night was a moment's madness, for lack of a better description. You've known Harry too long not to know he's a good man."

She stared at the floor. She had withdrawn from her face and was not listening. Though she could stop listening, I could not stop explaining.

"You're sad because I betrayed your father. I would feel exactly the same in your place. What I'm offering is not a defense, but a promise that it won't happen again."

It was useless but I continued compulsively. "There's so little we can give people we love when they're suffering, Miranda. Soft words and our touch. That's it. I had no right to give Harry more than soft words." My energies were draining down the well of her silence. Suddenly, I could think of nothing to say.

She turned, lifted her face, and looked directly into mine. "Are you finished?"

I nodded. "I must be."

We were invited to the Fitzroys' that night to watch from their front porch the fireworks in Humphrey Park. Bart begged off to work but promised to cook brunch the next morning. "Invite Daisy and George," he told me.

Miranda put her arms around him. "I'll help."

He smiled and squeezed her. "You're on."

A good girl, our Miranda, hurrying to fill the imagined vacuum in her father's life. Men seem lonely creatures to women. We keep rushing headlong into their loneliness, sometimes finding it a mirage; sometimes finding it so immense we become lost in it.

The day was long, but at least I could sigh and pace and throw myself on the sofa and get up again, in privacy. The evening at the Fitzroys' was longer because I couldn't. Fireworks weren't sufficiently compelling to wipe Miranda and Harry from my thoughts.

I settled into a wicker armchair, drinking gin on the rocks, crossing and uncrossing my legs. For a while I sat on the porch balustrade, swinging my free leg. I went to the bathroom, freshened my lipstick, and leafed through a copy of *Forbes*. Twice I made myself a drink.

Finally, Daisy rose and asked, "Larry, would you give me a hand with the chicken salad?"

She closed the kitchen door behind us. "What in hell is the matter with you?"

I sank down on a stool, set my drink on the counter, and ripped a paper towel from the dispenser on the wall. Dabbing it below my eyes to prevent my mascara running, I told her. I told her about the two men from Good Hope whose argument Harry and I had overheard, and about the pantry, the passionate kisses and ardent phrases I didn't remember but knew had been spoken, about Miranda finding us and running away from me and my running away from Harry.

"Oh, my God," Daisy whispered.

"Exactly."

She put an arm across my shoulders. "There's not much I can do, I suppose, but I'm here."

I picked up my glass. "Thank you."

"Have you talked to Miranda today?"

"Yes. But it was pointless. She doesn't understand. How could she? I don't think she'll ever forgive me."

Daisy patted my shoulder and moved toward the refrigerator. Removing a bowl of chicken salad, she handed it to me. "Put this on the tea cart." From the cupboard she took down plates.

The kitchen door opened. Sarah came in. She studied my face for the briefest moment. "Let me help."

Daisy gave her the plates, then pulled a bag of croissants from the bread box. I opened a drawer and asked what napkins she wanted. Sarah found the flatware. We all went knowingly about our business.

22

When I woke Sunday morning, Bart was already up. Wrapping a light cotton robe around myself, I tiptoed to the kitchen and closed the door behind me.

Since Friday night I'd tried not to avoid Bart. Normally, there was no question of avoiding him. He simply was "incommunicado." But with the children on hand he was in greater evidence and I was having to play out little scenes with him. I was very sensitive to Miranda's evaluation of us. To spare her any more doubts, I tried to offer a picture—neither cold nor cloying—of her father and me, which would reassure rather than undermine her sense of us as a unit. She didn't need, at this point in her life, an upheaval driving her pell-mell into an ultraconventional marriage.

As Bart and I shared such a slim piece of common ground (meals and the children were the only places we could consistently meet), it wasn't easy to present an encouraging picture. But the effort had to be made.

"Starting already?" I asked. He was mixing homemade Bloody Mary base. "Would you like some help?"

"Yes to the first question. No to the second."

I poured myself coffee. "I told them ten o'clock. Was that right?"

"Oh, yes. I just wanted this to chill for a couple of hours." He spooned some out and tasted. "Very good. Very good. Want to try it?" Ladling some into a juice glass, he handed it to me. "What do you think?"

"Delicious. But you should taste it with vodka to be sure."

He grabbed a bottle from the cupboard and poured vodka. "There. Now stir it a little."

"Yes. It's perfect. Here, you finish it."

"You're right. I think this is my best. I used a tad more chili powder than last time."

"Well, whatever it was, you've created a masterpiece. Brillat-Savarin would be pleased." I looked at the canning kettle in which he'd mixed it. "You've made an awful lot, haven't you?"

"Well, there'll be eleven of us. Do you think it's too much?"

"Eleven?" In my mind I counted couples. "I count only eight."

"I forgot to tell you," he began, pouring the base into pitchers. "Last night while you were at Daisy's, I had a brilliant flash. I said to myself, 'The thing to do is call Roberta and Harry and ask them and Bobby to come out.'" He turned, beaming.

"You did *what?*"

"I called Roberta. After the nonsense last Sunday at the Kaffee Kafe, I thought it wouldn't be stupid to show the world we're all friends and that I know there's nothing between you and Harry."

"I don't believe this is happening," I said, folding down onto a chair.

"I did it for you."

"I loathe and despise Roberta Arneson."

"I didn't know you felt that strongly. You always seemed to make an effort in the past. I'm a little sorry for them—having their lives divided up by this river brouhaha."

"Roberta Arneson is the Bitch Empress of the world! I only made an effort for Harry's sake. And Bobby! Did you consult Miranda? This is going to put her in an awkward spot. How could you, Bart? How could you do such a stupid thing?"

"Because I don't like uproar."

"You did this because you don't like uproar?"

"Yes. I told you last Sunday, I don't like mess and unpleasantness. There's no reason there should be unpleasantness between us and the Arnesons. We can all be the friends we used to be. As for Bobby, he and Miranda haven't dated for years. He's going to hit it off just fine with Dennis." He threw a spoon into the sink. "Tuesday when the children leave, I can go back to my writing knowing I've restored order and civility to our lives."

"You blind... fool." The acid in my blood curdled the words in my mouth. It was as though I flung some awful spoiled thing at him.

His face was covered with stark surprise and with that expression he turned toward Miranda, who had opened the door as my words flew across the kitchen.

She'd been wearing a smile and now she didn't know how to dispose of it. "Can I help you, Daddy?"

23

The poor girl was developing a habit of opening the wrong doors, and I a habit of providing heartbreaks behind them. I left the kitchen immediately. I don't know what explanation, if any, Bart gave her. Until the guests arrived, she spent her time helping him with the food.

As I showered and dressed, it seemed impossible that Harry and Roberta and Bobby were coming to brunch. There was nothing about the event that I could visualize. It was too absurd to be imagined and therefore surely wouldn't happen.

Fortunately, Daisy and George arrived before the Arnesons and were thus warned of Roberta's imminence. Roberta, Harry, and Bobby were twenty minutes late, twenty minutes during which I could pray they'd all been put under quarantine. In the midst of innocents, Daisy and I sat, disbelieving, hoping for high winds and rain.

Bart and Miranda set out the food on the screened porch.

Except for the sliced ham, which was keeping on a hot tray, it was a cold buffet so that guests could eat immediately or later, assuming they had any appetite. People had been told to bring swimsuits if they wished. Clark and Dennis drove to the Caspersons, our nearest neighbors, to borrow their canoe. That provided us two in the event we were all desperate to paddle away, which I had little doubt we would be. Clark and Dennis didn't seem aware of any discord, but I thought Sarah had got downwind of it.

Roberta, descending like a bogus Russian princess with a pair of recalcitrant borzois on her leash, swept in wearing a stunning white sharkskin pantsuit. She was overdressed by river standards, but beautifully overdressed. I wondered what she had threatened in order to secure Harry and Bobby's presence. Bobby was sullen, Harry looked as though he yearned to fly on the wings of morning.

Roberta jingled and jangled around the group, a king's ransom in gold bracelets on her wrist carrying her leitmotif through our tragicomic opera. She brushed cheeks with those who could be counted on not to empty their Bloody Marys on her. That was the men and Miranda. To Sarah, Daisy, and myself she raised her lovely hand in a Queen Mother wave, at once greeting and dismissing us. The two borzois, slipping the leash, were sniffing around the bar table.

"Well, Roberta, what's this we hear about a new career?" Bart asked ingenuously, marching into the center of the fray.

"Isn't it exciting? I can't quite believe they asked me to represent them," Roberta declared, accepting a Bloody Mary from Bart as though it were a nosegay of violets and lace.

"How did it happen?" George wanted to know.

Roberta settled herself gracefully on a redwood chaise. "I suppose they heard about the work I've been doing with the Belleville Welcoming Committee."

"Imagine. I wonder how they heard?" Daisy mused.

"Had you been in touch with them?" Dennis inquired innocently.

Casting a quick, sidelong glance toward the porch, where Bobby and Harry were pouring drinks, she explained hastily, "Well, naturally I had written them to say how delighted most of the people of Belleville were about Belle Rive Estates."

Coming down the porch steps, Bobby put in, "And didn't you tell them you were organizing a committee to smooth the way?"

"I pointed out the various goals of the Belleville Welcoming Committee. Certainly, one of them is encouraging new business and new residents."

"When do you begin work?" Bart asked.

"Tuesday they're flying me to Dallas to meet with management and begin a couple of weeks training with their public relations people."

"If and when the company completes the project, will your job end?" Clark inquired.

"Oh, dear boy, not 'if' but 'when,'" Roberta lightly assured him. "*When* they complete Belle Rive Estates I may be kept on, I'm told. If I'm successful in communicating Valhalla's message to this community, I may be hired to do the same in other communities. I think there's every chance I will be."

From the porch steps where she'd taken a seat, Miranda asked, "Would that mean a lot of travel or relocating?"

Roberta didn't answer immediately. Gazing thoughtfully at the gold bangles on her wrist, she ran a hand over them, causing them to tinkle softly. "I'm very torn by all of this, Miranda. I can't expect many people to appreciate that but, as a liberated career woman, perhaps *you* will."

Sarah, Daisy, and I exchanged glances.

"I'm afraid poor Harry doesn't quite understand," she went on, a sad little smile flickering momentarily across her face. She cast Harry a look drenched in equal parts of adoration and remorse. Except on Madonnas and the faces of those suffering flatulence in crowded elevators, one doesn't often see a look of such pain.

Harry said nothing. He studied the drink in his hand, got up from the canvas chair, and carrying his glass, wandered toward the steps that led down to the dock. Watching him go, I thought he'd lost weight during the past three weeks.

"What doesn't Harry understand?" Daisy wanted to know.

"Any of it," Roberta lamented wistfully. "My feelings about Belle Rive Estates, the Belleville Welcoming Committee, or this wonderful opportunity to plug into something big," she explained, caressing the final word.

During all of this I occupied myself drinking, rattling the ice in my glass, and watching Miranda watch Harry, Roberta, and me. She was trying to discover how the pieces fit together. Sickened and fascinated as a detective at work on a grisly case, she would pick through the sordidness seeking explanations. Not that what she found would alter things between us. She had seen what she had seen: her mother and Harry Arneson, behind the delphinium-blue door of Daisy's pantry, hurling themselves into the dark chasm between the sixth and eighth commandments and, this morning, the nasty little scene in the kitchen.

The best I could hope from this day was that nothing further should distress her. What she'd observed couldn't be excised. The pain of it had blotched dark circles around her eyes and drawn a tight line at her mouth. No new doubts must be planted. I would be civil, if understandably distant, with Roberta. I wouldn't go near Harry. I would sit quietly, doing and saying nothing provocative, and with any luck, retire early with a severe migraine.

"*Whom the gods would destroy...*" I mused, dragging myself to the bar to wet down my ice cubes. I wished desperately that I could run away from what I'd done. Maybe the Beast would take me in.

Gesturing with his glass, Dennis drawled to Roberta, "I'm not sure I've got this straight. Do you have a job you're giving up to go with...Valhalla Projects or whatever the hell it's called?"

"Mother and I own Arneson Printing here in Belleville," Bobby told him.

"And what's going to happen to that?" Miranda's fiancé continued.

"Bobby will run it," Roberta said. "Bobby's more than capable of full responsibility."

I thought it odd that Bobby said and did nothing to affirm this but instead wandered to the furthermost periphery of the group, almost out of earshot, and sat down beneath a birch to gaze away from us toward the river, much as his father had done. Miranda's eyes followed him but she remained where she was.

"Well, but you might have to move away from here," Dennis gently pressed Roberta.

"It's conceivable. If I'm successful."

"And your husband? He runs the paper?"

"Yes. The *Courant*."

"You know, I'm not opposed to couples relocating for the wife's work, but it appears to me you've got a problem. Harry's not going to leave the paper, is he? Seems like a pretty big commitment. You're going to have yourself a long-distance marriage," he observed with what sounded like skepticism. "I'm not sure how I'd feel about something like that," he said, glancing at Miranda.

Miranda was annoyed. "Really, Dennis, none of this is *our* business. I'm sure Roberta will work it out."

"I'm not trying to poke into her business, honey, but this is the kind of thing *we* might have to face. People have to think about the possibilities. *I* wouldn't stand for a long-distance arrangement."

Miranda bridled and would have answered but Roberta snatched back the reins. "Actually, I don't think Harry would mind all that much if I were to relocate," she observed with a quick, plucky smile. "He probably wouldn't notice I was gone." She waited a swollen moment to be certain she had our undivided attention. "I'm afraid I'm an embarrassment to him. And he has his work and"—she paused, looking at me, begging for my mercy, dolor filming her great green eyes and setting her lower lip to quivering— "...and other involvements." The way her eyes clung piteously to mine, the slow, delicate manner in which she turned her head and lowered her chin so that her hair fell around her face, these spoke of unspeakable injury.

Resounding silence followed. The moment floated in a jar of formaldehyde, preserved in all its ugliness for future consideration. Dennis and Miranda, Sarah and Clark would study the scene again and again, holding it to the light, turning it this way and that, examining its surfaces and guessing at its interiority.

At length Miranda crossed the yard and sat beside Roberta on the chaise. "Roberta, come swimming with me. I'd like your advice on the gowns for my wedding."

Tossing back her black hair, closing her eyes tightly, then quickly opening them, as if to banish her desperation, Roberta reeked of soldierly grit. "I'd love that." As they started arm in arm across the grass, Roberta explained, "I've always wished I had a daughter to share things with. Wedding gowns and...other problems."

Clark and Bobby followed them, to change into swim trunks. Dennis filled a plate with food and passing my chair asked, "What's *that* one up to, Snooks?"

"I think Roberta's suffering from water retention, Dennis."

Daisy had wandered away to join Harry. Pouring himself another Bloody Mary, George sat down with Dennis, who wanted to know more about our efforts to keep out Belle Rive Estates.

Bart studied me. "She's still convinced there's something between you and Harry," he pointed out acerbically. "Why is that, Larissa?"

"Because she's a little girl looking for someone to blame for her problems."

"That's rather unfair, don't you think? I thought she behaved like a trouper. I felt damned sorry for her."

"Oh, for God's sake, Bart. How do you think poor Harry felt?"

"Poor Harry? If he gives her reason to doubt him, I hope he felt acutely uncomfortable."

"How do you think he does that? What is it you think Harry's doing?" I pursued.

"I'm not sure," he said slowly, then added, "but you could help matters by being a friend to her the way Miranda was. She's our guest, after all. It wouldn't hurt you to show the woman a little human kindness."

"She's our guest because *you* invited her. I told you I couldn't stand her. She's a manipulative bitch and I'd like to shove her off the end of the dock and let her goddamned bangles pull her under. But I haven't. *That's* human kindness, Bart."

"Larissa!" he spat.

He was looking past my shoulder. I turned. There was Roberta and beside her Miranda. Her eyes filling, Roberta gave Bart a grateful smile, grasped Miranda's hand for reassurance, and headed stalwartly toward the river. Another woman would have jumped right back into her white sharkskin pantsuit and got the hell out.

Miranda divulged nothing to Dennis or to Sarah and Clark. The children all spent the greater part of the following day, Monday, in Belleville with friends. In the afternoon there was a picnic in Humphrey Park and in the evening a movie, *The Virginian*, at the Little Palace.

Bart worked on the book and I tried to draw. The cottage was as hushed and humorless as a mortuary. I needed to see Pan, but I didn't want to pick over the skeletal remains of the weekend so I passed a languid day at home, rubbing salt in my wounds.

There is a certain perverse and childish satisfaction in being miserable if one has done nothing to deserve it. One awaits with toes curled the day of delicious vindication, when one's husband, daughter, or what-have-you deplores the awful injustice that has been done, tearfully begs forgiveness, and vows never again to be cruel to one so undeserving. There is no satisfaction in being miserable if one has earned it.

The children were home by eleven, and except for Sarah, they were tucked into their beds soon after. Bidding them "Good night, sleep tight, and don't let the bedbugs bite," I went swimming. Sarah was standing on the dock holding a big towel when I emerged from the river.

"Thank you," I panted. "You're going to be exhausted in the morning. Clark said you have to be up at six if he's to be at work by eight-thirty."

"I'll be all right."

"Well, don't let the mosquitoes eat you alive."

"There aren't many out tonight." Hugging her neat bulk (she managed to make even pregnancy a tidy, not too graceless affair) and scanning the cloudless night, she explained, "I wasn't sleepy. Now that I'm this size, sleeping isn't as pleasant as it used to be. It's hard finding a comfortable position."

She wasn't anxious to go in, and with the big towel wrapped around me I wasn't cold, so we made our way slowly up the steps and sat in yard chairs.

"I've had a wonderful weekend," she said. "I hope you'll let us come often, especially when we have children."

"This place is for all of us. You don't ever have to wait for an invitation. And you mustn't wait for Clark. If you need to get away, come."

"Thank you. I feel at home. It's serene."

I swallowed caustic laughter. "When the children are running in and out the screen doors, wet and sandy, carrying dead fish or garter snakes, you may find it less than serene."

"Will you mind that?"

"No. I'm pretty good with children. Grown-ups are more difficult. They're not so forthcoming—up front, I suppose you'd say— as children. One has to tiptoe more."

"I hope you won't tiptoe with me," she said earnestly.

"I don't think I will," I told her and found that I meant it.

"You weren't awfully happy when Clark married me." There was no accusation in her voice.

"I'm sorry if it showed. It wasn't *you*. I don't believe in early marriages. I hoped Clark would travel and do something unconventional before settling down. I worry he'll turn to wood. I'd hate that for you."

"What makes you think *I'm* not conventional?"

"There's something old and wise about you. I don't know how that came to be, but old, wise people are rarely stodgy or conventional." We sat facing each other. I leaned forward to touch her hand. "I love him dearly, Sarah, but if he settles into a comfortable, rigid world and you help him maintain it, you'll end up crackers or you'll leave him. I want you to be part of this family so...please drag him through some adventures."

"I understand."

And she did. She understood a great deal more than we'd been discussing. "A daughter-in-law is lucky," she observed. "She has a fairly clean slate with her new mother. There aren't a lot of guilty or resentful memories from the past. And there isn't that blinding ego involvement that exists when it's your *own* mother or your *own* daughter. We can be friends if we like each other. I know from experience how difficult that is with one's own mother. There's so much history to be set aside, so much role-playing to be forgotten."

"Yes." I wrapped the towel more tightly. "You haven't said— are you hoping for a boy or a girl?"

"A boy first, I think. Until I get the hang of it. My mother always said her two boys were less worry than her one girl. I suppose it's difficult for a woman not to see a daughter as a piece of her own fabric. What the daughter does is then her *own* defeat or triumph. And if the mother thinks she herself is beyond the possibility of triumphs, the daughter's defeats must be twice as painful." She considered. "And it's surely the same for men, don't you think? I mean, with their sons."

"I suppose, although Bart has always managed to keep his ego separate from Clark, I think."

"Maybe because he's been so well satisfied with *himself*," she said without a trace of irony or criticism.

"Yes."

She pulled herself forward in the chair, preparing to rise. "I think it will be easy for us to be friends. When you need a friend, will you remember?"

My throat ached. I held her hand and got to my feet. With my arm around her comforting bulk, we went into the cottage.

24

"They started bulldozing the buildings out at Ernie Duffy's this morning." It was Daisy. She'd caught me as I was about to leave the cottage.

"So soon?"

"I thought you'd want to know."

"Yes." Feeling suddenly tired, I sat down at the kitchen table.

"I drove out as soon as I heard. The man in charge—someone from St. Paul—said they're going to leave the house standing for a while and use it as an office. Roberta will operate from there, I guess."

"Did she know about this on Sunday when she was out here?"

"Probably. We're calling an emergency meeting of Save the River Thursday night. I've got my publicity people busy phoning everyone. It'll be in Thursday's *Courant*, but that won't be enough notice for some people."

"I can't be there."

"Oh?" She waited for me to explain.

"After what's happened, there can't be any more contact between Harry and me."

There was a moment's silence on the line. "Well, I understand, I guess."

When she'd rung off, I loaded olives, retsina, and ouzo into the canoe, along with lunch for Pan. I wasn't hungry. It was noon and hot. The children had left for the city at seven—Miranda coldly and silently, without a touch.

When they were gone I was too depressed to strip the sheets and pillowcases, so I climbed into Miranda's bed and pulled the covers around me. But I couldn't sleep and half an hour later I got up, dressed, and washed the breakfast dishes.

Bart was back at work in his study, the door shut firmly behind him. He'd failed to restore order and civility to our lives. It was hard to forgive me for that and so much more. We hadn't spoken ten words since Roberta'd heard me say I'd like to push her off the dock.

Unloading my cargo on the east bank, I reflected how life was crumbling like a dried-out sand castle. Wasn't it fortunate I had the Mythical Beast?

After I'd carried everything up on the bank and spread out the cloth, I went swimming. It was important during depression to get plenty of exercise. That and gin would put you to sleep at night.

My hair was nearly dry and I'd drunk a beer when Pan came softly through the woods. "How did it go with your children? I thought they'd never leave." He came forward and lowering himself onto the bedspread, began to sort through the provisions. Holding aloft a bottle of retsina, he grinned a vast, beastly grin. "These are for me?"

"If you share."

He kissed my cheek. "Thank you."

"It went horribly." I told him everything, beginning with the children's arrival on Friday and the little talk Miranda and I had had on the dock before dinner—"I had some hope. It didn't go too badly"—and ending with her silent departure that morning. "She hurried into the car and slammed the door when she thought I might touch her."

I got up and walked away. I couldn't sit beside him, with his pity and concern lying heavy on me like an obligation. Across the water was the dock and the old steps and the trees and back between them, the cottage, rank now with festering memories. I withdrew from it, returning to Pan. Kneeling beside him, I pleaded, "Let me stay with you. I won't be any trouble. I'll do whatever you like."

"This place wouldn't do for you to hide," he explained not unkindly. "Unless you were willing to run away, really away, there would be no use. In a day or two your husband would have police dogs in here searching for you. You couldn't live in the woods hand to mouth as I do. If you want to escape, you must be practical. Do you understand?"

"Yes."

"Now, have some retsina. Do you like it?" He filled my glass.

"Yes. It's awful, but I like it. I haven't had any for years."

He narrowed his eyes, screwed up his mouth, and considered me. "What you have here with me in the woods is *stasis*. It's a comforting nonmovement, a standing still in a quiet place. Someone like you can't live that way for long. You must move in some direction."

"I don't want to talk about it." I tore a hard roll open and ate the inside. "I have something else depressing to tell you."

"Enough. You make yourself more unhappy."

"No. I have to tell you this. They've started tearing down the buildings at Ernie Duffy's farm. For the condos."

"When?"

"This morning."

"I'll look into it," he said.

"What will you do?"

"I don't know. Maybe nothing. Sometimes things settle themselves."

"Well, for God's sake, don't get caught."

"If I'm an invention, how am I going to be caught?"

I recalled both his fear of being "a public grotesque," and Nellie Bergen speaking of "One more beater moving through the tall grass."

"When I was a child, sometimes Jamie took me pheasant hunting in the autumn. I went because it was an honor and because the days were crisp and it was always satisfying to be alone with him, even if we couldn't talk for fear he'd miss a shot.

"But when the pheasants rose up startled, and Jamie raised his gun and brought them down, I was sick. I had helped flush those lovely creatures. It was an awful price to pay to be with Jamie. The cock pheasant is so beautiful, right out of an oriental tapestry, with his elegant ringed neck and long tail and rich colors...lying broken on the ground among the crackling, brittle cornstalks, with his feathers running with blood..." I fell silent, bruised by those old memories and frightened for Pan.

Reading my thoughts, he said, "You needn't worry. I'm not so easily tricked as the pheasant." Then, laughing and teasing, he tried gallantly to cheer me. In gratitude I attempted first to throw off my mood and failing that, to hide it. To carry my colors half so high as he did would make me proud.

Before I left I went to rummage through the basket.

"What is that?" he asked when I faced around.

"A tape measure. I'm going to measure you."

"Why?"

"I want to buy you some clothes."

147

"Why?"

"You might need them. Stand up, please."

"Will I enjoy being measured?" he asked, getting to his feet, a glass of retsina in his hand.

Dragging the canoe out of the water, I tied it to a tree root, then lugged the basket up the steps. The trees were sullen and I passed them, paying no heed. I let the screen door slam, went to the kitchen, set the basket down, and turned on the radio to a country-music station. They were playing a favorite by Hank Williams, Jr., and I turned up the volume so I wouldn't miss a word. There was a note on the kitchen table.

"I've made myself a sandwich. I'll work through the dinner hour."

He was going to sulk. Hell. I needn't have come back at all. I began unpacking the basket, putting the soiled glasses in the sink, the leftover hard rolls in the bread box. As I worked, I sang along with Hank. He had such a fine twang, like an old fiddle. I couldn't imitate it, so I sang backup.

I was stashing a slice of melon in the refrigerator and singing about country folks surviving, when Bart went silently past me and turned the radio off. I finished the phrase without Hank, crossed the room, and turned him back on, louder than before.

Glaring at me, Bart turned him off and stood defiantly rooted. "I can't hear myself think," he bellowed in the quiet.

"*That* must be a relief." I snapped Hank on again, nearly brushing Bart as I passed. I turned but didn't retreat from the radio. "If you touch that radio, I'll cut off your balls," I promised, every word falling between us heavy and true.

So rarely was Bart backed up against the wall of hard emotion, his features were unschooled. Now, with a comically disorganized face, he screamed above the music, "You are insane."

25 ❧

In the morning I knocked lightly on the study door, opened it, and reported, "I'm going to Minneapolis for a couple of days. The refrigerator is stocked. If you need a car, Daisy will lend you hers. The tires on your bike have air." He didn't look up.

Reaching the city, I drove directly to my bank and withdrew money from my savings. At the house, I hid most of it inside a roll of toilet paper. The remainder I took shopping. All Wednesday I dashed from store to store, up escalators and down elevators, into dressing rooms and out revolving doors. At midday I downed a salad and beer and pressed on.

By five the car was stuffed, back and front, with boxes and bags. For Pan there was a suit, shirts, trousers, sweaters, jackets, underwear, ties, handkerchiefs, a toiletries kit, and two large pieces of luggage. For me, two washable knit dresses, walking shoes, a heavy jacket, and a couple of pairs of slacks. My closet at home contained everything else I would need. Pulling the car well back in the drive, I parked near the kitchen door.

When I'd switched on Dan Rather and thrown together a very dry martini, I dug around in the freezer until I found a lamb chop, which I slid into the broiler for dinner. There were no salad greens in the house so I opened a package of baby carrots and put them in the steamer.

The bags and boxes had already been carted up to the master bedroom. Settling myself at the kitchen table, I slipped off my shoes, put my feet up on a chair, and watched the news events hurry self-importantly across the five-inch screen. The telephone rang. I set down the martini and went to check on the lamb chop. The telephone rang ten times and stopped.

Dinner dishes washed and put away, I made another martini, flicked off the kitchen light, and went hunting for the cassette player. It lay on the living room coffee table with the Duke Ellington tape in it, the one I'd played last time I was in town. I flipped the tape and pressed "play." "Take the 'A' Train" flooded the room.

In one corner of the living room a tall secretary stood, the writing surface never used, the drawers and shelves overflowing with family clutter. Shoving aside the desk chair, I lowered myself to the floor, opened the bottom drawer, and lifted out half a dozen photo albums. Poring through them for forty-five minutes, I removed several pictures, returned the albums to the drawer, and climbed the stairs with the photos in hand.

From Belle Riviere I'd brought a small portfolio containing a number of sketches of Pan. These I spread out on the king-size bed, and alongside I laid the photos I'd pulled from the family albums. I studied the entire array for some time, then began to sketch on a fresh pad, hurriedly combining features from several portraits.

At ten the phone began ringing. Nine, ten, eleven rings. I continued drawing. When I'd completed ten or twelve quick sketches, I laid them in rows on the floor and stood over them, considering each, removing them one at a time until there were only two remaining. These I put in the portfolio. The others I carried down to the kitchen and burned one by one in the sink.

Grabbing up the cassette player and half a dozen tapes, I extinguished the downstairs lights and padded back up to the bedroom. Duke Ellington was replaced by Benny Goodman's "Sing, Sing, Sing." The two new Pullman cases I opened, removing the wadded gray paper from their interiors. Unwrapping the day's purchases, I packed most of Pan's wardrobe and toilet articles into the luggage, closed and locked the cases, and dropped the keys into my handbag. I dragged the dressing-table chair into my closet. By standing on it, I could lift the bags up to the luggage shelf and lower my own bags.

When I'd finished packing those, I returned the luggage again to the closet and the dressing-table chair to its customary spot. The empty shopping bags and boxes I would put in the car tomorrow, to be disposed of in a public trash receptacle.

The phone woke me at eight. When the neighbors on either side had driven off to work, I dressed and hauled to the car the trash I intended dumping, my portfolio, and the parcels for Pan.

Since nothing in the refrigerator resembled breakfast, I closed the house and drove to an International House of Pancakes. Ordering toast, cantaloupe, and coffee, I inquired about a public phone, and dialed a couple of numbers. Before driving out of the parking lot, I tossed the bag of trash into the restaurant dumpster and brushed my hands together in a satisfied gesture.

The orthopedic supply company opened at nine, so I stopped there first. From the glove compartment I removed a roll of toilet paper and from its core withdrew a number of bills, which I stuffed into my handbag. Returning the toilet paper to the dashboard, I locked the compartment, then the car, and hurried into Abernathy Orthopedic Supply.

There were two more stops on my itinerary and then I was back in a public phone booth, this time calling an ophthalmologist, whose name I'd picked because he practiced in a neighborhood where I knew no one.

"I'd like an appointment for next Monday. Late morning or early afternoon. One-thirty is fine. Mr. Pan. One *n*."

That small matter dispatched, I stood in the booth studying its location. Where to have lunch? It was past two. Someplace nearby. Whipping along to the IDS Building, I took the express elevator to the top floor and sat at a window table in the Orion Room. The waitress brought me a Reuben sandwich and a bottle of Heineken.

My beautiful city lay below. Off to the right the Mississippi moved purposefully along the route of its obligations. My eye grazed the closer scene. Miranda's bank was in one of the nearby buildings. Like a rejected suitor, I longed to lay eyes on her, longed to be included again in the circle of her favor.

In odd moments I would find my spirits buoying, as though it were inevitable that Miranda and I would be reconciled. Each time they fell again, deeper than before.

I paid the check and stopped in the rest room. It was nearly four. I was going to be caught in rush-hour traffic. There was no hurry to get back to the river. Maybe I should stay in town and drive up in the morning. I didn't know what to do, couldn't even make an arbitrary little decision. When I thought of Miranda, I lost faith in myself. In my wallet I found a dime and tossed it in the air. Belle Riviere.

Emerging from the rest room, I hesitated not far from the elevators, digging in my bag for car keys. A young couple passed on their way to the restaurant. They argued in low, intense voices. I swung around. Their backs were to me. The woman shook her head, the man touched her arm. She seemed almost to give in to him, then pulled away and preceded him briskly into the Orion

Room. He glanced quickly over his shoulder, as though he felt my reaction. His eyes were startled, but they skimmed me with contrived nonchalance, pretending not to have seen me. Miranda and Bobby Arneson.

During the descent in the express elevator I felt ill. In the street I sucked air into my lungs and tried to get my bearings. Crossing to the opposite side of Marquette, I sat on a bench and concentrated on the distance. Jamie had advised that for motion sickness. It wasn't working. I bent forward, putting my head between my knees. A girl in a Northwest Airlines flight attendant's uniform put a hand on my shoulder.

"Can I help you?"

"I can't remember where I parked the car."

"I see," she murmured and backed away.

Having left the parking ramp ticket on the dashboard, I had no clue to the whereabouts of the Volvo. For an hour I sat on the bench, watching pedestrians move with purpose, anticipation, and expedition. I wished to move in that manner. People would observe of me, "There's someone who knows where she's going." Someone who knows where the car is.

At length I rose and began a serious search for the car. I remembered that I'd left it on the second level of wherever it was. The third ramp I investigated brought success and I was soon on the road.

An hour later, approaching the cottage, I flicked off the headlights, killed the engine, and let the car coast to a stop a couple of hundred yards from the drive. From the back, I unloaded the wheelchair, folded and in its packing carton. I headed toward the cottage, dragging the cumbersome box by the rope I'd requested the salesman tie around it. When I reached our drive, I veered left with my freight and cut through the yard, keeping as much distance as possible between me and the house. Only the study light was on.

Gaining the embankment, I was forced to carry the box down the steps, backwards and a step at a time. From there it was only a few feet to the canoe, still tied to the tree root. There was a dreadful racket tipping the unwieldy thing into the canoe. I stood absolutely still, listening for Bart, but he didn't come. Back to the car to retrieve the remaining parcels.

With everything loaded, I left my shoes on the dock, untied

the rope, heaved the craft into the water, and climbed in gingerly, expecting to capsize. On the other side I unloaded the goods and hid them in a thick growth of sumac. Immediately I paddled back, uneasy about leaving the car on the road. As I recrossed the yard, the kitchen light went on, spilling through the open window and nearly spotlighting me. I froze. The refrigerator opened and, after a moment, closed. A cupboard door squeaked, a drawer of flatware jangled. I withdrew into the shadows and waited. Presently, the light was extinguished and I continued on.

When I climbed into bed, Bart pretended to be asleep. I lay, my back to him, staring into the moonlit trees outside. Miranda and Bobby Arneson. There could be only one explanation. She'd confided what she knew about Harry and me.

26

I got up and showered at five-thirty, partly because I couldn't sleep, partly because I wanted to be about when Bart got up. After setting the coffeepot on the stove, I boiled him an egg and made toast.

Yesterday's *Courant,* still furled, lay on the table. I sat down and opened it. The state was requesting an environmental-impact study for Belle Rive Estates. That was expected but nonetheless reassuring. Arvin Reinholdt, of Reinholdt, Harris & Swenson Contractors, was quoted as saying no construction would begin before spring. The land would be cleared and other preparatory work completed before snowfall, however. Reading between the lines, it was obvious they expected a battle and were considering this in the schedule. There was a notice of last night's meeting of Save the River.

Bart finished his shower. I poured coffee and orange juice. He didn't look overjoyed to see the table laid out. "Sit down and have an egg before you begin work."

He grunted assent, sitting opposite me, but not looking up. It was a compromise.

"I see that Belle Rive Estates is having to file an environmental-impact study," I told him.

"That should make you happy."

"Yes. Doesn't it make *you* happy?"

"I suppose."

"But?"

"I'm sick of it. The whole business is becoming pernicious, if you ask me."

"And so we ought to give in and let them have their way?"

"Look what it's doing to Roberta and Harry."

"*It's* not doing anything to Roberta and Harry except providing a dramatic backdrop for her antics."

"Vicious, aren't you?"

"Yes, I suppose." I rose to fetch the coffee.

"Always quick to defend Harry."

Returning, I explained, "Harry's my friend. Roberta isn't."

"That's obvious."

Refilling the cups and setting the pot aside, I told him, "You're needling me. I guess I'm needling you, too. In a simple sentence or two, I'd like to know what you're thinking about me and you and Roberta and Harry, but especially about me and you. Do you think Harry and I are having an affair? Do you care?" I sat down, trying to appear calm and reasonable. "Tell me what you're thinking."

Applying marmalade to his toast as though marmalade-spreading were an art form, he explained, "I'm not sure I want to get into this. I *am* sure I don't want to get into it now. Everything has to be deferred until the book's finished. I've got to husband my energies."

"When will the book be finished?"

"If there aren't too many interruptions, this draft should be done by Labor Day. Then it's only a matter of reworking parts that are ragged."

"Three months or so?"

"Possibly."

"And you can defer everything that long?"

"Can and will."

"You're remarkable."

"Thank you," he said without sarcasm, and stirred sugar into his coffee. "If you go into Belleville today, would you pick up a couple of typewriter ribbons and a bottle of correction fluid?"

"You found the chair and the clothes?"

"The chair is a wonder," Pan exclaimed, and lifted an open bottle of retsina to his lips. "It must have cost a fortune." He wiped his mouth on the back of his forearm.

"Will the clothes fit?"

"Oh, yes. I tried them already." He grasped my hand to help me over a fallen tree. "I took everything to my place."

"In Minneapolis there are two suitcases of clothing for you. The things here are just for the immediate future."

We were strolling along the river, behind the first line of foliage. Between the trees and bushes the water lay bright in the noonday sun.

"How immediately will I be wearing them?"

"Monday."

"Today is Friday."

"Yes."

"That's soon. Where will I wear them?"

"I'm taking you to the city."

He handed me the bottle and I drank. "What will we do there?" he asked.

"You'll be fitted for contact lenses. Do you know what they are?"

"Yes. But I have no problem seeing."

"They'll be colored. Blue. When you wear them, your eyes will appear blue."

"Extraordinary. But why?"

"So they'll match the color on your passport picture."

He stopped. "What are you saying?"

"That you're going home."

He turned. The face, so animated a moment ago, was slack with disbelief. Glancing away and back again, he whispered, "Home?"

I nodded.

His eyes filled. I held out the bottle, thinking he might need it. He didn't notice. "Again."

"You're going home."

*   *   *

155

I couldn't stay. I'd come to see if he'd found his things. There were groceries and Bart's writing supplies to be picked up in town. I must call Daisy about last night's meeting.

"Come back tonight," he told me as I left.

Beverly Apple, sister of Delores Apple, cashier at the Little Palace Theater, was doing housework for Daisy, so Daisy suggested we meet someplace. A house where Beverly Apple lurked, hand on the O-Cedar mop and ear to the wall, was not a place where one would speak one's mind freely. Daisy and I agreed that for backstairs, hole-and-corner business, you'd go a long way to beat Al's Place.

Backing the car into the road, I got out to check the mailbox. There was a letter from Miranda, addressed to me. I was panic-stricken. My hands shook as I climbed back into the car and sat paralyzed with trepidation, staring at the envelope. At length I tucked it into my handbag, unopened. Unhappy words could wait an hour or two.

I stopped in Belleville to buy typewriter ribbon and eradicator, and in Blind Moose to pick up a few groceries before meeting Daisy at Al's. Daisy's white Buick and Al's ancient pickup with the faded Goldwater sticker were the only vehicles in the lot.

"We're organizing a Labor Day flotilla to protest Belle Rive Estates," Daisy explained, when Al had deposited two light beers on the table.

"A flotilla?"

"The two farms north of Ernie Duffy's are Johnson's and Black's. They're both opposed to the condos and they've agreed to let us use their river access. Anyone who's interested is invited to paddle or sail a nonmotor craft from there to Humphrey Park. We'll have an all-day rally at the park, with speakers and music and other entertainment.

"If we start the boaters early in the day and keep them coming all day, we can launch and beach them without too much backup. Both the Minneapolis and St. Paul papers have promised to cover the story, and it looks like we'll have TV coverage, too.

"We're hoping to attract people from all over the state, maybe even snare a politician or two into committing himself. There'll be buttons and bumper stickers and T-shirts for sale. We've promised to pay for extra law enforcement to keep order and prevent anyone from drowning. We'll have volunteers to help with the boats." She ran the cold surface of the beer bottle across her brow. "Let's see. What else?"

"That's quite a bit."

"One more thing. The series of pictures you're doing on Belle Riviere history? Is it possible you could lend it to us? Lydia Comstock is putting together a multimedia history of the river, to be set up at the museum."

"I don't know. I don't know how much I'll have done. That's ... what? Six or eight weeks?"

"Whatever you've got, we'll use." Removing a linen handkerchief from her bag, Daisy blotted her face. There was no air conditioning and with all the windows closed, the big overhead fan did little more than keep the flies circulating. "I haven't seen you since Sunday. How are things with Miranda?"

"Bad."

"They may get worse before they get better," she said.

"Do you know something I don't?"

"Harry's getting a divorce."

"What?"

"He stayed after the meeting last night. I think he only told me because he knew I'd tell you."

I was stunned. Daisy went on, "Miranda's bound to see a connection between you and Harry's divorce. Would you like me to talk to her? She needs to know that you're not behind it."

I shook my head dismally. "She wouldn't believe it. Thanks anyway."

"Roberta knew Sunday that Harry wanted a divorce. He told her before the fund-raiser."

"So?"

"So—Poor Pitiful Roberta Torn Between Husband and Career was an act. Act one of 'Roberta Wronged,' a five-act tragedy in blank verse."

Driving home from Al's, I thought, Miranda will be as inaccessible as the moon after this. There was nothing to be done.

I made a light dinner for Bart and when I called him from his work, explained, "I'm going to lie down. I have a headache. Probably from the heat."

"Yes. It's warm. I've nearly suffocated in the study this afternoon."

"Just put the dishes in the sink when you're through. I'll do them later."

"All right." He sat down and cracked fresh pepper over his salad. "Did you remember the ribbon and eradicator?"

"Oh, dear. I must have left them in the car. I'll get them."

"I'd appreciate it. My bottle's bone-dry."

Closing the bedroom door behind me a few minutes later, I turned on the bedside lamp and removed Miranda's letter from my bag. It had been written before I saw her and Bobby yesterday, before she'd learned about the divorce.

Sitting on the bed, I opened the envelope and pulled out the piece of ecru stationery. Trembling, I leaned against the headboard to steady myself.

Tuesday P.M.

Mother—

It's been four days since the party at Daisy's and the shock hasn't worn off. Everything I've believed in the past about you and Daddy and Harry has been a lie. Nothing is what I thought it was. How many years have you been trying to take Harry away from Roberta?—And you treating her as though *she* were the villain!

When did you stop loving Daddy? And why didn't you have the character to leave him when you stopped? Or the backbone to make the best of things? You're too old to be so selfish and foolish.

I'm surprised Daddy has stuck around. He's an intelligent, attractive man. The marriage can't have been much fun for him. He must be very devoted to you.

I won't tell him about you and Harry. It isn't my place and I can't hurt him that way. But, if you imagine that you're getting away with adultery, remember—for the rest of your life, every time you look at me, there'll be something in my eyes you won't want to see.

I'd honestly rather you weren't at my wedding, but there would be no way to explain to Daddy.

Miranda.

The period after her name was like a door-slam. Stuffing the letter into the drawer where her last note lay, I rushed from the room, grabbing a sweater lying across the sofa arm, and flinging out the screen door and down to the river.

The sky was still light. Running through the trees, I searched for Pan. Beyond the slough, in the clearing where I'd run the old tramp to earth, I found him. He rose when he heard me and closing the book he'd been reading, waited, his hands held out.

Throwing my arms around him, I clasped him as though he were the last tether holding me on the face of the earth. "Tell me about Arcadia, about the mountains. Tell me about Olympia and how the games used to be. Tell me..." I pulled away and asked suddenly, "Will you be afraid to fly?"

27

We lay down together where he had been reading his book. He told me about the Peloponnese, the great peninsula that is the southern portion of Greece, and about Arcadia, that part of the peninsula where he and his father Hermes were native. He pictured for me mountains, some wooded, others barren, and rivers and vineyards and the seemingly endless coast, with vistas first on one sparkling gulf and then another.

Describing his home and the deities, major and minor, and the nymphs and satyrs and all his old amours and cronies, he grew animated, his gestures large and fluid, his voice mellow and theatrical. Nearly in reach of his past life, his old spirit revived. Even his dimensions seemed to expand, his chest to broaden, his body to lengthen.

Without our noticing, it had grown dark. He led me back through the trees and the slough to the river's edge. I peeled off my clothes, and we swam back and forth across Belle Riviere, giggling no louder than the river. I felt strong and tireless.

When we climbed out, I retrieved a towel from the canoe and dried myself. Turning to Pan, I briskly rubbed the downy white fur that covered his lower body. It was a cloud in the moonlight. Spreading the towel on the bank, we reclined.

"You're running away with me," he said.

"Yes. Do you mind? I would have taken you home in any case, but now I can't come back. If you like, I'll leave you when we get to Arcadia."

"Don't talk foolishness. You'll fall in love with it and I'll be good to you. But you're going to miss your family and Harry, I think." He spread his arm. "And this place. The river."

"I'm going."

"When will we leave?"

"September tenth. After Sarah's baby is born."

"What have you told your husband?"

"That I'm taking a trip."

"And when he finds out you're not coming back?"

"In the end, he'll be greatly relieved."

He let the remark pass. "You won't be here for your daughter's wedding."

"She doesn't want me. If I were here, I'd cry hysterically from beginning to end and embarrass everyone." I grabbed his hand and held it tightly. "It's wrong that she's getting married."

He held me close to him. "She'll be all right." He was warm and strong as a father, and his kisses were like chocolate-covered cherries, lickerish at their heart.

For the next two days, evening meals and a few household chores were the only demands that kept me from the far side of the river. While I worked on the Belle Riviere sketches, Pan and I chatted endlessly about our trips, first to Minneapolis and then, more important, to Greece. Each day he added to the list of places and things I must see.

I'd brought the cassette player and Greek-language tapes up from the city. I practiced answering the tapes with proper little phrases; Pan laughed and answered with what were, I'm sure, improper little phrases.

If I could have remained through the night, I would. The moment I returned to the cottage, everything weighed on me again. I was being pressed to death like a witch.

At night I had terrible dreams of missed planes and misplaced passports, of lost children and lost fathers, and life slipping away like pellets of mercury rolling across the floor. As soon as the window was light, I was up, and after brewing a thermos of coffee to pack in my basket, I was gone.

At dinner Sunday evening I told Bart I was driving to the city the next morning and would probably spend Monday night in town.

"I'm getting ready for my trip," I explained. "There's a lot to do."

"When do you leave?"

"September tenth."

He didn't ask when I would be returning.

It was a quarter past seven Monday morning when I picked up Pan and loaded the wheelchair into the back of the car. I'd told him to wait for me by a narrow graveled road that ran from Blind Moose down to the river, passing near the dalles. He was to remain concealed until he saw the car.

As I approached, he suddenly stepped out from the shadowy woods and I was startled. Dust billowed up from beneath the wheels as I slammed on the brakes. I hadn't been prepared to see him clothed. I knew, of course, that he would be, but I hadn't imagined the effect. He looked like a Greek Paul Bunyan, bigger than life, very handsome, a lumberjack god. I wondered if people seeing him wouldn't know at once that he wasn't mortal.

It was half an hour before he spoke more than a greeting. "This is my first trip in an automobile," he said finally. "Once I climbed into one and sat for a while, but I've never ridden." He watched everything I did and asked questions. He wanted to know what each knob and dial on the dashboard was, how the floor pedals worked, and whether I minded if he operated the radio. Playing the radio—changing the stations and adjusting the volume—offered him a sense of participation, of doing his part, in the driving. We listened to rock, country, opera, farm news, and cooking hints. He most enjoyed the cooking hints, although they made him hungry.

As soon as we reached the city we stopped for breakfast. Setting up the wheelchair in the parking lot, we rolled right up to a table. His appetite whetted by the radio, Pan ordered the He-Man No. 2: pancakes, sausages, hash-brown potatoes, two fried eggs, juice, and coffee. The waitress was good-natured and skillfully solicitous. Pan feasted on her attention and the breakfast, grinning and confounding her with invalid humor.

"She was ready to adopt you," I told him when we were back in the car. "You're shameless in that wheelchair."

That afternoon it was the same story at the ophthalmologist's as Pan joked and charmed his way through a thoroughly unfamiliar situation with the aplomb of a Ringling Brothers aerialist.

The ophthalmologist naturally was curious to know why he

wanted blue contact lenses and Pan explained suavely that, as a photographer's model, he did not want to miss employment calling for a blue-eyed model. This made patent good sense to Dr. Handel, and events progressed without a hitch until the doctor tested Pan's eyes.

"My God," he murmured several times and cast confused glances at his patient. Advising us the date when I could pick up the lenses, he exclaimed, "I've never tested anyone with vision as acute as yours, Mr. Pan. It's extraordinary. If you wouldn't mind, I'd like to keep in touch. I think your eyes should be studied. I'd need to contact a couple of doctors at the university, but I know medical people would be interested. You're ... well, it's almost extrahuman, your vision." He chortled nervously. "No kin of E.T.?"

We left while he was covered by confusion. "What if Doctor Handel tries to contact us?" Pan asked as we drove across town.

"I gave them a bogus address. Since I'm going to pick up the contacts and pay cash for them, they have no need of a proper address."

We bought lunch at a drive-through fast-food and headed for Lake of the Isles in the heart of the city. Spreading a blanket on the grass, we settled ourselves beneath a maple and ate.

"This is a beautiful city," Pan declared.

"I wish I could show it all to you. It's filled with lakes and parks like this. The population is insane for outdoor recreation."

"Could we come back again before we leave the country?"

"Yes. Once at least. Maybe more." I pointed in the direction of Lake Calhoun, which we could glimpse from where we sat. "Bart and I live just over there a few blocks."

"It's difficult for me to believe there are no gods here," he observed, gazing at the sylvan setting. "Maybe they're hiding, waiting for men to make the world safe for them."

"The once and future gods?"

"Perhaps. Gods won't live in places not fit for humans. Men who have so little regard for themselves that they destroy the beauty and even the structure of nature are not safe companions for gods." He assessed our surroundings. "This place looks promising."

"Most people in the world think they *have* a god."

"Aha," he cried, thrusting a forefinger at me pedagogically. "He doesn't show *himself* either."

"Why don't the great gods destroy men and start over with something better?"

"It's unnecessary. Men are destroying themselves." He plucked a blade of grass and sucked the sweet root. "It's only a matter of time."

"And when men are all gone, what then?"

"Perhaps nothing. The gods may have had their fill. If the family pet became a mad dog, one might swear off pets for good."

A robin alighted close by, poking his beak into the grass, searching for worms and insects, cocking his head at Pan and hopping closer. Pan tossed a bit of bread beyond the bird. The red-breasted fellow cocked his head on the other side, studying Pan with his left eye, as though not believing his right; then, bounding after the bread, he flew off to dine in seclusion.

Pan lay back, clasping his hands behind his head. "You know, myth has it that I died when Christ was born."

"I'd heard that rumor."

"Elizabeth Browning even wrote a pompous, self-satisfied verse to that effect. But, to quote Twain, 'The report of my death was an exaggeration.'"

On our way to the house, I pulled into a drugstore parking lot and ran in to buy hair dye, enough for two applications, and a pair of weak-magnification nonprescription eyeglasses with tortoiseshell frames.

"We won't tackle your hair until later," I told him, heading toward the house on Thomas Avenue. "I want to take you to dinner tonight. We'll have a go at it when we get home."

After a refreshing shower, we dressed for dinner. I fetched one of Pan's bags from the closet shelf and found him proper clothes. The lightweight suit required pressing, but shortly we were admiring ourselves in the long mirror in the guest room, silly as children several steps ahead of the truant officer.

For an hour we sat in the twilight on the little flagstone terrace, sipping white wine. If Pan were an illusion, and these hours a lonely mind's invention, I prayed not to wake and find myself in a scrubbed and faceless room with a scrubbed and faceless doctor studying my chart and inquiring with brisk satisfaction, "Now, isn't this better, Mrs. Demming?"

We were seated in the Orion Room just before darkness fell. Pan watched enthralled as lights blinked on among the trees and lakes and along the river.

"Enchanting," he observed, "especially when viewed from this Olympian height." He smiled disarmingly.

"You are the most attractive creature I ever encountered," I confessed. "I'll have to be careful not to fall in love."

"Why?" he asked, tilting his head.

"Because it would be a dreadful complication."

"You discuss love as though it were a disease."

"Oh, but it is. I have no doubt of it. Many have died, others linger in agony. Those who are only mildly uncomfortable are feigning the disorder."

"Nonsense. It's a limitless natural resource."

"Oh, God, you're a romantic."

"I like to think so." He sipped champagne. "Gods are evolved enough to be genuine romantics, rather than mere sentimentalists."

"What's the difference?"

"We know that the emotion is more important than the object."

"You're right. I'm not that evolved. For that matter, I'm not sure *you* are."

"Well, I confess that minor deities are somewhat more subjective than the Olympian upper crust." He set his glass down and slightly away from him. "What about your Harry? What's going to happen there?" He had diverted the conversation very suddenly in order to catch me unprepared.

"Happen?"

"He's divorcing his wife. Don't you imagine that he'll want to marry you?"

"I hope not. In any case, I won't be around."

"Ah, yes," he said, opening his menu and looking at me over the top of it.

"I've bought enough hair dye to color your hair twice. It may take two applications to get the proper color. If not, we'll have enough to redo it before we leave for Greece. It'll start to grow out by then."

"Why not wait and dye it just once?" he asked.

"I'm not sure how successful this is going to be. We don't want to wait till the last minute to find out."

We'd driven home from the restaurant and, at my suggestion, Pan had removed his clothes and hung them up. I knew from Miranda's experiments with hair color when she was a schoolgirl that it was a thoroughly messy business.

We were in the downstairs bathroom, a Willie Nelson cassette playing in the living room, Bart's passport, opened to his photo, lying on the vanity. It was like a slumber party. Pan drank Michelob, and I'd poured myself a glass of wine, which I set on the back of the toilet while I stripped off my dining-out dress. Over my panties and bra I planned to tie an old kitchen apron when we got down to cases.

Seated on the edge of the tub, Pan read aloud the hair-color instructions, making them sound as devious and complicated as a CIA plot.

I recalled that there were several old towels in the back-hall broom closet. They would suit our needs, and I went to find them. Returning, I heard the front door knocker thump firmly several times. Oh, hell. At ten o'clock, it was probably someone looking for a house number. Tossing the towels over the back of a chair, I pulled Bart's raincoat from the hall closet and wrapped it around me. Flipping on the porch light, I flung open the door, the glass of wine still held in my free hand.

"Yes?... Harry! What on earth? I was just... I was just having a glass of wine." Glancing down at the raincoat, "I don't have any clothes on, so I grabbed this..." Slowly I looked up at him. "I'm surprised to see you."

"Are you alone?"

I stared. I opened my mouth. Reaching for the door frame, I braced myself, and still staring at him, turned my head imperceptibly toward the rooms behind me. The raincoat fell open and the porch light picked out the black lace panties and brassiere. In the living room Willie Nelson sang "I'd Have to Be Crazy." Slowly, I moved my head from side to side. I could hear the bones in my neck as they negotiated this painful maneuver.

28

He was covered all over in disbelief and I felt a moment's elation that he did not think me capable of what his eyes took in. No, there was a mistake. He allowed the smallest pause into which I could inject a giggle and a zany explanation. As it became apparent I had no zany explanation, he drew upon the meaningless, civilized effusions commonly used to cover a humiliating retreat.

"Didn't mean to barge in. Should have called. I was in town with Sam. Sorry. I ... uh ... I'll be in touch." This saw him down the steps. He turned quickly and hurried to his car.

"Harry," I groaned as he backed away, "it's not what it seems."

And then, of course, Tuesday night Daisy called. Pan and I had returned to Belle Riviere in the afternoon.

"Did Harry reach you?" she asked. "Last night?"

"Yes."

"I saw him yesterday morning at the *Courant*. He said he and Sam had to go into the city. I mentioned, simply by the by, that you were in the city. He thought he would call you while he was there. He'd decided to tell you about the divorce, I think. He did call?"

"He came by."

"I tried to reach you about dinnertime to tell you to expect him, but you didn't answer."

"I ate downtown."

"So he came by."

"Yes." She waited for me to amplify. "Don't ask anything."

"You sound sick. Are you sick?"

"I don't know. I have to go now."

Sitting high on the riverbank on the Blind Moose side, sketching the boat landing in Humphrey Park, I reflected on my twenty-year friendship with Harry. We had met when Bobby, Miranda, and Clark were taking Red Cross swimming lessons at the municipal pool at the south end of the park. In those days it was called River Park.

Bart was in Turkey picking over ruins with a team of archeologists. Roberta was—well, I forget just what Roberta was doing, possibly visiting her parents in Scottsdale, Arizona. She did that a lot.

The two young swimming instructors requested the parents not to hang about for the first couple of days, until the children got over their initial fears and shyness. I'd brought along a pad and pencil so I wandered away to sit on a bench and draw.

The log cabin that housed the Historical Society intrigued me as a subject. Its rough surfaces and firm, natural grip on the landscape pleased the eye. I'd been sketching for fifteen or twenty minutes when someone commented, "Hey, that's good."

A tall blond male with wide shoulders stood behind me, scrutinizing my work. When I glanced up, surprised, he straightened. "I didn't mean to startle you." His eyes were a light, intense blue in a darkly tanned face. At their corners, pale lines radiated toward his temples, deep laugh wrinkles that failed to tan with the rest of the face. It wasn't a handsome face but it was very pleasant, unguarded, not at all closed up.

"Sorry to interrupt," he said. "My name is Harry Arneson. My son Bobby's in the swimming class."

"I'm Larissa Demming. Most people call me Larry. My little girl Miranda and my son Clark are in the class, too. You're not interrupting. I was just passing time."

"Larissa? Beautiful name. Unusual."

"It's the name of a city in Greece. My father saw it on a map and couldn't get it out of his mind."

"Are you an art student?" he asked, ambling around the end of the bench and taking a seat. He didn't seem forward, only eager for conversation.

"I used to be."

"I like the sketch. Would you mind if I used it in the paper?"

"The paper?"

"I publish *The River Courant*. Do you live in Belleville?"

"We bought a cabin on the river last summer. During the school year we're in Minneapolis. My husband teaches at the university."

"I've wanted to run a series of photographs of landscapes and landmarks in Beau Bois and Three Toes counties. Seeing your sketch, I'm thinking that drawings might be more effective. Could I talk you into doing some work for me? I can't pay much, but if you're interested in selling your things, the exposure would be good."

"Can I think it over?"

"Sure." He took out a pen and wrote his name and telephone number on the back of my pad. "There. Give me a call when you decide."

I worked for Harry all summer. We met occasionally to discuss projects. Craving conversation with another adult, I talked incessantly. Harry listened incessantly. I put it down to his newspaper training.

Although I talked about Bart and the children, Harry rarely mentioned Roberta, except perhaps to say, "Roberta and I would like you and the kids to come fishing with us Sunday." After the first such occasion, I was pretty certain Roberta didn't want me along, but with Bart away, I accepted anyway. And some part of me took perverse pleasure in annoying Roberta with my presence. Although she was intelligent and well educated, Roberta was aggravatingly mismatched with Harry. She was brittle and shallow, a person who lived her life with an audience in mind. I would have dismissed her out of hand, but she was Harry's wife and that made it difficult.

The following summer Bart was included in the Arnesons' invitations. This eased the strain between Roberta and me, and we settled into a more or less permanent, if wary, truce. Through the drawings in the *Courant*, I met Daisy. She wanted my work for her shop. She might still be handling my watercolors, but the fifth summer I lived on the river she was nearly killed in an automobile accident. The shop was closed and never reopened. Daisy was hospitalized for weeks and bedridden for months. I visited her almost every day, often running into Harry.

As I sat on the riverbank now, quickly penciling in the details of a one-man sailboat moored at the landing, I remembered the jokes, the gossip, and the arguments with which Harry and I entertained Daisy. Daisy and George and Harry and I grew close that summer. Daisy's daughter, Georganna, spent most of the summer at the river with Miranda and Clark. Many afternoons Harry's son, Bobby, rode his bike out to join them.

In daydreams I married Clark to Georganna and Miranda to Bobby. They would settle in Minneapolis and enjoy noisy weekends at Belle Riviere, and I... I would soak them up and warm myself at them. I would be the factotum who cooked their favorite dishes, read and recommended current best-sellers, ferreted out ethnic restaurants, and clipped provocative articles from magazines and newspapers.

I would see that there was suntan lotion, plenty of fresh batteries for portable radios, a dish of mints beside the bed. I would cull village gossip, saving the choicest morsels for them, and drive country roads to find the freshest corn and berries.

All I asked was that they should once in a while sigh contentedly. That was all I asked. But what a great deal too much that had been. They did not owe me fulfillment of my daydreams.

---

* * *

I was washing dishes Thursday evening when Clark called. Clark almost never called. Sarah called and Clark said hello. I was immediately worried.

"Is Sarah all right?"

"Sure. She's fine. I'm at the office. Had to work late and thought I'd call you before I left."

This was strange. "Oh?"

"There's no point beating around the bush. Have you talked to Miranda lately? What the hell's going on with her?"

Dear Clark. All subtlety. "Going on with her? In what way?" I was cautious now.

"Something's going on between her and Bobby."

"Why do you think that, dear?" I asked, not for a minute wanting to know.

"She's been seeing him. Did you know that?"

"Seeing him? You mean those few minutes in Daisy's backyard?" My voice was full of phony incredulity.

"Well, that too. But I was referring to last night."

I clutched the receiver so tightly, the joints in my hand ached. "What about last night?"

"Sarah and I went for ice cream about eight. We decided to pick up an extra quart and drop it by for Miranda on our way home."

"Yes?"

"Bobby was there. Miranda was so flustered when she saw me, she damned near slammed the door in my face. What in hell's the deal?"

"Clark, I think you're making too much of this. Bobby was probably in town and stopped to say hello."

"Come on, Mom," he said with exasperation. "Miranda'd been crying. Her face was all red."

No glib lies came to mind.

"Mom? What do you think? Is he bothering her or what?"

"Darling, I don't know what to say. Miranda is a grown woman. Whatever is happening, obviously she wants to deal with it herself. If she doesn't ask your advice, you can't interfere. It's probably nothing. You may be reading things into this that aren't there."

"He hurt her before."

"He was a *boy*, a callow college boy."

169

"She's engaged."

"Trust her."

"I trust *her*. But what if he's trying to talk her out of marrying Dennis? I don't think that's cricket."

"Clark, I'll tell you honestly that I don't think he's doing that. But if he were, it's his right and it's her right to listen." Absolutely panicked, I was pretty certain I knew what Bobby and Miranda had discussed. Sweet Jesus, I wondered, leaning against the wall, eyes closed, how long before Clark knew about Harry and me and Harry's divorce? I would lose my son then, too.

29

"There's so many people wanting to talk about the river these days," Grandma Mercy exclaimed cheerfully on the phone. "My social calendar is filling up like a debutante's. I hope you won't mind if you're not my only caller."

"Oh, no. And I hope you won't mind if I bring a tape recorder."

"Well, I feel like a celebrity. That'll make two tape recorders in the same afternoon. If you can come about two, we'll make a regular tea party out of this."

At two o'clock Friday afternoon I turned the Volvo into the long drive leading to John Mercy's farmhouse. The pine grove through which the driveway passed was shady and sweet-scented. The white Victorian house sat in the middle of a sprawling farmyard planted with weeping willow, lilac, and climbing roses. A table was laid with a hand-embroidered cloth, unmatched china cups and saucers, a platter of homemade biscuits, and a jar of the fabled strawberry and rhubarb preserves.

I parked the car in the drive and walked up to the front porch, tape recorder and sketch pad in hand. I had no idea whether the pad would be needed, but I was prepared. A big dog of mixed breeds sashayed around the opposite end of the porch, wagging his way toward me.

From inside the screen door a voice called, "Otis, don't bother the lady," and the dog turned his head momentarily toward the sound, then back to me, prancing slowly, carefully, in the way of old and friendly dogs.

The door opened and a small woman stepped out. A conductor of strong currents of energy even at ninety-odd, she moved briskly to meet whatever was there and did not expect it to come to her.

"Don't mind Otis. He loves the ladies." She took my hand. "You're Mrs. Demming. I'm Caroline McCorkle Mercy of Good Hope, Belleville, and the Universe, you might say. Did you see *Our Town* at the Guthrie Theater? It was wonderful, wasn't it? Remember when the young girl recited a big, long mailing address that ended, 'the Solar System; the Universe; the Mind of God'? Wouldn't it be heaven if everyone thought he was a citizen of the Universe and the Mind of God? If we thought we were inside the Mind of God, we'd feel responsible for all of it, wouldn't we, not just our little two hundred and eighty acres." She raised a gnarled but strong-looking hand to indicate the land surrounding us.

"Come sit down here. This is the most comfortable rocker. It has a nice, thick pad and plenty of room for your arms. You'll need room if you want to draw." She sat on the swing. "My other caller was delayed, but he'll be here any minute. By the way, you can call me Carrie. Not Carrie Nation. Carrie Universe." She laughed at her own bon mot.

"I brought you some leaflets and several articles from the paper about the condominium project on Belle Riviere. You've probably seen them, but Nellie Bergen said you'd be interested." I handed her a manila envelope.

"Aren't you dear! I try to keep up. The river means more to me every year, even though I haven't lived on it since I married John Mercy, Senior, and moved to this farm. I lived on it all my life before that."

I reached across and turned on the tape recorder.

"We lived just north of Good Hope, sort of on the outskirts, on the west bank of the river. It was quite near the cemetery, which I loved. It was so pretty, like a park. I never thought about the dead people. I just thought, 'Isn't it nice they've put this beautiful place right where I can enjoy it?'" She leaned a bit toward me. "I have to tell you something funny. When I was little I thought the word was 'cementery.' I came to the conclusion they must cement people into the ground, like fence posts, so they wouldn't float away if there was a flood."

As unobtrusively as I could, I pulled a pencil from my bag and began drawing Grandma Mercy as she talked. Her hair was white, short, and naturally wavy. It looked buoyant, like a cap of goosedown trying to float on the air. Her skin, crosshatched by a million fine lines, had a soft, talcumed appearance. A child would want to touch and pat it.

"I had a wonderful childhood, living on the river. I loved the river so much, my dear, it was almost pagan," she confided, sharing something she had decided I would understand.

"What did your father do?" I asked, sketching hurriedly the white collar that concluded at her bosom with an old filigree silver brooch.

"He was the iceman for Good Hope. He drove an ice wagon and he let me ride with him sometimes when he made his deliveries. In the winter he cut the ice from the river and stored it underground. So you might say we made our living from the river. People bought the ice for their iceboxes."

A yellow VW turned off County Road 19 and bounced up the drive, coming to a stop behind my Volvo. "Here's my other caller," Carrie Mercy exclaimed happily and stood to meet Harry as he hurried up to the house with his tape recorder, camera, and yellow legal pad.

"Carrie." He bent and kissed her cheek, urging her to resume her place on the swing. "You didn't tell me you were going to be entertaining," he said. "We could have postponed our visit until tomorrow." He nodded at me quickly, then sat in the rocker on the opposite side of the table.

"I thought this would be more fun," she explained. "Like a party. Do you know Mrs. Demming, Harry?"

"Harry and I have met," I told her, adding, "Please call me Larissa."

"Harry has been my friend since he bought the paper," Grandma said, smiling affectionately at Harry. "He used to drive out here and pump me for—what do you call it—background information. Lately I haven't seen hide or hair of him."

"The committee's keeping me pretty busy."

"How's it going?" she wanted to know.

"Fair, I guess. It's a long, slow process." He gave her a rundown of the committee's work and described the planned Labor Day demonstration. "Sam and I drove to Minneapolis Monday to meet with state bigwigs, like Senator Ammens and Senator Zeidler. We'd like to line up some big guns to speak at the rally. Zeidler's agreed and several others are maybes."

"You look tired," she remarked. "You're working too hard. And you're not getting enough to eat. We can do something about that right now. I'll put the coffee on. You two visit. I won't be a minute. We have one of those Mr. Coffee things."

When she was gone, Harry got up and walked down the porch steps. The dog, Otis, sat in the shade at the side of the steps. Harry bent and ran his hand along the dog's back and spoke the meaningless, kind syllables one speaks to animals.

I put down my pad. "I'm sorry about this, Harry. I didn't know you were the other caller."

He didn't look up. "It doesn't matter." His voice was weary and detached.

I'd never heard that tone from him, as though I were a stranger he wouldn't meet again. It stung. I took up the sketch pad, nervously penciling in a suggestion of the bachelor's buttons that were scattered across Grandma Mercy's dress. My eyes burned and I tried to concentrate on the portrait.

Harry went in the house and moments later emerged with the coffee carafe, Carrie Mercy behind him, carrying a couple of large scrapbooks. "There are old pictures and newspaper clippings here you might like to see," she said, laying the albums on the table beside my tape recorder.

I poured coffee and Harry passed the plate of biscuits. "The biscuits are better when they're hot," she told me. "Next time, I'll bake them *after* you get here." I wasn't hungry and I didn't think Harry was, but we made an effort.

"Was the river very different when you were a girl?" I asked.

"Not so many people lived on it, of course. And there was logging off and on for many years. That went back way before I was born. What a mess!" she said with spirit. "The jams! The passenger steamboats had terrible trouble getting through when the logs got jammed. They used the steamboats sometimes to try to break them up. Men got killed going into a jam to find the key pieces that were holding it. Dear God, that was awful. But when the jam broke, everything closed down and folks ran down to the river to watch. It was something to see.

"I wasn't born yet when they had the worst jam. But my daddy told me about it often enough. Several men on the jam crews were killed in that one. And according to a piece I read about it a few years back, there was one hundred and fifty million feet of timber caught between the dalles. Can you feature it? Belle Riviere isn't all that wide to start with, so you can about imagine how high those logs were piled.

"To tell the truth, I was just as glad when the lumber companies ran out of profits and stopped the logging. This river wasn't ever meant for commotion. It's what I'd call a 'still waters' river. It runs pretty deep in some places, but mostly gentle. The woods where they were cut down have grown back and it's a hidey place for things that need to be safe."

I planned to paint at least one watercolor of the steamboats. There were several rough sketches in my portfolio that I'd done from photographs at the Historical Society, but there might be something new in the pictures Grandma had. I'd already finished several studies of loggers and jams, but I ought to have Grandma look them over for errors in detail. I began paging through the first of the two scrapbooks. Harry picked up the second.

While we winnowed the pictures, clippings, and memorabilia, Harry for items he could weave into a long background piece he was writing about the river, I for sketch ideas and emotional grist to put into the graphic process, Carrie Mercy pattered entertainingly about her father's ice business and his customers. She revived ancient scandals, love affairs, bankruptcies, suicides, and murders.

"I wish I could remember last week the way I can remember eighty years ago," she sighed. "I think television is ruining my memory. It fills up too many crannies where more important things ought to be. Think of what it's doing to the little children, putting all that cheap nonsense in the places where real life should be."

I was reading an account of a train hitting a cow two miles south of Good Hope, the grisly details of which went on for several paragraphs, when I turned the page and was so startled I exclaimed "Oh, my!" before I could stop myself.

There, in sepia tones, was a photograph taken on the lawn of the Hazeltine cottage. Alice Hazeltine and a little girl wearing a sunbonnet stood one on either side of a wheelchair in which a laughing, fabulously handsome Pan sat reveling in female blandishments. It was an achingly merry and unshadowed moment.

Grandma Mercy leaned forward. "What is it, dear? Is anything wrong?" Harry, too, had paused in his reading to glance at me.

"It's . . . it's just this picture. It's so happy, it makes me sad. Who's the little girl in the sunbonnet?" I held the album up for Carrie Mercy to see.

"Why, that's me," she said. "The young woman was Alice Hazeltine. I must tell you about her. And the gentleman was a Greek who was a houseguest at the Hazeltines'." She smiled, remembering, "I fell head over teacups for him. I couldn't have been more than six or seven, I suppose."

Harry came around the table and stood behind me, looking down at the photograph.

"Grandma, may I please borrow this?" I begged. "I'll guard it with my life. I want to paint this scene." I would not only paint it, I would have copies made. One for Pan and one for myself.

"Goodness, of course."

"I'll bring it back soon, I promise."

The old woman eased herself back in the swing and folded her hands in her lap. "Alice Hazeltine died but a few weeks after that picture was taken. Drowned in the river. Sleepwalking, was the story they gave out, but I always thought otherwise."

"What did you think?" Harry inquired, returning to his chair and taking up his notepad.

"Suicide."

"She looks awfully happy for someone who's going to commit suicide," Harry observed. "Why would she do it?"

"I'm not sure. It had something to do with the Greek, I know that in my bones." She pulled a small linen handkerchief from inside her dress, patted her brow and neck and temples, then played nervously with it in her lap. "And it may have had something to do with the Devil of the dalles."

Awkwardly I jumped in to steer the conversation in another direction. "How did you happen to have your picture taken with Alice Hazeltine?"

"I knew Alice and her aunt from going with my daddy on his ice deliveries. They'd always tease me a little and give me a treat. They were so pretty, both of them, like pictures. And warm-hearted. I cried terribly when I heard about Alice. She was like an angel."

"The Devil of the dalles?" Harry asked. "I heard about him once years ago. What is this mythological creature?"

"I wish I could tell you exactly. I don't even know when the story started. While I was a girl, I think. At any rate, I first heard it when I was eleven. My daddy told Mama and me one night at dinner that a fellow, whose name I don't recall—he was a worker on the railroad section crew—had been whispering around town about a Devil he'd seen in the woods north of the Hazeltine place. This fellow wasn't making a general announcement, mind you, since he'd been trespassing at the time. Daddy said the man was a Hungarian and Hungarians would believe anything. But the story took hold of my imagination.

"I know I was eleven because I graduated from elementary school that June and I spent the summer searching the woods for the Devil."

"Then about 1916 maybe—it was during the war, I know— there was a piece in the paper. It's in one of those books you're looking at. A fellow from Blind Moose who had taken some lads on a nature hike had reported seeing a monster who looked like the Devil. None of the boys had seen the creature and the poor man was laughed out of town.

"Well, a few years later there was a story going around about a woman who was living in the Hazeltine place. She was friend to a couple of Good Hope young ladies, daughters of a minister, and she went all to pieces one night, had to be taken to the city and put in a hospital. Said the Devil had been coming to her and tempting her into all sorts of things she shouldn't be doing. Something about the story made me think of the others. Maybe she was just a poor crazy thing, but it was a coincidence, wasn't it? That's about all I can tell you."

Harry riffled through the album in his hands until he found the clipping Grandma had mentioned.

"'The fiend had white fur growing on its body,' Loomis stated, 'and hoofs instead of feet, and its eyes were of awful fire,'" Harry read. "No mention of a tail," he added wryly. "Loomis probably encountered the beast head-on."

We spent another hour with Grandma Mercy. Although I was uncomfortable being with Harry, there were many questions I wanted to ask about Belle Riviere and about Grandma. I felt nourished by her memories and her person. To think I might have missed her! When I kissed her good-bye, I didn't want to leave.

At the car I hesitated, waiting for Harry. As he approached, looking annoyed because I was still there, I told him, "I'm not in a position to ask favors of you, Harry, but if you'll make me two copies of this, I'll pay you for your trouble." I held out the old photo of Alice, Pan, and Carrie McCorkle.

He took it. "I'd like a sketch of Grandma for the paper. I got some shots of her, but I'd prefer something like the one on your pad."

"Fair enough," I said. "I'll drop it at the *Courant* Monday if that's soon enough."

He nodded and started to walk away.

"Harry, are you going to write about the Devil?"

"Yes. I'm doing a long piece covering the river over the past one hundred years. One installment will run in the *Courant* each week until Labor Day. The Devil is part of the story and the sort of silly thing that will make people read the rest of the history, I hope."

"I wish you wouldn't write about him."

"Why not?"

"I don't know. Presentiment."

Without reply he walked past me to his car. I started the Volvo's engine, turned around in the big drive, and headed back to County Road 19.

30

Bart was up at his usual hour the following Monday. I put a pot of coffee on the stove and soft-boiled an egg for him.

"I have to drive down to the university," he said, sitting at the table and spreading a napkin across his lap.

"Oh?"

"There are several facts I left dangling in the manuscript until I could get to the stacks at the library."

Buttering toast and setting it beside him, I suggested, "You might call Miranda and have lunch."

"I'll call her, but I don't know about lunch. Maybe dinner. I'll give her your love."

"Yes. Do that."

He spread lemon curd on his toast. "Are you finding things to do?" he asked.

"The pictures I'm doing for the Historical Society are keeping me off the streets."

"Oh, yes. I'd forgotten. When I finish this draft of the book, you might like to proofread it," he suggested, carefully stirring exactly one and a half teaspoons of sugar into his coffee.

"Yes, well, it's ... something to think about." I studied him across the breakfast table. He was someone who sits next to you in a crowded place—a train station or a diner—only because it's convenient. I knew him less well now than when we were married. I hadn't the science or art of engrossing a preoccupied person. Perhaps if I'd followed a career, I would have contributed more to the family pool of vitality. I wondered if he found our marriage as disengaging as I did. It might seem perfectly normal and satisfactory to him. Was having creature comforts and being left alone a man's idea of a good marriage?

Later, I walked with him to the car. "When will you be back?"

"Around nine, I guess."

More than twelve hours. In fact, it was only 8 A.M. when I poured another cup of coffee and washed the few breakfast dishes. Carrying the cup to Bart's study, I set it on the desk, raised the shade and then the window. I drew his chair near the window and placed a small table beside it. Laying his manuscript on the table, I picked up my coffee, kicked off my sandals, and settled into the commodious chair.

I felt like a child consumed by nasty-minded curiosity, poking through a parent's desk, a treasure trove of personal correspondence, inexplicable clippings, mysterious telephone numbers, and snapshots of strangers—how was it that the parent knew strangers?

I expected to be less than engrossed. I was prepared to admire the style and deplore the plot. What, after all, did Bart know of action? In short, I was reading, not for entertainment but to discover whether there was a hope that Bart could have some success with this book, a success significant enough to carry him across the frontier of my leaving.

The work had the physical heft of a so-called blockbuster. There were, I noted, six hundred and fifty-odd pages. Obviously, I couldn't read it all today, but I would read what I could and page through the remainder. I stayed with it until three in the afternoon, breaking only for a bit of lunch.

The story chronicled the exploits of Alexander the Great in

India. It was spellbinding. All the stock phrases and hackneyed adjectives applied. It had grandeur, tumultuous passions, and broad brush strokes of action. The characters were truly wrought and well-fleshed. Among the most affecting was the youthful Prokles, a scholarly officer, and a character in which there was, I thought, a bit of Bart. Something in his attitude toward study.

The bittersweet core of Prokles's story was his love for a young slave girl in his father's household. Cleis, as she was called, was destined for the old man's bed, and Prokles, despite his love, might not touch her. Translating desire into tutelage, he taught the girl to read and shared with her poetry and history. Devotion was spoken through the phrases of pedagogues and poets.

At his father's bidding, Prokles accompanied Alexander across the Hellespont, through the Middle East, into Egypt, and eventually to the ill-fated campaign in India. During the years of war and travel, he wrote poetry, half of it love poems, half descriptions of war and the places he'd seen and, occasionally, destroyed; all of it was for Cleis.

When he returned, she would know what had passed with him through the years. She would know that he had loved her. After eleven years of exile and the death of Alexander, Prokles made his way home, only to learn that Cleis had died in childbirth a year after his leavetaking.

With the manuscript on my lap, I sat, my breath rather taken away. At length I returned the chair to its proper spot, reassembled the manuscript on the desk, and tidied up. Lowering the window and shade, I left, closing the door behind me.

So. There was the Bart I couldn't find. We knew each other even less than I'd supposed. Had the novel begun as a sort of Mythical Beast, an almost clandestine escape? Writing it must have been a great adventure. It was filled with bold undertakings, imaginative sex, and many sorts of love and hate.

I was proud of Bart. He was a fine novelist. The book would be well received critically, I was almost certain. And I was just as certain it would sell millions if properly exploited. Bart would be a rich man. He could leave teaching, write full-time. He would be famous and grudgingly pleased.

This book would surely suffice for my absence. I rather thought it would fill the place of two or three of me. Once negotiations got under way, Bart would be swept up in a real-life adventure. For all that, I was thankful and pleased. But a streak of bitterness cut across my feelings. If the book's energy and excitement were in Bart, where had they been all these years?

I rode the bike to town to drop the Grandma Mercy art at the *Courant*. I left the pen-and-ink work with the woman at the *Courant's* front counter, requesting that Harry receive it today. In return she handed me a manila envelope containing the original and two copies of the picture of Alice Hazeltine, Carrie Mercy, and Pan. There was no accompanying note.

31

"Mrs. Demming."

I turned to see Bobby Arneson emerge from Arneson Printing, next to the *Courant*. "Bobby."

"Where're you headed?" he asked.

"I was going to collect my bike from the rack at the public library and head home."

"Okay if I walk over to the library with you?"

"Well...all right." It was just across the street in Humphrey Park.

He fell in with me, walking with his head down, his hands thrust deep into his trouser pockets. Now that he'd committed himself to escorting me, he was ill at ease and silent except to remark that the day was unusually hot. Actually, the day wasn't unusually hot for July on the river.

When we reached the library parking lot, he said, "Do you have a minute? I mean, do you have to get right home and fix dinner or something?"

"No. Bart's in Minneapolis."

"Could we talk? I won't keep you long and I can throw your bike in the back of the Jeep and give you a ride home afterward." He kept glancing toward River Avenue, afraid possibly that Roberta might happen along and see us together. Or maybe it was Harry he didn't want to encounter.

"Where's the Jeep?"

"Parked in the alley behind the shop."

"If you give me a ride home now and we talk there, could someone lock up for you?" It was nearly five.

He appeared relieved. "Sure. Millie Boyle was going to close up anyway. I'll get the Jeep. You wait here." He took off across River Avenue, dodging cars and calling, "I won't be a minute."

Piling out of the Jeep, Bobby unloaded the bike and I put it away in the garage. "Would you like something to drink?" I asked. "Beer? Lemonade or something stronger?"

"Beer, please," he said, following me into the kitchen.

I poured myself gin and lemonade and we carried our glasses to the porch.

"Will Mr. Demming see Miranda while he's in the city?"

"He may have dinner with her. He's coming back later this evening."

"I see."

"Does that bother you? That he may see her?"

"No. Well, I don't know. Miranda's not too happy with me."

"You're afraid she'll discuss you with her father?"

"Not really. Maybe I'm afraid he might guess at something, you know, kind of 'read' things."

"I wouldn't worry. In any case Miranda's very close about her personal life."

"Yah. That's true, I know."

I felt sorry for him. He didn't know which end of the porcupine to grab. "You've seen Miranda recently."

He nodded. "You saw us at the Orion Room, didn't you?"

"Yes. And Clark said he'd run into you at her apartment."

He fidgeted with the glass, set it down, and asked, "Do you mind if I smoke?"

"No. You might as well know," I told him, "that Clark said Miranda had been crying. He assumed you were to blame."

He lit a cigarette. "He was right." Sitting forward, elbows on his knees, he stared at the trees in the yard and puffed hastily on the cigarette. "Mrs. Demming, I hope you won't get mad if I say this, but I don't want Miranda to marry Dennis. He's not right for her. He's a nice enough guy, I guess, but it isn't going to work. You've got to talk to her. She won't listen to me." He cast an imploring look in my direction.

The unhappiness in my answering laugh was unmistakable.

"Oh, Bobby, she'll never listen to *me*. Miranda's terribly angry with me."

"Then what're we going to do?" he asked, assuming I was sympathetic.

"I don't know. What is it about Dennis that you think is 'wrong' for Miranda?"

He looked uncomfortable. He didn't want to bad-mouth Dennis, and he could see, too, that I might suspect his motives, since he and Miranda had once been close. His concern for her overcame these considerations, however, and after taking a harsh drag on his cigarette and slowly expelling the smoke from his lungs, he began, "He's so all-American, so...macho. He was a four-letter man at school and I don't mean nasty words. Mr. Fraternity Jock." He caught my glance. "I know, I know—none of this is a hanging offense."

"And they don't give out law degrees for a wicked backhand," I reminded him.

"He isn't stupid." He stood abruptly and paced to the screen door. Leaning against the jamb, he stared out at the river. His face was filled with regret and I surmised that he was recalling the afternoons here with Miranda and Clark and Georganna Fitzroy. What had gone wrong?

"Whatever I say, it doesn't convey what I *mean*," he continued quietly. "It all sounds like sour grapes." He glanced in my direction. "I promise you it isn't. I can't marry Miranda. I couldn't, even if there weren't any Dennis. But I want her to be happy. More than anything, I want that. I feel closer to her than to anybody in the world." His voice caught. He cleared his throat quickly and went on, "Dennis is solid and stolid. He'll provide her with kids and cars and season tickets to the symphony, but he'll never have the imagination to know what she wants."

How well he understood and what pain it gave him to understand.

"Bobby, I've tried to talk Miranda out of marrying Dennis. I should say, I've tried to convince her to postpone the marriage. For different reasons from yours, perhaps. I don't think she's ready for marriage to anyone. I don't think she's had enough...experience. She hasn't ridden life up high enough or down low enough."

He gave me a strange, unsettling, sideways look. "Oh, I think she's had some real lows, Mrs. Demming."

I was startled. Did he refer to Harry and me? I wondered. What did Bobby know or guess? What had he been told? I'm not sure even now why I didn't press him to tell me. It wasn't simply that I didn't want to hear that Miranda had been devastated by her weekend on the river. I don't suppose I longed to hear it but I could have stood up under it. Perhaps there was something in Bobby himself, in his person, that constrained me.

"Well...I don't know," I said falteringly. "Perhaps you're right. Mothers don't know everything," I said, backing off. "In any case, I don't see that there's anything you or I can do to keep Miranda from marrying Dennis. Maybe it's a mistake she has to make. And maybe she'll be happy despite our hand-wringing. What we can't change, we must accept—isn't that what they say?"

I felt like an awful hypocrite throwing this last at him, for I had no intention of accepting Miranda's marriage until it was irreversibly achieved. But there was no need for Bobby to charge himself with the responsibility of dissuading her. He appeared to need a respite from his burdens. Perhaps I was myself part of his burden, if he worried about his parents.

"I don't want to think this marriage is a mistake Miranda has to make," he said wearily, "and I'll tell you why—she's so damned stubborn, she'll go down with the ship." He looked hard at me. "She'll stick with it till it's too late, maybe forever. She won't admit it was a mistake. She'll figure out that it was somehow all her fault and she'll stay." He threw himself down on the chair, grabbed his glass, and finished the beer.

Without speaking, I fetched another and set it beside the glass. For a long time we sat, not speaking. I don't know where his anguish took him, but mine carried me back to other summers.

The four youngsters everywhere—in the river screaming and half-drowning one another; lazily drying out in the sun on the dock, speaking in sleepy murmurs; playing volleyball in the backyard; or cooking up disgusting snacks in the kitchen. Then later, their summer bodies, so clean and fresh and taut, biking into town to the movies.

Georganna had been a great tomboy and tireless kidder, always ragging Clark about something. When they came up from swimming, she would chase him around with a damp towel, snapping at his buttocks and finally breaking down his primness.

Miranda and Bobby...well, they talked. By the hour they sat

here on this porch, or down on the dock, and talked. About everything: what they wanted to be, where they wanted to live, how many children each would have. They argued books and television and movies and politics and religion. They preferred arguing with each other to any pastime with someone else. They were each other's best friend and, while they might disagree heatedly with each other, they stood together against the rest of the world.

I wanted to cry out, "Oh, Bobby, what happened?" But lest he think I held him somehow to blame, I didn't ask. Whatever it was, the break between them had come during their junior year at the university. Bobby went to Europe in June and Miranda went to summer school.

"People do what they must, Bobby." I was full of empty phrases. "If Miranda marries Dennis, we have to be fatalistic: it was meant to be, it's in the cards or the lap of the gods, or wherever."

The phrases were not entirely empty. They did at least carry my own sympathy, my own love for Bobby. It came back in waves that I tried to control. My tenderness toward him should be something of which he was only subliminally aware, something that comforted without taxing.

The sensitivity and decency of the grown-up Bobby were the same I'd seen in the child Bobby. I recalled a conversation between him and Miranda when he was only seven or eight. At the time it struck me so sharply I came undone and had to hurry into the bedroom and close the door.

The two children were sprawled on the cool porch floor playing with Lincoln Logs, building a village. I was in the living room working a crossword puzzle. I remember that even now.

I heard Miranda ask Bobby, "Where should we put the graveyard?"

"There ain't gonna be a graveyard."

"Don't say 'ain't.' It's stupid."

"Well, there ain't gonna be a graveyard," he repeated defiantly.

"Why not?"

"'Cause I say so."

"That's stupid."

"No, it ain't. Did you ever kill anything?"

Silence, then, "Bugs. Worms when we go fishing. Fish, I guess, if catching them is killing them." Silence. "Did you?"

"Not me, but I was there."

"Where?"

"In the car. My mom took me out to Johnson's farm to get corn. When we were coming back, an old farm dog ran out on the road. I think if we'd been going a little slower, maybe we could have missed him."

"You ran over him?"

Silence. Perhaps he nodded his head.

"Was it all bloody?"

"I don't know. I heard him hit the car—whomp, like that—and I looked back and he was lying in the road."

"What'd you do?"

"We didn't do nothin'. I wanted to stop and put him over in the grass even if he was dead, so nobody else would run over him again. He didn't deserve to get run over again."

"Wouldn't she stop?"

"She said there wasn't anything we could do for him now."

"She shoulda stopped anyway. It would've made you feel better."

"She was in a hurry and she said she didn't want to get her good pants all messed up and there wasn't anything we could do for him now."

Silence. He concluded, "So we ain't gonna have a graveyard, 'cause I want to be able to do something for 'em."

"I'm going to fix another drink," I told him, rising from the swing. He rose also and followed. "I'm to blame for Miranda's refusal to postpone the wedding." I took the pitcher of lemonade from the refrigerator. "When she came home over the Fourth, I think she was vulnerable to persuasion. She might have put the wedding off until Christmas." He sat down at the table. "But...things happened over the weekend to drive her away from me." Stirring gin into the lemonade in my glass, I carried the drink to the table, then went back to the refrigerator and pulled out salami and cheese and laid those on the table, along with crackers and a knife. "Fix yourself a snack." I got a plate from the cupboard and put it in front of him, then set a cutting board on the table. From a basket on the counter I took an onion and began slicing it thin on the board.

"When you stopped me outside the *Courant,* I thought you wanted to talk about your parents' divorce." My hands were trembling and I nicked my thumb with the knife. "Damn." I wrapped a paper napkin around it and continued. "Miranda thinks Harry and I are having an affair, that we've been having one for some time." I pushed the sliced onion toward him, moved to the opposite side of the table, and sat down.

"I've known your father twenty years. During those years a lot of what seemed harmless flirting went on, as it often does between two people, each of whom is rather determinedly married to someone else. In all that time, only one kiss was ever exchanged. I do not consider that an affair. Unfortunately Miranda was a witness to it."

He smiled thinly and gave a sad little shake to his head.

"Yes. It was a helluva moment for all concerned, but mostly for Miranda. I thought perhaps she'd told you about it."

"No."

"I'm sorry to divulge all of this, but I didn't want you to leave here thinking it was your fault Miranda's getting married in October."

He said nothing. He ate a little, but I think it was only to please me. He looked underfed, his shoulders too sharp beneath the light summer shirt. I wasn't sorry to make him eat. His quiet didn't offend me. He'd always been quiet (except with Miranda), rather autonomous and a trifle brooding. A wary little boy, he had required drawing out, without a hint of patronizing. When he dropped his guard, he was gentle and eager, tentatively playful.

At seven-thirty he rose to leave. I walked out to the yard with him. As he prepared to climb into the Jeep, he turned back. "Thank you." He jumped into the driver's seat, then looked at me for several seconds. I thought he'd returned to that brown study where he wrestled, but he asked, "Are you in love with my dad?"

I was little prepared for the question or his importuning gaze.

"Oh, Bobby . . . please."

The dark gray eyes were unwavering. He made no move to put the key in the ignition. "Just between you and me, Mrs. Demming."

Taking several steps toward the Jeep, I reached out a hand and placed it on Bobby's. His lay on the steering wheel and I clasped it tightly before I spoke, hoping, I suppose, that this physical connection would give him assurance of my good intentions despite my answer, which must necessarily alarm and distress him.

"Yes," I said and backed away.

Then he put the key in the ignition and started the Jeep. Shifting into reverse, he backed out into the yard, leaving me to implore my absent daughter, Why aren't you marrying this one?

---

32 🌺

"Will you show me where the Hazeltine cottage stood?" I asked Pan Thursday morning. I'd been sketching and painting all week and this was yet another setting I needed.

"It's overgrown now. The house burned to the ground years ago, you know."

"Yes."

"There's not much to mark where it was."

"I understand, but unless it's painful for you to go over the ground with me, I'd like to do it."

And so began the last unhurried day we would share for some time.

"It's too far for you to tramp with your equipment," Pan explained. "We'll take the canoe." Nimbly seating himself, he wrapped the lower half of his body with the bedspread. "I'll paddle," he said as I stepped in.

"Have you ever done it?"

"What difference does that make?"

I shrugged.

He took the paddle, dug it into the river bottom, and pushed off, bringing the canoe about adroitly and heading downstream. "You see," he told me kindly, "much of what humans must learn, a minor deity knows instinctively. There are, after all, some compensations for immortality."

"But you had to learn to read English. Alice taught you."

A smile crossed his face, chasing a sunlit memory. "Ah, that was because it was a pleasure."

We passed a couple with casting rods, fishing from the bank. They waved. We waved. They held up casting until we were safely past. They didn't know us, nor did I recognize them. This sort of encounter occurred with regularity. In the beginning it unnerved me, but I had grown accustomed to it.

"This is it," Pan announced, nosing the canoe toward shore.

The boathouse and dock were long gone. He'd been right. There was nothing along the shore to say that a man of vast holdings and influence had built a lodge here and entertained others like himself, that a young woman had died pointlessly, perhaps in this very spot. Or that another woman had fallen down mad at the feet of a cleric.

Pan alone bore witness, connecting me and this morning with Nancy and 1925, and Alice and 1895, and others before them, back forever to a mist-shrouded cleft in the universe from which all mystery poured, an unquenchable river coursing through the shantytown world of our smug and meager certainties.

For a moment I stood in the river with Pan, drowning in memories of endless eons and numberless worlds, drowning in a thoroughly cloudless vision that forgave all pain and understood all injury.

"Are you all right?"

"Yes. I was ... dizzy for a second."

He knew better. The river would not have flowed through me without his allowing it. It had been a gift to which one could not refer without demeaning both the gift and giver.

We dragged the canoe up to the trees and began picking our way through the forest and undergrowth that hid decaying evidence of human lives. Pan, carrying the basket and wearing the bedspread draped across his shoulders, led the way. I brought a pad, pencils, and a small easel. We'd hiked maybe seventy-five yards inland when Pan called back, "Here's what's left of the gazebo."

I quickened my pace to catch up with him. Ahead and to the left was a stone foundation that formed the floor, and beside it, steps leading up. Parts of the wooden superstructure remained like the splintered hull of a ravaged vessel; nature and vandals had destroyed most of it. The roof was gone and the beams had fallen in, many of them to be carted away, probably for campfires on the beach. Woodbine, ruthful and forgiving, clung to the remains, creating a gentle memorial.

I'd never been to this place, but the atmosphere was thick with memory. Ghosts of my past brushed my cheek and spoke against my ear, old forbidden words, forbidden deeds. I wondered if Pan didn't feel the breath of Alice on his skin. His face didn't betray him. He stood beside the steps, absently plucking a leaf from the woodbine. Tucking it into the hair above his ear, he flashed me a rakish smile and turned rather quickly away. We moved on, Pan leading us at an angle, to the right and farther from the river. About two hundred feet from the gazebo was the stone-and-masonry foundation of the north wall of the cottage. We walked the entire circuit of the enclosed area. Within the rectangle where the house had stood, trees grew and amongst them sections of great charred disintegrating beams lay nurturing the young growth.

When we reached the east, or rear side, of the foundation, we could glimpse through the foliage a gracefully sagging building, its roof delicate as netting. It stood nonetheless and was more beautiful in age than in youth.

The roof shingles were long gone from the stable, and the woodbine connecting the joists filtered all but thin strands of sunlight. These strands seemed to hang in the air and to sway like satin streamers.

Leaning against a topless bin that must once have held hay or feed, I began to sketch. Another day I would come back with watercolors but now I could get the structural elements on paper. It was warm and close, even with the big stable doors missing. Gnats hung and darted in the air like tiny minnows, and high in the rafters a hive of bees mumbled like monks at their prayers. While I worked, Pan cleared an area where he spread the picnic cloth.

As I put the pad away, he handed me a paper cup of Riesling and I joined him on the ground. Actually, it wasn't ground beneath us, but a thick mattress of pine needles and below that, the old concrete floor of the stable.

Pan drank part of his wine, then set it aside and pulled the *Courant* from the basket, inquiring, "Anything of interest in the newspaper?"

"Nothing that can't wait."

He cast a narrow glance at me and raised an eyebrow. "Something unpleasant."

"Something . . . a little unnerving."

He unfolded the paper and spread it out before us. "Which article?"

"'Belle Riviere: Story of a Great Beauty.' This is the first installment. There'll be one each week until Labor Day."

"Yes, that's what it says here." He read quickly, then turned the pages to the "jump" on page four. "Mmmm," he murmured, perusing my study of Grandma Mercy and the photograph of himself with Alice Hazeltine and Carrie McCorkle. Reading on, he found, under the subhead "Devil of the Dalles," the paragraphs that made me uneasy.

Finishing the article, he refolded the paper and stuffed it back into the basket. "Your drawing is good," he said.

"Thank you."

"What is it that concerns you?"

"I don't like your picture appearing in the paper. And the piece is going to stir up interest in the Devil of the dalles, something we don't need. It could bring a couple of dozen nuts of assorted varieties out here beating the bushes for you."

"I've lived here for eighty-seven years. I'll manage for another six weeks."

"If they find you, you'll end up in a zoo."

"You exaggerate."

"Well, on *Good Morning America,* then."

"Stop worrying now." He brushed hair back from my face. "Your cheeks are flushed. It's most attractive." Kissing my mouth in a soft, kneading way that never failed to arouse me, he began to unbutton my shirt. He slid the shirt down from my shoulders and helped me to shrug my jeans.

With animal playfulness he nuzzled my neck below the ear, then nibbled downward to the shoulders, exploring their hollows. My fingers, locked in the mass of his black mane, caressed the two small nubs lying hidden there.

Gliding without haste over my ribcage, lingering on my flank and along my thigh, his fingers were sorcerers, delicate as the brush of silk, but striking the skin with a fine spray of lightning.

Brute power and endurance he translated into the most tender and patient skill, and he delighted to discover that the strength he surrendered, I absorbed, returning it to him in ardor.

Our lovemaking was all contrarieties: my body was at once heavy and slow with molten languor, light and quick with an upward rush of heat. His lips at my breasts sent exquisite fear and the sweetest revulsion filtering through me. The sight and touch and taste of him were of such appalling dearness, tears lay just beyond abandon.

With a sense of impending loss, like someone soon to lose her homeland, I wandered back and forth and back again across the landscape of his body: the broad, ancient plateau of his chest, the hard plain of his belly, and the rich valley of his groin. His great, tawny penis, which was as precious to me as his hands or any other part of him, I took into my mouth, exciting and contenting myself as much as him.

I would lose him irrevocably in Greece, and I knew memory could be a cold banker, hoarding meaningless receipts, so I tried literally to absorb him into my flesh: tears, sweat, sperm, and saliva. He answered my greed with generosity.

The sun lingered over the afternoon, moving with kindly procrastination. The streamers of light hanging from the rafters threw a golden corona around Pan's head and gilded his curls as he lowered himself over me.

Finishing the last bit of the picnic lunch, Pan sat, his back against the wooden bin, and took up his pipes. Before beginning to play, he said, "Any man who makes love to you in the future is bound to suffer by comparison, you know."

I laughed. "I've considered entering the convent."

He began to play and I, with my head on his thigh, lay ravening each note and moment as they unfolded. Later we napped and, waking, drank more wine. Then, suddenly, he marred the outing.

"Before you leave this place, I want you to realize why."

I straightened. "What does that mean?" I asked defensively.

He studied the cup in his hands. "Before you become an expatriate, consider carefully."

"If you're worried about being stuck with a crazy, middle-aged American woman, I told you before I'll leave you when we get to the Peloponnese."

"You mistrust everyone's commitment but your own," he said without impatience.

"You think I should come back here."

"I think you shouldn't emigrate until you know why. You're running away from something that will swim the Atlantic and beat you to Athens." His gaze was level and sad. "It's not the break with Miranda. No, I don't believe that. And it's not the fiasco with your friend Harry. Those are problems one expects from life. They *are* life." He looked at me until I diverted my gaze and felt above me the chill of a single cloud drifting over the day.

33 🌿

"L. Demming?"

"Yes."

"Gerald Sperling here."

There was nicety as well as impersonality in the voice. Under the circumstances—my total ignorance of the caller's identity—the "Gerald Sperling here" was presumptuous and intriguing.

"Yes?"

"I own Homestead Gallery."

"Oh, yes." I had, after all, heard the name Gerald Sperling before. I'd been to several showings at the Homestead, a tony Minneapolis gallery whose specialty was Midwest landscapes and rural life.

"I saw one of your paintings yesterday," he went on.

"Is that so?"

"A personal friend, Phil Amstel, won it at some sort of fund-raiser up your way."

How remote "up your way" sounded in his rococo inflections.

"Yes. Oh, yes. The St. Paul attorney."

"The very same." He paused to a count of three. Gerald Sperling did not wish to seem eager or perhaps even interested. It was he who'd called me, however, and so at length he was forced to further the conversation. "I'm not familiar with your work."

"There's no reason you should be."

"You don't have a gallery outlet?"

"No. I haven't made a point of selling my paintings for quite some time."

"Any particular reason?"

"Many reasons."

He waited for me to amplify. When I didn't he continued in the unhurried and elaborate manner of one for whom others wait gladly. "Well, of course I couldn't say without seeing considerably more of your work—every Sunday dauber has one decent painting in him, even if it occurs by accident, which it usually does—but if you had a sufficient number of salable pictures, I'd be tempted to present one or two of them."

His words and tone were overweening. If I were an anxious young artist fairly desperate to be noticed, I might even have been intimidated, but since I'd long looked upon my painting as therapy and escape, and my paintings as personal, frequently painful expressions of self-doubt, I was only curious and a little flattered by Gerald Sperling's elegant and dismissive voice.

It was the flattery, I suppose, that drew me to Sperling and Homestead Gallery. In fact, once off the phone, I found a great yearning for praise grabbing roughly ahold of me and pushing me to an impetuous response.

That afternoon, which was Monday, I drove to the Minneapolis house, taking with me sketches and drawings of Belle Riviere to add to the work stored in my studio closet on Thomas Avenue. Driving into the city, I didn't consider how strange it was to jump to Sperling's call; I only raced around in my mind, gathering together the best possible representation of my work.

Tuesday morning I called Sperling to make an appointment. He tried at first to put me off until the end of the week. His practiced reticence was nearly pathological, but I determined to match his ploy.

"I'm sorry you can't see me today. I'm leaving soon for Greece." I added lightly, "Our paths may cross again. Fate often paints with a fine Italian hand."

He glissaded gracefully but quickly into the breach. "I *do* see a small patch of blue on my schedule around four."

Unloading my things on the sidewalk in front of the gallery, I was overcome by fear and paralyzing second thoughts. Homestead was one of the oldest and most prestigious galleries in the Midwest. I didn't have an agent, hadn't sold anything—except to Harry—for many years. Did I really want to put myself and my work in the line of Gerald Sperling's criticism or contempt? Worse yet, his thinly masked pity? Did I want to confess myself publicly? For wasn't that what one did by showing work that had been privately rendered for private purposes?

A woman twenty-eight or thirty years old opened the door of the gallery and inquired, "Mrs. Demming?"

"Yes."

"Mr. Sperling should have told you about the alleyway entrance. It would have been easier for you. Here, let me help you with those." She propped open the door and came to meet me, shaking my hand before hoisting a couple of bulging portfolios. "Madge Allhouse, Gerald's right hand," she explained.

We quickly carried the framed and unframed art through the gallery to Sperling's office at the rear right side of the long narrow building. Despite a lack of natural light, the room seemed airy and pleasantly bright. To the left and toward the back an open stairway led to a loftlike walkway or gallery running around the entire perimeter of the room. More paintings and sculpture were displayed there.

When we'd deposited my things in the office, Madge motioned me to a chair and exited through a door leading to an adjacent loading area and workroom.

"Gerald will be right with you."

Despair and excitement twisted together in me. I'd felt this way as a child waiting to proffer crayon drawings to Jamie.

In the dining room of the Dupont Avenue house that Jamie sold when I started college, I would hand over to him one at a time for his consideration the day's output of garish imagination. Dessert out of the way (always something like apple Betty or fruit ambrosia) he remained at the lace-covered table with his coffee. Standing beside his chair, I would place the first sheet of cheap, slightly freckled paper on the table before him, keeping the others behind my back.

No matter how many times we played out the ritual, a knot of anguish and hope all but stopped my breathing. Although Jamie was never cruel, he was straightforward about my work.

"Oh, yes, I see what you were trying to do here," he would remark, holding up a drawing. "This was supposed to be a man, very big and good-looking fellow, standing on the back of a circus horse, right? With a little girl on his shoulders? Too bad the little girl's head got cut off by the edge of the paper. Next time you ought to sketch it with a pencil before using crayons, don't you think?"

With one of my shoes I was stepping down hard on the toe of the other, punishing myself for ineptitude and telling myself I would let up as soon as Daddy said something really good about my work.

Of the next picture he might say, "Well, yes, this one's another

---

matter. This fellow on the horse really looks as though he's riding away from us through those trees. The perspective's very good. The road gets narrower and narrower as it goes away, doesn't it? Is this the same handsome devil as in the other picture?"

I nodded, cheeks red with praise. Laughing, he would draw me to his chair and deliver a noisy kiss to my neck, a kiss that tickled. I would laugh from the kiss and from relief at pleasing him.

The long, low rectangular mirror over the buffet had reflected a scene yellowed by a chandelier whose incandescence was filtered through frosted glass. In that mirror, in that light, we looked like memories, as if even the present were not quite ours. It made me fairly frantic to grasp hold of what was loved and, digging in my heels, to struggle against the natural reeling-out of time. I resisted the moment when Jamie must get up from the table, take up the folded evening paper, and settle with it into the soft dark arms of his chair. How could one know with certainty that he would smile, laugh, kiss on another evening in just that perfect way?

Mother was in the kitchen cleaning up. After that, she would be in the guest bedroom reading or embroidering or working crossword puzzles or listening to the radio or cutting recipes from magazines. From this distance of years I'd begun to understand or, more accurately, to guess at the nature of her remoteness. Shutting herself off from us was a form of penance. As a small child I'd felt to blame for her misery. When gradually it became apparent that, do what I might, her condition was irremedial, my feelings turned to resentment. No child can endure knowing that she's incapable of making her parent happy. It is the ultimate failure.

The door to the workroom opened and Gerald Sperling's monumental middle thrust into the office. Humpty Dumpty, I thought. But if Gerald Sperling fell off a wall, he would merely collapse on the cobblestones with a muffled "flump." He was of medium height and must have weighed nearly three hundred pounds. It was difficult to estimate precisely, since he wore a kind of loose-fitting smock, which extended to his knees. The smock, I learned, was his uniform. He had them custom-tailored in various fabrics, from expensive Scottish woolens for winter, to lightweight seersucker and sharkskin for summer. They were worn as a suit jacket, with a dress shirt and tie. That day a tan-striped seersucker smock tented his bulk above tan twill trousers. So small were his feet, he looked like a tethered balloon.

"L. Demming?" That was the way I signed my canvases. He glided into the room and past me, seating himself opposite me behind an enormous piece of Jacobean furniture, which I hesitate to call a desk. It seemed more like a sovereign state. "What have you brought, L. Demming, to tempt, tease, or transport me?"

I took the framed work and arranged it here and there in the room, leaning pictures against furniture and walls. As I began to unpack the first of the two portfolios, Sperling threw up a hand.

"Wait, wait. Let me look at these first." He rose easily from his chair and began circumnavigating the room, pausing now and again to study a painting, returning once or twice to review one he'd already seen, sweeping suddenly across the office, and wheeling dramatically to observe a canvas from a distance. He said nothing, nor did he reveal anything by his face. When he'd thoroughly studied what I'd presented, he picked up one of the portfolios, tossing it on the immense Jacobean table and, without glancing at me, suggested, "You might like to look around the gallery while I take my time with these."

I was glad to be released. It was unnerving to sit by, watching the dealer appraise the pictures. I felt protective, defensive, and not a little hostile, like the mother of a misconceived but obstinately adored monster. My progress through the gallery was reluctant and distracted, however, since once I was out of Sperling's office, I wanted to be back, detecting in each tilt of his head, each light or heavy breath, the critical, quite likely contemptuous, thought behind it. The suspense was like holding my breath and I lasted only ten minutes.

When I reentered the office he inquired without looking up, "What do you think about when you paint, L. Demming?" The watercolor before him on the desk was of Belle Riviere and the woods, late on a summer afternoon, the sunlight a golden veil thrown over the trees.

"Anything. Nothing. My grocery list. The stain on the living room sofa." I slipped down onto the chair in front of his desk.

"I think you frighten me," he went on, ignoring my empty response.

I could only assume he was being facetious or sardonic in some way I didn't comprehend. Nonetheless, misgivings now skittered around my brain pan like mice in the attic. I felt myself to be scrutinized. I sat straighter and made my hands lie sleeping and graceful in my lap, so that when he looked up I might appear tranquil and limpid.

Straightening abruptly, as if to catch me in a private lapse, he interrogated, "What is it you're guarding so jealously?"

"My privacy, perhaps."

"Then you're surely in the wrong business."

"I'm not in any business. I'm not asking to have my paintings shown."

"Aren't you." This last was not quite a question. "In this painting," he continued, referring to the one on his desk, "the brilliant light is guarding the dark, don't you see? And in this one..." He moved away from the desk to an oil leaning against open shelves. "In this one, the woods themselves are guarding something." He swung slowly about. "What a state of siege you must live in, L. Demming."

34

"Aren't you happy?" Sarah asked. "You don't seem very excited."

"I don't know."

"Don't you like him—Sperling?"

"He doesn't invite liking. He's..." I tried to think what he was. "He's a connoisseur, a critic, a judge, an observer, and a self-styled psychoanalyst. One minute he gives an impression of godlike detachment and the next, impertinent curiosity. He reminds me of a priest I knew when I was a child, Father White. English extraction— a mistake in a priest. He was clinical and finical. He dealt with me as if I were a particularly unyielding Sunday *Times* crossword and he the instrument chosen by God to 'crack' me. People like that create puzzles where none exist. Father White made me feel fraudulent. I couldn't find anything that answered his curiosity and I feared breaking the Eleventh Commandment: Thou Shalt Not Disappoint. So I stopped going to his confessional and as soon as I could I slipped away from the Church altogether."

"I didn't know you'd been a Catholic."

"My mother was a convert and obliged to raise me Catholic."
I rose from the Queen Anne wing chair and headed for a butler's
table where several liquor decanters wearing sterling silver identification bracelets stood prim as palace guards. "May I pour a shot
of gin?"

"Would you like ice?"

"Please."

She returned from the kitchen with a tray of cubes and trans-
ferred them to the silver-plated bucket beside the decanters. Ignoring the silver tongs, I dipped a hand into the bucket and withdrew
several cubes. "I may be dramatizing what happened at Sperling's
gallery, but I have the uncomfortable feeling that he's seeing things
in my work that just aren't there. If that's the case, eventually he'll
be disillusioned. It would be so much better if he saw me as a dull,
middle-aged landscape artist of moderate technical skill."

"I'd love it if people thought I was mysterious."

"If people expect mystery," I told her without turning around,
"eventually there has to be a payoff, something must happen to
satisfy the supposition, otherwise they end up feeling taken and
put-out."

"Well, mystery or no mystery, Sperling wants to show your
work. You have to be pleased at that."

"I am flattered." I walked slowly around the pleasant, orderly
room, trying to anchor myself to it and keep from floating away
into doubt.

"And he said he might give you a one-woman show," she reminded me.

"Yes."

"Don't you feel a little thrilled?"

I had been thrilled for a moment. Then I'd reminded myself
that if one were the darling, one could soon be the spurned. It was
one thing to have a small, local reputation along Belle Riviere, and
another to satisfy the expectations of the Gerald Sperlings of this
world, the professional knowers.

"I shouldn't have brought my bad mood over here," I apologized.

"You're feeling vulnerable because you don't know what to
expect. It's perfectly reasonable. It's the down side of up."

Plain and perfect as a tulip, my daughter-in-law sat calmly
treating my discontent and uncertainty. I'd called her immediately

upon leaving Homestead Gallery. Clark was working late and wouldn't be home until nine. It was Sarah's kindliness and simplicity I'd sought and I'd driven directly to their home.

"What a good mother you'll be."

"Let me fix you something to eat," she said, ignoring the compliment.

"No, really, I can't stay. I should get back to the river tonight. But you need to eat so I'll leave soon."

I wanted to remain in her quiet realm of gentle reason, but I wanted also to run away from Gerald Sperling, to put distance between me and the gallery and the need to make a decision about them. I finished the drink and set the glass on the butler's table.

"I'll let you know what I decide," I told her. "Don't get up, dear heart. Give Clark my love and tell him I'm sorry I missed him."

It was only seven, still light as day when I left Sarah. Anxious to reach the highway and put my foot down firmly on the accelerator, I didn't linger in town for dinner. I sought space. I wished to turn the car west instead of north, and drive until I was surrounded by emptiness.

That was how Jamie and I had felt when we drove across the country after my mother's death. We seemed to be chasing space, vastnesses empty of personal identification, places where we could find disencumbrance in anonymity. And we did find it, the disencumbrance, in many places.

The first night out of Minneapolis we had camped in the Badlands in South Dakota. How I had loved its wildness, its absolutely impersonal and evenhanded menace. The place was alive with gods and ghosts, but we were not their especial target. They crouched and hovered and drew themselves up behind peaks and pinnacles and looked out of their great, sleeping grief and now and then sighed, having waited so long for the sign that would rally them to vengeance. Anyone who slept out on the Badlands, and doubted that one day these spirits must be taken account of, was blind and deaf.

We spent a couple of days and nights in the Badlands and then headed south into the tableland of Nebraska. The day we stayed at Kizer's Kabin Kourt on the ragged hem of Hester, Nebraska, was the rare instance of our feeling dogged by my mother's Calvinist shadow. Jamie and I were running away from her, though we never spoke that way, and only in that one place, Hester, did she catch up with us.

Kizer's Kabin Kourt *looked* like a good place to be. It stood in a sheltering tent of giant elms, with here and there a nervous poplar shaking itself and rattling dryly at the least provocation. Built of smooth logs and painted a dark, lustrous green, the eight little cabins and a slightly larger one that was the office were pulled into a rough circle like wagons.

It was night, maybe ten o'clock or so, when we came upon the sign: KIZER'S KABIN KOURT, REASONABLE RATES DAY OR WEEK, KLEAN. The wooden sign was lit from above by a single large bulb, beneath which moths fluttered in great numbers. Except for another bare bulb outside the office, the grove was dark and quiet when we turned off the highway and into the graveled drive.

Jamie knocked at the office door and a moment later knocked again. At this a male voice, raspy with sleep, came to us from the dark depths of the still cabin.

"All right. All right." The door was opened and beyond the screen we perceived the dim form of a man in dark trousers and undershirt, who stood fussing with his left suspender. He twisted an electric switch by the door and several small yard lights blinked on. The man, presumably Mr. Kizer, peered at us and at the car behind us.

"I want a cabin for myself and my daughter," Jamie told him.

"Number three has twin beds," Kizer said, reaching for a key from somewhere just inside the door. Pushing the screen open, he handed the key to Jamie. "It's ten dollars. We'll settle in the morning."

We drove around the graveled circle to number 3, standing opposite the office, across a grassy verge. When he knew us to be in our cabin and the door closed behind us, Kizer turned out the yard lights.

There was a single bulb of maybe forty watts hanging from a cord in the middle of the room. A dimestore shade had been fastened over it in a makeshift way, so that the room was washed by muddy light. We looked like swimmers moving through turbid water.

Directly across the room from the door was an old painted bureau—who knew what color in this light? The flaking, spidery mirror above it gave the startling effect of revealing two other people entering from the opposite side of the room. Jamie and I recoiled when they spied us.

To our left was a small open closet with several wire hangers on a thick wooden pole, and next to the closet a dark bathroom, its linoleum rough and cracked like old glue. The two beds, their heads against the wall to the right, were tubular steel, brown like wood, but shiny and cold. Beside them were two windows draped with floral plastic curtains.

I set my bag on the farther bed and hurried to open the windows. Thick, fragrant night air rolled in, shifting the curtains and causing them to crackle and hiss like crisp newspaper pages being shaken and turned.

I faced around and caught Jamie's glance in the mirror. He was standing in front of the bureau laying out the contents of his toilet case. He smiled broadly and I smiled back. I began to laugh and I bounced on top of the bed and sat, legs hanging over the side, bouncing and laughing uncontrollably. The old metal bedspring screamed like a termagant. Now Jamie laughed. He stopped short, gazed about the room, began abruptly to laugh again, throwing his head back and letting all the stops out. Finally, he staggered, helpless, to the other bed and bounced onto it. There we sat facing each other, bouncing and laughing, tears on our faces. The sharp edge of raucous bedsprings and abandoned laughter sliced through the soft Nebraska night.

It could not have been much past ten-thirty when we turned out the light. I was awake at dawn. A breeze was snatching at the plastic drapery, making a sound like gull wings clacking against heavy air. I slipped stealthily from bed—as stealthily as one could from a bed whose springs cried out painfully at every slight pressure—and tucked the flapping ends of the long curtains out of the way behind the headboards.

There was a single straight-back chair against the wall between the two beds. I sat down for a few minutes to watch Jamie sleep. His great long body looked like a rugged landscape beneath the sheet. It lay peaceful as old mountains, very different from the first weeks after the funeral. Then sleep had been a continuous raging battle full of awful woundings and losses. Even upstairs in my room I could hear him cry out and I took to sleeping on the sofa as if he were a sick child. He didn't know I was there at first.

When he woke himself with his own crying, he'd haul out of bed and roam the back rooms of the house, the kitchen and breakfast room and even the sun porch, which was closed off in winter and unheated. It was March when my mother died and the porch was cold and bleak as Purgatory. Sometimes he would sit there in the dark for an hour or more. I hesitated to intrude, but I was afraid he might freeze or catch pneumonia, so one night I brought a wool blanket and tea.

He was sitting and staring and his skin was cold as stone. He couldn't hold the cup at first and I held it for him as if he were an infant being weaned. He trembled terribly and I put an arm around him to steady him. He turned away from the cup and clung hard to me, discovering at last how cold he had been.

Watching him now, I warmed to see how indulgently sleep lay on him and how he smiled at her.

Pulling on a pair of shorts and a shirt, I let myself out. The leaves on the poplars were shiny as glass and they switched ceaselessly. I walked around the circle of cabins, noticing for the first time a car parked on the far side of the cabin nearest ours. It was an old black prewar Mercury sedan, looking like a big black snail. Had that been there last night or did someone arrive after us?

Aside from the office, only one other cabin had a car. A white Fleetwood with dozens of travel stickers on the windows was pulled up close to the front door of the last cabin before the highway.

Hands thrust deep into the pockets of my shorts, I walked through the wet grass, circling the car slowly to read the many stickers. The Cadillac had been to the Everglades and Our Nation's Capital and Plymouth Rock and Niagara Falls and Yosemite Park and Carlsbad Caverns and many other wondrous-sounding places.

A grandmotherly woman in a blue chenille robe appeared at the cabin door. "Do you like our stickers? You might wonder what'll happen when we trade for a new car. Well, Herb has another set of stickers—he bought two each place we visited—and he's going to put them on the new one when we get it. I think that was using his noodle, don't you?"

I asked her about some of the places they'd been. She was friendly and open as a best-loved child. "If you'd like to play gin rummy later, come on back," she called as I headed toward the highway.

Kizer's Kabin Kourt was half a mile out of Hester, and halfway between Kizer's and the town was the Big Time, a truck stop and gas station with an enormous dead clock swinging from a twenty-foot standard near the road. I walked as far as the café, checked the menu, and turned back toward the cabin court, this time cutting across a field of timothy grass and through the grove of elms and poplars surrounding the cabins.

Approaching this way took me again past the cabin next to ours where the faded black Mercury was parked. I was startled to see a towheaded youth sitting on the single wooden step before the door. He had on a pair of dark, tweedy-gray corduroys and a white shirt which was too big for him. He was about my own age, and while his features were regular, something about him made me want to look away.

His hair was pale as homemade butter and his skin was lighter than that, as if he'd been out of the sun a long time. Expressionless, he watched me coming down the rutted gravel lane. I tried to look at everything but him until I'd drawn alongside. Then I cast him a glance, a nearly imperceptible nod, and a tentative smile.

He struck me with a look of such cold and righteous denunciation, it fairly blinded me. He had saved it until I was close so that I might receive the full force of his cruelty. I stumbled along the remaining distance to my own door.

I didn't tell Jamie. What would have been the point? He was up and dressed when I came in.

"Walking?"

"Yes. I just want to wash my face," I told him, going straight for the bathroom and closing the door. "And then we can go eat," I called, trying to sound hungry. I ran water and wet a thin, faded washcloth hanging above the sink. Sitting on the edge of the tub I held the cool cloth to my burning face. The water from the tap was cold even in midsummer. It must be from a deep well. I wrung the cloth out again. "I found a place to eat, up the road. The Big Time. That's what it's called. They have Swedish pancakes." I'd said the last before I thought.

Swedish pancakes had been a specialty of my mother's. Delicate and pale like her, the pancakes had been a treat she made us at holidays. Swedish pancakes with lingonberry jam. We used to ask for them frequently, but she saved them just for holidays. When she made them she was both pleased by the compliments and saddened by the associations. They were part of the Swedish background from which she'd been severed.

I wondered then why she cared so much. If the Andersons could be that cold and implacable, why did she yearn for them? And if she yearned so unrelievedly, why had she left them in the first place? Jamie and I should be enough for her, I thought. What was wrong with me that she took so little pleasure in me? Jamie was the instrument of her fall from family grace. Not I.

I hung the cloth on the rack. I wished that I hadn't mentioned Swedish pancakes.

"Ready for a big breakfast?" Jamie asked, his face bright and unclouded. "You must be hungry after your walk."

"Starved." I took his hand. Maybe the indirect reference to my mother had gone by him.

When we stepped out of the cabin, the boy was sitting on the grassy circle between us and the office. Jamie went across to "settle up" with Mr. Kizer, lest he think we were taking a powder. I rolled down all the car windows and slid into the front seat to wait. I didn't look at the boy but I knew that he was still sitting on the grass, knees drawn up and arms locked around them. He was staring at me, willing me to look at him.

I wouldn't turn my head, even though I was curious in a morbid way to see if he was screwed up to the same pitch of revulsion and condemnation as earlier. Jamie stood for a moment outside the car, studying a road map. Folding it, he tossed it into the back seat. As we neared the highway, I looked back. From this distance the boy's face would be indistinct. He was watching us drive out. Hair, face, and shirt all blanched, he was a ghostly figure in gray trousers.

We spent the hot middle of the day driving aimlessly through the countryside, fresh fruit, hard rolls, and bottles of pop in a grocery bag on the seat. We followed creek beds and wagon trails. Thousands of prairie schooners had rolled west through Nebraska, etching lines that a hundred years could not erase.

Jamie and I hardly spoke. When we did it was mostly nonsense. Our spirits were awed and cowed by the space and the loneliness and by the phantoms who filled it. We drove out to see Scott's Bluff, a landmark for pioneers heading west on the Oregon Trail. When they caught sight of it, they knew exactly where they were.

It was past five when we turned again into the drive of Kizer's Kabin Kourt. We'd been singing "Across the Wide Missouri" (which we were), and "Sweet Betsy from Pike," and we were started on "Big Rock Candy Mountain." I waved to the lady of the Fleetwood, who was walking a cocker spaniel among the trees.

"There's a tire swing down there behind those end cabins. I saw it this morning. I'm going to go have a swing," I told Jamie.

We left the car beside our cabin and strolled down the rutted lane to its farthest turning. "See there, Jamie?" I pointed to one of the tallest elms. The bottom-most branches were high up. To one of these a thick rope was secured and from it swung an old rubber tire, twisting ever so slightly in the breeze.

I settled myself in the swing and Jamie gave it a push. He kept it going, higher and higher. The arc was great owing to the height of the branch, and I was frightened at either end of it, but I wouldn't for the world have told him. "Higher, Jamie!" I called and laughed to cover my fear.

At last he let the swing die down. "Are you tired? Would you like a nap before dinner?" he asked, giving me a hand.

"If you would, yes. And I could use a bath. Godalmighty, I'm dusty."

As we started away, behind us an owl gave a soft, early-evening hoot and I swung around to look. There, beyond the swing, was the boy. He must have come up behind while I was laughing and squealing. He didn't give way. He wasn't unnerved at being caught spying. His eyes, hot as brimstone, were fastened on me and they didn't waver. The white dress shirt hung from his bony chest and shoulders as if a skeleton were holding it up.

I backed away, hollowed by fear and guilt. Jamie reached for me as I caught my foot in a Virginia creeper vine.

"Careful."

I fell against him and held tightly to his arm, scarcely able to stand. He gave me a quick, narrowed glance. "That boy is sweet on you, Larissa."

When we returned to the cabin court after a nearly wordless dinner at the Big Time, it was late twilight, still lavenderish but barely so. The outdoor lights weren't yet turned on. Thin yellow showed through the windows of the Fleetwood cabin. Everywhere else it was dark. There was no sign of life next door, though the black hulk of the Mercury was discernible in the deepening shadows.

"I feel like driving," Jamie told me as he pulled the car up close to our door. Cutting the engine, he sat with his hands on the steering wheel. "Would you mind if we packed up and left tonight?"

Although Kizer's Kabin Kourt with its towering elms and homely little cabins had looked like a good place to be, it had turned out otherwise. My mother had cast her pall like a net and caught us there, caught us in Hester, Nebraska, in the deathly features of a boy.

That night we drove to Laramie, Wyoming. Laramie was beyond my mother's reach. In a land of sun, dry space, and leather faces, we left her tangled net behind and lived together on the simplest terms, abandoning memories and questions for plain kindness and love, unexamined and unmeasured.

35

Crying, I reached across the seat for my bag and pulled a Kleenex from it. I knew a rest stop waited a mile ahead. There was no hurry to reach Belle Riviere.

For years I'd shut Jamie out of my thoughts. Only if his name was spoken, and that happened rarely, or one of his postcards arrived, another infrequent occasion, would his image be allowed into my daytime mind. When the postcard was put away or the conversation passed to other matters, I shut him out.

But this summer I had little control over what went in or out of my mind. I fell into great, long reveries, like tonight's of traveling with Jamie, and emerged shaken, crying, "My God, how did that happen?" More and more my mind was a companion with whom I was constantly at odds.

The rest stop was empty of cars. I parked, got out, and headed for the rest room. When I'd splashed with cool water, dried off, and applied fresh lipstick, I left, turning the light off behind me. Rather than sit on the damp grass, I would rest in the car before continuing on. Tuning the radio to slick, wordless music, I sat, eyes closed, with the windows rolled down.

The face that rose like a moon behind my eyes was my mother's. It had been a face closed off, except for the eyes, which spoke a great deal but always a language so uncompromisingly her own that I couldn't understand.

She did not set herself to be enigmatic. That would have gone against her upbringing. She set herself instead to be unadulterated by popish Irish influences. Though her family had given her up, she remained stubbornly loyal to the character and values of the Andersons. Their way was reassuringly strict, blessedly unequivocal. One knew what was *right*.

Contrast that to the quicksilver nature of Catholicism as she perceived it. Why, being a Catholic was like having a tricky lawyer. You could always find a way around the law. The Church could "get you off" if you knew the ways. It was big and showy but it wasn't solid. More like an art form than a religion. At bottom there was something rather wicked about it, wasn't there?

Yes, she married Jamie and married him in the Church, a course I don't believe he demanded. As a child I had never thought to press for details of my parents' marriage. As an adolescent I had intuited the hazard, but at some indistinct turning I had concluded that my mother had been pregnant with me when she married, that she'd "had to" marry Jamie. Marrying in the Catholic Church was an ongoing self-punishment, a lifetime reminder of one's weakness and folly. She was trying to square things with her own intractable God.

They slept in the same bed. There was sexual accommodation of some sort, because she became pregnant again when I was eight.

Mother had been "sick" for several weeks. I thought it was the flu, or the grippe as she called it. Hadn't I had it myself only a month earlier and been kept home from school a week? That had been late in March when everyone got sick from boredom and stayed home to find the strength to get through till spring. On the calendar, spring comes March 21. In Minnesota it comes when it damned pleases but never as early as March.

It was nearly the end of April when I learned that Mother didn't have the flu. The doctor had been to the house once, and Mother had subsequently gone to his office. Jamie hired a Mrs. Hayes to come in and do for us, and Mother stayed in bed. I thought it odd that the longer Mother was in bed, the cheerier Jamie grew. He and Mrs. Hayes had some secret between them and it had to do with Mother's illness. It was confusing. None of us had ever before stayed in bed a month. Surely it had to be serious, possibly fatal. Then how could Jamie and Mrs. Hayes be so pleased, unless of course Mrs. Hayes had persuaded Jamie to marry her when Mother was dead!

From the beginning I hadn't liked the idea of having Mrs. Hayes around, although admittedly there was more work to be done than I could do. I detested the way the woman mothered Jamie and treated me like a child. And Jamie in his high spirits flirted shamelessly with her, putting on his brogue and chucking her chin. The latter was so obscene it made me flinch.

Although Mrs. Hayes was always offering to play Monopoly or Authors, I preferred to be alone. To allow her friendship would have been a disloyalty to Mother and an encouragement to Jamie to carry forward plans to remarry.

April that year was chill and melancholy. Thawing began late and the ground was mushy with cold runoff that oozed around and into shoes, then socks, turning your feet white with cold because you'd forgotten your rubber boots at school. The sun shone bravely but could never quite get the upper hand. Winter still won in the shadows and in the wicked little winds that snapped at your flanks like a small, mean dog.

After school I stayed out in the backyard, although I was cold. I put my books down on the back porch steps and went to play in the muddy puddles around the garage and in the alleyway where there was always a gathering of sparrows, the cheerful lower class of bird society. Sometimes, I sat on the back steps waiting to see an early robin. Spying one, you must quickly pull off your mittens, wet your right thumb on your tongue, touch it to the palm of your left hand, then make a fist of your right hand and hit it smartly against your left palm. If you did all this before the robin flew away, it was good luck.

I was looking for as much good luck as I could find. With a mother who was probably dying and a father who was being led down the path by a hired woman, my only friend was luck, if I could find some. During that bleak April I became so accustomed to this line of worry and self-pity that the truth, when it came, took days to absorb.

I was sitting on the back steps watching for robins. It was getting near dinnertime. Mrs. Hayes had tried earlier to lure me into the kitchen with freshly baked peanut butter cookies, but she was mightily fooled if she thought I could be so easily won. I would rather be hungry and cold than betray Mother and yield Jamie to her.

The back door opened. Assuming it to be Mrs. Hayes, come

to tempt me again, I continued to stare into the yard. Jamie sat down beside me and seeing how I was huddled, put his arm around me and drew me close.

"Have you been worried about your mother?"

I nodded.

"Mrs. Hayes said you were."

"How did she know?"

"Just guessed, maybe. She's a kindly person." He gave me a squeeze. "I should have explained what was happening, but I've been busy and let things ride longer than I ought."

"What's wrong with Mommy? What's she got?"

"She's pregnant. She's going to have a baby. Some women get pretty sick in the first couple of months, but she'll soon be past the worst of it." He went on talking, explaining, sharing his warm hope, but I couldn't hear.

A baby. It was worse than I'd imagined. There was only love enough for *one* child and I was that child.

I had but brief, strained moments with my mother during that time. Even if she'd been a gregarious woman, she was too wretched and weak to endure much company. Mrs. Hayes came and went, carrying trays of pale nourishment, like broth and soda crackers, tea and dry toast. Now and then she told me I could "look in" for a minute.

"Tell your mother about all the pretty May baskets you got and how your papa took you around in the car to deliver the ones we made."

And so I would sit on Mother's dressing-table bench for a few minutes while she, preoccupied with nausea, lay limp against her pillows staring through me.

"Mrs. Hayes and I made May baskets from paper cups and tissue paper. We filled them with cookies and jelly beans. Daddy and I delivered them after school. Daddy took me in the car. We delivered twenty-one baskets. One to Miss Huber at her apartment. I'm such a fast runner, I ran away before anyone but Miss Huber could catch me."

Mother looked quizzical or maybe she was having a bad moment.

"You know, if they catch you, they get to kiss you. Well, they didn't catch *me!*" I started to laugh but caught myself. It didn't seem right to laugh if she was about to vomit.

Mother's cream-colored hair was pulled back with an uncharacteristic pink ribbon. Mrs. Hayes's work, I thought. Her pale face was flushed and very beautiful in illness. As I rose to leave, she grasped my hand and held it tightly, closing her eyes. Then, without opening her eyes, she set my hand deliberately aside as if she were angry. Never bantering or gay, she was now hot and sullen and under a new duress. It didn't seem to me that she was very happy to be having a baby. Could it be she didn't want it?

Well, Jamie certainly did. He had fastened extravagant hopes on this baby's coming. He believed, I surmise, that no one had ever taught my mother tenderness. About this he was probably correct. He imagined further that he and I would create a surround of tenderness in which mother and baby would flourish, warm and rosy. In this featherbed of fond care, Mother would by degrees soften, grow lenient and easy.

His desire had put him out of touch with hard reality. Mother didn't want to change. Happiness would cut short her penance and prove her unworthy of her cold, distant heaven. Jamie could only have satisfied her spirit by turning away, disdainful, dour, and blaming. Even if he'd understood this, he wasn't prepared to do it.

At the close of a blue-and-yellow day in early May, Jamie stopped at the florist on the way home. Springing up the steps and into the hall, he extended to the raw-boned and perpetually rubicund Mrs. Hayes a bouquet of pink carnations and baby's breath.

"For the angel sent to make us fat and jolly." He gave a deep bow.

Laughing and curtsying, she took the flowers. Then, suddenly, she pulled a handkerchief from the pocket of her apron and put it to the corner of her eye. "Thank you, Mr. McClanahan. You're a good man and a genuine fool, the Lord knows."

There was another bouquet, this one of yellow roses, for Mother. He set them on the hall table and unwrapped a single red rose rolled in tissue paper. Breaking the stem short, he fastened the flower in my black hair. "Larissa, mavourneen." He held me by my shoulders. "Mavourneen," he repeated. Then straightening, he inquired of Mrs. Hayes, "Is that pork roast I smell? I'll just take these flowers in to Marie and see how my girl is."

"I'll get a vase," Mrs. Hayes offered, striding away toward the kitchen.

There was roast pork with browned potatoes and carrots, spicy applesauce, cole slaw, and, for dessert, tiny cream puffs drizzled with chocolate. Mrs. Hayes's bouquet, arranged in a milk-glass vase with a piece of ribbon tied around the rim, was in the middle of the dinner table and the meal was festive and noisy.

Mrs. Hayes and I had gotten rather chummy since I'd learned that she wouldn't be marrying Jamie. She was robust and open-hearted and I liked to pretend that she was my aunt.

Jamie insisted on helping with dishes that night. He wiped while Mrs. Hayes washed, and I put away. We got to singing songs we all knew and when we turned out the kitchen light, Jamie pushed the dining room table against the wall, rolled the carpet back, and put a record on the phonograph. I don't remember what it was but it was lively and had a lot of trumpet and trombone. He took turns dancing with me and Mrs. Hayes.

He'd removed his suit jacket before dinner. Now he loosened his tie and rolled up his sleeves. His color was high and as he whirled, a lock of dark hair fell across his forehead. He looked nineteen.

"Wait'll Ginger Rogers sees Mr. McClanahan," Mrs. Hayes called as Jamie lifted me and twirled me off the floor. "Fred Astaire will be looking for work."

"James! Please!" It was my mother, standing at the doorway.

Mrs. Hayes ran to the phonograph and lifted the needle as Jamie rushed to my mother. There was blood on her feet and on the floor and as Jamie lifted her I saw that the back of her pink gown was drenched in dark blood.

The new baby was no more. With the passing of that hope, Jamie turned away from my mother as he had never done in the many disappointing years before. Though he didn't say as much, he seemed to blame her for the miscarriage. She accepted his resentment with equanimity. He had at last played into her unhappy needs.

When Mother came home from the hospital, Mrs. Hayes stayed on another two months while the patient got her strength back. Although Mother assured Jamie she could get along fine, he insisted the housekeeper remain. I don't think he could face coming home evenings without Mrs. Hayes's strong, positive face to greet him.

Her "two motherless children" is the way Mrs. Hayes referred to Jamie and my mother one afternoon. And indeed they were a strange, beautiful, despairing couple. Mrs. Hayes and I were sitting in the kitchen at the table after I'd come home from school. I was telling her about Jamie's parents, who had died of influenza in Baltimore when he was a year old. A great-uncle and his wife brought little James to Minneapolis and raised him as their only child. But they had been a good deal older than his own mother and father, and both adoptive parents passed away before Jamie met my mother.

"And your mama's family?" she asked.

"They've turned their backs." I savored the drama of the phrase, picturing two silent figures dressed in black, turning narrow, disapproving backs and walking slowly away.

"Your mama said that?"

I nodded, dunking a cookie into the weak tea and milk Mrs. Hayes allowed me for a treat.

"Poor thing." Elbows on the table, she held her cup between both hands. "Where do they live?"

"St. Cloud."

"That close. A shame." She sighed heavily.

Before Mrs. Hayes left us in mid-July, she sat me down one day in the backyard, where I had wandered to watch her hang clothes. Glancing up at the house, to be certain Mother wasn't at the window, she took my hand and led me to an old bench by the garage.

"You are a big strong girl," she told me, "and I like you."

It made me feel important to hear that she liked me. I looked straight at her and listened hard.

"You mustn't get discouraged by your mama's sadness. She can't help it." She tucked a strand of hair into the big, loopy bun on the back of her head. "*You* have to be your papa's cheer." She gave me a long, keen look. "You understand, don't you?"

I was glad that there were two of us who understood.

Six months later, after I'd turned nine, after Christmas vacation had come and gone and I was back in school, Jamie sat down on the bed beside me one evening as he was preparing to say goodnight.

"Mrs. Hayes is dead," he said dully.

"No." I started to cry. "No. Don't say that. I don't want you to say that."

"I'm sorry." He held me while I cried and told me that she had died in a car accident. She hadn't suffered, he said. Later, he went to get a cold cloth to wipe my face and I saw that he was crying.

Returning, he sat down again and, gently wiping my face, he said, "I never thought life would be like this, mavourneen."

I put my arms around his neck. I would be his cheer.

36

"Ma'am?"

The female voice was soft and hesitant, but I jumped, startled from my near drowse.

"Ma'am? I'm sorry to scare you."

"It's all right. I didn't hear you coming...I didn't hear a car."

"I don't have a car. I was just sitting over there beyond the rest rooms."

There was still light, but it was dying. It must be past eight-thirty. The woman standing beside the Volvo was in shadow and it was difficult to judge her age. From the voice I assumed she was between twenty-five and thirty-five. It was a sweet voice, but filled with anxiety.

"Are you driving north?" she asked.

"Yes, but not far. Only to Belleville. Do you need a ride? Where are you going?"

"Duluth. But I could ride as far as Belleville. Anything's better than being stuck here. It doesn't look like anybody's going to stay here tonight—you know, any tourists or anything—and I don't want to stay out here alone. It's spooky with no one around." She added, "I don't want to stand out there on the road and thumb tonight." She seemed to shrink almost physically from the prospect.

"Do you have a bag?"

"Nothing."

"Well, get in. I'll take you as far as Belleville."

Indeed, she had no baggage, not even a purse. That was odd, but at least she wasn't carrying a weapon. She opened the car door and slid in gingerly, her breath catching. The interior light revealed an unhappy darkness on her left cheek and over it the shine of swelling.

"You've been hurt," I said quickly. "What happened?"

"I'll be all right," she promised, frightened that I might after all decide to leave her in the darkening park. She forced a smile. "Honest. I'll be all right. And I'm not an addict or a maniac or something like that."

"No, of course you aren't." I started the car, turned around, and drove out to the highway. I was intuitively so certain she wasn't an addict or maniac, it was shocking to hear her even deny it. "I'm Larissa Demming, more often called Larry."

"I'm Hildy. Hildy Smith. Smith's my real name. I'm not making it up."

"Where are you from?"

"Denver."

"You're a long way from home."

"Yeah, well, I'm not sure it's home anymore."

"What does that mean?"

"Before I came out here, I lost just about everything I had in a fire. The apartment building where I was living burned down. Did it ever! I'm a cocktail waitress by trade. I'm good and I make decent money, but when you lose all your clothes and *everything,* you know, like your sheets and dishes and even your toothpaste, you are in trouble."

"Didn't you have any insurance?"

"Not a nickel. That was stupid, I know, but I never dreamed. I figured sometime the TV or stereo would get ripped off, but a fire? I didn't think of it."

She shifted position, moving tentatively, but hurrying on with the narrative, not wanting to call attention to her pain. "A girlfriend let me move in with her temporarily, but then I got word that my kid brother was killed in St. Paul. Piled his car up on a bridge and they were holding his body. If I didn't come get him, the city would bury him. Maybe I should have let them, I don't know. Eddie, that was my brother, he would have told me to save my money, but save it for what? He was the last relative I had that I know of, so I sold my car and flew out here to take care of him."

I grew increasingly uneasy. Her story tumbled out with a headlong impetus that seemed unnatural, as if she'd lost control of words.

"The thing was," she rushed on, "I didn't have enough money to get back to Denver. I tried a few places to get a job, but they weren't hiring just now or they wanted a deposit for the uniforms, you know. And then I met this guy who said he was driving to the Coast and for certain considerations I could go along as far as Denver. Well, that sounded about as fair as I could ask, under the circumstances. But he said he had a couple of days' business to finish before we started, so I stayed with him at his motel. I didn't mind as long as I got back to Denver."

She stared ahead as she spoke, embarrassed, I think, yet compelled by some shock. "We checked out of the motel Sunday and started driving south because he wanted to connect up with Interstate 80 in Iowa. We stopped for lunch in a place called Owatonna. I ordered fried chicken. He got up to go out to the car and get his reading glasses, which he needed to read the menu, even though I said I'd be happy to read it to him. And that's the last I saw of him." She added tonelessly, "And I'd given him two of the sweetest days and nights he'll ever have, the ungrateful sonofabitch.

"The woman who owned the place was a real pissant. I offered to work off the bill but she was going to call the cops. There were three guys in the next booth having lunch, and one of them came over and said he'd pay for the chicken if I'd join them. God, I was so relieved. I've never been in jail.

"The guy who invited me to eat with them said he'd make some phone calls to see if he could get me work. He said the three of them worked for a construction crew and he thought the boss was looking for someone to do simple office work, nothing real complicated. I rode with them out in the country, where they said the office trailer was parked by the construction site. Sure enough, there was a construction project, all right, and a trailer that said Hoenig Construction. They drove around to the far side of the trailer and parked.

"There wasn't anyone else around and no one could see us from the highway. I'm so stupid, really stupid. They didn't work for a construction company, not *that* one anyway. Oh, God." She whimpered just once, almost inaudibly. It was more alarming than a cry. "I screamed and tried to run, but no one could hear and I couldn't get away from three of them. For a couple of hours or so they kept me there, holding me down and taking turns."

She was silent. Tears slipped down her face and she caught them with the tips of her fingers, because her cheeks were painful.

I reached into the bag beside me on the seat, pulled out a packet of Kleenex, and handed it to her.

At that moment I felt as related to Hildy as to my own children. Finally, I asked, "Did you go to the police?"

She shook her head. "They said if I did, they'd tell the cops I'd been hustling them. I haven't got any money or job. Who would the cops believe when they heard I'd been dumped there by a stranger I'd been shacked up with for two days? I'd end up in jail for vagrancy and prostitution, you can bet on it."

"Where have you been since Sunday?" Owatonna was only a couple of hundred miles away.

"I couldn't move when they left me. I slept beside the trailer. I thought about breaking a window and sleeping inside but I couldn't stand up long enough. I kept falling asleep or fainting or something and then coming to. And I was dreaming. I dreamed I broke into the trailer. When the foreman came in the morning, I was sort of off my head, and I kept apologizing for breaking in.

"He thought my boyfriend had beaten me up and left me. He drove me to a truck stop, where I could thumb back to Minneapolis, and he bought me breakfast. I cleaned myself up the best I could in the rest room. When I looked in the mirror, I swear I thought it was someone else. My face..." She put a hand lightly to her cheek. "After my food came, he left, but he gave me a five-dollar bill. That was nice, wasn't it?"

She rested a moment. "A truck driver gave me a ride to Shakopee. But getting a ride from there into Minneapolis was damned near impossible. I didn't look like somebody you'd want to pick up, you know. I must have walked half the way. A couple of high school kids finally gave me a ride into town to a place called Lake... Lake ... I forget. It started with a C."

"Lake Calhoun?"

"Yes. Calhoun. That was it. It was almost dark. I got a sandwich and then I walked around the lake until I found a place where I could sleep without getting caught."

She'd spent the night two or three blocks from our house.

"And why are you going to Duluth?"

She didn't answer for a moment. I thought perhaps she'd dozed off.

"I don't know anymore. When that foreman left me at the truck stop, Duluth was stuck in my head. My first mother was born in Duluth. I guess I thought I might find a relative. But now I think it was one of those ideas you get when you're off your head, you know, like a dream. It makes sense at the time, but when you wake up, you see that it's crazy." Her voice was growing slow as fatigue pulled her down. "Maybe I'll find work there."

"The lights in the distance are Belleville," I told her. "I can't leave you out on the highway at this hour. You can stay with us tonight and rest up before you go on."

It was after nine when we reached the cottage. I found Hildy a cotton gown, gave her towels, and left her in the bathroom to shower, while I explained to Bart that I'd met a girl in town who was spending the night. He looked up from his reading.

"I won't interrupt you now," I said. "I'll explain more in the morning. I'm putting her in Miranda's room."

He nodded. Sloughing off my city clothes and shoes, I pulled on a robe and went to the kitchen to heat a can of soup for Hildy. When she sat down at the table, a towel covering her wet hair, I saw that behind the many bruises and the still swollen face, there was a very pleasant-looking young woman. She was probably in her early thirties, skin still tight as a girl's. From beneath the towel, biscuit-colored tendrils fell around her face. With large, confounded blue eyes, she seemed a rose grown to maturity on vines too tender for support.

About ten the next morning I was seated on the porch, drawing, when Bart took a break for coffee and stopped to inquire, "Your friend's still sleeping?"

"Yes." I put aside my pencil. "Can you spare a moment?"

He took a chair and I told him the entire story. "She's sick and penniless and half-starved. I couldn't leave her."

"No. Of course not," he said, not at all discomposed. I'd half-expected him to view it as a pother, another of the minor plagues to which he was subject in a universe in perpetual conspiracy against the contemplative and ordered life. "You're sure she's all right?" He inclined his head in the direction of the bedroom. "Maybe you should have taken her to a doctor."

"I think she'll be all right. I'll keep an eye on her."

He finished his coffee and went to the kitchen for a second cup. Returning, he mused, "The outside world doesn't often come into my house—not in person, so to speak."

"No."

"I suppose a person has to choose."

"Choose?"

"Between the outside world and the inside one. Life viewed or *re*viewed." He shrugged slightly and went along to his study.

Bart was a born scholar and researcher, but occasionally when he'd been closeted too long, he grew disoriented and a trifle unsure of the reality of his existence, the import of his sequestered occupation. His doubts would temporarily drive him into the world or cause him to invite some part of the world in. He shortly measured what he saw, was appalled by its incivility and mediocrity, and returned to his clerestory, feeling redefined and certain, satisfied not to be part of the throng. It was a war out there and only the mad went abroad. I suspected that Hildy's arrival coincided with such a period of doubt.

Hildy woke, apologetic and half-frantic, at four that afternoon. She'd slept eighteen hours.

"I can't believe the time," she moaned. "Oh, God, I should have gotten up hours ago. Can you give me a ride to the highway?"

"Don't be silly. It's too late for you to start now. Wait until tomorrow. One more day isn't going to make a difference."

"Oh, but I can't ask you to put me up another day."

"You don't have to ask. It's settled. I've got some clothes I think will fit you," I told her and went to fetch a pair of denim putter pants and a knit shirt. "Here, put these on. Your things are out on the line drying."

At six-thirty Bart joined us for dinner. He was chatty, convivial, and urbane, the way I recalled his being when I was a student, the way he must be with his students even now. I watched him as though he were an actor performing particularly well in a Noël Coward role, but he wasn't acting. This was as much a part of him as his solitariness. It was another facet of his professionalism. He *was* his work.

Hildy was charmed. With her chin cupped in her hands she listened, nodded, smiled, dimpled, dropped her gaze, and finally laughed from sheer good spirits. I laughed too.

Bart needed a student. Why had I not noticed that? When I was young, I'd sat at his knee. Then Miranda had slipped into my place without ado as I became Mother. When Miranda left, Bart had lacked a student at home. He'd withdrawn more and more into the other side of his profession, the other side of his nature.

After a second glass of wine and two cups of coffee, he at

length tore himself away from the dinner table. "Have a pleasant evening," he admonished and departed, whistling softly. I could only gape.

Hildy rose, carrying dishes to the sink. "You have an adorable husband, Mrs. Demming."

She spoke of someone I had not known for years.

37

When Hildy padded into the kitchen Thursday morning, it was apparent that she was ill. Her cheeks were flushed and she was clinging to herself with chill.

"It's all caught up with you," I told her. "I'm going to take you to my doctor in the city."

"No, please. It's just a cold." Her voice was a squeaky rasp.

Her temperature was one hundred and three. I had her to the doctor and back again, settled into bed with prescription bottles on the bedside table, before three that afternoon. She had a severe bronchial infection and was going to require rest and recuperation before going on her way.

Carrying a dinner tray into the bedroom, I saw that she'd been crying. "What's wrong?"

She played nervously with the ties at the neck of her gown. "I'm running up a terrible bill here."

She didn't speak literally but I knew her worry. I set the tray in front of her, unfolded the napkin, and handed it to her. "I have a daughter, Miranda. She's twenty-four. At the moment there's a helluva mess between us. I hope other women are doing for her what I can't. I'm only doing for you what your mother can't."

"I have some things here for Hildy," Bart said, emerging from his study, "to help pass the time." He set a stack of books on the bedside table. "There may be something there that will amuse you," he told her. "I'd be happy to answer questions, if you have any."

"Thank you." She smiled. "I'll probably have plenty of questions."

"Good. I like to answer questions. I'm very good at answering questions. Unfortunately, it is the talent of a second-class intellect. The really bright minds *ask* the questions," he assured her, moving toward the door where I waited. "I'm keeping you from your dinner. *Bon appétit*, Hildy."

Friday and Saturday I stayed in, working on the Historical Society retrospective and keeping an eye on Hildy. By Sunday she was a good deal improved and I was suffering from cabin fever, so I got the bike out and rode into town.

I stopped at the Kaffee Kafe to buy a Sunday paper. In the window a red-white-and-blue placard proclaimed, THIS BUSINESS SUPPORTS THE BELLEVILLE WELCOMING COMMITTEE. The line below importuned, DO YOU?

Helen Wilhelm was running the cash register. I ordered a large coffee to go. Thrusting my change on the counter, Helen asked in a lean, carrying voice, "How's your husband?"

"Fine. Very busy."

"Never see him anymore. Used to see him in here now and again. Especially Sundays. Not anymore."

I felt accused and glanced around to see if we were being overheard. "Well, he's really buried in work right now."

"That's a danger," she observed enigmatically.

Peddling down into Humphrey Park, I found a bench near the river and settled myself with the paper. Since it was just past nine, I had the park nearly to myself. When I'd read as much as interested me, I put the folded paper in the bike basket and began stalking the water's edge. I couldn't blame my restlessness on a couple of days' confinement in the cottage. It was Gerald Sperling and Homestead Gallery that gave me the fidgets. It was whether or not to hand my work over to him.

I was not an artist, that was part of the problem. Georganna Fitzroy, Daisy's daughter, was an artist. I was someone who had studied art and who painted. I wasn't sure what the difference was, only that there was a difference. To allow Gerald Sperling or anyone else to think I was an artist was an imposture.

Before he decamped, I had painted for Jamie. After, I painted to shut him out. To me that did not sound like the mentality of a *real* artist. A neurotic dilettante is what it sounded like.

Now here was Gerald Sperling saying silly, puffery things:

"Fascinating. You've stopped just short of personifying nature. Look how the clouds flee, escaping, looking over their shoulders, you might say, at what pursues. And here—a tree, ruthful, bent down with pity." And moving on, "In this, you've quarreled with the river and painted vicious anger all over it." And more such nonsense that might better have been saved for gullible buyers.

Although I had laughed aloud and been irritated at the same time, now I was only amused recalling that in his critical summation, what Sperling regarded most highly in my work he refused to credit to any talent or intelligence on my part.

"It's purely a matter of technical skill—which any cretin may have—and abnormal psychology. Without the abnormal psychology, L. Demming, you'd be just another boring landscape artist."

Yet, despite great misgivings and certain scruples, I was tempted to say yes to Sperling. I liked the idea of being feverishly absorbed until time to depart for Greece—where my Beast and I were still going. Between the Historical Society show and the work for Homestead Gallery, I would be thoroughly occupied until September 10.

The Homestead Gallery one-woman show, if it came to pass, would likely take place in the spring of next year. I'd warned Sperling that I wouldn't be on hand, and he had taken that in stride, explaining, "So long as you've prepared the work, it isn't important. Frankly, it may be a plus. It will enhance the general air of mystery the canvases evoke. The public may assume I have you tucked away in a clinic, squeezing your psyche onto canvas, like so much undiluted color from a tube."

Emerging from the park a little before eleven, I glanced quickly across River Avenue at the *Courant*. It was closed, of course, on Sunday. Was Harry at his desk, sleeves rolled up, writing the weekly fishing report or wondering what to do if more businesses pulled their ads and their money from the paper? How many windows in town displayed placards announcing, THIS BUSINESS SUPPORTS THE . BELLEVILLE WELCOMING COMMITTEE?

I turned the bike toward Daisy's house. Her car was in the drive. "Are you busy?"

"No. I just finished making some phone calls for Save the River."

"Can you come riding?"

We rode west through town on River Avenue, which, beyond

the county fairgrounds, became County Road 19. Sunday midday was somnolent and ghostly. A smell of fried chicken drifted across one of the broad lawns and out to the street. Past the fairgrounds, big cottonwoods grew along both sides of the road, and their sprawling branches stretched over the road, like arms reaching across a gulf to embrace.

I told Daisy about my meeting with Gerald Sperling.

"Larry, that's wonderful."

"I didn't promise him anything."

"Don't be silly. It's the chance of a lifetime."

"I'm leaving for Greece in less than six weeks." I felt a kind of stage fright. "I don't know when I'm coming back. Or if I'm coming back."

"You're leaving Bart, that's what you're saying."

"Yes."

"How's he taking it?"

"I haven't told him. I'll tell him later, after he's finished the book. He deserves to finish it in peace."

"Why not wait until he's finished before you go? It can't be so long, can it?"

"No. A couple of months at most."

"Well?"

"I can't."

The sun on the cottonwoods caught the waxy side of the leaves and glistened like fresh rain.

"What about Harry?" she asked. "You've told him you're leaving?"

"Not yet, but it doesn't change anything."

"I can't believe that."

"Things have happened that I can't talk about, Daisy." Without pausing, I told her, "We have a young woman staying with us out at the cottage. Her name's Hildy Smith." I explained briefly.

"What will happen when she's well?"

"I don't know."

We rode for a while in silence, then Daisy asked, "Why Greece? Why so far? Couldn't we compromise? How about Chicago?"

I laughed.

"It's not funny," she snapped. "I hate your going that far." She was serious. "We're not just friends, you know. People as close as we are—it's more than just friends. There's no word for it, maybe, but you know what I mean. We're closer than most sisters. Oh, hell."

She was weeping. Pulling the bike off the road, she swore, "I can't pedal this goddamned thing and cry, too." And she threw it aside.

I dropped my bike on the grassy verge and we stood beneath the cottonwoods, helpless, our sense of futility estranging us.

"It shouldn't be this easy to walk away from friendship," she said angrily. "Just good-bye and 'I'll see you every few years.'"

"We'll still be friends."

"Oh, fuck, we will. Letters that get fewer and fewer, seeing each other for a few days every couple of years? You call that friendship? If you moved to one of the coasts even, it wouldn't be so bad. But Greece. God."

We sat in the long dusty grass.

She cried, "I'm being a bitch, I know."

"No, you're not."

"Yes, I am. But give me this one tantrum." Tears were still welling in her eyes and she put a wadded Kleenex to them. "Why am I crying? Look at me. I have a good husband, right? A busy life?" She turned to me. "So why am I so damned upset?"

"Daisy..."

"Those things aren't the same. They're not the same as you. As us. There are different kinds of marriages, Larry. There's husbands and wives, and parents and children, and there's friends like you and me. It's very unlikely that we're going to find anyone to take our place. We're not kids anymore." She reached for my hand. "I wouldn't run halfway around the world and leave you—if I wasn't coming back."

38

Like stones in a tumbling box, Daisy's admonishing words rolled over and over in my brain, as the wheels of the bike turned over and over down the road. Dispirited, I rode the bike into the garage, then walked around the cottage, tossing the Sunday *Tribune* in on the porch floor and continuing on down to the river.

On the far beach I pulled the canoe up on the sand, climbed the shallow embankment, and pushed into the woods. I hadn't seen Pan for a week. Friday morning early I had scribbled a note and left it in the cache. It was still there.

Hiking through the trees, I shucked off my sneakers and waded across the slough. Finally, I stood in the small clearing where he sometimes came to lie in the sun. There was no sign of him.

I turned north and trudged perhaps half a mile, beyond the northern end of the slough, before swinging west and back to the river. Twice, I spotted other hikers, once a lone young man, the second time a boy and girl, teenagers. Uneasy, I returned to the canoe and sat down to wait.

I had neglected him the past week. But he wasn't the sort to sulk, so where had he gone? At four I paddled back across Belle Riviere, feeling reluctant and guilty. And about half a cup short of whatever it was the recipe required.

Monday morning the lively, efficient voice of Madge Allhouse, Gerald Sperling's assistant, greeted me long-distance. "Good morning, Mrs. Demming. Mr. Sperling asked me to call you. He needs to know your decision. Harvey Gray Eagle wants a spring show and Gerald will give him your spot, I'm afraid, if he doesn't have a firm commitment from you."

"*Today?*"

"Yes, I'm afraid so. I'm sorry. I know it's difficult."

Whatever I decided, I would find it was the wrong thing, I knew that. As soon as I hung up the receiver, a dozen trenchant arguments would rise up to smite my choice.

"Mrs. Demming?"

"Yes. I'm here. Thinking—or wishing I could."

"Would it help if I called back in twenty minutes?"

"No. Not at all." With the heel of one sneaker I kicked the toe of the other. "Tell Mr. Sperling we have a deal. Tell him I would like something in writing. I don't want him to change his mind when I'm out of the country. Tell him I'll be down to see him Friday."

When she had hung up, I lowered myself onto a kitchen chair, the pulse in my throat leaping so violently I put a hand to my neck.

Late that afternoon I went again to the opposite side of the river, again without success. He might at least leave a message in the cache, but no, there was nothing. Tuesday the same. I was genuinely worried now.

The rest of life went forward unawares. Tuesday Hildy was up and dressed in the jeans and shirt she'd worn the night we met at the roadside rest. Her voice was still a little hoarse, but she'd regained much of her strength. In appearance she was somewhat worse, however, since the bruises on her face had gone from blue to green and yellow.

I was at work at the drafting table when she sat down on the sofa across the room and told me, "I'll be leaving tomorrow, I think."

"You're supposed to see the doctor again. We have an appointment Friday."

"I know, but I don't think it's necessary and I'm getting crazy, thinking about money. I'll be a lot happier when I'm earning my way again. I thought maybe I'd call the guy I work for in Denver and ask could he wire me a hundred bucks. I can work it off when I get back."

"Don't be silly. I'll lend you the money when you leave, but you can't go before Friday. What if you had a relapse? Where would you be then? In Denver with no place of your own, unable to work and out of money. You'd end up on welfare." It was unscrupulous to use that last argument, but I knew it would hit a vital organ.

"Oh, God," she groaned.

"Do you have a boyfriend waiting for you?"

"Nobody right now. That's a mercy, I guess."

"You'll see Doctor Minnelli Friday. We'll abide by what she says. I'll lend you the money to get back to Denver and get started again. It's settled. Stop looking so miserable."

She sat worrying a long, loose coil of hair that fell to her shoulder. Suddenly her face brightened. "I'll make you a bargain," she said, flinging the strand of hair back over her shoulder. "If you'll let me work around here, I'll do what you say."

"Not while you're still sick."

She stood. "I don't think you know how strong I am. I'm wiry, but I'm that *strong* kind of wiry. Mrs. Heddison that I used to live with said I could outwork any two hired girls she ever saw. Do you and Mr. Demming like homemade bread?" she asked, not giving me time to protest.

"We don't have any yeast."

"I'll go get some. It can't be much of a walk to town."

"Take the car. The keys are on the hook by the back door. My wallet's on the kitchen counter." Listening to the Volvo grumbling down the rough road toward town, I thought, What's to say she'll come back? I put aside the charcoal, wiped my hands on a rag, and wandered out to the porch to stand staring at the river, the river that ran away forever and yet, thank God, was never gone.

Hildy was back in less than an hour. From my worktable at the north end of the little living room, I could observe her at the kitchen table, up to her elbows in flour. She had piled her hair on her head in a jaunty if not quite successful attempt to keep it out of the way. The day was warm and humid and the humidity coaxed wisps of hair loose from their mooring and set them drifting across her forehead and along her temples, so that she had to straighten from her work every few minutes to thrust out her lower lip and blow upward, sending the errant strands flying.

Her face as she worked the dough was earnest, and it shone with perspiration and a kind of affection for the pliable mass in her hands. Without looking up, she recalled, "Mrs. Heddison showed me how to make bread. I used to make it once or twice a week when Eddie and I were living there. Eddie *loved* homemade bread. Did he ever."

"Who was Mrs. Heddison?"

She paused in her work, the heels of her hands resting against the dough. "When Eddie was born, my dad took off. My mom didn't know where to turn. We were living in Oklahoma then. Some people by the name of Heddison lived next door. They said they'd keep Eddie and me until my mom could get on her feet. Anyway, she went to Tulsa to look for work and she wrote us for a while about how she was going to come and get us as soon as she could, but after about a year the letters stopped. I think she maybe met some guy who didn't want a couple of somebody else's kids, you know.

"We stayed on with the Heddisons. Then when Eddie was five, Mrs. Heddison got cancer and died and Mr. Heddison couldn't keep us, he said, so the county took us and we lived in foster homes after that. Mrs. Heddison was like a mother so I always call her my second mother."

"Was Eddie much younger than you?"

"Ten years." She buttered a bowl, placed the dough in it, turning it to grease the smooth skin. "I felt like a mother to him sometimes." She covered the bowl with a damp towel and placed it in the unlit oven. "When you don't have somebody to look after, you really feel alone."

"Why did Eddie come to Minnesota?"

"Looking for family."

When she'd wiped up the table and washed the utensils, she looked droopy. I got a swimsuit from the bedroom. "Put this on and go lie in the sun while your bread's rising."

Late lunch was a feast of warm bread and butter. Hildy fixed a plate for Bart and carried it in to him, along with a mug of tea and milk. I heard her teasing, "I put a whole lot of words in the dough—good ones I got from that dictionary in the living room. You'll find them rising to your brain this afternoon."

Later, when she fetched the empty plate, he told her, "You were right about the words. And they were the very ones I needed."

His appreciation of her rather awestruck attendance was genuine. He did not condescend but treated her as a valued student as well as a charming member of the household. She for her part was deeply flattered but uncowed. She'd been to schools he would never attend.

Friday. I still hadn't seen the Beast. Dr. Minnelli pronounced Hildy well, or well enough that she needn't book another appointment. "Take it easy for a week or so. Get plenty of rest."

I dropped Hildy at the movies before my appointment with Gerald Sperling.

"Remember," she admonished before jumping out in front of the theater, "*you're* the one in the catbird seat."

That wasn't true, of course. Sperling could dump me and fill my place with any number of other artists. There was a nearly limitless supply of artists, but a dearth of good galleries, a good gallery being one where the artist was presented well and paid promptly and fairly.

Again, it was Madge Allhouse who greeted me. "The work you're doing for your Historical Society, how's that going?" she asked as we headed toward the office.

"Pretty well. I only have a couple of pieces left to do and then the framing. Mr. Sperling doesn't object, does he?"

"Oh, no, but I think he's going to keep you pretty busy until you leave for..."

"Greece."

The ground level of the gallery was currently filled with work by a South Dakota woman, Grace White Deer, whom Sperling had discovered on the Rosebud Reservation. He had three American Indians in his stable of artists. The huge works on display were filled with powerful, clear color in geometric designs of such movement that they fairly leapt around the canvas like an exploding Catherine wheel.

"My God, they're good, aren't they?"

"Yes," Madge agreed. "Grace is causing a stir. Galleries on both coasts are interested. We've already sold several pieces from this show to museums."

Beside a talent like this, I could not conceive what Gerald Sperling saw in my work. I would surely and shortly be found a fraud. Would it not be more sensible to back off now, before I was found out? Grace White Deer, if she were strolling past *my* work and pressed for a comment, would say, "Well, it's...it's nice."

"Gerald's waiting," Madge said as I followed her into Sperling's office. And indeed, there he sat at his huge desk like a great bear who might rise and deal me a killing blow, or dance on his hind legs and play the tambourine.

"L. Demming," he said, rising only slightly, then settling back in the tall Jacobean chair and resting an elbow on one of its slender arms.

I sat without being asked.

"L. Demming, with your permission I have sold two of your pictures."

I was pleased but perversely refused to enthuse. "Which two?"

"Let me see." He put a small hand with strangely pointed fingers to his temple. "One was a clown, all white, on a white horse. The other...oh, yes, a cottage, with blank, staring windows, high on an embankment above a river."

The pictures had gone to a wealthy Lake Minnetonka broker, William Greighley, a well-known arts patron in the Twin Cities area, who sat on the board of the Minnesota Orchestra and contributed heavily to the Minneapolis Art Institute.

"Your work is an investment," Sperling told me. "Greighley will make money on you. What's more, Greighley is a bellwether.

Where he goes, others follow. To make a sale as significant as this with an unknown is a minor miracle and owing almost entirely to my own acumen and reputation."

If he thought to intimidate me with this last, he was mistaken. I had no intention of turning down the money, but it was the praise inherent in the sale that lifted me, the choosing of me from among others (if only as an investment). I felt distilled to the essential child, unsure and eager to be prized, discovering a means by which to please.

Sitting forward in a confidential attitude, the dealer asked, "How do you feel about all of this?"

"Surprised. Grateful. Frightened."

"Frightened? Of rejection? Of success?"

"Of rejection, yes. And of being... exposed. Of exhibiting myself. Don't you think that's a frightening thing to do?"

I was with Sperling for half an hour. At the end of our meeting he summoned Madge, who led me into the next room, where my work was stored. We pored over various unframed pieces Sperling wanted readied for showing.

"Gerald is a pain in the ass," she told me, "but he's good. I wouldn't be here if he weren't. He'll never tell you that he likes your work, but you wouldn't be here if he didn't. He doesn't handle work he doesn't like, no matter how salable."

"I'm glad you told me that."

"Some artists get emotionally dependent on the people who represent them. Gerald has artists whose validation is based on his acceptance or rejection. He's not above exploiting that. But I think you deserve to know your work is appreciated."

Did she see me as one who might become emotionally dependent on Gerald Sperling?

As I was preparing to leave, Sperling suddenly appeared at the door to his office and hailed me. "L. Demming, wait. The white clown on the white horse, was he dead or was the blood someone else's?"

I stared at him for a moment, then turning, walked out the door Madge held open for me. Yanking a pair of sunglasses from my bag, I hastily clapped them on my face.

I had nearly an hour until I must pick up Hildy at the theater. Parking the car in the Dayton's ramp, I dashed through the department store grabbing up essentials for Hildy: a pretty cotton dress, a pair of shorts and a shirt, a sweater, a swimsuit, underwear, a pair of sandals. She needed toilet articles and makeup, a bottle of cologne, a pair of earrings, and a handbag.

When I pulled the car to the curb in front of the movie house, Hildy was standing beneath the marquee biting her lower lip and peering anxiously up the street.

"Sorry I'm late," I told her, reaching across to open the passenger door.

Glancing in the back where the portfolios and parcels were stowed, she exclaimed, "Sure looks like you've been busy."

It was late afternoon. We'd be home in time for dinner. To Hildy, I'd noticed, ritual and routine were luxuries from which she derived deep satisfaction. She would be gratified to be home for the evening meal, to lay out the table carefully, to fold the napkins precisely and polish the wine goblets, as if preparing communion.

As we headed north I told her, "If and when you want to leave for Denver, I'll lend you the money you need, although I hope you'll wait at least a week until you're completely well. I don't want to hold you here if you're eager to get back, but if you're in no special hurry, I could use your help."

"How's that?"

"It's five weeks until I leave for Greece. I have work I must do for Gerald Sperling before then. It'll require running back and forth to Minneapolis. I have the show for the Historical Society to finish and endless other details to clear away. If you don't mind staying for a while and keeping house for us, it would be a godsend. You could earn the money to go to Denver. There wouldn't be a loan to repay." I added, "If you want to think it over, take your time."

She thought she would like to stay awhile. At dinner we celebrated, Bart and Hildy and I. Mozart's String Quartet No. 17 ("The Hunt") played on the kitchen radio as Bart took his seat. Hildy wore her new pink cotton dress and pink lipstick. She looked no older than Miranda or Sarah.

She emptied a pan of hot corn muffins into a napkin-lined basket and tucked the corners of the napkin around the muffins to keep them warm. Placing it on the table near Bart, she observed, "It just seems more than chance, doesn't it, the way things work out sometimes? It could have been a hundred other people who stopped in the roadside rest that night. And where would I be now? I know I wouldn't be this happy."

Pouring innocent white jug wine into our sparkling goblets, Bart raised his glass to Hildy and me. The corners of his mouth lifted in the grip of satisfaction as he closed his eyes to recall a line from Shakespeare:

"My crown is called content;/ A crown it is that seldom kings enjoy."

39

I knew that women did not always fit so neatly into one another's households as Hildy fit into mine.

After my mother's death, quite soon after, a woman named Norma Farmer came several times to our house to make dinner for Jamie and me. She was a bookkeeper who had been with Jamie since he'd taken over the hardware stores belonging to the great-uncle who had raised him. Three stores were a heavy responsibility for a young man, and at first he had to rely a good deal on the judgment and loyalty of a handful of experienced employees. One of them had been Norma Farmer.

Norma was one of those women who, once grown to maturity, never vary more than a pound or two in weight the rest of their lives. Neither do they abuse their bodies with excessive alcohol, cigarettes, sunbathing, work, illness, or desperate love affairs. Their faces are unlined by passion or migraine. In consequence of this, at twenty they look thirty, and at fifty they still look thirty.

They are tenacious, not tempestuous. While they do sleep with men, they rise from it looking as if they'd spent the night playing canasta, no trace of frowzled, open-faced euphoria or peevish disappointment clinging to them. And yet I do not believe they are sexually cold—perhaps just the opposite—only that they're profoundly unaffected beyond the moment. To such a one, a good fuck is like a good steak, not a thing over which one laughs or weeps. I suppose such women are a great relief to men. They do not invest themselves heavily and therefore do not anticipate a large return. Beyond the marriage license, they do not tax their men unduly. They are self-satisfiers first and last.

All of this was Norma Farmer, and I suspected her from the moment she walked into our house in her tailored brown skirt and silky beige blouse with the cameo at the neck. Cameos were ruined for me from that day forth.

After Jamie introduced us—"This is Miss Farmer, who has kindly offered to cook a proper meal for us, Larissa. Norma, this is mavourneen, Larissa"—she was neither friendly nor hostile to me but ignored me as if I were the family dog and she no great dog-flesh enthusiast.

Jamie mixed them drinks. She had vodka and Coca-Cola. They sat in the breakfast nook, a cozy booth at the end of the kitchen, and talked about taxes. Women of Norma's sort talk a good deal about taxes and accounts receivable and the latest postal increase and other hugely uninteresting topics pertaining to business.

Although I set the table in the dining room at seven, we didn't eat until eight. Was Norma trying to starve me into making myself a peanut butter sandwich and disappearing to my room? I was damned if I would. With the aid of a little book from Betty Crocker that Mother kept in the buffet, I set the table as Mother might, had the Duchess of Windsor been coming to dinner: water goblets and wine goblets, three forks, salad plates, and bread plates with butter knives. Folded like little accordions were our best linen napkins. The china was Mother's Haviland, the flatware her Wallace sterling, and the goblets Irish crystal.

At seven-thirty I brought Jamie a bottle of wine to uncork. From the refrigerator I pulled out a package of pork chops and set it beside the stove. Opening a jar of spiced apple rings, I arranged them in a cut-glass dish. It was too late to bake potatoes, so I put a kettle of salted water on the stove for noodles. Buttered and sprinkled with grated cheese, they would do. There was a package of baby peas in the freezer and salad makings in the lettuce drawer.

At length I interrupted Norma and Jamie in the middle of equipment depreciation write-offs. "Would you like me to cook the pork chops?" I inquired amiably.

Noting my tentative posture and helpful expression, Norma saw some hoped-for advantage slipping away. She smiled at Jamie. "I've lost track of time, James. Excuse me while I fix dinner. You just sit there and talk to me while I work."

At eight o'clock I lit the candles, poured wine, and tossed the salad with my own dressing. I sat in Mother's chair at the foot of the table. Jamie sat at the head and Norma sat between us, to my left.

I raised my glass. "To the cook," I said without a trace of irony.

Jamie contributed a gentlemanly "Here, here."

"You drink wine?" Norma observed most casually. I knew that butter was melting in her mouth, however.

"Jamie says I'm a young woman now and he allows me a glass on special occasions."

That I called my father Jamie was a point of curiosity and mild irritation to her, but she let it pass. Since she was sure to bring it up later in a by-the-way manner when I wasn't present, I explained, "Since my mother died and I began keeping house, Jamie has allowed me to call him by his first name. He says I've taken on a lot of grown-up duties and I may assume some grown-up privileges." I cast him a fond glance. The subject was closed. "Have you read any good books lately, Miss Farmer? Do you prefer American or European authors?"

Anyone who thought to capture Jamie, I would have opposed. But Miss Farmer it was a pleasure to combat. How had she dared to insinuate herself into our home less than a month after my mother's death? I believed then and I still believe that Jamie honestly imagined she'd come to cook us dinner. It wasn't that he was naive or unused to women's attentions, but during those early days after Mother's death he walked around in a storm of remorse. It was a comfort to him that Miss Farmer was so concerned with the business. Heaven knows, he could not give it his best attention.

She came twice more, both times at her own invitation. Jamie now recognized her intent, however, and the occasions were kept light and comradely. The last time I met her at the door. It was a warm evening in early June, shortly before Jamie and I set out on our cross-country journey.

"Miss Farmer, how nice to see you. Come in." I was genuinely gracious, as I could now afford to be, and led her into the living room, where wineglasses glittered in lamplight, champagne chilled in an ice bucket, and hors d'oeuvres tempted from a silver tray on the coffee table.

Jamie, who had driven her to the house from the office, opened the champagne and poured three glasses. "Old friends," he said, lifting his glass.

"Have you been to California, Miss Farmer?" I asked.

"No. Only as far as Colorado."

"Jamie and I are going to California. We'll be gone a month, but I guess you already know that. We're driving. We haven't definite plans, except to enjoy ourselves."

Miss Farmer's brave sociability in the face of defeat aroused admiration and a fleeting tristesse. Accepting an hors d'oeuvre, she told me, "You're a clever girl, Larissa. Very grown-up."

If Jamie had brought home someone like Hildy, what might have happened? Sabotaging her chances would have pricked my conscience a good deal more, but I would have done it, nonetheless.

Hildy went to bed early. I sat at the drafting table fussing with a logjam drawing. I'd sketched the scene numerous times, never to my satisfaction. It was essential to the Belle Riviere retrospective, so I continued grappling with it.

Bart, in his study, was hunched over his writing pad. Everywhere in the cottage, windows were open and night sounds drifted through them: crickets, owls, and country dogs barking. At the window beside my table, a moth occasionally hurled itself against the screen with enough zeal to produce a tiny thump, which did not so much startle me as draw off some small portion of my attention.

About eleven-thirty a sound at the window jerked my head around. A leering face pressed itself against the screen. The scream rising in my throat I muffled to a grunt. "My God," I breathed. Then, tossing my pencil down, I ran to the porch and out the door.

Throwing my arms around Pan, I giggled and cursed and trembled with relief. Angry with him for the fear he'd caused me, I was insanely happy to welcome him back. "Damn you," I spat. "Where have you been? Why didn't you leave a note? Why didn't you come before? I've missed you. I have so much to tell you."

I fetched the old damask bedspread and we laid it under the trees in front of the cottage, but near the embankment, out of sight of anyone glancing casually from one of the windows. He lay back, clasping his hands behind his head. I sat beside him, my fingers idly playing along his furry thigh, afraid to let go for fear he might evaporate.

I described Gerald Sperling and Homestead Gallery and what had transpired there. I told him about Hildy and her agreement to remain with us until I left. "But where have you *been*?" I pressed, bending to nibble at his belly, then resting my head on his breast as he related a strange tale.

"The morning after I saw you last, a Friday morning, I woke at dawn. Through a high crevice in the rock walls of my shelter a pale-blue morning breeze slipped in. A morning fit for man or beast, I thought. Just as I'd begun to slide back the rock concealing my door, a sound reached me from beyond it. It was not at all a customary sound for these woods.

"A dolorous male tenor was singing some kind of hymn, quite chastening and Germanic. And there was the sound of an animal, presumably a dog, pawing and snorting immediately outside my door.

"For an hour the singing fellow continued to reproach the morning. And the dog, which must be his, went on digging at my portal.

"Then for half an hour or more the man was silent though I knew he remained, since there were no retreating footsteps. I believe he was praying or meditating, for he paid no attention to the dog who dug ever deeper until at one point a great white paw appeared beneath the rock on my side.

"I would not injure the creature, but I did deliver him a sharp crack on the knuckles. He yelped and withdrew. I quickly filled up the hole with loose dirt and stones.

"He was soon again at his occupation, but the tenor now hailed him. 'Here, Michael,' he commanded and started away through the woods. The dog remained.

"The man returned. 'Come along, Michael.' But the dog turned and gave a growl which was not so much a threat as a declaration of determination.

"'Stay, then,' the man said in a dour tone and marched off.

"Throughout the remainder of the day the dog worried the earth beneath my door. His paws, which now and then I glimpsed, grew ragged and bloody."

I asked, "Why didn't you slide back the rock?"

"And confront him."

"Yes."

"It's difficult to answer. Needless to say, it was not physical fear that constrained me. A single kick from one of these hoofs would crack the skull of even a very large dog."

His arm around me pressed more tightly, as though he were sending the answer to my question through my entire body and not trusting to words only. "There was a profound resolve in what the dog did. It was his *lot* to hound me." He laughed sardonically at this little wordplay. "If I slid back my gate and went out, he would have to try to overcome me. Then I should have to kill him or be pursued, a risky thing these days with so many people wandering in the woods—thanks to your friend Harry and his Devil of the dalles."

"What did you do all day?"

"I stayed in and read by oil lamp. There was food and drink at hand. When the light outside my window slit waxed purple the dog left digging and lay down with his nose close by the hole. Now and then I heard him sigh and snort. And in the night several times he whined softly.

"Shortly after dawn his master came singing down through the woods, again his song full of scourge. He brought the dog some food. Either it was a small portion or the dog ate only part of it, for the creature was immediately back at his task.

"As on the previous morning the man sang his unhappy hymns for nearly an hour, then was silent. When he left, he called sharply, 'Come along, Michael.' Several times he ordered the dog but was ignored as before and finally left, chiding coldly, 'Stay, then.'

"The second day was like the first. I wondered how long the dog's persevering paws could hold out."

I interrupted, "Surely you could have gotten away at night. If he chased you, no one would see."

"And where would I run? To you? What would you do with me? There was no point in running. And, besides, his doggedness deserved my presence, do you see?

"The ritual continued exactly the same for a week. Each morning the man returned with his unforgiving song, brought food for the animal, and admonished it to accompany him away. Each time the dog disdained. On the seventh day as he prepared to leave, the man rebuked, 'Stay, then. No hare is worth this.' He left and did not return again.

"But the dog remained and kept at his duty. By now his paws were blood-matted stubs, unrecognizable. The second day he was without food I was sure he would abandon the digging. Think of the frustration to him when I, on the inside, am laying down rock after rock below my door, to defeat him. And how could he go on in his condition with no food? That night as he slept, his breathing was stertorous and full of anguished little sighs.

"The following two days he stayed by the excavation but could dig only interruptedly. That he had the stamina or will to continue at all was evidence of his great strength and indomitable character.

"I knew that the next morning I could slide back my door. I would give him food and water until he had the strength to find his way home. In this way only could I hope to win, outlasting him, wearing him down, until he understood at last who was the master.

"I slept very poorly that night, alternating between fits of great sadness for his suffering and an uplifting relief knowing that when dawn came I would minister to him. I listened for the sound of his breathing and knew that each labored breath brought us closer to my mastery and his comfort. In the early morning, an hour or two before dawn, I fell into a heavy sleep and when I woke, the sky at my crevice was very light.

"I jumped up and began to haul back the stone gate. The dog lay with his nose nearly against it. Running back into the cave to fetch water, I grabbed up a clean cloth to bathe his broken feet. Kneeling in the loose dirt I lifted his huge head and saw that I was too late."

"Oh, no," I whispered.

"Oh, yes. If only I hadn't been so determined to master him." He held me gently while I wept. At last he exclaimed, "What a great white hound he was. Magnificent." He hugged me to him. "I carried him into the cave and covered him over. That night I buried him in the woods. Since then I've stayed in the cave and fasted. It's not penance so much as honor due him. Tonight I came because I knew you would worry."

"You must try to forget."

"Ah," he breathed with patient, unhappy amusement at my ignorance. "Forget. Forgetting is not a possibility. What I must do is accept."

"Accept his death."

"No. Accept his living. Now that I've brought him down, he will always be with me. He is twice alive to me."

We lay together until the sky began to pale. I had no palliative to ease the heaviness of his soul. Nor any power to still the deep vibrations of disquiet the story had set humming in my own. I felt a new urgency to fly with him where the dog couldn't reach us.

40

Monday night an open-forum meeting was called in the high school gymnasium. The village council and Mayor Smiley, along with Roberta and Daisy, would present themselves for questioning about the Belle Rive Estates project and the move to stop it. I had promised myself to stay out of the conflict since Harry was so deeply embroiled, but I needed one or two sketches for the Historical Society reflecting this bargaining and politicking over the river. And since the gathering was bound to be sizable, I should have no difficulty avoiding Harry.

The gymnasium was not air-conditioned. Windows high above the bleachers were opened, as were the great double doors at one end. Panel and audience sat beneath a harsh blaze of wire-protected illumination.

Folding chairs were set up on the floor of the gymnasium, and a raised dais with a long table was positioned at the end of the room opposite the double doors. At one of the entrances Harry and Bobby were stationed, Harry with a yellow legal pad, Bobby holding a tape recorder and microphone. As townspeople filed in and milled in the aisles, the two men waylaid them randomly, plying them with questions. This was surely a new and possibly explosive situation, Harry and Bobby working together.

Mayor Smiley gaveled the forum to order. On either side of him were council members, and at opposing ends of the table, Roberta and Daisy. Harry and his son took their places in the first row of folding chairs, reserved for the press. Representatives of all the small papers along the river were there, as well as a couple of reporters from Minneapolis and St. Paul.

I sat in the balcony where I could observe and sketch the key figures. I spotted librarian Nellie Bergen and husband Hoot in the second row of folding chairs, near Lydia Comstock of the Historical Society and Phil the high school principal. Several rows behind them sat Save the River's legal counsel, Sam Fergus, with George

Fitzroy. The gymnasium was as jammed as for a district basketball final.

Beau Bois and Three Toes counties had been settled by northern European stock—Swedish, Norwegian, German, and English. These people rarely shouted or raised their fists. They'd grown ruminant and stoical. But they had a history of fighting for their rights. They believed in education and tended—albeit slowly—down the paths where it beckoned.

The first half-hour of questions and answers was polite, tentative, and selfconscious. Then a farmer identifying himself as being from near Good Hope rose to inquire, "Who in hell's gettin' anything outa this except town people with businesses? I'm downstream and when the river floods, which it does often enough, what's gonna happen to the land? I mean, if you got a river full of gas and oil and garbage, what does that do to the soil? And what does it do to my livestock if they drink it?"

Daisy explained that this was a concern of Save the River and a question the environmental-impact study would have to answer. "What will happen to wildlife as well as domesticated stock?" she added.

"There won't be any untreated sewage going into the river from Belle Rive Estates," Roberta hastened to point out.

"Treated or untreated, who wants it?" someone called.

"It's your damned marina that's going to foul the water!" another male voice contributed. "What about the fish—they got no rights at all?"

"I understand your concern," Roberta assured him, "but this is a river, not a pond, we're talking about. Fresh water will constantly carry off whatever *minimal* pollution there may be."

"Yah. It'll carry it right down my way," the first farmer rejoined, to applause.

Reverend Braun, the Methodist minister, remarked, "We have the example of the Mississippi around the Twin Cities. I for one would not want to swim in it. While the pollution problems in the city are naturally bigger, so is their river."

Roberta steered around comments like these, emphasizing at every opportunity the economic benefits of Belle Rive Estates. She was prepared with projected tax revenues and increased employment figures. So far as most residents were concerned, this was the only argument for Belle Rive Estates.

Frankly, almost no one was eager to welcome and assimilate several hundred newcomers. When they descended in numbers, newcomers had a way of taking things over. First thing you knew, it wasn't *your* town anymore. *They* were the ones running the church bazaar or standing in a loose knot gossiping in the dimestore. *Their* children were the football heroes and valedictorians. You weren't, well, so much at home anymore, so much in control. That was frightening.

Roberta was allowed ten minutes to present a slide show of facts, figures, and artists' renderings of Belle Rive Estates. The drawings were impressive. Renderings of proposed construction are nearly always impressive.

The Belle Rive Estates of these drawings was hybrid stock of Scarlett O'Hara's Tara and Arthur's Camelot, rising serenely from a sun-dappled knoll above the river, velvet lawns, sculptured shrubs, and manicured planting beds a cinema setting. It spoke of antebellum grandeur, broad verandas, fluted columns, live oaks, and Spanish moss. It had nothing to do with long winters when life was perpetually bent against the wind.

During her presentation Roberta appeared to avoid looking at Harry and Bobby. Her eye swept back and forth over the crowd beyond the first row but never, it seemed, did it come to rest on son and husband.

As the evening wore on, the meeting heated up. One unaccustomed speaker followed another. Delia Mercy, Grandma Mercy's granddaughter-in-law and herself a fifty-five-year-old woman, got up. "I'm thinking I know a little how the Chippewa felt when my great-grandparents came out here to homestead. I don't mind sharing, but I don't want the place wrestled away. I don't want our childhoods plowed under.

"If you go traveling much, you come across tourist traps where they've made spanking cute imitations of the real thing—brandnew ghost towns and Indian villages and mining camps. They're sad and expensive and don't have a nickel's worth of character. The real thing got plowed under while people were looking the other way.

"*We're* the real thing, and we ought to go slow and careful about plowing ourselves under. Plenty comes along that calls itself progress. It's only change. And not for the better, either."

I nearly felt sorry for Roberta. The bandwagon had broken

down. It was going to be a foot-soldier's war, with victory uncertain. It was a war to which Daisy was more emotionally suited, Daisy who loved work almost for its own sake.

I didn't stay behind to talk to Daisy when the meeting adjourned at ten. She was snared in a net of townspeople who converged on the dais, so I hurried down the balcony stairs and out the nearest exit. I had parked across the street and half a block north. I cut across the broad lawn in that direction.

"Mrs. Demming...Larry. Wait a minute. Can I talk to you?" It was Bobby Arneson, without Harry.

"What's on your mind?"

"I need ten or fifteen minutes of your time. Buy you a beer?"

Minutes later we sat on opposite sides of a booth at the Blue Ox. We were the first to arrive from the meeting.

"Anything get decided up at the school?" Benjy Bledsoe, the bartender, wanted to know.

"Nope."

"I wishta hell I'd never heard of Belle Rive Estates. Guys come in here, they get inta the damnedest arguments you ever saw. Who needs it? I thought the Soderman boys was going to kill each other one night. What can I get you?"

We ordered draft beer.

"I'm going to write a book about the struggle over the river," Bobby launched.

"A book?"

"A chronicle of contention between real people over something they care about. I'm hoping it might be helpful to other communities that have to come to grips with something like this. I see it as almost entirely interviews: interviews with town people, farmers, people in government who're involved, with the Belle Rive Estates people, and prospective buyers who've already put their names down..."

"With your mother?"

"Her, too."

"Do you have a publisher?"

"Not yet. And maybe I won't be able to get a commercial publisher. It's possible I might be able to get some grant money. I'm looking into all that right now. Dad's put me in touch with an editor friend in New York. I've started the interviews. Maybe you saw me with the tape recorder tonight."

"Yes."

"You were working, too, weren't you?"

"Yes."

"Can I see what you did?"

I showed him my sketch pad. He pushed his beer glass aside and wiped the table with napkins before opening the pad in front of him. I hadn't gotten much tonight. I'd only put down general ideas and the details I was afraid of forgetting: Harvey Black and his two sons, whose farm bordered Belle Rive Estates, sitting side by side in identical gray suits and identical loosely knotted rep ties, all of them similarly hunched forward, elbows on their knees, attention fixed on the dais.

"May I see?" Harry sat down next to Bobby.

I hadn't seen him come in. The Blue Ox was filling up with people from the meeting at the gymnasium.

Harry flipped through the evening's sketches. "These are what you had in mind," he said to Bobby. Bobby nodded.

"What do you mean?" I asked.

"I'd like some of your pen-and-ink work, like the one of Grandma Mercy you did for Dad, in my book. Unfortunately, I'm not in a position to promise you anything, since I don't even have a publisher."

"That wouldn't matter if I were going to be around. I like the idea. But I'm leaving the country in a month."

"What?" Harry's head shot up.

"I'm leaving for Greece the tenth of September."

"For how long?"

"Indefinitely."

"What's that—six weeks, six months?"

"I don't know."

When Harry saw that Bobby was absorbed in this exchange, he quickly went on to say, "Of course, your being away wouldn't have to queer the project. You could do preliminary roughs here and work them over during your vacation."

"Harry, please." I took back the pad. "Do you know how much work I have to do? Besides getting ready for an extended absence, I have to finish the stuff for Labor Day—the Historical Society show—and I'm working with Homestead Gallery in Minneapolis. I may have a show there in absentia."

"I understand, Mrs. Demming ... Larry," Bobby began, but was interrupted by his father.

"No, Bobby." Harry shook his head and turned to me. "Okay, I understand your problems, but you may already have a lot of work Bobby could use. There must be pictures you've done for the Historical Society that would be appropriate, that they'd lend him after Labor Day. If you went with him on a few of his interviews between now and September tenth..."

"Harry," I broke in, "Bobby doesn't need me. There are other artists, probably better suited. Why not use photographs instead of drawings?"

"He doesn't have time to find someone else," Harry argued. "He needs someone *now*, on the spot, with an understanding of the situation."

Bobby added, "I thought about photos, but I want the book to have the feel of a novel—every word will be true, the words of real people, at any rate—but I want the tensions and characters to come through. Photos seemed too journalistic."

"Could you give him a day or a day and a half a week?" Harry pursued. He hated begging me for anything. He would have done it for no one but Bobby.

"Harry, please. This isn't fair."

"Goddamn it, Larissa, will you *try*? Try for one week!" He didn't say, "You owe me this," but it was there in his voice. His face was bent close across the table, a face that had always been open to me and was now closed. I could see small beads of perspiration just above his brows, and smell a wisp of cologne. I wondered how he was paying the help at the paper and meeting his other obligations.

"I'll try it for a week."

Bobby thanked me. Harry ordered a beer and studied the crowd. I left five minutes later. Rising, I saw Roberta at the bar with Hollis Gibney and Mayor Smiley. And she saw me.

41

Thursday morning I drove out to Ernie Duffy's. I wanted a picture of the apple orchard, the yawning spaces where the farm buildings had stood, and the lonely silo. The barn, henhouse, machine shed, and corn cribs were already gone, I knew. Only the house and silo remained. I wondered why the silo still stood.

At the driveway an enormous white sign of vaguely antebellum design announced: BELLE RIVE ESTATES—GRACIOUS CONDOMINIUM LIVING, 612-555-7382, BELLEVILLE, MN. OFFICE AHEAD, and an arrow pointed the way.

Roberta's black BMW was the only car in the yard. I parked at the far end of the farmyard and legged it toward the river. The bulldozers and trucks were not in sight. I regretted that I hadn't sketched the farm before they'd gone to work on it.

Most of the trees on the property, except around the house, were deciduous—oak, box elder, cottonwood, and apple. They were unharmed—so far. The twisty, reaching limbs of the apple trees were heavy with green apples that might never be harvested. How many other farmers on the river would lose their land? How many developers waited with money that was never enough to pay for the loss?

I'd brought a Polaroid, thinking that Roberta might ask me to leave before I could finish sketching. I threw down my pad and began snapping pictures. Working quickly, I finished a roll of film in a few minutes and reloaded. Halfway through the second roll, I caught sight of Roberta stepping rapidly across the lonely yard and through the orchard. She stopped fifty yards away.

"Come up to the office, please."

"Now?"

"Yes." Without further word she turned and started back to the house.

I finished the second roll of film, slipped the pictures into an envelope and the envelope into my shoulder bag. Picking up the drawing pad, I made my way slowly through the grove, reluctant to have a confrontation with Roberta. Though perhaps it was time.

Closing the screen door behind me, I stood in a central hallway. To the right was the former parlor. On a long table in the center of the room was an architect's scale model of the project. Here was tangible evidence of what might come to pass. I felt defeated by it.

"Beautiful, isn't it?"

I didn't answer but looked up to see Roberta standing in a doorway across the room. She turned back into her office and I followed. This had been the dining room.

"Are people putting money down to reserve units?" I asked, not knowing how to begin our encounter.

"Not yet. We're taking applications and registering requests for particular units. I've been swamped with applicants." She walked to a window and stood looking out at the ravaged farm, as though it were her fiefdom. "When the project has been approved by the agencies who must be satisfied, these people will be contacted for earnest money." How confident she sounded.

Without turning around, she asked, "What are you doing out here?"

"Taking Polaroids of the farm for drawings I want to do." I was near her desk. A visitor's chair sat close by, but I continued to stand. I wouldn't be staying long.

"Why didn't you ask me first?"

"I was afraid you'd say no."

"You're trespassing."

"Are you planning to have me arrested? I could have come by boat and taken the pictures from the river. That seemed a little silly."

"Don't think I don't see through you." She swung slowly around. "I see through you so well."

"What does that mean?"

"You're quite a schemer, aren't you? The book was a stroke of genius."

"The book?"

She took a couple of steps over to her desk, but didn't sit. "It's a legitimate excuse to see my husband. It's a perfect opportunity to come between my son and me. To ... lure him into an unstable, arty world away from Belleville. And your so-called talents will have an outlet."

"Are you talking about the book Bobby's doing on Belle Riviere?"

"A schemer," she repeated.

I thought she might cry, and I didn't know what to do if she did. Under the circumstances, it was difficult to imagine comforting her and yet I felt sorry for her. She was not normally a person to risk what she would consider humiliation. This outburst sprang as much from pain as hatred.

Without thinking, I moved closer. Without considering that it would be the last thing she'd want to hear, I insisted, "The book wasn't *my* idea, Roberta. Harry and Bobby came to *me*. *They* wanted me to do it."

I didn't know I'd been struck until the sharp heat in my cheek told me the cracking sound had been Roberta's hand against my face.

Climbing out of the Volvo, I stood for a moment, hand on my cheek. In the kitchen, I tossed my bag and pad on the table, stepped out of dusty espadrilles and let my shoulders sag. Hildy wasn't around. She might be down at the dock or maybe she'd taken the bike to town.

From the refrigerator I drew out a can of beer, pulled up the tab, and drank, then wandered back across the room to glance at the day's mail lying on the table: a notice to Bart from the university library that a book on Hellenic art had been returned if he still wished to withdraw it; a car insurance premium; and—all I needed—a postcard from James John McClanahan.

> Temporary digs—with young widow, Angeline Goodblood, Great
> Slave Lake, District of Mackenzie, Northwest Territory. Are you
> still there? Someday, maybe soon, we'll sing the old songs and
> dance the hornpipe I taught you, like I was never gone at all.
>
> Love, J.

Lies. He was not moving closer but away. Carrying the card and the can of beer, I went to the bedroom and lay down. I placed the card on the bedside table and set the sweating can on top of it so that the drops running down would smear the exquisite script of Jamie's hand.

"What happened to your face?" Bart asked. Dinner was over. Carrying a brownie on a saucer, he prepared to return to his study. Now he paused beside the table, noticing my cheek. "What on earth happened?"

"I was out in Ernie Duffy's orchard taking Polaroid shots. I made a wrong move and got a branch in the face."

"Was this for the thing you mentioned this morning? The Bobby Arneson book?"

"Yes."

He hadn't approved of the book, though his objections were vague. "Do you think you should see a doctor?"

"No."

"Does it hurt?"

"Only when I laugh."

"Should you put ice on it?"

"I think it's too late, but I'm taking aspirin."

"Pretty ugly-looking. People are going to wonder."

"If you hit me?"

"Yes, I suppose." He glanced uncomfortably in Hildy's direction. She was at the sink, back to us, scraping a pan.

I smiled.

"Is that funny?" he asked.

"Yes," I retorted. That the world might imagine Bart feeling so strongly toward me as to strike me seemed maybe not funny but ... well, yes, funny.

"I'm sorry," I said, feeling suddenly contrite. "Pretty soon you'll be famous. This summer will only be a poignant paragraph in your memoirs. You're going to be rich and famous and happy."

"Is that why you're doing the book with Bobby Arneson?" He nearly always used Bobby's last name, as if that would keep Bobby at a distance.

I looked up. "What?"

"Aren't you trying to steal a little thunder?"

Hildy dried her hands and left the room. In the twilit silence, I stared at Bart.

"You've come to resent me." He set the saucer down on the counter. "You weren't prepared for the children leaving. You expected me to fill the void. When you saw that my work would go on as before, you began filling your days with middle-age nonsense. You interfered with Miranda's life, you carried on a dalliance with Harry Arneson. You've made a mess of things this summer. And you blame *me!* What better way to get back at me than Bobby Arneson's book?" He snatched the brownie from the saucer and left.

The problem in shutting the world out week after week, as Bart did, was that it went about its business, and when you returned, it was not the same and you understood nothing of how it came to be different. It seemed callous and inhospitable, even a little treacherous. To reassert yourself over it, you might do something dramatic, possibly embarrassing, like upsetting a fruit basket.

42 ❧

On Friday afternoon Bobby with his tape recorder and I with my sketch pad went to the courthouse to interview Mayor Smiley, the village council, and members of the county government. It was like trying to catch fish with bare hands. Only old Mrs. Jasperson, who owned three of the best farms in the county and had for years been a member of the council, was willing to open up. Her opinion was that condominiums were a form of self-incarceration. The others equivocated. It was all "under review" and they were not at liberty to discuss it. After a dozen such interviews, the political forestalling itself emerged as a theme.

Whatever Bobby's difficulties, I had a field day in and around the courthouse, with its marble columns and stairways, Palladian windows, and beautifully polished wood paneling. Some of our subjects were interviewed on the lawn or on the wide stone steps leading up on four sides to ten-foot oak doors. The lawn was shaded by stately evergreens and graceful elms, which had inexplicably survived Dutch elm blight. The beauty, even grandeur, of the setting mocked the functionaries who played out their lives against it.

At four o'clock, sitting on marble steps with late sun filtering down through lacy elms, and dust out in Main Street hanging in the air like an early mist, we looked at each other and laughed. The entire day's work had been a kind of elaborate circular folk dance, Bobby and I in single file behind an assortment of village officials dancing in quick, herky-jerky sidesteps away from us.

After dinner I went at once to the drafting table and spent a long evening bent over it with my pencils. Hildy cleaned the oven and later read in Willa Cather's *My Antonia,* one of the books Bart had lent her.

At one point she looked up, irritation pulling at her features. "I can't stand it that Jim and Antonia didn't get married. I don't like it when the right people don't end up together."

"But her husband—what was his name?—Cuzak, was a good man."

"Yes, but you could tell she loved Jim. Don't you think he was sorry he didn't marry her?"

"I suppose. But he made the best of it. He saw the friendship and good memories they would have. He saw that her husband and children would become his friends, too. Maybe he ended up with more than he would if he'd married her. Maybe they wouldn't have been happy."

"Oh, no, I don't believe that. She was the girl who would have made him the happiest."

"Well, remember, the ones who make us happiest also make us saddest."

"God, that's the truth. But I still believe you should marry the one who makes you happiest, even if he makes you miserable."

"It doesn't often happen, I think."

Wandering out of his study an hour later, Bart asked, "I was wondering when you might have a look through the manuscript. I know you're occupied with the Bobby Arneson thing and the whatever for the Historical Society. I don't expect you to *do* anything to the manuscript. I just want you to give me the average reader's reaction." Hearing what he'd said, he backtracked. "You know I do value your opinion."

"Thank you, Bart. Maybe after Labor Day. I have to finish everything for the Historical Society by then. Oh, dear—Labor Day's the sixth and I leave the tenth. No, I may not have time. I'm sorry. I'm sure it's wonderful."

Why not confess? "Actually, I know it's wonderful. I peeked at it one day when you were out. It's splendid. You'll be lionized. It will give you everything you want."

"But I don't want that much." He'd started to turn away. "Only respect."

"Would you like a nice glass of iced tea?" Hildy asked him, laying aside *My Antonia*. "It's probably very hot in your study and you need a little break."

Respect was at hand.

At eleven I put down the pencil. My right hand was cramped and shaking. At the kitchen sink, I washed my hands and massaged them. Shaking out three aspirin, I swallowed them at once with a half-glass of water. My cheek stabbed and throbbed as though I had a toothache. I'd taken aspirin off and on during the day but the pain was worse this evening. Being tired seemed to aggravate it. By tomorrow it would be gone, though yesterday's encounter with Roberta would continue to fester. She was most unhappy, convinced that she was losing not only Harry but—perhaps more important—Bobby. Neither was my fault, but I felt guilty.

I slopped gin into a glass, tossed a couple of ice cubes in, and carried the drink to the living room. "I'm going down and sit on the dock for a while," I told Hildy. "Would you like to come?"

"Thanks, but I want to finish the book."

Sitting on the edge of the dock, I closed my eyes and listened to Belle Riviere gliding serenely past, quite unlike life. For twenty years it had given me cheer. The hollows life created, the river filled.... Within minutes Pan's figure rose out of the water. He laid a hand affectionately on my cheek, and I winced.

"What's wrong?"

"Roberta landed a haymaker yesterday."

He turned my face to examine the cheek by moonlight. "You've got a big bruise. Makes you look a veritable demimondaine. Lucky not to have a black eye. How did it happen?"

"Roberta thinks I'm stealing Harry and Bobby from her. She's very threatened by the book Bobby wants to write. Since I'm involved, she imagines the project is my idea. I shouldn't have told him I would do it. I feel sorry for her."

"If you refused Bobby, you'd feel guilty," he pointed out.

"Yes."

"Dear Larissa," he sighed, "stop clucking over the world. Let some of it slip by. The part that isn't in imminent danger of extinction, you might trust to muddle through."

"What in hell part would that be?"

He laughed again. I loved to hear him laugh, all the more in recent days, as he was still brooding over the dead hound. He saw it in the night sometimes, he said, a white figure slipping through the woods.

"All the world's in jeopardy," I told him. "If I stop worrying, part of it will disappear. I stay up late and get up early, but there are those few hours," I said, only half in jest. "And for you I worry most of all."

* * *

Before hiking back up to the cottage, I implored him to drive with me to Minneapolis for the weekend. "I'll be at the framer's tomorrow. Sunday I'm going to see Miranda. *Please* come."

"What about the young woman, Hildy? Shouldn't you ask her? Won't she think it strange if you don't?"

"She has plans for fanatical housecleaning this weekend. She's glad to have me out from underfoot. I wish she didn't worry so about earning her keep."

"Perhaps she simply enjoys housekeeping."

"I suppose it's possible."

So it was agreed that I would pick him up early the next day, as I had done before. He was pleased to be going. Partly, I think, because of the hound.

With slow steps I climbed the wooden stairs from the dock. I was tired. Approaching the cottage, I heard Bart and Hildy in the living room.

"I'm going to have a glass of wine before retiring," he told her. "Will you join me?"

"I'll get it," she offered, little used to being waited on.

I opened the screen. They didn't hear me. From just inside the door I could see Hildy on the sofa, preparing to rise.

Bart, who was out of view near the kitchen door, insisted, "It will be my pleasure."

Please let him, Hildy.

43

I stood at a window wall in Miranda's living room, looking down at Loring Park. A few weeks ago in the park I had sat near the lake, riffling through travel brochures and sampling books of mythology. Mythology. Just when one thought the sunlit truth was immutable, history would flex and turn; the obscure would become plain, and what had been plain would be wrapped in mist, a myth. It was all truth and all dream. It was all stuff and nonsense, and yet it claimed one so brutally. In the park, a swan arched beneath the footbridge. For such a phantom would any Leda part her milky thighs.

"Sanka?"

I stepped away from the window and lowered myself into a huge, white, androgynous chair, covered in Haitian cotton, an intimidatingly "in" fabric. I was dwarfed by the thing and regretted sitting in it, in part because it was low and I felt rather upended. That was perhaps a sign of age. One did not leap nimbly from low chairs at forty-seven.

"What else do you have?"

"White wine."

"Bring me a glass and the bottle." After all, this would all belong to someone else's daughter were it not for me.

The bells of St. Mark's Episcopal Cathedral across the park rang out. The church where Miranda and Dennis were going to be married. A vague reproach tweaked Miranda's lips.

"Were you going to church?"

"No." She disappeared through a doorway to fetch the wine.

The room was clean and simple. A large, pale dhurrie covered much of the light oak floor. The couch and chairs were white, the tables glass. An aerie of purity. I had the uneasy feeling I was sloughing soil, corrupting the surroundings. Miranda returned, a glass and a chilled bottle of Hungarian Green on a tray, a linen tea napkin tied around the neck of the bottle. She was putting me at a distance with her niceties.

She sat down in the chair opposite, crossed her legs, clasped her hands, fingers laced, around one knee. She wore expensive white raw-silk trousers and a big, loose-fitting white cotton sweater. *Architectural Digest*, that's where we were.

"What is it, about five weeks until the wedding?" I asked.

"Yes."

I poured a glassful of wine and took a sip.

"I mentioned in my letter that I'm working with Bobby."

"Yes."

"I'm enjoying it. The work and Bobby. He's fine, a fine man."

"Yes."

"Very fond of you."

She nodded.

"He's upset about your marriage. I suppose you know that."

"Who hit you? Daddy?"

I'd forgotten the bruise. "Roberta."

"How you manage to look down on so much of the world from your level is an athletic wonder."

"Save your ammunition, Miranda. You're shooting at a moving target."

"What's that supposed to mean?"

"I'm leaving the country the tenth of September."

"Is Harry going?"

"Of course not."

"Then why are you?"

"I'm leaving your father. He doesn't know yet, so please don't mention it."

"The last to know."

"Yes. I wanted him to finish the book first."

"Why are you telling me this?"

"I guess so you'll realize I don't have much of an ax left to grind." I twisted the graceful stem of the goblet in my fingers. "I have no hopes where you and I are concerned. We've torn the house down to the foundation. The foundation remains. We're still mother and daughter. Whether anything will be built on top of that again, I don't know. I'm saying this because I want you to know I'm not clinging to bits of hope. I'm not looking for a last-minute reprieve."

I seemed to sink lower and lower into the chair. My knees rose at an ungainly angle, or so I thought. "I'll go to Greece on the tenth. I'll look for a place to rent there and settle in. You'll be married the following month. We'll be a little like divorced people, you and I, not knowing quite what to do with all that accumulated past. Time and distance will make it easier. I'm not dreading the future in the least."

"Nor am I."

"I guess if I really believed that, I wouldn't be here."

"Being omniscient must give you a great sense of power."

"I'm out of range now, Miranda," I lied. I set the goblet on the enormous expanse of glass coffee table. It stood elegantly alone, like a single sailboat on a placid pond. "I can't think why your friends, other than Bobby, haven't told you what a dreadful mistake you're making and how miserable you're going to be. They must be stinkingly discreet."

I couldn't bear to think of her living a safe, sorrowful life, what

Alice Hazeltine had called "death by comfort." I pulled myself forward in the sheepdog of a chair. "You've loved Bobby for as long as you can remember. I don't know why you're not marrying him, but marrying Dennis won't help."

"Don't start on Dennis."

"I don't intend to. There's no need. Dennis isn't a rotter or a fool. It's wrong for you to marry him merely because it isn't right."

"Would you rather I was lonely than married to Dennis?"

"I'd rather you were in love."

She sighed derisively. She considered me the very worst authority.

"You'll *be* lonely married to Dennis."

"Dennis is kind and loving."

"If you'd been married to him for twenty years and what was left of your feelings was appreciation of his kindness, it might be excuse enough to keep the marriage together. But going in, it's not enough. It isn't fair to Dennis. He deserves someone who's crazy about him."

"He's crazy about me. He says one person in a marriage always cares more than the other. There's no such thing as a perfect division of love. He's willing to be the one who cares more."

She uncrossed her legs and got up. Drifting restlessly toward the glass wall, she slid open the door to the tiny balcony and stood leaning against the jamb, gazing down at the park. "Dennis and I have the same goals and values. We like the same things. We have fun together and we respect each other. We are going to build an old-fashioned marriage on all of that. Romance is a modern invention."

"You're rather a modern invention yourself."

"I'll make it work. I'm intelligent and responsible, and *I'm* not a quitter," she said, glancing at me.

"Such grim determination. Are you getting married or filing a Chapter Thirteen?"

"Oh, stop! I'm sick of your cute assessments of things you know nothing about."

"Then tell me!" I demanded, springing up. "For God's sake, tell me why you're not marrying Bobby."

"Because he's gay, Mother."

I'd expected her to say something negotiable. I stood staring stupidly at her, flinging about in my mind for a mother's practical answers.

"I told him I wanted him anyway," she went on. "I said he could have lovers and I wouldn't mind, if we could be together. He said he couldn't hurt me that way."

This was the girl who had a banker's mentality, who didn't like surprises? The girl who wanted things to add up and come out even?

"I'm so sorry, Miranda."

"I feel... I feel like it's my fault in some way. If I'd been different, he might not need men. For lack of some phrase I couldn't know, or touch I hadn't learned, I lost him. I drive myself insane thinking about it." She turned her head away.

"Miranda." I crossed the room to put my arms around her. "Instinct tells me you're wrong, that there was nothing you could have said or done."

"There was something. I failed."

"If he'd fallen in love with another girl, you wouldn't feel this way, as though you'd failed him." Wouldn't she? I turned her face, daubed with tears, toward me. "You're obsessed by what you can't have. Let go. Otherwise no one can make you happy." What to say that might release her? "As long as you hang on, Bobby feels responsible for your unhappiness. That's wrong. If you care about him, let go." I added cruelly—because I didn't know another way to reach her—"But maybe you don't care *enough*."

That hit. She whipped away from my touch, whirling to face me halfway across the room, features contorted. "Where do you get off, playing the expert? Look at *your* failures! First Granddad. Then Daddy. Granddad pulled out and never came back. What did you do to *him*?"

A child's voice, full of self-pity, begged, "Please don't, Miranda." Groping for the handbag beside the chair, I lurched toward the door. The room tipped and tilted drunkenly.

In the elevator, slumping against the wall, I closed my eyes. Birth was not this hard. I drove home, to the Minneapolis house, feeling old and slow and careful.

For dinner Pan and I drove out of the city to Lord Fletcher's Restaurant on Lake Minnetonka. We sat at a table near the water and watched hundreds of boats, motor- and sailboats, beginning to make their way home. The scene was one to gentle any pain: the retreating sun leaving a path of gold on the water; white sails, colored sails, spinnakers like tropical birds, coursing down the gilded ruffling. But despair hung on tight.

We stayed late beside the water, drinking coffee. Now and then Pan broke off the silence with snatches of philosophical advice.

"You've bundled together all responsibility for all failure and thrown the bundle on your back. It is perverse and excessive. Additionally, I believe it is self-indulgent."

"I shouldn't wonder."

"No call for sarcasm. Constantly feeling guilt relieves you somehow of having to square things, of having to figure out who *is* responsible."

"Please let's not talk about me."

Down the shore a loon cried. Lights began to wink on in the misty late twilight.

"She's looking for the most comfortable misery in which to live out her life," I told him. "Is there absolutely nothing I can do to stop her?"

"Nothing." Later, as we prepared to leave, he said, "She's not yours anymore. Blow her a kiss and let her go."

But I was thinking of Jamie now and how I had failed him, Jamie who clung at this moment perhaps to young widow Angeline Goodblood on the shores of Great Slave Lake. For lack of some phrase I couldn't know, or touch I hadn't learned.

44

"I sort of rearranged things in the kitchen cupboards," Hildy said. "I hope you don't mind."

I had called her from the Minneapolis house to say I was tired and wouldn't drive back to Belle Riviere until Monday morning.

"Not every woman likes someone messing with her kitchen cupboards," she explained. "Some women would take it really personal."

I laughed. "I haven't any personal feelings about kitchen cupboards. She who cleans them gets to arrange them. I hope you didn't spend the entire day working in the kitchen."

"Oh, no. Mr. Demming gave me a swimming lesson this afternoon. I don't know how I got so old without knowing how to swim. I guess I didn't find the time. But I was going to go down and lay in the sun a while and he said, 'Do you know how to swim?' I said, 'No,' and he said, 'What if you fell off the dock?' I said, 'It's not all that deep at the end of the dock,' and he said, 'You can't be too careful,' so he gave me a lesson. Wasn't that nice?"

"Yes, it was."

And after the swimming lesson, I wondered, what then? But of course I couldn't ask. It would have been too alarming, too shocking to her. She would have misunderstood.

But didn't Bart, like Dennis, deserve at last to have someone who was crazy about him? Someone who did not feel toward him like a sister, for whom sex with him was not incestuous?

Once he put his mind to it, Bart was a skilled if somewhat painstaking lover, leaving no i undotted, as it were. Well, that was hardly an unforgivable flaw in a lover. I was suddenly conscience-pricked to note how coldly analytical I could be about all of this. A conniver, Roberta had said.

Before we rang off, Hildy recalled, "You got a postcard in the mail yesterday."

Not another one so soon.

"Would you like me to read it? It's right here. Let's see. It says ...Well, the first word's M-A-V..."

"Mavourneen."

"Is that a name?"

"Sort of."

"'Heading for Winnipeg at the end of the month. Love, Jamie.'"

I sat drinking gin in the dark on the terrace. Pan appeared at the back door.

"Come to bed."

"I can't sleep."

"Come to bed. It's two A.M. You're going to see your daughter-in-law in the morning before we leave. She'll know you've been drinking all night."

"Yes. You're right." I got up and followed him into the house and upstairs.

When I closed my eyes, my head spun dizzily. I seemed to hear a child crying. Getting out of bed, I went to the windows overlooking the street. There was nothing, no child.

"I saw this in a quilting store the other day. What do you think?" I asked Sarah, spreading the crib quilt on the sofa.

"It's beautiful. It looks Amish."

"I know scarlet and brown and black aren't exactly baby colors. If you don't like them, the woman said we can exchange it."

"Oh, no. This is something the baby can use forever. You know, it could be a wall hanging later."

"That's what I thought. I'm so glad you like it." I pushed the quilt aside and sat down.

"You look tired."

"I had too much to drink last night."

She inclined her head.

"A row with Miranda."

"Would you like to talk about it?"

"Not till I can disengage myself a little."

"Well, then, can I show you something I made?" she asked, heaving her eight-month bulk up out of the chair. She left the room and returned minutes later with a canvas bundle.

"What's this?"

"I made this for a girlfriend's little boy. When she comes over with him, I never have anything to occupy him."

She undid the bundle, which was tied with bright ribbons, and spread the unrolled piece of canvas on the floor. It measured perhaps a square yard or more. In one corner was a zippered pocket containing little plastic cars and people and animals and such. "These were very inexpensive," she said. "I'd prefer wooden ones and I'm looking for the right size."

On the canvas was drawn in brilliant crayon colors a sort of aerial view of a village: village square, railway station, school, hospital, and so forth.

"I drew it with indelible markers," she explained, "and a set of indelible markers goes with it, so the child can decide what to name the streets, who lives where, and things like that. If he's too small to print the names, the mother can. In other words, the child could decide, 'This will be Grandma's house,' and the mother could label the house 'Grandma's.' There are all kinds of details and names they can add to the basic layout: the drugstore may be 'Hanson's,' the market, 'Gelbart's,' and so on."

"It's enchanting!" I exclaimed.

"One thing I like about it is that the child can learn some basic words by seeing them again and again on the cloth, words that *he* chose, that mean something to him."

"This is a marvelous idea. And it's portable. You ought to take it to a toy manufacturer."

She laughed. "Actually, I thought I might set up my own small company. What do you think?"

"I think you're foolish if you don't. Let me know if you need money."

With girlish excitement and a good deal of laughing we discussed the idea of Sarah's toy company. "What will you call it?"

"Ms. Goose."

"I can't wait. Oh, I can't wait." Suddenly I glanced at my watch. "My God, it's almost noon. I've got to run."

Sarah walked out to the car with me. Again I felt that longing to stay with her. "Ms. Goose," I said, squeezing her hand, "you're a tonic."

I picked up Pan at Lake Calhoun, where I'd left him sunning himself and reading a book on modern Greece. The colonels and Melina Mercouri. He would return to his homeland prepared for changes.

We stopped for lunch at the Rainbow Café at Lake and Hennepin, then headed out of town. The temperature was nearly one hundred, so we rode with all the windows rolled down, hot wind whipping us. We sped past a highway crew mowing the roadside grass.

"Doesn't that smell good!" The country air was heady with references to other times. To rides in Jamie's car...

When my mother's self-mortification reached out to pull us all into a sinkhole, Jamie would grab my hand and slam out of the house. Screeching away from the curb, we would leave billowing dust and spattering grit behind us. By the time we reached the corner, Jamie regretted his childish recklessness, not because it was reckless but because it was evidence that Mother could strip him of his nature, could make him a person he did not recognize or admire.

Before pulling away from the stop sign at the corner, he would beckon me over to him and ask, "Which way should I turn, mavourneen?" I would point left or right, and at the next corner the same until we were on our way, away, away.

Off to the country we flew. We might search out a hill to climb or a meadow to picnic on. Sometimes we'd end up at a lake. Jamie would rent a boat and we'd go rowing, taking turns on the oars. One time we stripped down to our underwear and went swimming from the boat, and a snapping turtle bit Jamie's toe.

If it was winter, we'd skim across the white landscape planning what to do should a terrible snowstorm blow up, like the Armistice Day blizzard of 1940. We would not be able to get home, of course. We might have to dig a cave in the snow. It was an adventure for which I prayed devoutly, but it never came to pass.

Wending homeward from our truancies, humor restored, Jamie would take one hand from the steering wheel to hold mine. "Mavourneen, you always save me," he would say.

Well, I thought to myself, that's what little girls are for.

Just after two, Pan climbed out of the car on the Blind Moose side of the river, pulled the folded wheelchair from the back of the Volvo, and lugged it into the woods. I waited to see him disappear, then drove to the cottage.

At dinner I relayed the news from Sarah and Clark. The toy-company idea appealed to Hildy. "Now that is clever. If she needs any help, I'd sure like to work for her."

"With a new baby, it will be some time, I daresay, before Sarah will get a company, even a small one, off the ground," Bart noted, dismissing the idea of Hildy's working for Sarah.

During dessert Hildy asked, "How did it go at the framer's? Did he get all your pictures framed?"

"It'll take several weeks to finish them. Before I leave for Greece, I'll pick up what he's completed and give it to Sperling. The rest he'll have to deliver to the gallery later."

"Is it expensive?"

"Yes, quite. But the pieces Sperling sold will pay for this batch. Usually I prefer to frame my own things, but there isn't time now."

"I hope I'm still around here when you have that show. I'll be proud as a peacock. For sure I'm going to the one at the Historical Society. I'll wear a sign, 'Friend of the Artist.'"

Coffee in hand, Bart rose to leave. "I must away, fair ladies." At the door he paused. Like a turtle thrusting forth its head from its shell, Bart extended his mind from under a blanket of preoccupation. "Speaking of history, when you read my book, did you find it slow? I mean, did it seem to you the history got in the way?"

Hildy had put the card from Jamie on top of my bureau. Picking it up, I read, "Heading for Winnipeg at the end of the month. Love, Jamie." Winnipeg. How far was that, four hundred miles? My hand shook. I threw the card down. It was the closest he had ventured in many years.

45

The three weeks that followed were squeezed full of work. Without Hildy to relieve me of virtually every household task, I could not have accomplished all I did. I was up early and late, struggling at the drafting table, flying out to meet Bobby, dashing to the city to buy frames and matting for the Belle Riviere retrospective, and conferring with Gerald Sperling (who'd sold another piece of my work, an oil study of my mother).

Centrifugal force spun me through the daily round. At the end of the day—usually after midnight—it flung me, with my gears still whirring, into the dark across the river where Pan waited.

I never glimpsed the white wraith who haunted him. But because I witnessed its effect upon him, I was prepared to glance up from the worktable late at night, and see beyond the window a ghostly hound reconnoitering.

Pan was not frightened in the sense that you or I would be by a pursuing revenant. But disquiet filled him. His spirit whirled in circles like a lighthouse beacon searching the dark.

"What is it he wants?" he asked as if I might have the answer.

At the cottage, Hildy maintained. Her prudence and pleasance blessed us all. Her motto: Something was better than nothing. And however small the something was, she polished it.

Bart saw her not as a vessel full of hard-won wisdom, but one empty of letters. Into this emptiness he would pour his erudition. The prospect excited him. And it dazzled Hildy. Not having been to college, she had an acute sense of intellectual unworthiness. That Bart considered her capable of sharing the astonishments and perplexities of learning, was nothing short of a miracle.

I wanted to beg her not to sell herself short, but I kept silent. Warnings to happy people have a faintly sour odor, especially when they blow from the direction of unhappiness.

On the Wednesday before Labor Day I delivered the Belle Riviere paintings and drawings to Lydia Comstock at the County Historical Society. We spent the afternoon hanging the pieces in roughly chronological order. Physically tired and emotionally depleted, I grew melancholy as we mounted the pictures. I had invested a good deal of myself in them. I was reminded that my feeling for the river was deep, and when I left I would grieve for it. My leaving was only days away.

"I know you don't have room to keep all of the pictures hanging after the Labor Day show, Lydia, and I don't mind if you sell some of the pieces, but I hope you won't sell the one of the Hazeltine place."

"I think we'll store part of the collection and rotate the pictures. I'll make a note for the board meeting saying that the Hazeltine painting is not to be disposed of without your permission."

The Hazeltine painting, done from the photograph Grandma Mercy had loaned me, showed Alice Hazeltine and the sunbonneted little girl who had been Carrie McCorkle standing on either side of a fabulously handsome Greek houseguest, who presided from an oak wheelchair. They were grouped on the vast lawn that swept down to the river where Alice was to die.

The big Save the River rally, with which Daisy had been occupied for weeks, was scheduled for Labor Day. The Belleville Welcoming Committee, Daisy's opposition, was holding a similar gathering Sunday, the day before.

On Friday a number of executives from Valhalla Projects and Harold Falworth, Inc., arrived in long, black rented limos. They checked into the Hotel Belleville. With funereal swank, the limos, three of them, sat side by side on Main Street.

These Texas magnates had come to meet with local politicians and business people, and to assess what Roberta had accomplished on their behalf. At Sunday's demonstration by the Belleville Welcoming Committee, they would appear on the platform with Roberta and Congressman Wesley Westerman, who had found his bread best buttered on their side.

Saturday morning there was a closed meeting with half a dozen business leaders; Saturday afternoon, an expanded assembly of the full Chamber of Commerce and press. For this meeting in the Crystal Room of the Hotel Belleville, Bobby and I turned up early, tape recorder and pad in hand, to buttonhole those from Valhalla Projects and Harold Falworth who would permit interviews.

Wearing a softly draped sailor dress of fine mauve lawn, Roberta was overseeing preparations for a champagne buffet, striding briskly between the manager's office, the kitchen, and the Crystal Room, metallic voice lassoing the hotel help.

With a curt hello to Bobby, she showed us to a table set aside for the press, then moved along to the head table, where she fussed with the flower arrangements and checked the flatware for smudges. Bobby wandered out into the lobby.

"When do you leave for Greece?" Roberta inquired, holding a glass to the light.

"Next Friday."

"You'll be back for Miranda's wedding?"

"No."

She set the glass on the table and took a step toward me, not sure she'd heard correctly. "You're not coming back for Miranda's wedding?"

"No." Trembling, I gripped the pencil tightly and began to sketch her as she stood beneath the room's namesake chandelier.

"Well...well, *I'll* do everything I can for her," she declared. Roberta would step in as my surrogate at Miranda's wedding. It was to be expected, but it stung.

"She's asked me to take charge of the gifts," she went on, "but whatever needs to be done, I'll do." *You don't deserve her,* her look said. *A child who doesn't haunt you or break your heart. By what fluke is she yours?*

* * *

I had dinner with Bobby and spent the evening at his apartment, working on the book. Riffling through the day's work, he saw the fragmentary sketch I'd done of Roberta.

A wry cast took his face. "Try not to mind my mother," he said. "She comes from a long line of people who believe defeat is immoral." Passing on to the next sketch, he remarked, "I'm one of her defeats."

A strong wind buffeted the Volvo as I drove home along River Road. Clouds raced across a moon that was still nearly full. The air smelled like rain.

I parked in the yard, rolled up the window, and locked the car. The wind whipped the trees. I felt a child's fear. The wind was pursuing me. Perversely, I moved with slow, deliberate steps toward the brightly lit kitchen. Hildy looked up from the teakettle as I came in.

"I was worried about you. The wind's awful. A branch blew down in the front yard a few minutes ago. It made a terrible cracking noise." She tipped up the kettle and poured boiling water into the teapot. When she had carried the pot to the table, she took down cups and saucers from the cupboard and filled a plate with peanut butter cookies. Everything she did, she did with preciseness, performing a charming ritual. She was like a child, albeit a wise child, playing house, and she smiled to herself as she carried out each small task. When the tea had steeped, she called Bart.

"Well, isn't this pleasant?" he said, beaming at each of us in turn. "And you've remembered that I like cream," he told her in a voice rich with praise, as though she were a winning child. It was a tone that made me stiffen when he used it on me. But Hildy slipped into her chair like a satisfied kitten and lifted the teapot, filling Bart's cup first.

Outside, the wind thrashed and moaned, heightening our homey cheer at being together and within. Gazing at Hildy and Bart as if they were my children, I smiled and passed them the plate of cookies.

46 ❧

The rain didn't come. Next morning the wind was down, but heavy clouds hung over the sun like damp, gray rags. Bobby and I found ourselves back at the Hotel Belleville for a fifty-dollar-a-plate fund-raising breakfast where Bobby was to interview Congressman Westerman. From the hotel, members of the Belleville Welcoming Committee would proceed to Humphrey Park for the day's rally.

We arrived at the hotel at eight. Breakfast wasn't until nine, but I needed to sketch backgrounds that I hadn't had time for yesterday, and Bobby hoped to pick up comments from the staff. As I sat in the dim lobby, Harry pushed open the door from the coffee shop and advanced, camera hung round his neck, yellow legal pad in hand. I pretended not to have seen him and went on sketching the front desk, where the manager stood looking nervously at his watch.

There were, I'm told, hard feelings on the part of the Wilhelms of the Kaffee Kafe, over the committee's selection of the Hotel Belleville for the fund-raiser. The Wilhelms had, after all, volunteered the Kaffee Kafe for the breakfast, would have closed its doors to the public, would have met the Hotel Belleville's price and probably thrown in little souvenir birchbark canoes besides. But the committee had chosen the hotel—it had a certain *je ne sais quoi*, as Brenda Bergquist had expressed it. The Wilhelms had to be satisfied with a one-day permit to sell Belgian waffles and cinnamon coffee in the park.

The lobby began to fill with reporters and committee members, the women in their best summer finery from Magnin's, hair freshly coiffed by a Minneapolis stylist. Roberta labored somewhere in the bowels of the hotel, riding herd on cooks and instructing waitresses.

I drew a hasty sketch of Harry as he bent to catch the words of the congressman. Wesley Westerman raised prizewinning Guernseys. In fact, he had a bull, a dram of whose sperm cost more than a fur coat. His congressional district abounded with jokes about

Westerman and his bull. Frisking along behind the congressman was Belleville's Mayor Smiley, smiling at everyone and nothing, commenting on American foreign policy and the politicization of outer space.

As the big money men from Texas began descending the wide, open stairway from the second floor, a hush fell over everyone but Mayor Smiley. Belleville was unaccustomed to wealth and power on this scale; the citizenry was abashed, sensing itself in the presence of royalty.

Roberta emerged to welcome the men as though she hadn't just spent the better part of two days with them. Her smile was as luminous as if she'd come to usher them into a higher state of delight than they'd ever known. Slipping her womanly hand into the kingpin's arm, she led him toward the Crystal Room, where at the piano, Ginger Gibney played "Everything's Coming Up Roses."

Bobby and I eased out of the Crystal Room at eleven, just before the breakfast gathering broke up. Walking out the lobby door, we stood gazing at the three fateful limousines, then headed toward the park.

Harry fell in beside us. I had shunned him and I expect he had shunned me as well. Seeing him had been too painful after the night he'd come unexpectedly to the house in Minneapolis. But my work for Bobby had thrown us together and as time grew short, it was a sad pleasure to see his face, to store up its reality against a day and place far away when it would become, like Jamie's face, a myth: Harry Arneson, crusading small-town newspaper publisher. Under a sky dark and still, the three of us marched wordlessly along together.

WELCOME TO BELLEVILLE, A FREE ENTERPRISE COMMUNITY, heralded a red-white-and-blue banner above the River Avenue entrance to the park. Inside the park, the band shell was draped with bunting. Close by the entrance, a concessionaire offered T-shirts with messages ranging from WELCOME TO BELLEVILLE to NUKE THE EPA. From a sound system rigged high in the trees, a Sousa medley shrilled "Stars and Stripes Forever." One had a sense of being called to arms. Near the band shell a scale model of Belle Rive Estates was set up and printed brochures were being passed out by Simone Signoret Bergquist, sixteen-year-old daughter of Arch and Brenda Bergquist.

Bobby and I and Harry wandered along to the Kaffee Kafe's

stand. My hands were cold, so I ordered a large coffee from Helen Wilhelm, who sported an uncharacteristic straw boater with a tri-colored band. I wrapped my hands around the paper cup.

Hollis Gibney's pink moon face materialized inches away from me. "Come to sign up on the side of the angels?"

"The Devil's looking better every day," I told him, easing toward Harry.

At noon the bell at St. Ignatius tolled. With its last peal, the Belleville High School band struck up "It's a Grand Old Flag," and began to march through the gate and toward the band shell.

Thursday's *Courant* had carried an account of the flap over the band's participation in today's event. Parents of some band members had objected to the use of a public high school organization for what they saw as a political gathering. Roberta let the furor froth for two or three weeks, garnering a good deal of publicity for the Belleville Welcoming Committee. Then she announced that the committee had received from Harold Falworth, Inc., of Dallas a liberal grant earmarked for "community service projects." One of these would be the purchase of badly needed new uniforms for the high school band. Taking their seats before the band shell, the boys and girls swung into their new number—"The Yellow Rose of Texas."

Near the Historical Society's log cabin a fire truck and ambulance stood ready for emergencies. At ten minutes past one, the limousines crawled through the gate and around behind the band shell.

As the last note of "The Star-Spangled Banner" hung in the chill, damp air, and the men on stage settled themselves onto folding chairs, Roberta walked to the microphone amid general cheering. She welcomed the dignitaries and the crowd. She spoke of the broad purposes of the Belleville Welcoming Committee.

If, watching his wife, Harry felt regret or wistfulness, he was careful not to show it. He listened intently, glancing occasionally at the press handout containing excerpts from the speech, and scribbling notes on his yellow pad.

My gaze went back to Roberta, who appeared so strong and bright. Harry and I had imagined that because there had been no sex between us, there had been no affair. We had been cruel in our ignorance.

Roberta introduced Wesley Westerman. The congressman

talked of deregulation and a healthier economy. New ventures like Belle Rive Estates, springing up in the wake of less government interference, were bringing jobs and tax dollars to depressed areas like Beau Bois and Three Toes counties.

As Westerman spoke, the sky, which had seemed entirely filled with sleeping elephants, began to stir. The clouds pressed in upon us. There was no strong breeze, only an occasional impatient switching of branches.

The next speaker was John I. Simpson, president of Harold Falworth, Inc., who spoke a few dry words over us. He took no pains to entertain. He was powerful. That was entertainment enough.

Following Simpson's brief remarks, Roberta revealed, "We have a surprise speaker with us—a college classmate of mine and one of the hardest-working men in Washington. Until late yesterday we weren't sure he'd be able to break away from his heavy schedule to join us. But he saw our need and he came. I know you'll give a big Midwest welcome to Secretary of the Interior Jennings Hooper!"

This was a surprise indeed. Hooper emerged from a door at stage left to frenzied applause. He was tall, with the lean good looks of a cowboy film star. The controversial cabinet member made his way to the microphone, where Roberta waited to clasp his hand and buss his cheek.

They stood together, Hooper's arm at Roberta's waist, facing the crowd and acknowledging the thunderous reception. Finally, Roberta backed graciously away, leaving the Secretary with the microphone and the audience.

The sky was growing darker and more hostile as Hooper began his speech. He was an engaging talker, armed with a great many amusing stories, most of them about himself. He also spoke humorously and candidly about the Washington scene. When he had the crowd in the grip of his down-home charm, he began serving his political philosophy to them, like buttered biscuits.

"I believe that God created the world," he began.

"I believe he showered us with gifts, varied and abundant."

The lights in the park came on automatically as the day began to look like night.

"I believe he meant his gifts for all men.

"But, I especially believe that he meant them for those who have worked and prospered.

"God loves work. He loves to see man work, and harvest the fruit of his work. In our society, one of the fruits of man's work is money.

"God loves money." He glanced around at us all. "Yes, friends, God loves money, I promise you."

Discontented little winds moved among us, snatching straw boaters and political tracts and tossing them into the air.

"*Why* does God love money?" Hooper asked rhetorically. "He loves money because:

"Money buys medicine.

"Money buys food.

"Money buys shelter.

"Money supports churches.

"God has created a world of abundance. He smiles on man's labor and its harvest of money. Can you then imagine that God wants to keep man from securing the abundance He has showered on him?—That He wants to prevent man from securing a bit of Paradise, like Belle Rive Estates, for which man has labored?"

The sound of distant tympans drew closer.

"No. And a thousand times no. God meant man to enjoy the gifts He put on earth. And those who say otherwise are the godless!"

The thunder came from everywhere: from the clouds that flowed down like lava from the heights to the very treetops; from the earth grinding and groaning beneath us.

The young musicians abandoned their instruments and scuttled backward to the base of the band shell, where they huddled behind folding chairs. Trees creaked and moaned and gave up branches like offerings.

From the boiling clouds a shaft of lightning shot downward, striking an elm that danced like a dervish in the wind, severing one of its great, flailing members, which fell down across the forestage. Jennings Hooper jumped backward, joining the little cluster clinging to the back wall, their lips moving soundlessly.

Close-following thunder deafened us and we stood several seconds in eerie, internal silence, staring into one another's faces.

Harry grabbed me, shielding me. The ground yawed violently, pitching a giant pine over, naked roots up, into the river. Would it lift and gape and fold us into itself?

And then the wind died, not in decrements, but all at once. In the sudden stillness, the bell at St. Ignatius tolled two o'clock.

As if released from an enchantment, the clouds let go their rain, washing dusty trees and yellowing grass and people who flowed through the gates and into River Avenue. Men and women ran through the streets like children, and children ran as they always had in summer rain, stomping in the puddles and lifting their mouths to catch the drops. Nature had withdrawn her fury, pressing it back into her bosom.

47

In sweatpants and sweatshirt I stood on the porch, looking at the morning and waiting for the coffee to brew. I'd worked until three, and my shoulders ached. I thought I might go back to bed for an hour when I'd had a cup of coffee. But I had to make sure the world was still there.

Although the worst of the storm had roared over us in minutes, hurling on into Wisconsin, where its anger dissipated, for those few minutes it had seemed we might all perish in the park, crushed beneath the leaden weight of a falling sky. That we hadn't, felt like a reprieve.

The Save the River rally was going at full tilt under an innocent sky in a world clean and sweet-smelling as a freshly bathed infant. Bobby and I hurried from group to group, from place to place, first the boat landing in the park, then the bandshell, and around the fence where stalls were set up as they had been yesterday. Later we drove out to Johnson's and Black's farms along the river, where hundreds of boats and rafts were being launched for the regatta, which wasn't so much a race as a parade. All day long they came down the river, many flying bright banners proclaiming, WE CAN'T ALL LIVE UPSTREAM.

Just like yesterday, T-shirts and buttons were hawked in the park, bearing such sentiments as CONDOS ARE MADE BY FOOLS WHO SCHEME, BUT ONLY GOD CAN MAKE A STREAM. Dave Fergus, whose band had played at the July fund-raiser, anchored a launch upstream in the middle of the river, where he and Backwater played for the amusement of those in the flotilla.

A juggler juggled, and a small troupe of mimes in whiteface entertained in front of the public library. Two clowns, a man and a woman, did simple slapstick routines while selling balloons. A pair of acrobats somersaulted across the green, and an old man in a hobo costume put a pair of black poodles through balletic paces.

I was impressed by the number of people from outside the village, and even from beyond the state, who had come to volunteer time and talent. Politics and religion and commerce and sex had made cynics of us all, and yet, when we closed the door and no one could see, we still entertained hope as if it were a kinky passion. Occasionally we took our hope out in public, as today.

I spent a few minutes in the Historical Society museum, admiring my exhibition. Lydia Comstock, museum director, amused, I suspect, by my rapt interest in my own work, stood beside me, following my gaze as I evaluated the showing.

"The opaque watercolors are the most successful," I told her.

"I like the ink drawings best," she countered.

"You may be right."

"You were here in the park during the storm yesterday?"

"Yes. Were you?"

"No. It must have been horrible."

"Scared hell out of me."

"Some people are saying it was a judgment. They really believe that." She smiled her embarrassment.

"Well, we've had windstorms before."

"The big tree that went into the river, that wasn't the wind."

"We'll have to see what the seismologists tell us."

"Yes. It's easy to see, though, how legends get started. They say it was like there was a giant under the earth."

Minutes later librarian Nellie Bergen waved a petition at me from a booth where signatures were being taken to stop Belle Rive Estates. "When do you leave?" she asked.

"I leave Minneapolis Friday. Belleville tomorrow."

"How long will you be gone?"

I shrugged.

"Going to paint while you're away?"

"Oh, yes."

"The retrospective's good," she said, inclining her head toward the museum. "Some of the watercolors of the woods make you feel you'd never come out if you went in." In the same breath she said, "You're not coming back, are you?"

I didn't answer, but touched her hand and glanced at my watch. "I have to find Bobby. I told him I'd only take ten minutes."

The official program began at two. Daisy started it off, introducing the others on the stage: one of the state's Senators, Ben Zeidler; Lieutenant Governor Fridley; a former EPA head; and Grandma Mercy. I remember vividly parts of Grandma Mercy's talk.

In her blue print georgette with the hand-worked lace collar, she began, "Civilization is very uncivilized. When I look through my *National Geographics*, the decent people are mostly the ones without clothes. The ones with clothes are the savages...

"Civilization isn't what we had hoped. We were misled by those who stood to make money from it. Civilization has cured diseases and created new ones with pollution. Civilization has given us the means to end hunger, and the politics to withhold food. It's freed us to spend time with our loved ones and destroyed the family.

"A while back we decided it was wrong for little children to work in mines and factories. When laws were passed to stop it, business didn't come to an end. We decided it was wrong for one company to have a monopoly and control the price of goods. When we passed laws to stop it, business didn't come to an end.

"Isn't it time to say it's wrong for industry to pollute and destroy the environment, whether it's the quality of the air or the beauty of the countryside?

"Still business cries 'This will be the end.' I say, if business is half so wise or clever as it purports to be in advertising, it'll find a way, as it has in the past, to obey the law *and* make a dollar."

Late in the afternoon I closed my eyes a minute and the park sounded like a big party. It was a party occasionally marred by a drug arrest or a drunken fistfight. Part of the crowd was too mellowed out to support its own weight, much less the weight of a commitment. But in the reading room of the Historical Society, extra chairs and benches had to be set up for a workshop in environmental protection. Mark Braun, minister of the United Methodist Church, operated an all-day child-care service in a roped-off area at the far end of the park, so that parents of small children could attend workshops and films. Everywhere Daisy's hand was apparent.

She even had a command post in the basement of the public library. From there she kept in radio contact with lieutenants scattered from Johnson's and Black's farms, to the southernmost in a string of rescue craft anchored along the route of the flotilla.

Early in the evening Bobby and I dropped in on her. "We're still totting the figures, but I estimate that five thousand people celebrated the river today," she said. "For a village this size, that's impressive. I haven't any idea until the stalls close how much money we made.

"As you maybe noticed, there were two camera crews here. One from commercial TV in the Twin Cities, one from public television. We're hoping to be seen outside the state.

"Realistically, none of this saves the river, but it draws attention, raises money, and, I hope, it raises questions and consciousness. Many people signed up today to work in our campaign, many put their names to a petition for a referendum. It may be that we won't see the issue settled for a year."

When Bobby and I got up to leave, Harry asked his son, "How much longer are you going to work?"

"I'm done."

"I have a couple of backgrounds I have to fill in," I told Bobby, "so you go on home, and I'll call Hildy to come get me when I'm finished."

"I'll give you a lift when I'm through here," Harry said.

Bobby looked at me.

"All right. In the morning I'll drop off the sketches that are ready," I told him.

Daisy followed us to the door. "You'll stop by the house in the morning?"

"When I leave Bobby's."

Half an hour later I stopped drawing. It was growing dim. Snapping several Polaroid shots of settings I would need, I packed up my gear and carried it to the office.

"Can I leave this stuff here while I walk around the park?" I asked Harry.

"Sure. If you hold on, I'll walk with you."

There were still quite a few people around, although the stalls had folded and the rally was officially ended. In two or three places young people were gathered around a guitar player. We walked down a path that led toward the museum.

"I'm grateful, Larissa," Harry said.

"For what?"

"The book. You've thrown yourself into it. Bobby's pleased as hell with it."

"Have you seen what we've done?"

"Yes. The drawings are your best."

"I think so, too."

We were nearly at the municipal swimming pool. "Twenty years ago I met you there," Harry recalled, pointing to a bench. We turned left onto a path carrying us to the river. "I haven't done anything right with you this summer," he said.

"And nothing wrong. It was a no-win situation."

"I should have made my move years ago when we were younger."

"There was never a right time."

"Where will you settle?"

"I'm not sure. I'll send Bobby an address right away so he can reach me. I'm going to miss him."

"Why are you going so far?"

"So that I'll be entirely gone. If I were in Chicago or Denver, I'd always be thinking how easy it would be to come back. I'd let my mind play with the idea. And I'd spend my energy trying to stay away. When you're torn like that, you're nowhere at all."

"When the kids were young," he said, following his own thoughts, "I felt close to you, connected to you through them. I didn't mind so much that you were married to someone else, because the children seemed almost like *ours*. But when they were older and gone, I was left looking at you across a chasm."

"We missed the tide, Harry."

"Tides come more than once." He sat on a bench facing the river.

"A tide can be so strong it carries you way beyond where you could begin again."

"Are you so stubborn because of Miranda?"

"Partly."

"I went to Brad Haney." Brad Haney was a Blind Moose attorney. "He's going to handle my divorce."

"Why are you telling me this?"

"You don't have to go halfway around the world to stay out of Miranda's way," he said.

Farther down the beach, near the landing, young people were singing about ninety-nine bottles of beer on the wall.

"Are you asking me to marry you?"

"Yes."

Oddly, the assurance that he still cared about me gave me the strength to leave him.

"What about the night you came to the house in Minneapolis?"

"I don't know what that was about and I don't want to know." He rose, walking slowly down to the water's edge. "It hit me like a truck. The timing was so bad. I hated you."

The fevered devotion I kept repressed, flushed to the surface. The line of his back, the curve of his neck where it met his shoulder, these almost overwhelmed me. A strong man's vulnerability was nearly my undoing. I turned my gaze away.

"But when it came down to it," he said, "when it came to losing you, what happened that night meant very little." He swung around. His voice low, bewildered, he asked, "Are you listening to me, Larissa?"

"Every word, Harry."

"It doesn't feel as though you're hearing."

"Harry, if it could have worked with *anybody*, it would have been with you."

"Couldn't we see at the end of a year?"

"Living on hope is like being hungry all the time." I grasped his hand and put it to my cheek.

He sat down close beside me and, sighing, put an arm around my shoulders.

"Sleep with me tonight, Larissa."

"Please don't, Harry."

"Bart?"

"No."

"The man in Minneapolis?"

"No. I can't explain. It's as though I've lived two lives. The first wasn't ended when the second began. I have to find a way to end the first. Or perhaps the second. I have to give myself completely to one or the other."

"That's pretty cryptic."

"I know and I'm sorry. I'm not playing games."

The voices in the park grew fewer. Finally, there were only straggling, disembodied good nights, like remembered summer-night good-byes of childhood, floating through the park and down the years:

Jamie, like God the Father, standing on the front porch steps, summoning me to him from the darkness up the street, a white aureola of porch light spread around him. Me, walking backward down the sidewalk, stumbling over uneven sidewalk seams and calling, "Good night. Good night. Good night. Good night," until Jamie said, "That's enough," and ushered me into the house, where we sat reading together in the intimate exclusivity of his lamplight.

Long after everyone was gone from the park, Harry and I remained amid the soft echoes of their many good-byes. When the night had stretched into early morning hours, we rose to leave. We kissed, a kiss at first sweetened with friendship, then filling up with all the rich passion I felt for him and this place, all the sorrow I felt at leaving them.

48

I left the cottage at eight the next morning. The farewells were light and not at all unpleasant. It was thought that I was taking a vacation. Hildy was staying to keep the house for Bart while I was away.

It was cowardly to leave in the way I did, but I would do it again. I've never understood Bart so dispassionately, nor felt as close to him as I did in leaving him. He was not unkind. He was intelligent and accomplished. He only required someone who was totally dependent upon him intellectually. In return he offered the security of his household, recondite cocktail-hour conversation, and the simple, unquestioned physical dependence of an infant. Many women were well suited by such a man, especially those women who yearned for a more or less continual motherhood. I hadn't been the woman for him, I who had failed at daughtering and mothering.

Bobby was still in his apartment when I rang the downstairs bell at eight-twenty. Fully dressed and smelling of after-shave, he came down to let me in. I handed him the work I'd completed, and he carried it up with him and into the living room.

"Sit down."

"I can't stay, my dear, except a few minutes."

I stood at the window. If I lived in this apartment, I would stand at the window for hours. The river and the bridge were visible to the left. Directly across the street was the park, where half a dozen Save the River people were dismantling stalls and cleaning up.

I could see Nellie Bergen arriving early for work at the public library, her tread youthful and nimble as she ascended the broad steps, a great ring of keys swinging from her hand. Chatelaine of the stacks, of apprehensible secrets. Turning, I said, "There's a maple in the park that's changed color."

"Summer's gone by Labor Day."

"It's always a terrible shock, September is. If I could, I suppose I'd fly from summer to summer, like a surfer." I sat in a battered old wing chair. "I'll be in Minneapolis until Friday, as you know. I'll (I'd nearly said 'We'll') leave the car in the airport lot. I appreciate you and Hildy picking it up. Whatever work I finish between now and Friday, I'll leave in a portfolio on the backseat. You can call me at the house before then if you have any questions. I'll call you the minute I have a mailing address. Will you see Miranda when you're in town?"

"Would you like me to take Hildy to meet her?"

"That would be good."

We talked about the book, some minor changes in outline and an additional sketch we needed in one of the later chapters. Awkwardly, I told him what working on it had meant to me, the satisfaction and confidence I'd found in it.

"You have to get to work," I said finally, rising. "I've kept you too long."

"Any message for Miranda?"

"No." I hugged him tightly. "I love you, Bobby." Clutching my handbag, I rushed to the hall and down the stairs.

I sat on the front porch of the house on Fleur Street. Daisy sat opposite in another wicker armchair. The conversation was quiet and filled with intimate lulls and little sighs of recollection.

"I'll drive out to the cottage tonight and meet your Hildy," Daisy told me. "Until she and Bobby pick up the Volvo on Saturday, I'll bring her to town for groceries or whatever she needs."

"I wonder if she might decide to settle here," I ventured.

"There's not much in Belleville to attract a single woman."

"I meant in Minnesota." The many things I'd wanted to say were still unsaid.

"I'll come to Greece and visit you," Daisy promised. "Some time during the next year I'll fly to Paris and see Georganna, and then I'll catch the Orient Express to Athens. Does the Orient Express go to Athens?"

"It probably would for you." Time was escaping. "And you'll write."

"Yes." Then, without preamble, "Why are you going?"

I looked at her blankly, and she pursued, "It's because you've fallen in love with Harry, isn't it?"

"That should be reason to stay."

"It should be, but in this case I don't think it is. Are you afraid?"

"Afraid?"

"Of a blood-and-sweat, no-holds-barred love affair?"

"I don't think so." How old-fashioned "love affair" sounded.

"Of marriage, then."

I could only stare. Afraid of marriage? "A fascinating question, one we shall have to consider at our next meeting," I said, rising. "It's nearly noon."

"Why not leave after lunch?"

It was difficult saying good-bye to her. I put my cheek to hers. "Remember, Daisy, 'Reward is its own virtue.'"

She waved and called to me as I ran down the sidewalk, "Don't take any wooden drachmas!"

I hurried to the car.

"You've been upset the entire afternoon," Pan observed. "I'm to blame in some way."

He was settled on the tiny flagstone terrace outside the Minneapolis house. I had carried our things upstairs, opened the windows, and found a bottle of tonic. Now, with an untasted gin and tonic in my hand, I stood at the terrace door, cowed, like a child not wanting to come forward.

"Larissa, come sit down."

I came and sat down and even managed to sip my drink very much like a grown-up.

"What is wrong? Why are you upset?" Oh, his voice was indulgent and his eyes concerned, but he had changed. As I was going away from Bart, so he was going very rapidly away from me. He was more and more himself, the self he once had been. He had changed as naturally as the leaves around us were changing to yellow and red, without meaning to cause melancholy, without intending to inspire that autumnal stocktaking in which one always came up short.

"Tell me what's wrong," he invited, and his voice had a majesty that made him sound like an actor playing a father. He grew taller even as he sat in the lawn chair, I thought, and I shrank.

"Well?"

"It's . . . I'm not angry."

"What, then? You're upset at leaving your life behind. That's natural. But it isn't that."

"Partly it's you. The closer you get to home, the younger and stronger you are. Your immortality oppresses me."

"I wish immortality were mine to bestow."

"It's not for me, you understand."

He gave me a penetrating look and waited like a patient confessor for me to go on.

"Nothing. It's nothing." I sagged and held tightly to my glass.

"Are you afraid I'll leave you?"

"Don't ask me that again!" I shrilled. I was shocked then, but not remorseful, only confused. And weighted down, unaccountably weighted down. I got up before I became too heavy to move, and went into the house, carrying my drink upstairs with me.

Setting the glass on the table beside the little silver-framed pictures of the children and Jamie, I lay down across the bed. "I didn't expect him to look after me forever," I said and fell asleep. When the phone rang, I woke angry, as though I'd been angry in sleep. The purring clock beside the bed said 5 P.M.

"Hello?"

"Mother?" It was Clark.

"Yes. Who did you think it was?"

"I'm at the hospital. Sarah had the baby."

"She's the most beautiful baby I ever saw," I told Sarah. "And eight pounds! What a lovely size, not skimpy and unfinished-looking like so many babies."

Clark had fallen asleep in a chair by the window. His head rested against his fist, his cheeks were flushed, and his thick, dark hair was mussed. His stolidity had always stood between us, I thought, but now he looked assailable, fragile, and I thought perhaps I'd always misjudged him. You were continually assessing and reassessing, getting it all straight—who and what they were, and what you were in relation to them—and the next week finding it wasn't so or at least doubting that it was, and having to start sorting everything again.

"He didn't get much sleep last night," Sarah said. Maternity rolled from her in great, lush, ripened waves, washing over Clark and me. I felt so petty and unreal and soiled beside Sarah. Her serenity pillowed me, however, as though I were another of her children.

"You must be exhausted yourself."

"No. The baby was born at two-fifteen and I had a good long nap afterward."

"I hope Clark will take pictures of the baby and send them to me."

"How long will you be gone?"

"Quite a while."

She looked sidewise at me. "You won't be here for the wedding."

"No."

"I didn't think so. Miranda's father will be giving her away, though."

"Yes."

She lowered her chin in a half nod, her eyes fastened to the white cotton thermal coverlet. She'd guessed that I was clearing out.

"Do you have someone to help you when you get home?" I asked.

"My mother's coming tonight. Dennis is picking her up at the airport."

"That's nice." Dennis. He was already part of the family, picking up Sarah's mother, and doubtless ingratiating himself in other ways. Envy and resentment tweaked me as I pictured the family like a ring-around-the-rosy, hands joined. I was on the outside of it now. Further outside.

I had a sudden panic. "Is Bart coming?" I didn't want him to pop in on Pan and me. "I have the car. Bobby Arneson and a woman named Hildy are coming to pick it up on Saturday."

"Dad is driving down on Sunday. That would give us a chance to be settled at home, he said."

"I suppose he'll bring Hildy."

"He said he would. Who is she?"

So I told Sarah about Hildy.

"The poor girl," she said.

"Yes. You and Miranda will have your hands full for a few weeks, but maybe you could give Hildy a call once in a while. You might even find some little task for her to handle at the wedding, so that she feels part of things. Don't tell Miranda *I* suggested it, though."

"I'm sorry things are so bad between you and Miranda."

"It isn't fatal."

Sarah's eyes seemed very bright, glassy even, and I saw that there was a fine pencil line of perspiration across her upper lip.

"You're tired. You're riding on excitement. I'll come back to-morrow." I pulled a tissue from the pack beside the bed, blotted her face, and kissed her feverish cheek. "We won't wake Clark," I said. "Let's let him sleep." I had to force myself away from the comfort of her. "You haven't any idea what you mean to me, Sarah."

Heading to the door, I turned. "I forgot—have you picked a name for the baby?"

"Larissa. Larissa Ellen Demming. I chose it. Isn't it beautiful?" Her smile wrapped me, close and warm. I was a child again. A *happy* child.

"Hello." I picked up the clock, held it close to my face, peering at the dial—4:30 A.M.

"Mother." It was Clark.

"Yes? Clark, what is it? What's wrong?"

"She's dead."

"Who? What are you talking about? Is it the baby?"

"Sarah's dead."

I dressed, packed Pan, the wheelchair, and his bags into the car, and drove him to the Marriott Inn near the airport.

"I'll call you."

Again, the world had tilted on its side and I was falling off. Really falling off this time. Gullies of earth scraped away as my nails scrabbled for purchase on a swooning globe. Why not fall and be done with it? Could it be so bad?

Press your feet down firmly. That's what I'd said. If the world drops away like the deck of a tossing ship, you'll still be connected. But I hadn't pressed firmly enough.

At the funeral on Thursday I clung to the church pew in front of me. When we left the church, I let go and I slipped down through the afternoon, seeing it all go by and none of it anything to do with me anymore.

Everyone said it was too much to expect Sarah's mother to care for the baby, mourn her daughter, and worry about callers at Clark and Sarah's house, so family and friends came to the house on Thomas Avenue. Sarah's mother had insisted on caring for the baby. It kept her going, she said.

Well, she was feeling terrible guilt, too, wasn't she? For the times she'd quarreled with Sarah, for saying Sarah's brothers had been easier, for not having been there to save Sarah's life? If it had been Miranda, I'd have died of guilt; it would be worse than for Sarah's mother. Not that I was trying to win a Nobel Prize for guilt, but at least Sarah's mother knew that she'd been an honest-to-God mother, not a sham, on account of which, in some cosmic retribution, she was responsible for her daughter's death.

Hildy and Daisy were there at the house doing things with food. Strangers from Clark's office came and near strangers from the university. How had they all heard? And the neighbors?

I was underfoot, slipping down, slipping past them, like someone falling from the top of a tall building and seeing...at...each ...window...people she recognizes, but of course not being able to stop or even to cry out and not wanting to.

I would have liked to go upstairs and turn on the radio. I would surely have felt closer to Sarah. But when I turned on the radio in the kitchen, someone immediately turned it off. Miranda, maybe. Maybe not.

I saw Harry and Roberta and Bobby there, at the funeral and at the house. "Will you still leave?" Harry asked.

"Yes."

He studied me for a long while, then seemed embarrassed, as though by mistake he'd spoken to a stranger. Well, I suppose he was thinking about Clark and how Clark would have neither wife nor mother and how sad it was. I could have told Harry I knew how sad it was. I knew.

The baby was serene, rarely crying, but eating, then sleeping like a little hibernating thing who would wake when this strange winter of misfortune was over.

In the early evening Clark and the baby and Sarah's parents left. Clark held the baby. He was far away, inside his and his baby's world.

Hildy saw me to bed. Strange, because I don't remember drinking anything. People were drinking. I saw drinks in people's hands but I don't remember having a thing. Maybe I didn't.

I was sitting on the edge of the bed. Hildy came in and said, "I thought you'd gone to bed and here you are still up. They've all gone home. Where are your nighties?"

She opened drawers until she found one.

"How could it happen? How can she be dead?"

"Let me help you with your dress," Hildy said, urging me up from the bed. "She got this little infection," she explained, as it had been explained more than once without my yet believing it. How *could* it have happened that way, so quickly, so easily, as if it were nothing at all to snatch away the life of someone young and strong? There should be more to it.

"They gave her an antibiotic," Hildy went on patiently. "She'd never had antibiotics before..."

"Isn't that incredible?"

"There was no way the doctor could have known she'd be that allergic. Who would dream it?"

"God must lie awake nights thinking of these things."

"Mr. Demming will probably be up real soon."

"Who...what did you say?"

"Mr. Demming will probably be up real soon." She pulled back the covers.

"Oh, him." I sat on the edge of the bed.

"Don't you want to wash your face and brush your teeth?"

49

"She'd never been sick," I told Pan. "Never. It's hard to believe. I never heard of anyone who was never sick. She was allergic to the antibiotic. An infection had developed. Nothing serious..." I had said all this before, hadn't I? Yes, I was sure I had.

I put my head against the impersonally dusty-smelling airplane seat. It seemed to me that the plane was flying very slowly. Was that dangerous when we were so high in the air?

"Sarah was an extraordinary girl... Why am I saying this? What good does it do to keep saying these things? I can't stop." The weeping began again. Or maybe it had never ended. I saw the tears on my dress.

"She wasn't pretty. She didn't find it necessary. But she was wise. Something she was born with. The baby is like that. Maybe it's something inherited, an extra chromosome or gene."

Pan handed me a clean handkerchief. What did he expect me to do with that?

"Wipe your eyes. Would you like me to get you a cold cloth?"

"For Christ's sake, don't leave."

"The baby, she's dark like your son?"

"Yes, like Clark... Do you think she might inherit Sarah's allergy? What if she caught a cold or developed a little infection? Babies are always doing that. What would they do? Would they give her antibiotic, do you think? I'd better write to Clark about it. Tonight. I'll write tonight."

"I'll take care of it."

I don't believe she's dead. It has struck me through the heart. Am I only thinking these things or am I saying everything out loud?

"Have I been saying everything out loud to you?"

"Only just what one would say."

"I see."

Later, he said, "I think you should eat something."

"The one thing in life I know is right is leaving Bart. That's the *only* thing I know is right." *Where had I got the man's linen handkerchief I was twisting?* "Since the children went to college I've been waiting in the lobby of a respectable hotel for someone who's never going to come downstairs. The hotel tonight, what will it be like?"

"It will be pleasant."

"How do you know if you've never seen it?"

"We will only stay in a place that you like."

And how will I know if I like it? What if I look at it and don't know? He hadn't explained how I was to judge. "I don't think I can do it."

"What's that?"

"Choose the hotel. You must choose."

"Yes, all right." He pointed to the tray in front of me. "Please eat something. I've asked them to leave the tray, because I hope you'll eat. What about the fish—couldn't you eat some of that?"

I shook my head.

"The melon is good."

"I've lost my appetite." Yes, that was *just* how it was. It was lost. Misplaced or gone forever? "Poor Clark. He's never lost anyone close. He hasn't experience with losing. Do you think experience helps? I lost my mother when I was fifteen. But my mother was different, nothing like Sarah. My mother made us lonely. It's not fair for me to judge, I suppose. What do we know of our mothers if we don't grow old with them?

"She was only thirty-five when she died. Think of that. Twelve years younger than I am now. I thought she was old. Everyone said, 'Poor Marie. So young. So beautiful.' To me thirty-five didn't seem a strange age for a mother to die. I didn't want her to die. I hadn't gotten to know her, hadn't learned to please her yet. Still, when she was dead, I did wonder if I hadn't killed her."

"It's a natural thing for a young person to think when a parent dies."

"It's rare when parents and children are properly matched. We are mostly mismatched sets. It's like sending away to a crazy mail order house where the orders are all mixed up. A mother is ordered, they send a girlfriend or a distant cousin or even an enemy. A father arrives in the mail, clearly marked 'brother' or 'uncle' or 'husband.' People try to make the best of it."

I have the ticket stubs from the flights: Northwest Orient Airlines, Mpls/St.P to JFK; TWA, JFK to Athens. They are in a manila envelope, with postcards bought at JFK and never mailed and an assortment of things not worth keeping that I'm unable to throw away. But I don't remember much else about the flights, except that we took off from JFK at sunset, flying east, against the grain of time, so that night fell upon us with theatrical suddenness.

I do recall a pounding in my chest like footsteps running away. And I recall telling Pan, "Jamie lived in Greece. Years ago. I lose track. I have the postcards in little boxes."

Boarding and deplaning with a wheelchair-confined man involved a ceremony of attention and attendance, I'm sure, but I don't recall. Nor anything of clearing customs, though of course we *did*. By my ticket stubs I know we arrived in Athens at 11 A.M. I know further that we slept that night in a small hotel on the Ionian coast of the Peloponnese, not far from Pirgos, and beyond that, Olympia. The town was Theopropoi. The trip from Athens was by train.

Maybe it was on the train—it doesn't matter, I suppose—that I told Pan how Jamie had sold the stores, sold the house, sold the car even, and set off, with a single satchel, as soon as I was moved into the university dorm. He left me like a foundling on the dormitory steps.

The early days in the hotel on the Ionian shore are elusive. Nor do I recall much about the village or even the beach. I remember talking incessantly, not being able to stop. I remember in the morning when I woke, saying to myself, "Today I'm going to shut up."

But I didn't. "My identity in the dormitory derived partly from Jamie's postcards," I told Pan. "In the cafeteria or in the lavatory, the girls would ask, 'Where's Jamie these days?' They took to calling him 'the kid.' Julia, my best friend, suggested I tack the kid's latest postcard on the bulletin board in the lobby so everyone could keep track of him."

"How did you feel about that?" Pan asked.

"I hated having to share the little I had of him."

"Why did you do it?"

"It kept them from thinking of me as someone who had no one."

"I see."

"I lived in the dorm until I was married. Most of my friends pledged sororities or moved into apartments, and they wanted me to, but I couldn't see the point. The dorm was home. For the holidays I went to a resort, or sometimes home with a friend.

"A couple of times Jamie blew into town and descended on the dorm. He was still young, let me see, he would have been forty, forty-one, something like that, and he was handsome. But I've told you that." Maybe I'd told him several times. I didn't know. "Black curly hair and icy blue eyes, and wrapped around him, like a great, romantic cape, was the air of a sojourner. Girls were shameless, reduced to groaning adolescence.

"One night he took me to dinner at Charlie's—a restaurant that's disappeared now. We feasted, ate and drank like fools. I was still underage, but I made myself up and arranged my hair to make me look older and we drank two bottles of champagne. The waiter thought I was Jamie's mistress. It was that way when I was fifteen and we drove across the country. That was an unusual time, driving across the country.

"I felt very gay and witty at Charlie's, flirting across an expanse of white linen. I imagined that I *was* very gay and witty, putting him at his ease, making him happy so he'd come back soon, maybe for good.

"We went to dinner early because Jamie was leaving early the next morning for Cuba, which gives you some idea how many years ago this was. You could fly off to Cuba without thinking about it.

"It was only nine o'clock when we said good-bye outside the dorm. Light snow was falling and the air felt almost warm. It only lacked sleigh bells and the muffled beat of horses' hoofs on packed snow to land us in the middle of *Anna Karenina*. Although it was a miserable ordeal letting him go, I pulled myself together and smiled. Such noblesse was worth whatever it cost, since it was bound to bring Jamie back.

"Tipsy and all agush, I ran down the third-floor hall looking for Julia. I would tell her all about Jamie's great savoir faire. Savoir faire meant a lot to Julia. It was what college boys lacked, she said. Their fatal flaw. I didn't find her but I was waylaid by the others to describe dinner with the kid.

"'Squab and champagne, my God, what heaven.' Everyone agreed that the kid knew how to lay on the festal board. I went to bed early, hopeful and jaded.

"When I rang the Radisson Hotel the next morning to say

good-bye, Julia answered the phone. I hung up, of course, when I recognized her voice. I didn't know what to feel and so I felt nothing. Just empty. For several days, when anyone spoke to me, it was as though they were throwing pennies down an empty well."

50

"And what did you say to your father about this?" Pan wanted to know.

"I never mentioned it to Jamie or to Julia. Neither of them was married. Julia was nineteen and hardly a virgin sacrifice."

"But you'd had a shock."

"Yes. A shock. More than his selling the house and packing his grip, *that* night was his leave-taking. I didn't think I could recover."

I often woke from a dream of Sarah. The dream was very real. Sarah was alive. *I* was in the hospital bed and *she* was standing beside me, holding my hand and smoothing back the hair from my forehead. She smoothed back my hair as though I were feverish while, in fact, I was very cold but didn't want to admit it.

She tried to reassure me, but I had no idea what was wrong, so her words necessarily fell wide of their mark. But the concern and assurance were as welcome as mother love. She would say, "We're all crazy, you know. It's passed along on the mother's side. I'll stay with you, don't worry." And I would sit up, plucking her sleeve. "You will stay." And she would nod and stroke my forehead. I was washed over by a wave of cleansing relief at finding her alive. Then I would wake up.

Whatever shape and order those days had, Pan saw to. To me they were as formless and shifting as a rolling fog. It was a great effort merely to go downstairs to eat. Sometimes, Pan went out, managing the fragile elevator and doors and streets by himself or with the help of Nikos, a child who was some relation of the hotel owners. Other times, the boy would fetch us wine or bread and cheese so that we could make a simple meal in our room.

We were sitting by the window eating bread and feta the day Pan said, "I want to know how you met your husband."

"It's dull stuff."

"You don't want to talk about it?"

"You make it sound peculiarly significant or odd when you say that. It's only that it leaves a mean, copperish taste in my mouth."

He pulled at his ear and stared at me.

"I took Ancient Civilizations from Mr. Demming. Several of the dorm girls had told me they took Ancient Civilizations from him with a vague hope of getting a date. It was rumored that he occasionally dated students, a practice which was forbidden in those days, even if the girl was of legal age."

I crumbled the cheese on my plate into very fine crumbs. "I went into the class with this knowledge but hardly *because* of it. His was the only section which fit my schedule, and it was a course I should already have completed.

"When I saw him, however, I was reminded of what I'd heard. He was, in his own fashion, as handsome as Jamie. While Jamie's looks were dark, aggressive, and Irish, Mr. Demming's were ever so slightly faded, with a mellow patina of disillusion or dissolution or soulful ennui, depending on the time of day.

"After I'd finished the course, I ran into him occasionally, particularly at the library. We were on a tentative first-name basis, and one day during a summer session we bumped into each other on our way down the library steps.

"'Larissa, how is it going?' he asked. 'If you keep on at this rate, you'll graduate very early.'

"'I'll graduate at the end of next summer,' I told him.

"'Nearly a year early.' He looked at his watch. 'Can I interest you in a cup of coffee?'

"I thought he meant the student union or someplace close, but we walked several blocks beyond the campus, and into an old apartment building with a crumbling front stoop. The doors stood open but the foyer and stairwell still smelled of fried potatoes.

"His apartment was furnished in classic Campus Tawdry: a sagging brown mohair sofa and armchair, a Formica-topped Danish modern desk, a spindly wrought-iron bookcase, and underfoot, a puree-of-pea-green Axminster. There was a refrigerator. A double hot plate sat on a steel filing cabinet. An aura of many and meaningless seductions clung to the place.

"I perched on the arm of the brown chair. 'You've upholstered your sofa with hair of the mo,' I said. 'Where on earth did you find enough moes? They're nearly extinct.'

"He had carried a teakettle into the bathroom to fill, and when he came out, he said, 'I'm used to better.' Apparently, he'd taken umbrage at my silly remark.

"He put the teakettle on the hot plate, found paper cups, and measured instant coffee into them. I got up and walked to an open window. My life was turning on a moment's careless banter, for I believed that he was sensitive about his academic poverty and injured by my unintentioned ridicule.

"I would discover later that he was not poverty-stricken and that, further, he was a literalist. When he said he was used to better, he meant just that and nothing more. There had not been any rebuke, irony, or rue in 'I'm used to better.'

"He asked if I took cream or sugar, and I marveled at how quickly he'd recovered his composure. Surely, there was nobility in the way he'd turned his back on my deprecation.

"I sat on the sofa. He brought the two steaming paper cups and set them on the floor, since there was no table.

"'Would you like to hear about my doctoral dissertation?' he asked, sitting next to me on the sofa.

"'Oh, yes,' I exclaimed, turning to him with an enthusiasm meant to compensate for my earlier rudeness.

"I suppose he took me for one of those girls who signed up for Ancient Civilizations hoping to get a date. He made his moves quickly, and in no time Mr. Demming and Miss McClanahan were lying on the green Axminster, where Mr. Demming was sustaining elbow burns.

"When he'd uttered those fateful words, 'I'm used to better,' he'd been speaking of the comfortable upper-middle-class home in Creve Coeur, Missouri, where he'd been raised. Nurtured by a mother who was given to 'mind improvement,' he'd enjoyed a charming and eclectic library, season tickets to the symphony, and tickets to any *serious* theatrical production finding its way to nearby St. Louis. Not a hardship case." I shoved the plate of cheese crumbs away from me.

"And what did your father think of Mr. Demming?" Pan poured himself more wine.

"It wasn't until after Mr. Demming, by then *Dr.* Demming, and I were married that Jamie met him. Not much came of that except that before he left, this time for New Zealand, he screamed at me, the only time he ever did that, 'For Christ's sake, stop calling him *mister!'*

"So you see how prosaic my courtship and marriage were. But, lacking drunken brawls, crippling accidents, or abject poverty, we will make ourselves miserable out of what we have at hand."

Pan watched quietly, waited patiently, for what I hadn't said. He had a silent repertory of questions and urgings in the dip of his chin, the oblique cast of his glance, the pondering way he fondled his beard, which was once again growing out. Rarely, he would sigh and look out at the sea, then turn suddenly and ransack my gaze, thrusting into my storehouse of memory, knocking things over, tossing others aside, searching for something.

51

I didn't like to go out. I didn't like to do anything but sit and rest my mind. After those first days of talking, talking, talking day and night, I ran out of impetus and energy and I wondered how I could have done that, talked like a magpie about things of no importance and things of too much importance. I was exhausted and dazed and somehow ashamed, as though I'd done an obscene thing and been diminished by it.

I slept badly. That is the way, I think, when wakefulness is much like sleep, sleep becomes wakeful and it all becomes one thing. And within that depleted and torpid state, normal concerns, such as correspondence, meals, laundry, lose all significance; and matters of naught, such as the sound of the elevator door opening and closing, or the angle of moonlight entering the window, make fantastic demands on one's attention.

Exhaustion made me alternately heavy and inert as a dead

whale, and too light, as if I ought to hang on to things and press down firmly as I moved, lending gravity the collaboration it seemed to require. One day, when Pan had been urging me to go with him and the child Nikos to the beach, I told him, "Thank you, but I think I'll stay here. The sun hurts my eyes and I have no strength, no . . . substance. The wind will blow me down the beach. I'll flatten against a rock and remain there forever, like an old candy wrapper." He knew I would be distressed if they missed their outing, so they went, and I stayed in, sitting by the little balcony and watching incuriously as Nikos, the young worker in the hotel, pushed the wheelchair down to the beach.

I watched with the same impassivity the sailboats and fishing boats that came and went along the coast, distant and unreal. On particularly limpid afternoons I could see the island of Zakinthos, though I had no desire to go there. Pan had suggested that we take the ferry trip from Kilini, but I hadn't any curiosity about it.

Because of the changes that I had seen in him as the time had drawn closer when he would be home, I expected him to be a rampaging stallion locked in a stall when we reached the Peloponnese. I couldn't doubt that inside he must be raging to be free and gone, but to me he showed no restlessness, only tolerance and, at night, a gentle, indulgent touch.

On October 1 he rose early, announcing, "We're taking the train to Patras today. We'll buy a wedding present for Miranda and send a cable with your best wishes. If it will make the trip easier, we can take Nikos with us." It would have been unthinkable to refuse to send my daughter a wedding message. On the level of amenity where most of life's business is carried on, it *was* unthinkable. But in the sub-basement of mindfulness where I existed, there was narcotic apathy to sending a message, taking the train, or even walking out of the hotel.

The trip was accomplished. Nikos came along to help with the wheelchair. In the end, it was Pan who composed the wire to Miranda and Dennis: "Long life, good health, loving hearts, and careless laughter."

"She'll know I didn't write it," I told him.

He shrugged. "All the better. Let *her* wonder about *you.*"

We had lunch at a terrace restaurant near the water. Nikos enjoyed the outing. He was a big, strong, skeptical boy of twelve, with large hands and a shock of black hair that fell slantwise across his forehead and made me think of Bobby. I lowered myself to the chair as though I were a cumbersome trunk I'd lugged around all morning. I wanted only to sit in that spot the rest of the day, the big umbrella shading me, and gaze on the Gulf of Patras.

In the afternoon we shopped for Miranda's gift, eventually purchasing a vast, snowy acre of rug, exquisitely woven in an intricate white-on-white design. For the white aerie.

We were back at the hotel by evening and I allowed Pan to talk me into dinner in the dining room. Afterward we sat outside at a minuscule table, drinking brandy and watching natives and a handful of tourists promenade.

A long letter arrived from Daisy early in October.

Larry—
Come home. If you can't, then at least write. The one postcard with your temporary address, which looked as though it weren't even in your hand, won't do.

Belleville is quiet. Everyone who was leaving has left, including the regular summer people. Bart and Hildy have closed up the cottage and moved to the Minneapolis house. Fall quarter may have commenced by the time you receive this. Hildy is still keeping house for Bart, although she said she'll begin looking for a job when Bart's classes are under way.

We had them both to dinner the week before they left. She is a dear girl, you were right. I hope you won't be too shocked or disappointed if she doesn't move out of the Minneapolis house when she starts working.

Miranda's wedding was—what can I say?—perfect in every detail, except for your absence and Sarah's. Miranda has done the whole tradition of formal weddings proud. I won't go into details about it because, as you can see, I've enclosed snapshots, which George took of everything and everyone, including the caterers and the musicians. George is nothing if not thorough.

You had assured me you no longer wanted the clothes you left behind, so Hildy and I went through them and picked the beige lace for the wedding. My dear, she looked like a duchess. She was awfully pleased. Oh, damn, I wish you'd been here to see it all.

Sarah's mother, Grace, is still with Clark. She's not at all like Sarah, which is probably just as well, since she isn't continually saying and doing things that *Sarah* said and did. Grace is, as you know, rather headlong and blunt and always slightly distracted as if she were determined to carry on while trying to recall if she'd left the gas on.

The baby is as beautiful as her namesake. George took a great many pictures of her. She slept most of the time, and when she was awake she was so quiet, I think she was taking notes. Everyone wanted to hold her and she was quite undiscriminating.

Harry and Roberta were at the wedding and reception, together but not in yoke. Roberta, I must say, was a great help to Miranda. She went down to Minneapolis two days early and put herself at Miranda's disposal.

Harry and I managed a good long gossip at the reception. Both Bobby and Roberta want out of Arneson Printing. Bobby wanted to give it back to Harry, but of course Roberta wouldn't go for that. And in all fairness, she's put a lot of work into it and ought to realize something from it. The shift of ownership, as the lawyers are arranging it, is as complicated as the Treaty of Versailles. Bobby has found a publisher who's interested in the book. Harry says he's flying to New York to talk with them.

Harry has lost weight. He looks good. Quite svelte. He's the same old Harry, hail-fellow-well-met and all that, but wouldn't it be nice to order up a really satisfactory second act for him? Whatever you may think, I'm not hinting, Larry, just reflecting. Maybe another Hildy will come along to tidy up.

Not even Roberta was able to strong-arm Bobby into showing up for the wedding. I will never understand why it wasn't Bobby at the altar with Miranda. Remember our schemes, old girl? They were a lovely pastime, anyway. That's all that mothers' plans are meant to be, I suppose. Like tatting or painting by the numbers.

I have saved my surprise for last, and I do mean *my* surprise. Georganna flew back for the wedding. She was maid of honor in Sarah's place. I had called her to tell her about Sarah. She called Clark and then Miranda. Miranda begged her to come, then sent her the tickets, so Georganna had no excuse and of course she wanted to come anyway. Larry, it was grand having her here. And seeing the three of them together—Georgie, Clark, and Miranda. Only Bobby was missing. His absence was like an uninvited guest.

Georganna is staying until the end of the month. That way, she and Miranda will have time to visit when Miranda and Dennis return from Bermuda. It's four years, you know. I would have gone there if she had ever suggested it. I could never see "dropping in on my way through town." She'd have seen through that. She has staked out her territory, she's sure of it, proud of it, and it suits her. What more can I wish?

I see that we'll have friction before she leaves. If she feels herself being sucked back into our old hopes, she'll take it out on me as though I were scheming. We've had a couple of snappish moments. But it's all right. The day will come when she honestly believes herself stronger than me and then she'll forgive me for being her mother. In the meantime, temper and all, she's a treat.

My God, Larry, I nearly forgot to tell you—your father was at Miranda's wedding...

52

We stayed at that first hotel until November, when Pan learned of a small house for rent on the north edge of the village, up a gentle slope. It belonged to an old couple in frail health, who were going to Kerkira (Corfu) to live with a son and his wife. We moved on the eighth. It was a simple little house, all on one floor, with olive and fruit trees in a front courtyard where we sat in late afternoon to watch the sunset.

I had forgotten about the holidays or didn't want to remember, but the day after we moved our clothes into the house, we went again to Patras, this time to buy Christmas gifts.

"Your family is going to worry if they don't receive Christmas remembrances," Pan explained.

"Aren't you a fine one to talk about Christmas?"

We set off again with Nikos, who was almost entirely at our disposal now that there were few tourists at the hotel. We paid him well and his uncle, who owned the hotel, seemed agreeable to sharing him. I suspected that part or all of Nikos's earnings from us went to his family.

The day was bright and chilly, perfect for shopping if one had been in the mood. I was tired almost before we began, and we stopped for coffee early. But Pan and Nikos pestered me to persevere so that we could finish our Christmas purchases that day and see them on their way to the United States.

For Miranda and Hildy, Daisy, and Sarah's mother, Grace, we bought jewelry; for Bart a book of Peloponnesian antiquity; for Clark a sweater and for the baby a lace dress and a miniature of a woman who bore a striking resemblance to Sarah.

As I paid for the miniature, I noticed in a display case a man's ring, whose design struck me, and I asked to see it. The ring was silver, worked with black enamel and thin threads of gold, and it represented the classic head and shoulders of an athlete. On the head was a petasus.

"Hermes?" I asked Pan.

He nodded.

"I'll take it."

As we left the shop, I felt a small easing of the heaviness that bore down on me, as though from a great pile of rocks laid on me, one had been lifted. But with this slight alleviation, a sharp little knife point of emotion found an opening and nicked my consciousness. I thought it must be fear of some sort, since only fear, jealousy, and desire had such whetted points.

That night we sat before our small, glowing hearth.

"Those cards you bought," Pan said. "You'll have to write holiday greetings on them and post them soon. Before you know it, it will be December. And the ring," he added, "you didn't have it sent. If it's for Christmas, it should be on its way."

"Don't you want it? It's a likeness of your father."

"You're kind to offer it, but I don't think it was meant to be mine."

I looked away from him into the fire. One of the logs had reached that midpoint in its burning life when its seething, hissing center pulsed with the heat, expanding and contracting with a fiery breath.

I woke at two and found Pan gone from bed. Taking up my robe, I padded out to the sitting room. The house was cold, the fire long dead. There were no lights burning and only thin moonlight to reveal objects against the shadow.

"Pan?"

There was a stirring in the tall chair by the hearth.

"Pan? What's wrong?" I went to the lamp.

"Don't turn it on."

I sat down on the cot. "What is it? Has something happened?"

At length he replied very calmly, "He was out there, in the hillocks up behind the house."

"Who?"

"The white hound."

"That's not possible."

He chuckled softly. I shivered. Pulling my body tightly together inside the robe, I rose and crossed to the window.

"You won't see anything. He slipped among the hills and was gone. I stood a long time at the bedroom window but he didn't appear again."

"I'll make us a cup of tea." My words sounded idiotic but I needed to ground this strange conversation in something ordinary. I lit a small lamp in the kitchen, put the water on, and returned. "What do you feel? You're not frightened?"

"What he wants of me, I can only guess, but there's nothing to fear."

"Then why am I shaking?"

He laughed and grasped my hand. "Because you're cold, ninny. Get your slippers."

One day as I wheeled him on the beach, he asked, "The *first* time you fell in love, how old were you?"

"Fifteen."

As though picking his way across a bog, he spoke slowly, making sure of the ground under each word before proceeding to the next. "Were you perhaps in love with that first man when you married Demming?"

"Of course."

"Why did you marry?"

"I suppose I thought it might be a cure for loneliness."

"Was it?"

"It was a pastime."

I turned the chair to face the sea and pulled the brake so it wouldn't roll. Sitting on a smooth rock beside Pan, I gazed west across the water.

"When you fell in love at fifteen," Pan pursued, his eyes on the horizon, "did the man become your lover?"

"Oh, yes."

"You were a schoolgirl."

"Yes."

"He was older."

"Yes."

"Didn't this complicate your life?"

"Complicate it?"

"Wasn't it difficult being a callow, innocent girl and a woman with a serious lover, an older man? Didn't it cause you to wonder who you were?"

"I don't remember wondering. Being a student was unimportant. I'm sure I gave no concern to that part of my life. I was a voracious, single-minded lover."

"And then you ended it for some reason."

"No."

"He did."

"He walked away from it. He couldn't end it."

He said no more until I rose to continue our walk. Then, as I bent to release the brake, he grabbed my wrist cruelly and said in a voice so charged it hissed, "Think how alike we are, Larissa."

Did he mean us—him and me? Or my lover and him? I didn't ask.

Nikos had dinner with us at our house Christmas Eve. We would not open our holiday gifts until New Year's Eve, but we had a little Christmas celebration, the three of us, with lamb and rice and fruit and many sweets that I'd got in the village especially for Nikos.

After dinner I put on a jacket and walked him back to the hotel. The night was cold and so clear it seemed that if I were to squint out to sea, I could see the lights of Italy.

As we neared the hotel the boy said, "Uncle wants you and the man to eat dinner with us New Year's Day."

"Tell Uncle thank you, we'll be honored." We shook hands and he disappeared through the massive front door.

New Year's Eve Pan and I ate a late supper of cheddarlike *kaseri* and bread and fruit. When we rose from the table to have our coffee in front of the fire, I brought a plate of *pura*, a nut roll dipped in honey syrup, of which he was fond.

I opened my gifts from the United States: from Bart and Hildy a leather-bound album of Miranda's wedding pictures and a white cashmere sweater; from Clark an enlarged snapshot of himself and the baby in a silver frame; and from Daisy a subscription to *The River Courant*.

I gave Pan his gifts. All but one were copies of favorite books he'd had to leave behind at Belle Riviere: *Huckleberry Finn*, *Leaves of Grass*, *Return of the Native*, a complete Shakespeare, and several others. Additionally, I presented him with an opaque watercolor portrait of Alice Hazeltine posed against a backdrop of Olympian ruins, as he must have viewed her nearly a hundred years ago. I'd painted the picture at Belle Riviere, using color photos in books for the Olympia setting. I knew it wouldn't be exact but would evoke in his memory what the original had been.

He was moved and sat holding the portrait on his lap for a long time, studying it, then looking into the fire, then looking back at the painting. In the fire he saw the true picture.

I began to clear away our dishes and coffee cups.

"I have something for you," he said, rising and making his way to the bedroom we shared. A few minutes later he returned, holding out his hand, palm up. In it lay a gold chain, sparkling and delicate, and suspended from the chain was a small gold coin worn nearly smooth by the centuries, the head of Apollo on one side, an eagle on the other. The gold had that peculiar depth of luster which derives from repeated washing with blood and tears.

"From the colonies," Pan said.

I gave him a puzzled look.

"Near Troy."

"How can I thank you? It's breathtaking, but shouldn't it be in a museum?"

"No."

The chain he'd bought in Patras. Where he'd got the coin I would never know. He put the chain over my head. I was wearing a burgundy-colored dress with a deep neckline. The coin fell to where the cleavage of my breasts began and lay as soft as his breath against my skin.

At ten o'clock I wheeled him down to the hotel for drinks and music. As we made our slow progress through the village, he said, "You didn't open the photo album your husband sent."

"No."

"And I don't think you've ever looked at the pictures your friend Daisy sent you some time back."

He knew that I hadn't, so I didn't bother to respond.

"Don't you want to look at your daughter's wedding?"

"No."

"Because you're angry?"

"No ... no."

"Because there's someone in the pictures whose face you can't bear to see?"

"Be careful you don't drop the gifts," I told him. "One is a bottle of perfume and it'll break."

He held on his lap a basket of small gifts for Nikos's family and a leather jacket for Nikos. When we'd gone shopping in Patras, we'd asked the boy to model it for us, explaining that he was about the size of someone in America to whom we were sending it.

As I had the day we'd been in Patras, I felt a lifting of weight from me and an accompanying stab of pain. The gifts and the evening of festivity ahead were to blame, I thought.

When we entered the hotel, Nikos came running out from the dining room. "Why didn't you tell me you were coming?" he demanded. "I would have come up and helped you." His face, with a flush of gaiety in the cheeks, was so beautiful, I laughed for joy and warmed my hands a moment on the beardless skin. "Happy New Year, my darling Nikos," I cried and kissed him quickly before he could escape.

He wheeled Pan into the dining room. His aunt came forward and took our wraps, and the uncle poured wine. The room was alive with music and townspeople. Many were dancing and there was much shouting.

Pan handed Nikos his jacket and asked if he would distribute the gifts in the basket to his family. Nikos set the basket on a table, put on his jacket, ran his hands down the front of it appreciatively, stretched out his arms, first one, then the other, to appraise the sleeves, did a 360-degree turn so that all might admire him, then dropped his eyes in a fluster. "Thank you," he mumbled.

"What did you say, Nikos?" his uncle asked.

"Thank you."

Nikos's cousin Manilos asked me to dance, and Pan waved me away. This evening was the first socializing we had done in the village. Our position among its citizens was strange in a number of ways. For one thing, they didn't know, though I'm sure there was rampant speculation, what the relationship was between me and Pan. I still wore a wedding ring. However, my name was Mrs.

Demming—hardly Greek. The gentleman with whom I lived was obviously cultured, highly educated, and Greek, but he was living in a small house in an obscure village. Were we lovers or had the gentleman's injury or illness made him incapable? Should they be shocked or sympathetic?

Eventually, a story got around that I was an American widow who had fallen in love with the wayward son of a wealthy Athenian, that there had been an automobile accident in which I'd been the driver and Pan the tragically injured passenger, and I had now devoted my life to caring for him. I don't know who started the tale, though I suspect Nikos, but it so satisfied everyone's desire for a solution, both dramatic and tidy, that we let it stand.

We had come to the hotel as customers this night, but we were treated, despite my protests, as personal guests. Since we were invited to New Year's dinner, I hadn't expected to be a guest for New Year's Eve as well. Finally, I set aside my tourist's compunctions and had a grand time.

"You are happy?" Pan asked during a quiet moment.

"Yes."

"Tomorrow you'll be sad again?"

I was stopped by that, then I asked, "My dear friend, are you staying on until I'm happy, is that it? That was never part of our bargain. You only agreed to stay until I was settled. I want you to feel free now."

"Are you trying to get rid of me?"

I laughed.

"You're not ready yet," he said.

"How do you know that?"

"I know you...very well."

"I don't want to be a stone around your neck."

"I have forever."

At the stroke of midnight the *vasilopitta*, or fortune bread, was cut. There was more than one loaf, since the crowd was large, but Pan and I were given slices from Nikos's family's loaf. The first slice was set aside for Saint Basil, the second slice was the father's, the next the mother's, and so on through the relatives. When all had been served and we began to eat the bread, which was sweet and decorated with nuts, I explained to Nikos's aunt, "I'm very touched that you would include me in this ceremony."

"Eat," she admonished.

I took another bite of bread and bit down on something hard. For a second I thought part of a nutshell had gotten into the dough, and I was embarrassed to remove it from my mouth. I looked around, hoping no one noticed my predicament, but Pan was watching, an eyebrow cocked.

With my tongue I extricated the object from the bread and shoved it to the front of my mouth; then as daintily as I could I removed it.

"Look at it," Pan told me.

I wiped it with a napkin and found it was a small coin.

"Whoever finds the coin in the bread has good fortune for the next year."

At the bar Nikos's uncle raised his glass of wine to me. I smiled at him and his image blurred as sudden, unwarranted tears came between us.

53 ❧

There was a pounding at the door. I looked at the clock. Seven-thirty-five in the morning. Slowly, I dragged myself up and threw my feet over the edge of the bed. Groping with my toes for slippers that had disappeared under the bed, I reached for a warm robe on the chair.

"Nikos!" I exclaimed, opening the front door. "What on earth...?"

"Telephone. A call is coming for you at eight. Get dressed." He started away. "From America," he said, turning back.

"Hello, Larry? Daisy. Happy New Year!"

"Daisy. What time is it there?"

"Midnight. New Year's Eve. We all decided it would be a smashing idea to call you. And we're not even smashed. Well, not very."

"Are you having a party?"

"A small one. The Bergens and Comstocks, Sam Fergus and Harry, and a few others. Did you celebrate?"

"Yes. Here at the hotel. It was lovely. I had a wonderful time."

"Is it terribly Greek there, where you are?"

"Yes. It's terribly Greek. You'd never want to leave."

"That's what I was afraid of. You will leave eventually, won't you?"

"I don't know."

"Well, I'll see you in March. I've explained it all in a letter, which you'll be getting soon. Here's George. He wants to say hello. I'll talk to you again before we hang up."

I said hello to George and to Sam Fergus, who assured me that Save the River was winning the battle for Belle Riviere. It was impossible to tell from that distance if he was merely being reassuring. I said hello to Nellie Bergen, who insisted that when Bobby's book was published, I would have to sign the library's copies. The next voice was Harry's.

"Larissa?" His voice was more than six thousand miles away. It was beyond my reach. Someone had probably shoved the phone into his hand.

"Harry. Happy New Year. How are you?"

"Fine. And you?"

"Fine. How's Bobby?"

"He's fine. Very busy. The manuscript is nearly ready for the publisher. You'll be getting a copy of it soon."

"Oh, good. That's nice. Give him my love."

"Yes, I'll do that. Here's Daisy."

"Larry?"

"Yes, I'm here."

"Be on the lookout for a visitor."

"Who's that?"

"Your father. I don't know when he'll get there. I don't know what his travel arrangements were. It might be two days or weeks."

"Or years."

"Well, sweetie, I'll say good-bye for now. Everyone sends their love. You'll have a letter in a few days."

If this word of Jamie were good fortune, I thought, walking on the beach, I would return the coin from the *vasilopitta*. I was going to pack a bag, leave tomorrow, and tour the Peloponnese.

"You can't leave," Pan told me, before I suggested it.

"I *can* leave."

"No."

He was up and dressed by the time I returned. "There's cof-fee," he said.

I poured a cup and sat down in a big wooden armchair, over which we had thrown a bright-blue wool blanket.

"How many years is it?" he asked.

"Ten."

"How much time did you spend with him then?"

"Precious little. He stayed at a hotel. A hotel, for Christ's sake. He'd show up at the house in the afternoon when the kids came home from school. He didn't want to see *me*."

"Why was that?"

"How do I know? What had I done but sit waiting year after year, like Penelope waiting for Ulysses?" I said dryly.

"When had you seen him before that?"

"A year after I was married."

"And do you remember how that went?"

"Badly."

"How old was he?"

"Younger than I am now. And he looked younger than he was. He'd been in North Africa and he was brown as a Berber. He looked like one of those ancient bronze statues with the unexpected blue eyes."

"*How* did things go badly?"

"I don't know. There was terrible tension between us. He was very critical. He was never that way when I was a girl. But now I couldn't do anything right. The clothes I wore. My hairstyle, every-thing was wrong. And Bart was an idiot. Jamie seemed to despise me for marrying him." I shrank inside myself like a miserable child.

"And the next time? When he stayed at the hotel? Did he treat you with disdain?"

After consideration I said, "No. With pity."

Pan scratched together a little breakfast and when we'd eaten, he led me to the bedroom. We lay together silently.

He kissed me lightly on the lips and temples and eyelids. I felt like the girl I had been, strong, willing, selfish, and shy. He was delicate and unhurried as if I were that girl. Years telescoped and I could hear my muffled, voluptuous giggles and demanding little moans and I felt I must devour him rather than let him leave again.

* * *

At two o'clock I began to dress. I wore the same dark-red dress I'd worn the night before and, with it, the gold chain and coin. If I could have backed out of the dinner, I would have. I still intended to pack a bag and leave for Olympia the next day. I touched the coin as if it were a talisman, and walked out to the sitting room.

"You look Greek," Pan said. "You might be playing Elektra or Antigone."

"I'm a little long in the tooth for either of those."

"When you were fifteen," Pan said without warning, "how were you seduced?"

I sat down slowly on a straight chair. I was slightly nauseated. "I wasn't seduced."

"No? You were in love with an older man and presumably you slept with him, but you weren't seduced?"

"No. I seduced him."

"What makes you think so?"

"I remember. I remember how it happened. We met at my mother's wake. I sat beside him. I saw that he had been fond of her, had felt responsible toward her. There had been a charge upon him, which he seemed to feel he had failed. He was restless, cruel toward himself, as though he wished to shun himself. And I saw that he needed some assurance and I didn't know what assurance it was or how I could give it. When I saw him that way, so contemptuous of himself, I fell in love.

"There is always some small thing which disturbs our balance and sends us headlong. It isn't the totality of another's presence, however charming, but the small, fatal moment.

"I spoke to him, words I hoped would be reassuring, about my mother's illness and death and his old bitterness. He was deeply upset that I had read all his secrets.

"Later, when I saw him go into my father's study, I followed, closing the door so we could have privacy. I told him it hurt me to see the scorn he had for himself, that I knew he didn't deserve it and that I found his self-contempt terribly touching. I laid a hand on his arm and said, 'I'm so sad to see you this way. It's worse than Mother being dead.'

"He put a hand over mine and thanked me for my concern, but he was as bitter as before. I didn't know how I could cheer him. I bent toward him and lightly kissed his cheek. 'Try not to be unkind to yourself.'

"He caught my arm and held me against him as if to be assured, then thrust me away and began to weep.

"But don't imagine me a compassionate innocent callously seduced. Sympathy was one element of the affair and hardly the dominant one.

"After that day, when I saw the wretchedness going through him, I would cheer him with soft words and little jokes and a touch that told him I forgave him. He would stiffen each time as though to resist but then succumb and before long be himself again, laughing and content. I seduced him, there's no doubt."

"How long after your mother's death did you sleep with him?"

"A month maybe."

The sun porch was bitter cold. When I'd heard him cry out and stumble from his bed, I had waited. He did not need a fussing, distraught girl, trespassing and hanging over him. He rambled through the back of the house, lurching into furniture, uttering strange sounds like a sick animal. Eventually, he yanked open the door to the sun porch and wandered out there to sit in the frigid dark.

I waited what seemed like hours for him to return to bed. Finally, I got up from the sofa where I'd slept. I couldn't let him catch pneumonia or freeze. I went to the kitchen and quickly heated water for tea. I kept thinking, "Any minute he'll go back to bed and I won't have to intrude."

When the tea had steeped, I crept along to the sun porch. I didn't want to startle or embarrass him. In the doorway I spoke low.

"Daddy."

He didn't answer. I don't think he heard. Moving to the chair where he was slumped, I set down the steaming cup and knelt beside him, putting a hand on his sleeve.

"Daddy."

He turned his head.

"Daddy, it's very cold out here. You'll get sick. I've made you tea." I held out the cup.

He was trembling, so I held the cup to his lips. Suddenly he turned away from it and put his arms around me. Dressed only in a nightgown, I shivered and my teeth began to chatter.

He roused himself. "Larissa, you're freezing. My God, let me warm you." He got up from the chair. "You have nothing on your feet," he said, and picked me up, carrying me to the bedroom, where he set me down on the edge of the bed and wrapped a blanket around me.

He went down on his knees and took my feet one at a time in his hands and rubbed them until they were warm and his hands were warm as well with the chafing. Then he bent his head and kissed my feet. I put my fingers among his soft dark curls and gently lifted his head.

Pan was asking, "And for how long did the affair continue?"

"Until I started college."

"And then he walked away, as you say."

"Yes."

"Don't you ever long to start over, Larissa? To be a child, innocent of this?"

"To wipe it out of my experience, no. To have the pain end, yes."

He crossed to me and put a hand on my shoulder. "I wish I could make you a child again."

Half an hour later Nikos arrived to help wheel Pan down to the hotel. We'd reached the foot of the little hill on which our own house squatted, and as we turned left into another street, I glanced up where we had come. A white form rounded the courtyard wall and disappeared behind the house, moving toward the sharper, more forbidding rise that beckoned away inland.

The hotel dining room was closed for the afternoon and several tables had been pulled together to form a single long one, over which was laid a sparkling white banquet cloth. The dishes and flatware and glasses and candlesticks were polished to gleam in the slanting light of the winter afternoon. The oblique, pinky-yellow light from westward-facing windows cast a sepia tone over the white walls and linens and dark wood.

In a corner of the dining room an old upright piano stood. It had been much in use at the New Year's Eve party, and now a strange girl of twelve or thirteen sat playing simple but tenderly rendered pieces of the kind I associated with Miranda's second- or third-grade John Thompson book. The ancient piano's tone was stridulous and complaining. Like an old woman declining to dance even as she allows herself to be led to the floor, the piano reluctantly surrendered ardent little melodies.

In addition to the family members who operated the hotel,

other relatives had gathered for the New Year's dinner, some of them from as far away as Patras and Pirgos. We were perhaps thirty who sat down to the long table. It was a noisy, ebullient group, embracing and embracing again, laughing and toasting the day and the new year, as well as births and name days which had come and gone since the last coming-together.

The feast began with egg-lemon soup and ended with baklava and dark, spicy cake, accompanied by tiny cups of thick, sweet coffee. Between beginning and ending, we were served baked chicken, moussaka, salad, stewed green beans with garlic and mint, and fresh bread. When we had finished eating, everyone remained at the table, stuffed and euphoric. One by one the men stood in turn, speaking a few familial words or telling a humorous story, often about one of their number.

Recovering in this manner for an hour, and seeing the light in the western sky reduced to brilliant purple, the women began to clear the table, the men to clear the floor, in preparation for dancing. I begged to help and was returning from my second trip to the kitchen; Nikos's uncle was sorting through phonograph records; a number of men were standing along the bar smoking and speaking in intimate voices; a gentle hush enveloped us. The candles still burned on the long table and small wall lamps were lit, casting a hazy, golden light like the rich, sweet honey syrup of the baklava.

Pan sat at the table in his wheelchair, enjoying a glass of Metaxa. I bent over the table to gather up a platter. The chain around my neck hung loose, the gold coin catching the candlelight. Pan looked down my dress at my partially exposed breasts and smiled an intimate smile of admiration and affection. I thought that if one could capture a single moment of life, preserving its perfection forever in resin, I might choose this moment.

Across the room in the wide doorway to the foyer, a tall figure appeared, setting down a piece of canvas luggage and glancing around in the manner of one long accustomed to entering rooms full of strangers. The voices at the bar fell silent.

"Jamie."

Pan swung his chair around, looked long at my father, then back at me. I straightened and walked slowly around the table, my heels clicking in the silence, like a Spanish dancer's.

The wine-colored dress had long, fitted sleeves and a long,

fitted bodice that flared gracefully at the hips and created a sensuous swell around my thighs as I moved. I was as aware as a dancer of the swing of my hips, the straightness of my back, and the lift of my chin. I knew that the pale topaz light from the lamps and the color and cut of the dress flattered me. I knew that the delicate filament and ancient coin lying along my skin were like a golden beauty mark calling attention to the curve of my breast.

Approaching him, hands outstretched, I prayed that Jamie's mouth was full of gall.

54

He looked familiar, like someone I knew. As I drew near, I studied him, holding myself slightly away from him—to wonder who it was—as he embraced me.

He was seventy but still strong. He smelled like fresh air. His dark cheek, cool from the evening air, made mine burn. When I spoke, my voice was full and hoarse.

"Why did you come?"

"To talk. I'm old. I've come to talk."

"Excuse me." I turned. Pan was wheeling himself across the room, and I went to meet him.

"Go along," he said. "Take your father up to the house. I'll take a room here tonight."

As I bent to touch his cheek with mine he said, "Here is the chance to be a child again."

"But I don't want to be."

"You may."

He kissed his fingers to me as I moved toward my father.

The house was cold and dark. I turned on a lamp. "Take your bag into the bedroom. There's a tub if you'd like a bath. Can I get you a drink?"

"Later. I want to change out of these clothes."

I built a fire and made coffee, and when he returned I was drinking coffee with brandy. "Would you like the same?"

"Fine."

"Are you hungry?" Though I sounded calm, I didn't fool either of us.

"Not yet."

While I poured his coffee and stirred brandy into it, he asked, "How come you weren't at Miranda's wedding?"

"Your concern for Miranda is touching but please spare me any patriarchal duties you planned to perform."

"I asked a question anyone would ask."

"You can ask all the irrelevant questions you like, but now that you're here, we *will* get down to cases, and then you'll leave, or I will. This isn't ten years ago, when you could hide behind Miranda and Clark. We're alone in this house. No one is coming to rescue you." I handed him the cup and he sat in the armchair with the bright-blue throw. "When I heard you were coming, I was going to leave. If you'd got here a day later, I'd have been gone. But now you're here and you'll suffer for it."

He stirred the coffee once, twice around, then set the spoon on the saucer. "Yes."

I sat on a daybed at the opposite side of the hearth. "Miranda and I fought. I didn't want her to marry Dennis. That was the primary reason she didn't want me at the wedding and the reason I didn't want to be there."

"And the other reason?"

"She thought I was having an affair with someone named Harry Arneson."

"Were you?"

"No."

"Were you in love with him?"

For several seconds I sat playing with the cup in my hands. Finally, I looked up. "What do I know about love, Jamie?"

"A lot, I hope."

"Hmmmph." The pain I felt, looking at him, was unendurable. The lines running from his nostrils to the corners of his mouth were deeper. The lines at the corners of his eyes were like gullies, but his brow was smooth, his mouth had not the slack nor the pursiness of an old man's. His eyes were still clear and dangerous. Here and there among his white curls was a strand of black, a waning hold on youth that would soon be gone altogether. I was the stronger now, though he had a great deal of fight left.

"Why didn't you want Miranda to marry whatsisname?"

"She's in love with someone else, someone who happens to be homosexual."

"She's almost as lucky as her mother."

"Yes."

"There are a man's things in the bathroom. Are you living with someone?"

"Yes. Temporarily."

"This his house?"

"No. We rent."

"Is he...?" He picked up the spoon and stirred the coffee again. "You're not just sharing a house."

"No."

"I was through this town once, a good many years ago."

"Oh?"

"Didn't stay overnight or anything, but I remember the place, the beach."

"It's a beautiful beach."

"What's his name?"

"Pan."

"That's his name, just Pan?"

"That's all I know."

"How long have you been living with him?"

"Since I arrived in Greece."

"Quick work. Are you getting a divorce from Demming?"

"Yes."

"It was a stupid thing you did, marrying him." He spoke as though it had happened yesterday.

"Yes."

"Why'd you do it?"

"Don't play games, Jamie." Nervously I kicked off my shoes and put my feet up. "Why didn't you remarry?"

He ignored this. "Why'd you marry him?"

My toes were dug into the mattress. "To punish you. Did it work? Did you cry out in your sleep sometimes, when you dreamed about us, about Demming and me?"

"Wide awake sometimes."

"Why didn't you remarry?"

"I didn't want to. And I'd already hurt you enough."

"If you were so concerned about hurting me, why did you leave?"

"I had to do that."

"No, you didn't. You didn't have to leave and you didn't have to stay away."

He had put his coffee down. He didn't look at me. Instead, he stared into a dark corner. "You wanted more than I had a right to give you," he said finally.

"And so did you."

"That's true. And that's why I left."

"You ran away."

"You married Demming," he said almost petulantly, as if this were proof that I'd managed, that I'd survived.

"I was a girl, you son of a bitch! Was I supposed to get me to a nunnery or join a missionary order? Why, we might have arranged it so our paths would *never* cross."

"I had to leave."

"What if you'd come back? What if you'd tried to help me or I'd tried to help you?"

"How could I help you when I couldn't help myself?"

"You could have tried." I wanted to remain angry, but I began to cry.

"Did you want help, or did you want me?"

"I didn't get either."

"If it was help you wanted, you could have gone to a psychiatrist. But you didn't want that, did you? Did you, Larissa?"

"Why did you come here?" I got up and found a tissue and blew my nose.

"I'm old."

"Yes, you said that. Are you getting your house in order? Are you going to ask if I know a good priest? Ah, then what? A few minutes in a confessional and it's all over?"

"For God's sake, Larissa, leave the Church out of it. I may be looking for absolution, but not from a priest."

"You want *me* to forgive you?" I walked back and stood in front of him. "It was never a sin until this minute. I don't *want* to forgive you. And *you* damned well hadn't better start forgiving *me*. I don't want forgiveness."

"I'm talking about forgiving me for leaving."

"I don't think I can." I returned to sit on the daybed. "What difference would it make?"

"I need to rest. I need...some peace."

"Peace. You can find peace? *I* can't, not until you're dead."

He nodded. "That may be."

"Why should I give you peace?"

"Because you love me."

"Sweet Jesus, Jamie." I stared at him and then I laughed a laugh that scraped my throat. "Because I *love* you, I want to kill you where you sit. I want to rip out your eyes and strip the flesh off your bones. I want to throw you to the sharks and gather up your bleached bones on the beach and carve dildoes from them. Then *I'll* have peace."

"*That's* what you want to do because you covet me. What you want to do because you love me, is help me be peaceful."

"You're full of shit."

He picked up the cup and saucer he'd put down earlier and drank the brandied coffee. The cup shook in his hand and a drop of the coffee fell onto his white shirt. I looked away.

"You're doing an old-man act for me, Jamie, and I'm not going to buy it. You want me to pity you and because I pity you, forgive you."

"An act? What do you see when you look at me?"

Every movement, every word, every glance was a cruelty. "I see that your shoulders are still muscled and your belly's flat and your eyes aren't rheumy. I see a man who recently lived with a young widow in the outback of nowhere and is still a man."

"She cooked for me and put a pillow at my back when I sat reading at night, and she kept me from being cold all the way through."

"Stop it."

"What is it you don't want to hear—how she kept me warm at night or that I was cold?"

I didn't answer.

"I finally had to get reading glasses a few years back and now it's bifocals. I'm slow getting up from a chair and I like to nap in the middle of the day. My hands shake and I can't remember names and I'm more interested in my bowel movements than in what I ate. I'm not the god you thought."

"What do I care! What should I say, Jamie—'My God, how

disgusting! Now that you've got an old man's complaints, it's much easier for me to be your daughter. Your large ears that are probably hairy make it simple to forget everything else'?"

"I can't believe it doesn't make a difference," he said ambivalently. His joints that were old and often painful needed a daughter who would place the pillow of absolution at his back. But his blood was not so thin or cold that it didn't remember our past.

"I don't want to be your daughter. How can you ask it?"

"I need a daughter. Old age is getting the whip hand. I have to give in. Age is that way. It's a jealous thing, wants all your attention."

"Don't. Don't talk that way. I don't want to hear. You make it sound like a mistress."

"It is."

"Jamie," I said as calmly as I was able, "Jamie, there was a mistake. I don't know how such things happen, but they do. I was meant to be your wife, not your daughter. We were like jigsaw pieces. We tried fitting with others, but there wasn't another perfect fit." Rising from the daybed, I went to him and knelt before him, placing a hand on his thigh. My body hurt with desiring him. The hand on his thigh ached like something wounded that had come seeking remedy. "I could give you all the care you'll need or want if you share that bedroom with me."

He closed his eyes. He was on the point of capitulation. His thigh quivered beneath my hand. I stared through his closed lids and into his brain. "Whatever you need or want."

"No." It was hardly more than a breath. He opened his eyes and took my hand. "I need a daughter . . . before it's too late."

"It's always been too late," I whispered.

"If I believed that, I wouldn't be here."

I couldn't stand it. I had been so close. Getting to my feet abruptly, I pulled my hand roughly from his.

He went on, "I don't want to be old without being forgiven." He looked at his thigh. The memory of my hand lay on it. "You were all that mattered. The women, the chums—they were part of the background. You and I were the only ones front and center. The rest was a chorus. I left for your sake. You can't believe I wanted to leave." He turned to look at me where I stood. "You talked about a priest. I've never felt like going to one, not for forgiveness. I've had thirty years of penance for something we never thought was a sin. I'm not afraid to die."

"If you didn't think it was a sin, why did you leave?"

"You deserved better."

A cry escaped me. He had taken my life away when I was seventeen without even asking. He'd made the decision for both of us. I collapsed onto the daybed.

"If I'd stayed, you'd have hated me worse in the end." How he wanted me to understand, but I wouldn't give him any help. "After twenty years with nothing to show for it but an old man, you'd have hated the day I was born. I couldn't stand that. You'd have nothing then—no home or children, not even a father."

"You fool, you damned fool."

"There's not a person in the world who'd have been deceived, wherever we'd gone, Larissa. You wouldn't have had a friend to turn to when you got sick of the bargain, when you couldn't stand to look at me another day."

"Why didn't you say all this a long time ago?"

"Would you have understood?"

"No. But at least I wouldn't have thought that I wasn't... enough."

"Of course you would. You'd have said to yourself, 'If I were more of a woman, he wouldn't have all these doubts.'"

Yes.

"And another thing," he said. "I was living from day to day, not knowing when I'd weaken and come running back. If I'd left in a cloud of heroic dust, with a flare of trumpets, and then found I couldn't make it, you'd have felt such disgust, not just with me but with yourself for having been taken in, for having imagined me a man I wasn't."

"Then you didn't understand me."

"Maybe not. I've never really understood any of it. How God could plan it in the first place and then punish us so much."

"God didn't punish us, Jamie. You did."

He was bent forward, elbows on his knees, hands clasped together beneath his chin. His eyes were bleak. "Little girl," he whispered, "what are we to do?"

I saw in his eyes the old man he had dreamed I might let him become. He had hoped (knowing that he hoped hopelessly) that I would love him enough to give him up or to give up that part of him he'd pledged to me after my mother's death. But he knew now that he had no right to reclaim it. I'd paid too dearly for it. He wouldn't ask again.

He'd go away. Where this time? He'd been nearly everywhere. He dropped his eyes to close the curtain on despair. I couldn't breathe. I got up and went to the front door and opened it. The cold dark of the courtyard washed over me but carried no relief.

"Where will you go?"

"What? Oh."

He stretched his body elaborately, arms and legs, then clasped his hands behind his head, thrust his legs out long and straight and crossed them at the ankles, providing himself time to manufacture an answer. "Why, I'd planned to go to India from here," he lied. "I didn't see half of it when I was there." He threw me a jaunty smile. He was indeed a hero. Only to heroes did such costly gallantry come with illusory ease.

I closed the door and stood against it. "Oh, Jamie."

55

Waking with the first light the next morning, I lay in bed weeping silently. When I heard Jamie stirring in the other room, I wiped my face. I was the younger. I was the stronger. And I loved him enough—was it enough?—to try to be his daughter.

After a while there was a knock at the bedroom door. "I've made coffee, Larissa."

"I'll brush my teeth and be out in a minute."

After breakfast I walked down to the hotel. Jamie had slept late and it was getting close to noon.

"Mr. Pan left," I was told.

"Left? When? I didn't see him on my way."

"We put him on the train this morning for Olympia. You didn't know? There was another gentleman going to Olympia, a priest perhaps?" He put a hand to his neck to indicate the collar. "He helped us put Mr. Pan on the train. He promised to help him off at Olympia. He'll be fine, Missus. Mr. Pan will be fine."

"I'd forgotten he was going," I lied and turned away.

One by one the days passed. They passed slowly. I measured them off in small portions to be got through, and each portion was interminable. Worst were the long evenings alone together in the little house.

Routines evolved out of our struggle. We went for walks after dinner, stopping at the hotel for a drink before climbing the hill to the house. We took several walks some days, the first right after breakfast. Sometimes the walks were alone, but more often they were together. The important thing was to go out into the fresh air, to fling ourselves into space.

Jamie believed that the man with whom I'd formerly shared the house had left because of him, which of course was true in its way.

Jamie wasn't fluent in Greek but he spoke a good deal more than I, so his intercourse with the villagers was more thoroughgoing than mine. His friendship with them helped us through protracted days and nights. He sometimes spent the afternoon in the little square talking to old men about the war, or he stayed on at the bar in the evening for dice or checkers while I returned home.

How I missed Pan and cursed him for leaving without a good-bye. Two or three days after Jamie's arrival I noticed that Pan's books and the painting of Alice were missing.

"Jamie, did you see a watercolor of a girl sitting among some ruins? It was propped up on that bureau."

"No. It could have been there, but I didn't notice."

That was my own feeling. I'd been too distracted to note its disappearance. It seemed strange that Pan had returned for his belongings and left again without a word. Without these reminders of him, it was as though he'd never existed.

I tried to prevent Jamie seeing how painful his proximity was. The only thing more painful would have been his absence. We might be sitting before the hearth eating a light supper, Jamie regaling me with a story about his leave-taking from Ireland—"So I said, 'Darlin', you and your teapot and your cow I delight in. It's your bally weather that's finished me'"—and I'd laugh and reach to lay an appreciative hand on his. In midair my hand recalled itself.

317

I read a good deal. I didn't care for checkers. And chess—I don't doubt it sounds silly—was like an amorous battle, queens and knights having at each other, so we abandoned chess and played gin and sometimes Scrabble on a travel set I'd brought from the States.

When Jamie had been with me a couple of weeks, we took the train to Patras and leased a car. While we were there, I bought a new set of pastels and paper. By the end of February I was sketching a little; primarily because it took me out of doors. I sat on the beach and sketched the few small boats belonging to the village, or I took up a seat in the square and drew the locals and occasionally a tourist.

Just before Daisy's arrival in March, Jamie and I had our first blowup. How we'd managed to avoid it for two and a half months I don't know. Perhaps because we'd tried so hard to be polite, rather than intimate.

I'd spent the morning on the beach and Jamie had driven down to the hotel. At lunch he said, "Georgios's sister is visiting from Thessaloniki." Georgios was the hotel proprietor.

"Oh?"

"She's already bored, being away from the city."

"That's too bad. Does she have children?"

"Grown."

"Is her husband along?"

"She's a widow."

"Young?"

"Forty, maybe."

"I can introduce myself, if you think that would help. I could take her to Patras shopping or something."

"I'm taking her to lunch tomorrow."

"In Patras?"

"Yes."

I set my glass down. Noonday light flooded the room. It lit Jamie harshly but did him no harm. His skin was dark and exquisitely creased, without flab or downward heaviness. He'd gained five pounds since New Year's and I could have sworn there was more black in his beard. No day passed when his physical presence wasn't an oppression. No day passed when I didn't want to lie beneath him again. Most of the time I hated him and all of the time I wanted to scream. We weren't going forward. We were stuck. Pain was growing routine without growing tolerable.

"You invited her to lunch in Patras?"

He saw the storm coming. "Yes."

"How could you?"

"How could I?"

"How could you do this without telling me?"

"I'm telling you now."

"You know what I mean." I stood up, knocking over my chair. "How could you?" I screamed.

He didn't answer.

"She's beautiful. Tell me she's beautiful, you son of a bitch."

"I don't understand."

"I don't understand," I mimicked. "You understand, old man. Oh, yes, so *old* he needs a daughter, a family, a home base to philander from. Tell me you're free and over twenty-one and I'll drive a stake through your heart!" I snatched up a book from a small malacca table and hurled it at him. "I go to bed every night with nothing between us but a thin wall and my misguided worries about your happiness. I'm hanging on by my fingernails, and you're going to bring another woman in here? The hell you are, old man."

"I'm not bringing 'another woman in here.' This isn't that kind of lunch."

"Liar."

"I only felt sorry for her. I'll go down and tell her I can't go. I'll think of something. You're right. It was insensitive. I suppose I thought it would take some pressure off you."

I had started to cry and I ran into the bedroom. He followed me. "We're both under pressure, Larissa."

"Whose fault is that?"

I'd flung myself across the bed, and now he sat down beside me and would have reached to console me. I rolled away, screaming, "Don't touch me!"

He got up and went out. After a while I heard the front door open and then the car door. The motor started and he drove down the rutted little street in the direction of the hotel.

I lay crooning to myself and choking on tears. There was a wet spot on the spread as though someone had made love there. We couldn't make it work. I didn't have the strength. It was hopeless. I would tell him when he came home.

I fell asleep. Half an hour later I got up and rinsed my face. I began to clear away lunch. When I'd washed the few dishes and put the food away, I found the book I'd thrown, slipped on a pair of glasses, and went out into the courtyard to read.

319

The house didn't sit straightforward on its plot of land, but was canted slightly toward the west so that one could sit in the courtyard and gaze out at the sea. The book lay unopened in my lap and I sat staring at the blue Ionian. Off to the right out of sight, lay the island of Cephalonia, and close beside it, Ithaca, or Ithaki, to which Ulysses had come home. There Penelope had waited, a mere twenty years, for his joyful return.

At three-thirty the car grumbled slowly up the hill, bouncing and swaying like a broken-down perambulator. Jamie turned it around, parked facing downhill, then got out, carrying the white straw hat that he wore, climbed the stairs from the street and made his way toward the courtyard. I watched his progress. An old lion, still proud and parlous, loping home. No man could ever survive comparison.

"Wine?" he asked, passing my bench on his way into the house.

"Yes."

He brought out a bottle and two glasses. "She wasn't there. She'd gone to spend the afternoon with an aunt."

"I'm sorry about the hysterics. You must take her to lunch. I'd feel rotten if you didn't," I promised him, lying in my teeth.

He poured the wine and raised his glass. "Think how lucky we must be at cards, mavourneen."

56

Daisy arrived Monday, the fourteenth of March, after the environmentalist's Grand Tour. She'd met with groups in London, Stockholm, Brussels, Bonn, Paris, and Rome. She would rest with us for a week before flying home. Well, of course we had no plans actually to *rest*. That was a manner of speaking.

Jamie and I met her at the train in Patras. She glowed in her blond, luminous way and bubbled like a fresh bottle of seltzer. The trip had been rewarding and great fun. Her hosts had all been terribly kind, insisting that she stay in their homes, taking her around to as many local tourist attractions as there was time, begging her to stay on, and finally seeing her off like a lost cousin whom they were delighted to have recovered.

"Perfect. Perfect. I wouldn't have changed a thing. They were all very aware and so earnest."

"And Georganna? You saw her?"

"Yes. That was the least successful. She was all out of sorts, not with me, I don't think, but who knows? I'd seen her only four months earlier. Her trip home had its ups and downs, more ups than downs, and I was very pleased. Something has happened since she was home, I think, though God knows what and you could lose your sanity thinking about it.

"Once your children leave home, seeing them on visits is like randomly dipping into a novel you've never read. Everything's out of context. You don't know what line is important and what line is just the glue holding the important parts together. So you refer to something she has said that sounded important and get a look that tells you that next to a common, garden-variety rock, you are the densest thing she has stumbled over in six months. Naturally, you'd hit upon the mucilage. Let's talk about something else. Have you seen Bobby's manuscript? Isn't it marvelous?"

"Yes." I laughed. "Yes, I think it's marvelous."

"It's launched him out on his own," Daisy said. "Best thing that ever happened to him. Did I say yet that Harry and Roberta are officially unmarried?" She peered sharply at me, peeling back several layers of my social derma.

Jamie saved the moment by coming in with numerous tour books and maps, laying them out on a table in front of Daisy. "Now, then, the riches of Greece lie before us, *chères mesdames.*"

With an appalling lack of planning, and in no great hurry to arrive anywhere, we set out, Daisy, Jamie, and I, in the rented car, to "see a few things," as Jamie expressed it. We drove down the west coast of the Peloponnese, arriving at Pilos in the late afternoon. Pilos was a more than pleasant little town built amphitheatrically around the Bay of Navarino, site of the great sea battle during the Greek War of Independence. Closing in the bay on one side was the boding island of Sfaktiria, where in 425 B.C. the Athenians under Cleon defeated the Spartans in fierce fighting. But then, wasn't all fighting with the Spartans fierce?

We found rooms, washed up, and went out to walk through

the streets before sundown. The next day we would explore Neo-kastro, the fortress overlooking the town, and the remains of King Nestor's palace. Could it possibly be the King Nestor who was a contemporary of Ulysses? The thought made me giddy.

We had a simple meal of fresh fish, salad, and bread, washed down with white wine—unresinated for Daisy's sake—and sat long over the dinner table, poring over our maps. We were offered more advice than we could realistically follow, as locals gathered around to suggest the many sights we really *must* see on our unguided tour. The only certainty was that when we left Pilos, our next stop should be Kalamata. That seemed sufficient program for the moment. One did not after all want to inhibit spontaneity and astonishment on a junket such as this by overpreparing.

"Where did you live when you were here?" Daisy asked Jamie.

"The island of Milos for a year."

"Milos?"

"In the Cyclades. The armless beauty, Venus de Milo, was found there."

"Oh, yes."

"But I spent a good deal of time around Olympia and, of course, I was a rover, a few days here, a week there, visiting the islands and the rest of the country. Altogether I spent about two years in Greece. Then I moved along into the Middle East. I was restless."

"When did you begin traveling?"

"When Larissa went to college. Her mother died when she was fifteen." He looked at me. "We kept house for two years until she started at the university. I sold the business then and took off."

"Didn't you hate not being able to go to those romantic places with your father?" she asked me.

"Yes."

"And now?" She turned back to Jamie. "Will you go back to the States, do you think?"

"When Larissa's ready. I won't go without her." He wanted to go. He hungered for a taste of the sweets he'd forbidden himself on my account. He'd lived without home or family for thirty years. Was it time I took him back to live in the midst of his grandchildren and great-grandchild? When summer came and tourists descended like ravening birds, maybe we would fly in the opposite direction.

Two young musicians had appeared, a Greek with a fiddle and

an American with a battered guitar slung over his shoulder. They were unknown to each other, but traded off playing Greek and American songs, and on some of the American tunes familiar to him the Greek joined his fellow musician, contributing a second and haunting voice to "Across the Wide Missouri" and several others.

One by one, customers were standing up and singing. It seemed customary and was encouraged. They were thus far all Greeks and the songs were improbably sad-sounding. Even the lively ones were lively in a despairing way, as though the singer forced himself to clap hands while his heart broke and his life's blood poured forth in words. As each number concluded, the singer made a slight bow and resumed his seat with a smile of radiant good spirits, as if to explain, "That all happened a long time ago when I was young."

Then Daisy asked the American, whose name was Dooley, if he knew "Home on the Range," and of course he did and he accompanied her. The only song that came to mind all of whose words I could remember on the spur of the moment was "My Bonnie." Daisy and Jamie and the guitar player sang along rousingly on the chorus, "Bring back, oh bring back, oh bring back my bonnie to me!"

Jamie at his turn sang "Down in the Valley" with the straightforward and simple innocence of a youth. "Build me a castle forty feet high/So I can see her as she rides by," he sang, and a chill ran around my shoulders. *Throw your arms round me, give my heart ease.*

We reveled until late and then walked slowly back to our rooms, caught in the reverie that is the sweet downward side of skylarking.

Daisy and I whispered good night to Jamie outside our room, and he went along to his, which was separated from ours by one that had already been let. "To a German," our landlady had sighed.

As Daisy and I prepared for bed, she said, "I'm surprised your father became a gypsy. He obviously could have succeeded at any number of things."

"At anything."

"Was it your mother's death?"

"You might say."

"It seems a waste."

I pulled my nightgown from my bag. "You mustn't be mistaken, though. Jamie has succeeded in being a great man."

I lay awake listening to the quiet house in the still night. There is a silence so deep and limpid, one's thoughts seem to travel undeterred and undiminished, even to the stars.

My sharp love, and my rueful gratitude for what he imagined he'd given me, had only to travel down the hall two doors, past the German, so I knew that they reached Jamie pure and strong.

He imagined that he'd given me life by leaving. One had to be grateful for the intent, even while gagging on the gift. When he left, he wasn't driven by guilt or gods but by the certainty that the world would deal very unhappily with me if he stayed.

If there was a beastly crime in what had happened between us, it was difficult for me to grasp. There had been no moment of decision when the road divided morally and we were confronted by choice. We had simply made our way together down a single path that unreeled before us and burned itself behind us.

At last I fell asleep and dreamed that I went down the hall to him.

57

We had begun our peregrine party on Monday. By late Wednesday, when we drove into Kalamata, it was apparent that a week was not going to be half sufficient for Daisy's stay, so we called the airline in Athens and rescheduled her departure. A two-week visit was skimpy, but I supposed it would have to do.

During our remaining days we saw Megalopolis, Sparta, Mistra, Argos, Mycenae, Nauplia, Epidaurus, and ancient Corinth. When we reached Corinth I complained, "We've only a day left for Athens. She won't see Olympia!" This did not grieve Daisy so much as it did me.

"Well, she hasn't seen any of central or northern Greece, not to mention the islands," Jamie pointed out, "so she'll have to come back."

We saw her off at the Athens airport. "I think you and your father should come back to the States," Daisy told me.

"Yes, I think you're right."

"When?"

"I don't know."

We hugged, drew apart for a long, wordless look at one another, giggled and tried not to cry, hugged again, and parted quickly.

Jamie and I waited until her plane had taken off before we left the airport. As we climbed back into the car, Jamie deliberated a moment, then, "Shall we drive to Delphi instead of going right back home?"

"What a wonderful idea."

It was a golden spring day and we drove through the Attic countryside with the windows down. Once past Mount Cithaeron we were in the Boeotian plain, bare-looking, a prelude of expectation, an opportunity to jettison the common or uncommon concerns of daily life, to make oneself empty and humble, prepared to receive Delphi.

We passed through Thebes, where little remained to speak of its seemingly endless tragedy, of Cadmus, the founder, of Oedipus or Antigone. Beyond Thebes we came to a spot where three roads met. Here Oedipus killed his father. The country around began to change. We started to climb and the scenery, as it drew close to the sky, grew more fierce.

To the right we were able now and then to catch the spectacle of Parnassus. At length we came to the village of Arakhova, which appeared to be as high as we were going to climb. From here we wound slowly downward until, a few miles beyond Arakhova, Delphi materialized.

It is said that Zeus sent out two eagles from opposite ends of the universe and that they met at Delphi. It was the center of the world. I couldn't doubt it. We spent what remained of the afternoon wandering in the precinct of Apollo, from the stadium high up on the hillside, down through the theater, the temple of Apollo, where pilgrims came seeking the word of the oracle, the Sacred Way, the perfect little Athenian Treasury and more, much more.

The air was clearer than its common metaphors: water, crystal, glass. And its clarity put us closer to the sky. We walked with our heads among gods. Yet it was the men, battling private obsessions and public ambitions, building a homage and temple to Apollo, counselor of moderation, intellect, and moral purity, who prompted awe and pride.

We stayed that night in a hotel in the town of Delphi and the next day visited the Delphi Museum, whose bronze *Charioteer* staggered us. The fineness of temper, the gravity and sweetness of the youth better expressed the ideals of the ancients than anything I'd seen in Greece.

We lingered at the Tholos, or Sanctuary of Athena, which lies outside the precinct of Apollo, across the Arakhova road, then passed the afternoon again in the precinct. Sitting above the great retaining wall of the temple, I said, "I feel quiet here, lifted above my body."

He nodded and waited for me to go on.

"Do you ever think that maybe your body's a universe and all the gods and all the demons are in there, in your blood and your bones, struggling in a terrible endless battle? And you're caught in the middle? Does somebody win?"

He chuckled. "That's a pretty good explanation of agony. The Greek *agon* means contest, you know."

"I don't feel that contest up here." I lay back on the soft spring grass, which would soon yellow and dry under the summer sun.

"These past two weeks," he said, "despite the partying and racing around, have been halcyon days."

"Is that true?"

He nodded.

The only peace (was it peace, or defeat?) that I had felt was up here. I didn't tell him that. It was enough if *he* could find it.

I reached out and placed a hand on his. It was the first touch since the night he'd set his canvas bag down in the foyer of the hotel at Theopropoi.

"I never regretted what we were, Jamie. I wouldn't give it back. If a god came down off Olympus and said, 'You'll have to pay for this until you're sorry,' I'd pay forever. Do you think the gods could be satisfied if one paid for one's crimes without being sorry for them?"

"If I were a god, I would."

I gazed out at Apollo's precinct. "It says in the guidebook that Apollo was 'the beloved son of Zeus.' He believed that you could be purified by atonement rather than by revenge-punishment. This was contrary to the old ideas. For slaying Python, which surely couldn't have seemed like a crime at all, he went into self-imposed exile and served as a slave at the court of King Admetus, after which he returned to Delphi, 'his head crowned with laurel.'"

As afternoon began to wane, we prepared to leave for Athens, stopping first, however, to drink from the Castalian spring, whose waters purified those who came seeking the oracle.

58

Someplace between Patras and Theopropoi, Jamie asked, "Have you written to the lawyer, the one you mentioned? I forget his name."

"Haney?"

"That's it. Have you written him?"

"No. I'll do that in the next few days."

"Yes. Tomorrow wouldn't be too soon."

I laughed.

"Well, what's the point of delaying? Put it behind you and start over. Get on with what you want to do."

"I don't know what I want to do."

"Something will come up."

"There. You see?" Jamie said the next day as we sat in the courtyard of our little house, drinking coffee.

There'd been mail from the States. A letter from Clark contained snapshots of the baby, who looked quiet and full of her own humorous thoughts. Clark said that Mrs. Luchinsky, the housekeeper, was working out well. Business was hellish with tax season upon him, and he was particularly relieved to know that there was someone capable at home with little Larissa. He was muddling through. How chastened he sounded. How stripped of vanity and a young man's audacity. He went on to say that he had little time just now to see Miranda and Dennis, but Miranda stopped frequently to see the baby. He had had a letter from Georganna Fitzroy, saying she was looking forward to a visit from her mother. He made no mention of Bart or Hildy. At the end, "I'm glad Granddad's with you. Tell him hello from everyone here and give him one of the snapshots of Larissa for his wallet, if he keeps snapshots in his wallet. Love, Clark."

Jamie took the picture, pulled his wallet from his hip pocket, and opened it. "You're lucky," he said, "to have such a fine son." And then, "And I'm lucky to have such a fine daughter."

"Jamie, don't."

"I know it's hell for you and I appreciate it all the more."

"Well, isn't it for *you?* Or didn't you care that much?"

"Shut up," he flared. "Don't say stupid things."

I ran into the house, ashamed and miserable. From the courtyard, "Why don't you bring the coffeepot when you come?"

I stood in the kitchen holding a towel over my face. Finally, I got the coffeepot and returned to the courtyard, which was filled with flowering trees.

"Now open this other one," he said, holding up an envelope from Homestead Gallery. "What do they want?"

"I don't know." I set the pot down and took the letter from him. "It's from Sperling," I said, setting aside the envelope and unfolding the contents. "Oh, look, here are some ads that mention my show next month."

Jamie set those on the table and said, "Well, read the letter aloud. What does he say?"

"You're nosy as hell, James."

"Read."

L. Demming—

Progress is being made toward the showing of your work. Contrary to my first belief, it would be a good deal simpler if you were here.

We have decided to exhibit the work on both levels of the gallery rather than downstairs only. As you can imagine, this involves labor and decisions I have every right to believe you should share.

Is this not possible? Anticipating an immediate reply, I remain

Your servant,
Gerald Sperling

"There. You see?"

"See what?"

"Write the lawyer today, but first get on the phone and call this fellow and tell him you're on your way. By God, do you know it's already the last day of March and this ad says your show's the twenty-seventh of April?"

"Hush, Jamie."

"Let's go back, Larissa. I'll find us a house. You won't have to do a thing. I'll fix it up for you, whatever needs doing. Just tell me where you want to live."

As urgent as the appeal from Sperling was, I would not have gone back except for Jamie. Jamie was on fire with the idea of our setting up a household in the States, desperate for me to "start over."

"I can be near Miranda and Clark," he said. "And see the baby. She's a beauty, isn't she? Looks like Clark, I think.

"I could even stand old Bart, now that you're divorcing him. Can't imagine what that young blonde sees in him. What would you think if we bought a house on the river? You talk about that river like it was a cross between the Rhine and the River Jordan. It's getting late. Everything'll be snatched up for summer. Maybe we ought to rent till fall. The market'll open up then. What do you think?"

I thought his readiness bordered on the insane.

I couldn't bear the thought of frantic flight, throwing things hastily into bags and boxes, rushing around. In fact, I could hardly stand to think of leaving. I was deliberately slow in preparing, nearly driving Jamie up the wall.

"At this rate, you won't be there before the snow flies."

He wrote to Daisy and asked her to keep an eye out for a house. I was put out with him for doing that. "You know Daisy. She's not going to rest until she's found something. Really, Jamie, she has a life of her own."

There was no point in fussing. He was ruthless and relentless. I proceeded with all due inertia while he did as he damn pleased, driving up to Patras to order airline tickets on a flight from Athens, Thursday, April 14.

"That'll give me the weekend to rest before I start house-hunting," he explained.

We drove to Olympia Friday the eighth. I wasn't going to be dragged out of Greece without first seeing the place where Pan met Alice Hazeltine. And perhaps I secretly hoped to catch a final glimpse of him or exchange a final word.

Arriving about noon, we checked into the hotel, had lunch, and made our way to the sanctuary. The valley of Olympia is watered by two rivers, the Cladeus and the Alpheus, and it's between the two that the sacred precinct lies. For this reason the vegetation is, by Greek standards, very lush, with pine, olive, and plane trees and wildflowers, particularly in spring. The sanctuary was carpeted by grass and wildflowers when Jamie and I entered, although the tourists had begun to arrive in numbers and one supposed that by June it would be trampled to dust.

We wandered like children among the ruins. Where had Pan first spied Alice? I wondered. And where was he now? Had his friends and loves been here to welcome him when he returned?

I used two rolls of film taking pictures of Jamie against the ruins, and we prevailed upon a couple of willing English tourists to take several of the two of us together.

As we drifted among great overturned columns and along timeless paths, my eyes roamed the stone remains and the hills and groves. Pan was not there. His music like ribbons, his laughter that was all the best sins melted together, they were gone, into an olive grove up some mountain pass. Joy for his escape made me throw my arms around Jamie.

Midafternoon we walked back to the hotel, ordered drinks, and sat in the shade. "I bought you something last November," I told him as we sat chatting under an olive tree. "I put it away and forgot about it until this weekend, when I was sorting through the things I've accumulated here." From my handbag I took out the small box and handed it to him.

With a look of mild surprise and pleasure, he opened it and removed the ring with the head of Hermes worked in black enamel and gold. "Hermes was the god of travelers," I explained, "and since you've been a stepson of his... try it on."

He slipped it on his finger.

"It fits?"

"Perfectly. It's very impressive," he said, holding his hand out. "Thank you. I'll never take it off, even if it turns my finger green."

"That day at Delphi, you said you were hopeful. I wasn't. But today has been good."

"Let's not talk about it. I'm superstitious. The gods are listening."

"Well, then, let's order more wine."

When the sun fell lower, we ambled back toward the sanctuary, crossing it and climbing partway up a hill from which we could look down on the ruins, more satisfying in their ruin than anything modern and perfect.

Pretending to be ancients, two citizens of Athens come for the games, we pitched an imaginary tent where we sat, and watched the chariot race that opened the games.

"My servant has brought us wine," Jamie said, "and I'm showing my friend the magnificent ring given me by my daughter, Larissa." We laughed and turned to the race, which was being won by a chariot from Corinth. Corinth was very wealthy (the old Latin saying "It does not happen to everyone to go to Corinth" told something of the expensive life) and the owner of the lead chariot had spent a fortune in gold for his horses.

In the end the Corinthian threw a wheel and the race was taken by an upstart from Macedonia. "Aiyeee!" Jamie yelled, jumping up. "I had gold on that Macedonian long shot."

Before dinner we roamed through the town. "Come here," Jamie said, leading me into a narrow, dark little shop. "See what you can find that you like."

I looked at him.

"I want to buy you a remembrance—from my winnings on the long shot."

We searched through bracelets and necklaces, rings and earrings. Finally, Jamie held up a pair of finely worked gold earrings. "Do you like these?" They were olive garlands like those awarded Olympian victors. Swinging gracefully from delicate posts, they hung below the ear. I put them both on.

"What do you think?"

"We'll take them," he told the shop owner. "She'll wear them."

We walked out into the twilight and went to dinner. We laughed that night and danced and cried a little. It was after midnight when we returned to the hotel, and Jamie was whistling I don't remember what song, though I've tried. At the entrance to the hotel, he did a couple of soft-shoe steps, tipped his white straw hat to me, and collapsed on the sidewalk. I ran to him, knelt, and cradled his head, but he was dead.

59 ❧

I opened the last of the cartons I'd been sorting through. The contents of this one dated back over years, even to girlhood. There was a teddy bear I'd hung on to, transferring it from trunk to carton and from one carton to another. I lifted it out gently and set it on a chair. It looked at me rakishly and not at all accusingly for having been so long imprisoned.

There were old diaries and yearbooks and faded snapshots of girlfriends whose names had flown to Name Heaven. And in small boxes that once had held greeting cards, there were the postcards from Jamie. Like the snapshots, they'd faded, as though the sky had been so white-hot it had washed the color out of trees and hotels and even people. Hyde Park looked as if it were in the middle of a terrible, bleaching desert.

I shuffled them, reading a message here and there. From Scotland: "Cold." Just the one word. From Mexico where he'd first fled: "Try to understand. Love, Jamie." He'd written the same message from Tampico, Mexico City, and Veracruz. There were several from Greece, including one from Olympia: "You must come here one day. At the ruins I met three women from Minnesota traveling together! Spent the day with them. Thought of you... Love, Jamie." How I had hated those women when the card arrived.

I put large rubber bands around the packets, carried them into the hall, and set them on the stairs. I would read them later, at bedtime. The remainder of the things in the carton I put into the bottom drawer of the chest in the front hall. I took the empty carton to the back door and out to the garage.

Hurrying back into the house, I shivered and chafed my arms. With the door closed securely against the cold, I stood looking out the glass at the river, which lay white and solid at the end of the yard. If you stood at its edge, down by the old dock, you could see the dalles downstream, where Pan had waited so many years.

For the moment the river was safe from the threat of Belle

Rive Estates. This past spring, when workmen clearing the land had discovered an Indian burial site on the Duffy farm, the federal government, like a deus ex machina, had stepped in to halt all work on the condominium project.

Save the River had drawn a deep breath, but it was only a second wind. No one imagined that the siege of developers was ended. There were other farms on the river. Still, we were grateful for temporary favors. At Daisy's side I would throw myself into the next battle.

Harold Falworth had been impressed by Roberta's work despite the loss of the Duffy land, and Roberta was now a resident of Dallas and an executive in Falworth's public relations department.

The backyard had been brown and gray and bare, with a scum of dead leaves over it. Then yesterday it had snowed quietly, without ado, the entire day and into the night. Now the yard was all soft curves and flung fronds of driven snow. Across the river, along the Blind Moose side, the woods against the snowy hillside were a pen-and-ink drawing.

This house was the one Jamie would have bought. When I brought him back to bury him in the Good Hope cemetery, where I too would eventually be "cemented" away (as Grandma Mercy would say), Daisy had heard that the house was going on the market. The front faced Water Street several blocks north of the business district, several blocks beyond the Soo Line Depot. The lot, which was very deep, ran down to the river in back. There was an old dock that would be destroyed by the winter. In the spring the house must be painted and a new dock built.

In the backyard maple and Chinese elm stood with their boughs bent low. The idea had strayed into my head that a small gazebo among the elms would be a perfect spot for a little girl with black curls and witchy black eyes to play whatever games little girls played in these modern times. I could sit with her there and tell fairy tales and myths and show her all the postcards from her great-granddad's odyssey.

Blinking, I went back to the living room, which Daisy called the parlor. The house was built in 1917 and had the look of a midwestern farmhouse: a broad, open front porch, peaky roof, plenty of gingerbread, and a number of its original beveled-glass windows. The woodwork was dark and very plain, and the rooms gave a feeling not just of containment but of refuge. That feeling had decided me in favor of it. And Jamie being close.

The circumstances of his burial seemed strange. We had no funeral, only a graveside service. Grouped around the grave, in addition to the priest, were Bart and Hildy, Miranda and Dennis, Clark, Daisy and George, Harry, Bobby and I. Of these ten, only I really knew him. Next to me, Daisy had known him best, having spent two weeks with us in Greece. Bart, Miranda, and Clark had seen him so little, he was a virtual stranger to them. They came to bury a mythological figure, who after all had been human.

I hadn't known if there would be problems getting a priest to bury him, what with his dying without sacraments. I could have asked Reverend Braun, the Methodist minister, but I felt that one must take an Irishman's religion into account, even if he didn't. And so I told a number of what may have been unnecessary lies, but I didn't know and I couldn't take a chance, and in the end Jamie was buried by a priest.

After the short service we all went back to Daisy's for lunch and drinks. And almost at once it began: the children and Bart started to carve out a figure, fabulous and funny—mythic—from a monolithic block of unfamiliarity. Each had a few stories that outlined his figure; the years would fill in the details with half fabrication that would seem real, and eventually the legend would be complete.

"Remember the Christmas, Clark, when Granddad called from Casablanca and carried on the entire conversation in a Humphrey Bogart imitation?" ... "Do you recall, Miranda, the postcard from your grandfather that was in the mail for weeks? He'd posted it someplace on his trip on the Trans-Siberian Railroad. What did it say?—'On my way to salt mines. All this for an over-time parking ticket?'" ... "Why didn't he come to visit us oftener?" ... "It had something to do with our grandmother's death." And so it went, with Bart contributing as much as the children, although he'd never had a pleasant thing to say about Jamie. Now there was no need to fear him, and Bart could be generous. I saw for the first time that Bart *had* feared him.

I felt amused and indulgent and even grateful to them. They were constructing a monument over Jamie.

* * *

Without the demands of Gerald Sperling or the work on Bobby's second book, I don't know that I could have gotten through spring and summer. After final revisions on *The Still Beautiful River* were complete, Bobby flung himself into a new, more ambitious project, a book about the Indian dispute over rights to the Black Hills. We spent four months in South Dakota. My contribution was nearly complete when I returned to Belleville in October. Bobby stayed on to do more basic research. I'd told him I would come back if he required, but the last time we'd spoken on the phone, he'd said there was no pressing need. He was staying near Rapid City over the Christmas holiday to interview an American Indian Movement leader flying in from the West Coast. Do you want me to come? I'd asked. No, he would send me candid photos from which to work. He didn't want to disrupt my holiday and he was worried about Harry's being alone. Could I somehow include his father in my own plans?

I had seen little of Harry. I'd been occupied with the house, and he with juggling the newspaper and Arneson Printing. When I knew that Bart, Hildy, and the children were driving up from the city for Christmas Day, I called George and Daisy to invite them, then Harry. Counting the baby, we would be ten for dinner. A good number, though I should have liked to have had more.

This final day before Christmas a greeting card arrived from Gerald Sperling, a note scrawled inside in his painstakingly illegible handwriting.

> L. Demming—
>   New Year's Day I host a soirée of notable and stimulating friends. Included traditionally are a few of my protégés capable of eating with a fork and forming simple sentences, preferably in English. Since you appear to qualify, I have included you among the list. If you insist upon an escort, one hopes you will choose wisely, and present yourself punctually at two P.M.
>   Blessings of the Season!
>   Gerald Sperling

Darling Gerald, how he brightened his corner! I'd grown fond of him over the past year and a half. He was immensely knowledgeable, scrupulously honest, and unflaggingly industrious on behalf of his "protégés." Homestead was his obsession. It was marriage and offspring. Anyone doubting the abundant satisfaction of

Sperling's obsession was naive. The obsessed are disinclined to change places with the unobsessed.

"Mr. Sperling, dear," I said, phoning him at once. "L. Demming here. I'm happy to accept your gracious invitation. I will be escorted by an as-yet-undetermined male, who will eat with a proper utensil. I think you go too far in insisting on English, but I will do my best."

"*Chère madame,* your best is all I ever ask."

"Merry Christmas."

When I had rung off, I put on a coat, boots, and heavy scarf, and prepared to trudge through the new snow to Samuelson's Market for milk. I'd almost forgotten I would need extra for the baby, who was not quite a baby anymore, but walking and even talking a little, or so we all claimed.

Bracing myself, I hurtled into the out-of-doors. It wasn't unpleasant; the air was still and promising. I thought we would have another snowfall before tomorrow. A call should be made to Hildy, suggesting that she bring skates if she had some. I knew that Bart did.

I had always imagined Bart to be thoroughly conventional, but his unselfconsciousness about the arrangement with Hildy I found disarming. Our divorce wasn't final for some time, and I didn't know what Bart and Hildy had planned or if they even thought along those lines, but they were dwelling on that magic X where the favorable forces of life infrequently converge. Bart's book was an enormous success, but he was little changed by celebrity. It *was* the history that mattered and not the acclaim. He had just the one overriding passion. I wondered why I'd been so impatient with him.

Emerging from Samuelson's with a half gallon of milk, I was taken by a desire to see the dalles in winter. This was my first Belleville December. I plowed along Water Street for two blocks, crossed River Avenue just above the bridge, and entered the park. The street department hadn't come through with a snow blower yet, so the paths were covered, though footprints of children were everywhere.

Cutting through the fluff, I headed toward a bench by the river, where I brushed a thick batting from the seat and settled myself to gaze downstream at the great stone walls. Their color appeared darker, contrasted as it was by the white, lying along outcroppings and ledges. But their winter face had a stripped, rather bland look, quite innocent-seeming. Which made their secrets the more secret. I felt close to Pan.

I remained for some minutes. On the ice a pickup game of hockey caromed past me: boys of different sizes darting and gliding on clicking, hissing blades, smoke from their young fire hanging round their heads.

At length I rose and gathered up my grocery bag. There was cheer to be found in many places, but not peace. I'd given up looking, even begun to doubt its value. Peace was just a willingness to relinquish one's passions, a denial of the importance of one's obsessions. Peace was a consolation prize.

"If it was help you wanted," Jamie had said, "you could have gone to a psychiatrist. But you didn't want that, did you?" Jamie was right. If a doctor could remove your obsession, how much of you would be left? Lobotomizing, that was how the prospect of being cured had struck me. And it still did. After a while, you became your obsession. To lose it would be peace, perhaps, but death certainly. And the pain? It was a sharp assurance of life. You lived because of pain, not despite it.

Walking back through the park and out the gate I had entered, I waited at the curb for cars to pass, their tires munching the new snow. Most Christmas shopping was done in the cities or in the mail-order catalogues, but December 24 always saw a last-minute flurry of business along Main Street and down River Avenue, in the drugstore, the five-and-dime, and Nissen's Mercantile.

I crossed River Avenue. Colored lights strung back and forth across the street necklaced a gray afternoon, fuzzy and soft as rabbit's fur. Sounds were muted, the atmosphere snugged down for another snowfall. A strap of sleigh bells chinked as I pushed open the door to the *Courant*, chinked again as it closed behind me.

"Is there a drop of cheer in this place?"

Without greeting or expression, Harry pushed himself up from the chair, swung around to the filing cabinet, and poured two drinks into paper cups, one gin, one bourbon.

Pulling off gloves and scarf, I unbuttoned my coat. Harry nodded toward a coat tree in the corner where his own fleece-lined jacket hung.

"I can't stay."

He handed me the gin and raised his cup. "Cheer."

We drank. After the cold it was good to feel the gin burn its way down.

"It's been a while," I said, looking around.

His head dipped ever so slightly. Assent. He was seated in the swivel chair again. His hair was graying. It shocked me to notice this. I felt betrayed that it should have happened while I wasn't looking.

It was very quiet. The staff had the afternoon off. Christmas Eve. "I'm glad you're coming tomorrow."

"Are you?" Did he sound skeptical? Well, and why shouldn't he?

"Of course I am." I *was*. For twenty years we'd been friends. Rightly or wrongly was beside the point. He was one sweet son of a bitch and I wasn't going to let all the good times and trouble get tossed out. Just like that, as if it didn't matter. Not if I could help it. It wasn't so easy to come by, that kind of accumulation of good times and trouble.

"Do you have anything planned for New Year's Day?"

He shook his head.

"Gerald Sperling's giving a party. I'd like you to go with me." I added, "Everything considered, it's a nerve of me to ask."

"It sure as hell is, but I may be fool enough to go."

We shook hands. It felt like the thing to do.

60

Christmas Day rose quietly and slowly from a night of snow. Clouds were banked against the sun. That was good. Christmas should not be jingle-bells bright but, rather, closely wrapped around and woolly so that even people who are alone will feel gathered into it.

Harry arrived a little before the others. I didn't realize at once that he was there. Finding the snow shovel beside the front door, he cleared the porch steps and a path down the walk to the street.

He stood on the porch pulling off his galoshes. "I don't do windows," he laughed as I opened the door. Behind him the Fitzroy car pulled to the curb. Daisy waved. Soon the rooms were filled with voices raised a bit louder than usual, as they are at holiday gatherings.

Now I watched Clark trudging up from the river, pulling Larissa on the sled Santa had brought. Their cheeks were rouged by the cold. The baby in her cocoon of bulky snowsuit was smiling at something her father had said.

Sticking my head out the door, I called, "It's nearly time to eat, Clark."

"We'll be right in."

The house was a heavenly mélange of odors: Christmas pudding being resteamed, standing rib roast out of the oven, Yorkshire pudding still in, sweet potatoes in a bowl on top of the stove, likewise pureed chestnuts. I held a mug of hot wine for Clark. All the worst and best excesses of the season were mingling in the kitchen.

Hildy stood at the counter with an electric beater, mashing potatoes, Daisy applied a wire whisk to the rum sauce, and Miranda carried to the table horseradish, wine carafes, and hot rolls in a basket.

In the dining room she called, "Daddy or Harry, will one of you carve the roast, please?"

Bart stood up. "I'm your man, old girl."

"What's wrong with *me*?" Dennis asked without resentment. Their marriage still wasn't real to me. Like anything we've forbidden to happen, it could never be entirely real. In my mind they were merely living together. Of course, that was fine.

Only Bobby was missing as we sat down. He was in Rapid City. I was at the foot of the table near the door to the kitchen, Clark at the head with the baby beside him in a high chair. She looked like Clark, as Jamie had pointed out, but she resembled Jamie even more.

From where I sat, glancing through the broad oak archway into the parlor, I could see above the mantle the portrait of Jamie and me. I had painted it from one of the snapshots the English tourists had taken of us at Olympia. We stood before a giant drum of fluted column, which lay on its side absorbing and reflecting the bright warmth of the day. In his right hand Jamie held the white straw hat. His left arm lay across my shoulders. I had been squinting into the blinding Greek sunlight and there was a light-washed quality to the canvas, relieved only by our shadowed eyes and the shadows that we cast against the stone. We looked not unlike figures in one of the faded colored postcards from Jamie, figures from the past about whom one might reflect, "Isn't it fortunate that they were captured just at that moment which could never come again?"

I looked away. Elbow propped on the table, I fingered the gold olive wreaths at my ears. Oh, there was a strong presence of Jamie in the house. In the baby and in my children, but especially in the fact of our being together. Jamie had journeyed to Greece, demanding the impossible, not because he needed a daughter, as he'd said, but because he hoped to help me back into my proper role while there was still time. Out of love we had both tried to fool the other. He'd pretended to need a daughter. I finally had pretended to need a father. It was the last and only thing we could do for each other.

Well, Jamie, I thought, *I'm back in the drama. I don't think I'll ever have my part quite right. If the others are magnanimous and patient, perhaps they'll put up with the lightweight who's been dragged into the cast because she was a friend of the producer's.*

With an ardent glance I embraced them, a gathering rife with subtext: currents and tensions, living resentments and dead quarrels, old secrets and shame and diseases of the heart without remedy. The vulnerable flesh of family—proof that it was a viable organism, not a wax tableau. Our regard for one another was greater than our fear of injury.

Harry sat at my right. I reached to lay a hand over his. "After dinner let's call Bobby and everyone say hello."

"Yes," he agreed. "Yes, let's do that. I have a number where he can be reached."

Along some telepathic wire a message of distress went out from Miranda. My gaze skewed round the table toward her. A sharp line drawn between her brows, she studied her salad intently. She had known that Bobby would enter into the day, but there was never a way to prepare for all the small shocks and sorrows. You just hoped you could pull up your socks and slog through, with a tip of your hat to the Devil.

Miranda looked up suddenly and smiled at Harry. "One year when we were kids, Bobby wrote to me after Christmas about his toboggan. I could hardly read it because he had to print with his left hand. What was that all about, do you remember?"

"My God, Miranda, I'd forgotten completely." Harry laughed.

"Oh, my God, yes. Roberta's dad, who expected all kin of his to be precocious, gave Bobby a big toboggan when he was about eight, I guess. Gave it to him for Christmas. Well, Bobby was bound and determined he was going to ride the damned thing alone.

"The first day out, he broke off a tooth. I told him if he was going to ride alone, I thought we should put it away for a year. Oh, hell no, he wouldn't hear of it. The next weekend he broke his arm.

"You know what he said to me? We were sitting in the emergency room up at County Hospital. He said, 'Wasn't it a lucky thing I didn't smash the *toboggan*?' Here I was, every time he took it out, praying he'd come home with it in six pieces. And he thought it was lucky his arm was broken and not the toboggan. When you talk to him today, be sure to remind him about the toboggan. He'll get a boot out of that." He was looking at Miranda. "I miss him, Andy."

Well, there was something I'd forgotten entirely, that name Harry had sometimes used for Miranda.

George raised his glass. "To absent loved ones," he said.

We all drank, to Bobby and Georganna, and surely to Sarah. I looked quickly down the table at Clark and recalled how boyish and bland his face had been when he and Sarah had come up to Belle Riviere for the Fourth of July weekend. Now the fine lines in it were like delicate twine holding together his personal bundle of grief and reconciliation. He caught me studying him and smiled.

"I want to propose a toast," he announced, lifting his glass again. "To Granddad. He told us he'd bring her back and by God he did."

I sat up straight and held my shoulders back. With my chin raised, I took a deep breath and pressed both feet hard to the floor. "To Jamie."

They all fell to cleaning their plates then. I went to the kitchen and carried in the coffee.

"Anyone want to go ice skating later?" Dennis asked.

Miranda groaned.

"I'll go," Daisy assured him.

"Hildy, you'd like to go, wouldn't you?" Bart suggested.

"I'll go if the baby's asleep," Clark told them.

I set the coffeepot on the sideboard. Now, what was the mother's line here?

341